PRAISE

'Wilb

'The world's le

Daily Express

'Action is the name of Wilbur Smith's game and he's a master'

Washington Post

'The pace would do credit to a Porsche, and the invention is as bright and explosive as a fireworks display'

Sunday Telegraph

'A violent saga set in Boer War South Africa, told with vigour and enthusiasm . . . Wilbur Smith spins a fine tale'

Evening Standard

'A bonanza of excitement'

New York Times

'A natural storyteller who moves confidently and often splendidly in his period and sustains a flow of convincing incident'

Scotsman

'Raw experience, grim realism, history and romance welded with mystery and the bewilderment of life itself'

Library Journal

'Extrovert and vigorous . . . constantly changing incidents and memorable portraits'
Liverpool Daily Post

'An immensely powerful book, disturbing and compulsive, harsh yet compassionate'
She

'An epic novel . . . it would be hard to think of a theme that was more appropriate today . . . Smith writes with a great passion for the soul of Africa'
Today

'I read on to the last page, hooked by its frenzied inventiveness piling up incident upon incident . . . mighty entertainment'
Yorkshire Post

'There is a streak of genuine poetry, all the more attractive for being unfeigned'
Sunday Telegraph

'Action follows action . . . mystery is piled on mystery . . . tales to delight the millions of addicts of the gutsy adventure story'
Sunday Express

'Action-crammed'
Sunday Times

'Rattling good adventure'
Evening Standard

WHEN THE LION FEEDS

WILBUR SMITH was born in Central Africa in 1933. He was educated at Michaelhouse and Rhodes University. He became a full-time writer in 1964 after the successful publication of *When the Lion Feeds*, and has since written over thirty novels, meticulously researched on his numerous expeditions worldwide. His books are now translated into twenty-six languages.

Find out more about Wilbur Smith by
looking at his own author website,
www.wilbursmithbooks.com

THE NOVELS OF WILBUR SMITH

The Courtneys

When the Lion Feeds The Sound of Thunder
A Sparrow Falls Birds of Prey Monsoon
Blue Horizon The Triumph of the Sun

The Courtneys of Africa

The Burning Shore Power of the Sword Rage
A Time to Die Golden Fox Assegai

The Ballantyne Novels

A Falcon Flies Men of Men The Angels Weep
The Leopard Hunts in Darkness

The Egyptian Novels

River God The Seventh Scroll
Warlock The Quest

Also

The Dark of the Sun Shout at the Devil
Gold Mine The Diamond Hunters
The Sunbird Eagle in the Sky
The Eye of the Tiger Cry Wolf
Hungry as the Sea Wild Justice
Elephant Song Those in Peril

WILBUR SMITH

WHEN THE LION FEEDS

PAN BOOKS

First published in Great Britain 1964 by William Heinemann Ltd

This edition published 2009 by Pan Books
an imprint of Pan Macmillan, a division of Macmillan Publishers Limited
Pan Macmillan, 20 New Wharf Road, London N1 9RR
Basingstoke and Oxford
Associated companies throughout the world
www.panmacmillan.com

ISBN 978-1-4472-8516-8

1 3 5 7 9 8 6 4 2

A CIP catalogue record for this book is available from
the British Library.

Typeset by SetSystems Ltd, Saffron Walden, Essex
Printed and bound by CPI Group (UK) Ltd, Croydon, CR0 4YY

This book is for my wife

MOKHINISO

who is the best thing

that has ever happened to me

– I –
Natal

– 1 –

A single wild pheasant flew up the side of the hill almost brushing the tips of the grass in its flight. It drooped its wings and hung its legs as it reached the crest and then dropped into cover. Two boys and a dog followed it up from the valley: the dog led, with his tongue flopping pink from the corner of his mouth, and the twins ran shoulder to shoulder behind him. Both of them were sweating in dark patches through their khaki shirts, for the African sun still had heat although it stood half-mast down the sky.

The dog hit the scent of the bird and it stopped him quivering: for a second he stood sucking it up through his nostrils, and then he started to quarter. He worked fast, back and forth, swinging at the end of each tack, his head down and only his back and his busy tail showing above the dry brown grass. The twins came up behind him. They were gasping for breath for it had been a hard pull up the curve of the hill.

'Keep out to the side, you'll get in my way,' Sean panted at his brother and Garrick moved to obey. Sean was his senior by four inches in height and twenty pounds in weight: this gave him the right to command. Sean transferred his attention back to the dog.

'Put him up, Tinker. Seek him up, boy.'

Tinker's tail acknowledged Sean's instructions, but he held his nose to the ground. The twins followed him, tensed for the bird to rise. They carried their throwing sticks ready and moved forward a stealthy pace at a time, fighting to control their breathing. Tinker found the bird crouched flat in the grass; he jumped forward giving tongue for the first time, and the bird rose. It came up fast on noisy wings, whirling out of the grass.

Sean threw; his kerrie whipped past it. The pheasant swung away from the stick, clawing at the air with frantic wings and Garrick threw. His kerrie cartwheeled up, hissing, until it smacked into the pheasant's fat brown body. The bird toppled, feathers flurried from it and it fell. They went after it. The pheasant scurried broken-winged through the grass ahead of them, and they shouted with excitement as they chased it. Sean got a hand to it. He broke its neck and stood laughing, holding the warm brown body in his hands, and waited for Garrick to reach him.

'Ring-a-ding-a-doody, Garry, you sure gave that one a beauty!'

Tinker jumped up to smell the bird and Sean stooped and held it so he could get his nose against it. Tinker snuffled it, then tried to take it in his mouth, but Sean pushed his head away and tossed the bird to Garrick. Garrick hung it with the others on his belt.

'How far do you reckon that was – fifty feet?' Garrick asked.

'Not as much as that,' Sean gave his opinion. 'More like thirty.'

'I reckon it was at least fifty. I reckon it was farther than any you've hit today.' Success had made Garrick bold. The smile faded from Sean's face.

'Yeah?' he asked.

'Yeah!' said Garrick. Sean pushed the hair off his forehead with the back of his hand, his hair was black and soft and it kept falling into his eyes.

'What about that one down by the river? That was twice as far.'

‘Yeah?’ asked Garrick.

‘Yeah!’ said Sean truculently.

‘Well, if you’re so good, how did you miss this one – hey? You threw first. How come you missed, hey?’

Sean’s already flushed face darkened and Garrick realized suddenly that he had gone too far. He took a step backwards.

‘You’d like to bet?’ demanded Sean. It was not quite clear to Garrick on what Sean wished to bet, but from past experience he knew that whatever it was the issue would be settled by single combat. Garrick seldom won bets from Sean.

‘It’s too late. We’d better be getting home. Pa will clobber us if we’re late for dinner.’ Sean hesitated and Garrick turned, ran back to pick up his kerrie then set off in the direction of home. Sean trotted after him, caught up with him and passed him. Sean always led. Having proved conclusively his superior prowess with the throwing sticks Sean was prepared to be forgiving. Over his shoulder he asked, ‘What colour do you reckon Gypsy’s foal will be?’

Garrick accepted the peace-offering with relief and they fell into a friendly discussion of this and a dozen other equally important subjects. They kept running: except for an hour, when they had stopped in a shady place by the river to roast and eat a couple of their pheasants, they had run all day.

Up here on the plateau it was grassland that rose and fell beneath them as they climbed the low round hills and dropped into the valleys. The grass around them moved with the wind: waist-high grass, soft dry grass the colour of ripe wheat. Behind them and on each side the grassland rolled away to the full range of the eye, but suddenly in front of them was the escarpment. The land cascaded down into it, steeply at first then gradually levelling out to become the Tugela flats. The Tugela river was twenty miles away across the flats, but today there was a haze in the air so they could not see that far. Beyond the river, stretched far to the north and a hundred miles east to the sea, was Zululand. The river was the border. The steep side of the escarpment was cut by vertical gulleys and in the gulleys grew dense, olive-green bush.

Below them, two miles out on the flats, was the homestead of Theunis Kraal. The house was a big one, Dutch-gabled and smoothly thatched with combed grass. There were horses in the small paddock: many horses, for the twins' father was a wealthy man. Smoke from the cooking fires blued the air over the servants' quarters and the sound of someone chopping wood carried faintly up to them.

Sean stopped on the rim of the escarpment and sat down in the grass. He took hold of one of his grimy bare feet and twisted it up into his lap. There was hole in the ball of his heel from which he had pulled a thorn earlier in the day and now it was plugged with dirt. Garrick sat down next to him.

'Man, is that going to hurt when Ma puts iodine on it!' gloated Garrick. 'She'll have to use a needle to get the dirt out. I bet you yell – I bet you yell your head off!'

Sean ignored him. He picked a stalk of grass and started probing it into the wound. Garrick watched with interest. Twins could scarcely have been less alike. Sean was already taking on the shape of a man: his shoulders were thickening, and there was hard muscle forming in his puppy fat. His colouring was vivid: black hair, skin brown from the sun, lips and cheeks that glowed with the fresh young blood beneath their surface, and blue eyes, the dark indigo-blue of cloud shadow on mountain lake.

Garrick was slim, with the wrists and ankles of a girl. His hair was an undecided brown that grew wispy down the back of his neck, his skin was freckled, his nose and the rims of his pale blue eyes were pink with persistent hay fever. He was fast losing interest in Sean's surgery. He reached across and fiddled with one of Tinker's pendulous ears, and this broke the rhythm of the dog's panting; he gulped twice and the saliva dripped from the end of his tongue. Garrick lifted his head and looked down the slope. A little below where they were sitting was the head of one of the bushy gullies. Garrick caught his breath.

'Sean, look there – next to the bush!' His whisper trembled with excitement.

'What's it?' Sean looked up startled. Then he saw it.

'Hold Tinker.' Garrick grabbed the dog's collar and pulled his head around to prevent him seeing and giving chase. 'He's the biggest old inkonka in the world,' breathed Garrick. Sean was too absorbed to answer.

The bushbuck was picking its way warily out of the thick cover. A big ram, black with age; the spots on his haunches were faded like old chalk marks. His ears pricked up and his spiral horns held high, big as a pony, but stepping daintily, he came out into the open. He stopped and swung his head from side to side, searching for danger, then he trotted diagonally down the hill and disappeared into another of the gullies. For a moment after he had gone the twins were still, then they burst out together.

'Did you see him, hey – did you see them horns?'

'So close to the house and we never knew he was there—'

They scrambled to their feet jabbering at each other, and Tinker was infected with their excitement. He barked around them in a circle. After the first few moments of confusion Sean took control simply by raising his voice above the opposition.

'I bet he hides up in the gulley every day. I bet he stays there all day and comes out only at night. Let's go and have a look.'

Sean led the way down the slope.

On the fringe of the bush, in a small cave of vegetation that was dark and cool and carpeted with dead leaves, they found the ram's hiding-place. The ground was trampled by his hooves and scattered with his droppings and there was the mark of his body where he had lain. A few loose hairs, tipped with grey, were left on the bed of leaves. Sean knelt down and picked one up.

'How are we going to get him?'

'We could dig a hole and put sharpened sticks in it,' suggested Garrick eagerly.

'Who's going to dig it – you?' Sean asked.

'You could help.'

'It would have to be a pretty big hole,' said Sean doubtfully. There was silence while both of them considered the amount of labour involved in digging a trap. Neither of them mentioned the idea again.

'We could get the other kids from town and have a drive with kerries,' said Sean.

'How many hunts have we been on with them? Must be hundreds by now, and we haven't even bagged one lousy duiker – let alone a bushbuck.' Garrick hesitated and then went on. 'Besides, remember what that inkonka did to Frank Van Essen, hey? When it finished sticking him they had to push all his guts back into the hole in his stomach!'

'Are you scared?' asked Sean.

'I am not, so!' said Garrick indignantly, then quickly, 'Gee, it's almost dark. We'd better run.'

They went down the valley.

– 2 –

Sean lay in the darkness and stared across the room at the grey oblong of the window. There was a slice of moon in the sky outside. Sean could not sleep: he was thinking about the bushbuck. He heard his parents pass the door of the bedroom; his stepmother said something and his father laughed: Waite Courtney had a laugh as deep as distant thunder.

Sean heard the door of their room close and he sat up in bed. 'Garry.' No answer.

'Garry.' He picked up a boot and threw it; there was a grunt. 'Garry.'

'What you want?' Garrick's voice was sleepy and irritable.

'I was just thinking – tomorrow's Friday.'

'So?'

'Ma and Pa will be going into town. They'll be away all day. We could take the shotgun and go lay for that old inkonka.'

Garrick's bed creaked with alarm.

'You're mad!' Garrick could not keep the shock out of his voice. 'Pa would kill us if he caught us with the shotgun.' Even as he said it he knew he would have to find a stronger argument than that to dissuade his brother. Sean avoided punishment if possible, but a chance at a bushbuck ram was worth all his father's right arm could give. Garrick lay rigid in his bed, searching for words.

'Besides, Pa keeps the cartridges locked up.'

It was a good try, but Sean countered it.

'I know where there are two buckshots that he has forgotten about: they're in the big vase in the dining-room. They've been there over a month.'

Garrick was sweating. He could almost feel the sjambok

curling round his buttocks, and hear his father counting the strokes: eight, nine, ten.

'Please, Sean, let's think of something else . . .'

Across the room Sean settled back comfortably on his pillows. The decision had been made.

– 3 –

Waite Courtney handed his wife up into the front seat of the buggy. He patted her arm affectionately then walked around to the driver's side, pausing to fondle the horses and settle his hat down over his bald head. He was a big man, the buggy dipped under his weight as he climbed up into the seat. He gathered up the reins, then he turned and his eyes laughed over his great hooked nose at the twins standing together on the veranda.

'I would esteem it a favour if you two gentlemen could arrange to stay out of trouble for the few hours that your mother and I will be away.'

'Yes, Pa,' in dutiful chorus.

'Sean, if you get the urge to climb the big blue gum tree again then fight it, man, fight it.'

'All right, Pa.'

'Garrick, let us have no more experiments in the manufacture of gunpowder – agreed?'

'Yes, Pa.'

'And don't look so innocent. That really frightens the hell out of me!'

Waite touched the whip to the shiny round rumps in front of him and the buggy started forward, out along the road to Ladyburg.

'He didn't say anything about not taking the shotgun,'

whispered Sean virtuously. 'Now you go and see if all the servants are out of the way – if they see us, they'll kick up a fuss. Then come round to the bedroom window and I'll pass it out to you.'

Sean and Garrick argued all the way to the foot of the escarpment. Sean was carrying the shotgun across one shoulder, hanging onto the butt with both hands.

'It was my idea, wasn't it?' he demanded.

'But I saw the inkonka first,' protested Garrick. Garrick was bold again: with every yard put between him and the house his fear of reprisal faded.

'That doesn't count,' Sean informed him. 'I thought of the shotgun, so I do the shooting.'

'How come you always have the fun?' asked Garrick, and Sean was outraged at the question.

'When you found the hawk's nest by the river, I let you climb for it. Didn't I? When you found the baby duiker, I let you feed it. Didn't I?' he demanded.

'All right. So I saw the inkonka first, why don't you let me take the shot?'

Sean was silent in the face of such stubbornness, but his grip on the butt of the shotgun tightened. In order to win the argument Garrick would have to get it away from him – this Garrick knew and he started to sulk. Sean stopped among the trees at the foot of the escarpment and looked over his shoulder at his brother.

'Are you going to help – or must I do it alone?'

Garrick looked down at the ground and kicked at a twig. He sniffed wetly; his hayfever was always bad in the mornings.

'Well?' asked Sean.

'What do you want me to do?'

'Stay here and count to a thousand slowly. I'm going to circle up the slope and wait where the inkonka crossed yesterday. When you finish counting come up the gulley. Start shouting when you are about halfway up. The inkonka will break the same way as yesterday – all right?'

Garrick nodded reluctantly.

'Did you bring Tinker's chain?'

Garrick pulled it from his pocket, and at the sight of it the dog backed away. Sean grabbed his collar, and Garrick slipped it on. Tinker laid his ears flat and looked at them reproachfully.

'Don't let him go. That old inkonka will rip him up. Now start counting,' said Sean and began climbing. He kept well out to the left of the gulley. The grass on the slope was slippery under his feet, the gun was heavy and there were sharp lumps of rock in the grass. He stubbed his toe and it started to bleed, but he kept on upwards. There was a dead tree on the edge of the bush that Sean had used to mark the bushbuck's hide. Sean climbed above it and stopped just below the crest of the slope where the moving grass would break up the silhouette of his head on the skyline. He was panting. He found a rock the size of a beer barrel to use as a rest for the gun, and he crouched behind it. He laid the stock of the gun on the rock, aimed back down the hill and traversed the barrels left and right to make sure his field of fire was clear. He imagined the bushbuck running in his sights and he felt excitement shiver along his forearms, across his shoulders and up the back of his neck.

'I won't lead on him – he'll be moving fairly slowly, trotting most probably. I'll go straight at his shoulders,' he whispered.

He opened the gun, took the two cartridges out of his shirt pocket, slid them into the breeches and snapped the gun closed. It took all the strength of both his hands to pull back the big fancy hammers, but he managed it and the gun was double-loaded and cocked. He laid it on the rock in front of him again and stared down the slope. On his left the gulley was a dark-green smear on the hillside, directly below him was open grass where the bushbuck would cross. He pushed impatiently at the hair on his forehead: it was damp with sweat and stayed up out of his eyes.

The minutes drifted by.

'What the hell is Garry doing? He's so stupid sometimes!' Sean muttered and almost in answer he heard Garrick shout below him. It was a small sound, far down the slope and muffled by the bush. Tinker barked once without enthusiasm; he was also sulking, he didn't like the chain. Sean waited with his forefinger on one trigger, staring down at the edge of the bush. Garrick shouted again – and the bushbuck broke from cover.

It came fast into the open with its nose up and its long horns held flat against its back. Sean moved his body sideways swinging the gun with its run, riding the pip of the foresight on its black shoulder. He fired the left barrel and the recoil threw him off balance; his ears hummed with the shot and the burnt powder smoke blew back into his face. He struggled to his feet still holding the gun. The bushbuck was down in the grass, bleating like a lamb and kicking as it died.

'I got him,' screamed Sean. 'I got him first shot! Garry, Garry! I got him, I got him!'

Tinker came pelting out of the bush dragging Garry behind him by the chain and, still screaming, Sean ran down to join them. A stone rolled under his foot and he fell. The shotgun flew out of his hand and the second barrel fired. The sound of the explosion was very loud.

When Sean scrambled onto his feet again Garrick was sitting in the grass whimpering – whimpering and staring at his leg. The blast of the shotgun had smashed into it and churned the flesh below the knee into tatters – bursting it open so the bone chips showed white in the wound and the blood pumped dark and strong and thick as custard.

'I didn't mean it . . . Oh God, Garry, I didn't mean it. I slipped. Honest, I slipped.' Sean was staring at the leg also. There was no colour in his face, his eyes were big and dark with horror. The blood pumped out onto the grass.

'Stop it bleeding! Sean, please stop it. Oh, it's sore! Oh! Sean, please stop it!'

Sean stumbled across to him. He wanted to vomit. He unbuckled his belt and strapped it round the leg, and the blood was warm and sticky on his hands. He used his sheathed knife to twist the belt tight. The pumping slowed and he twisted harder.

'Oh, Sean, it's sore! It's sore . . .' Garrick's face was waxy-white and he was starting to shiver as the cold hand of shock closed on him.

'I'll get Joseph,' Sean stammered. 'We'll come back quickly as we can. Oh, God, I'm sorry!' Sean jumped up and ran. He fell, rolled to his feet and kept running.

They came within an hour. Sean was leading three of the Zulu servants. Joseph, the cook, had brought a blanket. He wrapped Garrick and lifted him and Garrick fainted as his leg swung loosely. As they started back down the hill Sean looked out across the flats: there was a little puff of dust on the Ladyburg road. One of the grooms was riding to fetch Waite Courtney.

They were waiting on the veranda of the homestead when Waite Courtney came back to Theunis Kraal. Garrick was conscious again. He lay on the couch: his face was white and the blood had soaked through the blanket. There was blood on Joseph's uniform and blood had dried black on Sean's hands. Waite Courtney ran up onto the veranda; he stooped over Garrick and drew back the blanket. For a second he stood staring at the leg and then very gently he covered it again.

Waite lifted Garrick and carried him down to the buggy. Joseph went with him and they settled Garrick on the back seat. Joseph held his body and Garrick's stepmother took the leg on her lap to stop it twisting. Waite Courtney climbed quickly into the driver's seat: he picked up the reins, then he turned his head and looked at Sean still standing on the veranda. He didn't speak, but his eyes were terrible – Sean could not meet them. Waite Courtney used the whip on the horses and drove them back along the road to Ladyburg: he drove furiously with the wind streaming his beard back from his face.

Sean watched them go. After they had disappeared among the trees he remained standing alone on the veranda; then suddenly he turned and ran back through the house. He ran out of the kitchen door and across the yard to the saddle-room, snatched a bridle down from the rack and ran to the paddock. He picked a bay mare and worked her into a corner of the fence until he could slip his arm around her neck. He forced the bit into her mouth, buckled the chin strap and swung up onto her bare back.

He kicked her into a run and put her to the gate, swaying back as her body heaved up under him and falling forward on her neck as she landed. He gathered himself and turned her head towards the Ladyburg road.

It was eight miles to town and the buggy reached it before Sean. He found it outside Doctor Van Rooyen's surgery: the horses were blowing hard, and their bodies were dark with sweat. Sean slid down off the mare's back; he went up the steps to the surgery door and quietly pushed it open. There was the sweet reek of chloroform in the room. Garrick lay on the table, Waite and his wife stood on each side of him, and the doctor was washing his hands in an enamel basin against the far wall. Ada Courtney was crying silently, her face blurred with tears. They all looked at Sean standing in the doorway.

'Come here,' said Waite Courtney, his voice flat and expressionless. 'Come and stand here beside me. They're going to cut off your brother's leg and, by Christ, I'm going to make you watch every second of it!'

– 4 –

They brought Garrick back to Theunis Kraal in the night. Waite Courtney drove the buggy very slowly and carefully and Sean trailed a long way behind it. He was cold in his thin khaki shirt, and sick in the stomach with what he had seen. There were bruises on his upper arm where his father had held him and forced him to watch.

The servants had lanterns burning on the veranda. They were standing in the shadows, silent and anxious. As Waite carried the blanket-wrapped body up the front steps one of them called softly in the Zulu tongue. 'The leg?'

'It is gone,' Waite answered gruffly.

They sighed softly all together and the voice called again. 'He is well?'

'He is alive,' said Waite.

He carried Garrick through to the room that was set aside for guests and sickness. He stood in the centre of the floor holding the boy while his wife put fresh sheets on the bed; then he laid him down and covered him.

'Is there anything else we can do?' asked Ada.

'We can wait.'

Ada groped for her husband's hand. 'Please, God, let him live,' she whispered. 'He's so young.'

'It's Sean's fault!' Waite's anger flared up suddenly.

'Garry would never have done it on his own.' He tried to disengage Ada's hand.

'What are you going to do?' she asked.

'I'm going to beat him! I'm going to thrash the skin off him!'

'Don't, please don't.'

'What do you mean?'

'He's had enough. Didn't you see his face?'

Waite's shoulders sagged wearily and he sat down on the armchair beside the bed. Ada touched his cheek.

'I'll stay here with Garry. You go and try to get some sleep, my dear.'

'No,' Waite said. She sat down on the side of the chair and Waite put his arm around her waist. After a long while they slept, huddled together on the chair beside the bed.

– 5 –

The days that followed were bad. Garrick's mind escaped from the harness of sanity and ran wild into the hot land of delirium. He panted and twisted his fever-flushed face from side to side; he cried and whimpered in the big bed; the stump of his leg puffed up angrily and the stitches were drawn so tight it seemed they must tear out of the swollen flesh. The infection oozed yellow and foul-smelling onto the sheets.

Ada stayed by him all that time. She swabbed the sweat from his face and changed the dressings on his stump, she held the glass for him to drink and gentled him when he raved. Her eyes sunk darkly into their sockets with fatigue and worry, but she would not leave him. Waite could not bear it. He had the masculine dread of suffering that threatened to suffocate him if he stayed in the room: every half hour or so he came in and stood next to the bed and then he turned away and went back to his restless wandering around the house. Ada could hear his heavy tramp along the corridors.

Sean stayed in the house also: he sat in the kitchen or at the far end of the veranda. No one would speak to him, not even the servants; they chased him when he tried to sneak into the bedroom to see Garrick. He was lonely with the desolate loneliness of the guilty – for Garry was going to die, he knew it by the evil silence that hung over Theunis Kraal. There was no chatter nor pot-clatter from the kitchens, no rich deep laughter from his father: even the dogs were subdued. Death was at Theunis Kraal. He could smell it on the soiled sheets that were brought through to the kitchen from Garrick's room; it was a musky smell, the smell of an animal. Sometimes he could almost see it: even in bright daylight sitting on the veranda he sensed it crouched near him like a shadow on the edge of his vision. It had no form as yet. It was a darkness, a coldness that was gradually building up around the house, gathering its strength until it could take his brother.

On the third day Waite Courtney came roaring out of Garrick's room. He ran through the house and out into the stable yard. 'Karlie. Where are you? Get a saddle onto Rooiberg. Hurry, man, hurry – damn you. He's dying, do you hear me, he's dying.'

Sean did not move from where he sat against the wall next to the back door. His arm tightened around Tinker's neck and the dog touched his cheek with a cold nose; he watched his father jump up onto the stallion's back and ride. The hooves beat away towards Ladyburg and when they were gone he stood up and slipped into the house: he listened outside Garrick's door and then he opened it quietly and went in. Ada turned towards him, her face was tired. She looked much older than her thirty-five years, but her black hair was drawn back behind her head into a neat bun and her dress was fresh and clean. She was still a beautiful woman despite her exhaustion. There was a gentleness about her, a goodness that suffering and worry could not destroy. She held out her hand to Sean and he crossed and stood beside her chair and looked down at Garrick. Then he knew why his father had gone to fetch the doctor. Death was in the room – strong and icy cold hovered over the bed. Garrick lay very still: his face was yellow, his eyes were closed and his lips were cracked and dry.

All the loneliness and the guilt came swelling up into Sean's throat and choked him into sobs, sobs that forced him to his knees and he put his face into Ada's lap and cried. He cried for the last time in his life, he cried as a man cries – painfully, each sob tearing something inside him.

Waite Courtney came back from Ladyburg with the doctor. Once more Sean was driven out and the door closed. All night he heard them working in Garrick's room, the murmuring of their voices and the scuff of feet on the yellow wood floor. In the morning it was over. The fever was broken and Garrick was alive. Only just alive – his eyes were sunk into dark holes like those of a skull. His body and his mind were never to recover completely from that brutal pruning.

It was slow – a week before he was strong enough to feed himself. His first need was for his brother, before he was able to talk above a whisper it was, 'Where's Sean?'

And Sean, still chastened, sat with him for hours at a time. Then when Garrick slept Sean escaped from the room, and with a fishing-rod or his hunting sticks and Tinker barking behind him went into the veld. It was a measure of Sean's repentance that he allowed himself to be contained within the sick-room for such long periods. It chafed him like ropes on a young colt: no one would ever know what it cost him to sit quietly next to Garrick's bed while his body itched and burned with unexpended energy and his mind raced restlessly.

Then Sean had to go back to school. He left on a Monday morning while it was still dark. Garrick listened to the sounds of departure, the whicker of the horses outside on the driveway and Ada's voice reciting last minute instructions: 'I've put a bottle of cough mixture under your shirts, give it to Fräulein as soon as you unpack. Then she'll see that you take it at the first sign of a cold.'

'Yes, Ma.'

'There are six vests in the small case – use a new one every day.'

'Vests are sissy things.'

'You will do as you're told, young man.' Waite's voice, 'Hurry up with your porridge – we've got to get going if I'm to have you in town by seven o'clock.'

'Can I say goodbye to Garry?'

'You said goodbye last night – he'll still be asleep now.'

Garrick opened his mouth to call out, but he knew his voice would not carry. He lay quietly and listened to the chairs scraping back from the dining-room table, the procession of footsteps out onto the veranda, voices raised in farewells and at last the wheels of the buggy crunching gravel as they moved away down the drive. It was very quiet after Sean had left with his father.

After that the weekends were, for Garrick, the only bright spots in the colourless passage of time. He longed for them to come and each one was an eternity after the last – time passes slowly for the young and the sick. Ada and Waite knew a little of how he felt. They moved the centre of the household to his room: they brought two of the fat leather armchairs from the lounge and put them on each side of his bed and they spent the evenings there. Waite with his pipe in his mouth and a glass of brandy at his elbow, whittling at the wooden leg he was making and laughing his deep laugh, Ada with her knitting and the two of them trying to reach him. Perhaps it was this conscious effort that was the cause of their failure, or perhaps it is impossible to reach back down the years to a small boy. There is always that reserve, that barrier between the adult and the secret world of youth. Garrick laughed with them and they talked together, but it was not the same as having Sean there. During the day Ada had the running of a large household and there were fifteen thousand acres of land and two thousand head of cattle that needed Waite's attention. That was the loneliest time for Garrick. If it had not been for the books, he might not have been able to bear it. He read everything that Ada brought to him: Stevenson, Swift, Defoe, Dickens and even Shakespeare. Much of it he didn't understand, but he read hungrily and the opium of the printed word helped him through the long days until Sean came home each Friday.

When Sean came home it was like a big wind blowing through the house. Doors slammed, dogs barked, servants scolded and feet clattered up and down the passages. Most of the noise was Sean's, but not all of it. There were Sean's followers: youngsters from his class at the village school. They accepted Sean's authority as willingly as did Garrick, and it was not only Sean's fists that won this acceptance but also the laughter and the sense of excitement that went with him. They came out to Theunis Kraal in droves that summer, sometimes as many as three on one bare-backed pony: sitting like a row of sparrows on a fence rail. They came for the added attraction of Garry's stump. Sean was very proud of it.

'That's where the doc sewed it up,' pointing to the row of stitch marks along the pink fold of scar tissue.

'Can I touch it, man?'

'Not too hard or it'll burst open.' Garrick had never

received attention like this in his life before. He beamed round the circle of solemn, wide-eyed faces.

'It feels funny – sort of hot.'

'Was it sore?'

'How did he chop the bone – with an axe?'

'No.' Sean was the only one in a position to answer technical questions of this nature. 'With a saw. Just like a piece of wood.' He made the motions with his open hand.

But even this fascinating subject couldn't hold them for long and presently there would be a restlessness amongst them.

'Hey, Sean, Karl and I know where there's a nest of squawkers – you wanta have a look?' or 'Let's go and catch frogs,' and Garrick would cut in desperately.

'You can have a look at my stamp collection if you like. It's in the cupboard there.'

'Naw, we saw it last week. Let's go.'

This was when Ada, who had been listening to the conversation through the open kitchen door, brought in the food. Koeksusters fried in honey, chocolate cakes with peppermint icing, watermelon konfyt and half a dozen other delicacies. She knew they wouldn't leave until it was finished and she knew also that there'd be upset stomachs as it was, but that was preferable to Garrick lying alone and listening to the others riding off into the hills.

The weekends were short, gone in a breathless blur. Another long week began for Garrick. There were eight of them, eight dreary weeks before Doctor Van Rooyen agreed to let him sit out on the veranda during the day. Then suddenly the prospect of being well again became a reality for Garrick. The leg that Waite was making was nearly finished: he shaped a leather bucket to take the stump and fitted it to the wood with flat-headed copper nails; he worked carefully, moulding the leather and adjusting the straps that would hold it in place. Meanwhile, Garrick exercised along the veranda, hopping beside Ada with an arm around her shoulder, his jaws clenched with concentration and the freckles very prominent on his face that had been without the sun for so long. Twice a day Ada sat on a cushion in front of Garrick's chair and massaged the stump with methylated spirits to toughen it for its first contact with the stiff leather bucket.

'I bet old Sean'll be surprised, hey? When he sees me walking around.'

'Everyone will,' Ada agreed. She looked up from his leg and smiled.

'Can't I try it now? Then I can go out fishing with him when he comes on Saturday.'

'You mustn't expect too much, Garry, it's not going to be easy at first. You will have to learn to use it. Like riding a horse – you remember how often you fell off before you learned to ride.'

'But can I start now?'

Ada reached for the spirits bottle, poured a little into her cupped hand and spread it on the stump. 'We'll have to wait until Doctor Van Rooyen tells us you're ready. It won't be long now.'

It wasn't. After his next visit Doctor Van Rooyen spoke to Waite as they walked together to the doctor's trap.

'You can try him with the peg-leg – it'll give him something to work for. Don't let him overtire himself and watch the stump doesn't get rubbed raw. We don't want another infection.'

'Peg-leg.' Waite's mind echoed the ugly word as he watched the trap out of sight. 'Peg-leg': he clenched his fists at his sides, not wanting to turn and see the pathetically eager face behind him on the veranda.

– 6 –

'Are you sure that's comfortable?' Waite squatted in front of Garrick's chair adjusting the leg and Ada stood next to him.

'Yes, yes, let me try it now. Gee, old Sean will be surprised, hey? I'll be able to go back with him on Monday, won't I?' Garrick was trembling with eagerness.

'We'll see,' Waite grunted non-committally. He stood up and moved round beside the chair.

'Ada, my dear, take his other arm. Now listen, Garry, I want you to get the feel of it first. We'll help you up and you can just stand on it and get your balance. Do you understand?'

Garrick nodded vigorously.

'All right, then up you come.'

Garrick drew the leg towards him and the tip scraped across the wooden floor. They lifted him and he put his weight on it.

'Look at me – I'm standing on it. Hey, look I'm standing on it.' His face glowed. 'Let me walk, come on! Let me walk.'

Ada glanced at her husband and he nodded. Together they led Garrick forward. He stumbled twice but they held him. Klunk and klunk again the peg rang on the floor boards. Before they reached the end of the veranda Garrick had learned to lift the leg high as he swung it forward. They turned and he stumbled only once on the way back to the chair.

'That's fine, Garry, you're doing fine,' laughed Ada.

'You'll be on your own in no time,' Waite grinned with relief. He had hardly dared to hope it would be so easy, and Garrick fastened on his words. 'Let me stand on my own now.'

'Not this time, boy, you've done well enough for one day.'

'Oh, gee, Pa. Please. I won't try and walk, I'll just stand. You and Ma can be ready to catch me. Please, Pa, please.'

Waite hesitated and Ada added her entreaty. 'Let him, dear, he's done so well. It'll help build up his confidence.'

'Very well. But don't try to move,' Waite agreed. 'Are you ready, Garry? Let him go!' They took their hands off him cautiously. He teetered slightly and their hands darted back.

'I'm all right – leave me.' He grinned at them confidently and once more they released him. He stood straight and steady for a moment and then he looked down at the ground. The grin froze on his face. He was alone on a high mountain, his stomach turned giddily within him and he was afraid, desperately unreasonably afraid. He lurched violently and the first shriek tore from him before they could hold him. 'I'm falling. Take it off! Take it off!'

They sat him in the chair with one swift movement.

'Take it off! I'm going to fall!' The terrified screams racked Waite as he tore at the straps that held the leg.

'It's off, Garry, you're safe. I'm holding you.' Waite took him to his chest and held him, trying to quieten him with the strength of his arms and the security of his own big body, but Garrick's terrified struggling and his shrieks continued.

'Take him to the bedroom, get him inside.' Ada spoke urgently and Waite ran with him, still holding him against his chest.

Then for the first time Garrick found his hiding-place. At the moment when his terror became too great to bear he felt something move inside his head, fluttering behind his eyes like the wings of a moth. His vision greyed as though he was in a mist bank. The mist thickened and blotted out all sight and sound. It was warm in the mist –

warm and safe. No one could touch him here for it wrapped and protected him. He was safe.

'I think he's asleep,' Waite whispered to his wife, but there was a puzzled expression in his voice. He looked carefully at the boy's face and listened to his breathing.

'It happened so quickly though – it isn't natural. And yet – and yet he looks all right.'

'Do you think we should call the doctor?' Ada asked.

'No.' Waite shook his head. 'I'll just cover him up and stay with him until he wakes.'

He woke in the early evening, sat up and smiled at them as though nothing had happened. Relaxed and shyly cheerful, he ate a big supper and no one mentioned the leg. It was almost as though Garrick had forgotten about it.

– 7 –

Sean came home on the following Friday afternoon. He had a black eye – not a fresh one; it was already turning green round the edges of the bruise. Sean was very reticent on the subject of how he had obtained it. He brought with him also a clutch of flycatchers' eggs which he gave to Garrick, a live red-lipped snake in a cardboard box which Ada immediately condemned to death despite Sean's impassioned speech in its defence, and a bow carved from M'senga wood which was, in Sean's opinion, the best wood for a bow.

His arrival wrought the usual change in the household of Theunis Kraal – more noise, more movement and more laughter.

There was a huge roast for dinner that evening, with potatoes baked in their jackets. These were Sean's favourite foods and he ate like a hungry python.

'Don't put so much in your mouth,' Waite remonstrated

from the head of the table, but there was a fondness in his voice. It was hard not to show favouritism with his sons. Sean accepted the rebuke in the spirit it was given. 'Pa, Frikkie Oberholster's bitch had pups this week, six of them.'

'No,' said Ada firmly.

'Gee, Ma, just one.'

'You heard your mother, Sean.' Sean poured gravy over his meat, cut a potato in half and lifted one piece to his mouth. It had been worth a try. He hadn't really expected them to agree.

'What did you learn this week?' Ada asked. This was a nasty question. Sean had learned as much as was necessary to avoid trouble – no more.

'Oh, lots of things,' he replied airily and then to change the subject. 'Have you finished Garry's new leg yet, Pa?'

There was a silence. Garrick's face went expressionless and he dropped his eyes to his plate. Sean put the other half of the potato in his mouth and spoke around it.

'If you have, me and Garry can go fishing up at the falls tomorrow.'

'Don't talk with your mouth full,' snapped Waite with unnecessary violence. 'You've got the manners of a pig.'

'Sorry, Pa,' Sean muttered. The rest of the meal passed in uneasy silence and as soon as it finished Sean escaped to the bedroom. Garry went with him hopping along the passage with one hand on the wall to balance himself.

'What's Pa so mad about?' Sean demanded resentfully as soon as they were alone.

'I don't know.' Garrick sat on the bed. 'Sometimes he just gets mad for nothing – you know that.'

Sean pulled his shirt off over his head, screwed it into a ball and threw it against the far wall.

'You'd better pick it up, else there'll be trouble,' Garrick warned mildly. Sean dropped his pants and kicked them after the shirt. This show of defiance put him in a better mood. He walked across and stood naked in front of Garrick.

'Look,' he said with pride. 'Hairs!'

Garrick inspected them. Indisputably they were hairs.

'There aren't very many.' Garrick couldn't disguise the envy in his voice.

'Well, I bet I've got more than you have,' Sean challenged. 'Let's count them.'

But Garrick knew himself to be an outright loser; he slipped off the bed and hopped across the room. Steadying himself against the wall he stooped and picked up Sean's discarded clothing, he brought it back and dropped it in the soiled linen basket beside the door. Sean watched him and it reminded him of his unanswered question.

'Has Pa finished your leg yet, Garry?'

Garry turned slowly, he swallowed and nodded once, a quick jerky movement.

'What's it like? Have you tried it yet?'

The fear was on Garrick again. He twisted his face from side to side as though seeking an escape. There were footsteps in the passage outside the door. Sean dived at his bed and snatching up his nightgown pulled it over his head as he slid between the sheets. Garrick was still standing beside the clothes basket when Waite Courtney came into the room. 'Come on, Garry, what's holding you up?'

Garrick hurried across to his bed and Waite looked at Sean. Sean grinned at him with all the charm of his good looks and Waite's face softened into a grin also. 'Nice to have you home again, boy.' It was impossible to be angry with Sean for long.

He reached out and took a handful of Sean's thick black hair. 'Now I don't want to hear any talking in here after the lamp's out – do you understand?'

He tugged Sean's head from side to side gently, embarrassed by the strength of his feeling for his son.

– 8 –

The next morning Waite Courtney rode back to the homestead for his breakfast when the sun was high. One of the grooms took his horse and led it away to the paddock and Waite stood in front of the saddle room and looked around him. He looked at the neat white posts of the paddock, at the well-swept yard, at his house filled with fine furniture. It was a good feeling to be rich – especially when you knew what it was like to be poor. Fifteen thousand acres of good grassland, as many cattle as the land would carry, gold in the bank. Waite smiled and started across the yard.

He heard Ada singing in the dairy.

'How rides the farmer
Sit, sit, so
Sit, sit, so – tra la
The Capetown girls say
Kiss me quick
Kiss me quick – tra la.'

She had a clear sweet voice and Waite's smile broadened – it was a good feeling to be rich and to be in love. He stopped at the door of the dairy; because of the thick stone walls and heavy thatch it was cool and dark in the room. Ada stood with her back to the door, her body moving in time to the song and the turning of the butter churn. Waite watched her a moment, then he walked up behind her and put his arms around her waist.

Startled, she turned within his arms and he kissed her on the mouth. 'Good morning, my pretty maid.'

She relaxed against him. 'Good morning, sir,' she said.

'What's for breakfast?'

'Ah, what a romantic fool I married!' She sighed, 'Come along, let's go and see.'

She took off her apron, hung it behind the door, patted her hair into place and held her hand out to him. They walked hand-in-hand across the yard and into the kitchen. Waite sniffed loudly.

'Smells all right. Where are the boys?'

Joseph understood English though he could not speak it. He looked up from the stove.

'Nkosi, they are on the front veranda.'

Joseph had the typical moon-round face of the Zulu, when he smiled his teeth were big and white against the black of his skin.

'They are playing with Nkosizana Garry's wooden leg.'

Waite's face flushed. 'How did they find it?'

'Nkosizana Sean asked me where it was and I told him you had put it in the linen cupboard.'

'You bloody fool!' roared Waite. He dropped Ada's hand and ran. As he reached the lounge he heard Sean shout and immediately there was the sound of someone falling heavily on the veranda. He stopped in the middle of the lounge floor; he couldn't bear to go out and face Garrick's terror. He felt sick with dread and with his anger at Sean.

Then he heard Sean laugh. 'Get off me, man, don't just lie there.'

And then, incredibly, Garrick's voice. 'Sorry, it caught in the floor boards.'

Waite walked across to the window and looked out onto the veranda. Sean and Garrick lay in a heap together near the far end. Sean was still laughing and on Garrick's face was a set nervous smile. Sean scrambled up. 'Come on. Get up.'

He gave Garrick his hand and dragged him to his feet. They stood clinging to each other, Garrick balancing precariously on his peg. 'I bet if it was me I could just walk easy as anything,' said Sean.

'I bet you couldn't, it's jolly difficult.'

Sean let go of him and stood back with his arms spread ready to catch him. 'Come on.'

Sean walked backwards in front of him and Garrick followed unsteadily, his arms flapping out sideways as he struggled to keep his balance, his face rigid with concentration. He reached the end of the veranda and caught onto the rail with both hands. This time he joined in Sean's laughter.

Waite became aware that Ada was standing beside him; he glanced sideways at her and her lips formed the words 'come away'. She took his arm.

– 9 –

At the end of June 1876 Garrick went back to school with Sean. It was almost four months since the shooting. Waite drove them. The road to Ladyburg was through open forest, two parallel tracks with the grass growing in between – it brushed the bottom of the buggy. The horses trotted in the tracks, their hooves silent on the thick powder dust. At the top of the first rise Waite slowed the horses and turned in his seat to look back at the homestead. The early sun gave the whitewashed walls of Theunis Kraal an orange glow and the lawns around the house were brilliant green. Everywhere else the grass was dry in the early winter and the leaves of the trees were dry also. The sun was not yet high enough to rob the veld of its colour and light it only with the flat white glare of midday. The leaves were golden and russet and red-brown, the same red-brown as the bunches of Afrikander cattle that grazed among the trees. Behind it all was the back-drop of the escarpment, striped like a zebra with the green-black bush that grew in its gullies.

'Look, there's a hoopoe, Sean.'

'Yeah, I saw it long ago. That's a male.'

The bird flew up from in front of the horses: chocolate and black and white wings, its head crested like an Etruscan helmet.

'How do you know?' challenged Garrick.

''Cause of the white in its wings.'

'They've all got white in their wings.'

'They haven't – only the males.'

'Well, all the ones I've seen got white in their wings,' said Garrick dubiously.

'Perhaps you've never seen a female. They're jolly rare. They don't come out of their nests much.'

Waite Courtney smiled and turned back in his seat. 'Garry's right, Sean, you can't tell the difference by their feathers. The male's a little bigger, that's all.'

'I told you,' said Garrick, brave under his father's protection.

'You know everything,' muttered Sean sarcastically. 'I suppose you read it in all those books, hey?'

Garrick smiled complacently. 'Look, there's the train.'

It was coming down the escarpment, dragging a long grey plume of smoke behind it. Waite started the horses into a trot. They went down to the concrete bridge over the Baboon Stroom.

'I saw a yellow fish.'

'It was a stick, I saw it too.'

The river was the boundary of Waite's land. They crossed the bridge and went up the other side. In front of them was Ladyburg. The train was running into the town past the cattle sale pens; it whistled and shot a puff of steam high into the air.

The town was spread out, each house padded around by its orchard and garden. A thirty-six ox team could turn in any of the wide streets. The houses were burnt brick or whitewashed, thatched or with corrugated-iron roofs painted green or dull red. The square was in the centre and the spire of the church was the hub of Ladyburg. The school was on the far side of town.

Waite trotted the horses along Main Street. There were a few people on the side walks; they moved with early morning stiffness beneath the flamboyant trees that lined the street and every one of them called a greeting to Waite. He waved his whip at the men and lifted his hat to the women, but not high enough to expose the bald dome of his head. In the centre of town the shops were open, and standing on long thin legs in front of his bank was David Pye. He was dressed in black like an undertaker.

'Morning, Waite.'

'Morning, David,' called Waite a little too heartily. It was not six months since he had paid off the last mortgage on Theunis Kraal and the memory of debt was too fresh in his mind; he felt as embarrassed as a newly released prisoner meeting the prison governor on the street.

'Can you come in and see me after you've dropped off your boys?'

'Have the coffee ready,' agreed Waite. It was well known that no one was ever offered coffee when they called on David Pye. They went on down the street, turned left at the far end of Church Square, passed the courthouse and down the dip to the school hostel.

There were half a dozen Scotch carts and four-wheelers standing in the yard. Small boys and girls swarmed over them unloading their luggage. Their fathers stood in a group at one end of the yard – brown-faced men, with carefully brushed beards, uncomfortable in their suits which still showed the creases of long hanging. These men lived too far out for their children to make the daily journey into school. Their land sprawled down to the banks of the Tugela or across the plateau halfway to Pietermaritzburg.

Waite stopped the buggy, climbed down and loosened the harness on his horses and Sean jumped from the outside seat to the ground and ran to the nearest bunch of boys. Waite walked across to the men; their ranks opened for him, they smiled their welcomes and in turn reached for his right hand. Garrick sat alone on the front seat of the buggy, his leg stuck out stiffly in front of him and his shoulders hunched as though he were trying to hide.

After a while Waite glanced back over his shoulder. He saw Garrick sitting alone and he made as if to go to him, but stopped immediately. His eyes quested among the swirl of small bodies until they found Sean. 'Sean.'

Sean paused in the middle of an animated discussion. 'Yes, Pa.'

'Give Garry a hand with his case.'

'Aw, gee, Pa – I'm talking.'

'Sean!' Waite scowled with both face and voice.

'All right, I'm going.' Sean hesitated a moment longer and then went back to the buggy.

'Come on, Garry. Pass the cases down.'

Garrick roused himself and climbed awkwardly over the back of the seat. He handed the luggage down to Sean who stacked it beside the wheel, then turned to the group that had followed him across.

'Karl, you carry that. Dennis, take the brown bag. Don't drop it, man, it's got four bottles of jam in it.' Sean issued his instructions.

'Come on, Garry.'

They started off towards the hostel and Garrick climbed down from the buggy and limped quickly after them.

'You know what, Sean?' said Karl loudly. 'Pa let me start using his rifle.'

Sean stopped dead, and then more with hope than conviction, 'He did not!'

'He did,' Karl said happily. Garrick caught up with them and they all stared at Karl.

'How many shots did you have?' asked someone in an awed voice.

Karl nearly said, 'Six' but changed it quickly.

'Oh, lots – as many as I wanted.'

'You'll get gun-shy – my Pa says if you start too soon you'll never be a good shot.'

'I never missed once,' flashed Karl.

'Come on,' said Sean and started off once more – he had never been so jealous in his life. Karl hurried after him.

'I bet you've never shot with a rifle, Sean, I bet you haven't, hey?' Sean smiled mysteriously while he searched for some new topic; he could see that Karl was going to kick the subject to death.

From the veranda of the hostel a girl ran to meet him.

'It's Anna,' said Garrick.

She had long brown legs, skinny; her skirts fussed about them as she ran. Her hair was black, her face was small with a pointed chin. 'Hello, Sean.'

Sean grunted. She fell in beside him, skipping to keep pace with him.

'Did you have a nice holiday?'

Sean ignored her, always coming and trying to talk to him, even when his friends were watching.

'I've got a whole tin of shortbread, Sean. Would you like some?' There was a flash of interest in Sean's eyes; he half turned his head towards her, for Mrs Van Essen's shortbread was rightly famous throughout the district, but he caught himself and kept grimly on towards the hostel.

'Can I sit next to you in class this term, Sean?'

Sean turned furiously on her. 'No, you can't. Now go away – I'm busy.'

He went up the steps. Anna stood at the bottom; she looked as though she was going to cry and Garrick stopped shyly beside her.

'You can sit next to me if you like,' he said softly.

She glanced at him, looking down at his leg. The tears cleared and she giggled. She was pretty. She leaned towards him.

'Peg-leg,' she said and giggled again. Garrick blushed so vividly, and suddenly his eyes watered. Anna put both hands to her mouth and giggled through them, then she turned and ran to join her friends in front of the girls' section of the hostel. Still blushing, Garrick went up the steps after Sean; he steadied himself on the banisters.

Fräulein stood at the door of the boys' dormitory. Her steel-rimmed spectacles and the iron grey of her hair gave her face an exaggerated severity, but this was relieved by the smile with which she recognized Sean.

'Ah, my Sean, you have come.' What she actually said was, 'Ach, mein Sean, you haf gom.'

'Hello, Fräulein.' Sean gave her his number one very best smile.

'Again you have grown,' Fräulein measured him with her eyes. 'All the time you grow, already you are the biggest boy in the school.'

Sean watched her warily, ready to take evasive action if she attempted to embrace him as she did sometimes when she could no longer contain her feelings. Sean's blend of charm, good looks and arrogance had completely captured her Teutonic heart.

'Quickly, you must unpack. School is just now starting.' She turned her attention to her other charges and Sean, with relief, led his men through into the dormitory.

'Pa says that next weekend I can use his rifle for hunting, not just targets,' Karl steered the conversation back.

'Dennis, put Garry's case on his bed.' Sean pretended not to hear.

There were thirty beds arranged along the walls, each with a locker beside it. The room was as neat and cheerless as a prison or a school. At the far end a group of five or six boys sat talking. They looked up as Sean came in but no greetings were exchanged – they were the opposition.

Sean sat down on his bed and bounced experimentally. It was hard as a plank. Garrick's peg thumped as he walked down the dormitory and Ronny Pye, the leader of the opposition, whispered something to his friends and they all laughed, watching Garrick. Garrick blushed again and sat down quickly on his bed to hide his leg.

'I guess I'll shoot duiker first before Pa lets me shoot kudu or bushbuck,' Karl stated and Sean frowned.

'What's the new teacher like?' he asked.

'He looks all right,' one of the others answered. 'Jimmy and I saw him at the station yesterday.'

'He's thin and got a moustache.'

'He doesn't smile much.'

'I suppose next holiday Pa will take me shooting across the Tugela,' Karl said aggressively.

'I hope he's not too keen on spelling and things,' Sean declared. 'I hope he doesn't start all that decimal business again, like old Lizard did.'

There was a round of agreement and then Garrick made his first contribution. 'Decimals are easy.'

There was a silence while they all looked at him.

'I might even shoot a lion,' said Karl.

– 10 –

There was a single schoolroom to accommodate the youngest upwards of both sexes. Double desks; on the walls a few maps, a large set of multiplication tables and a picture of Queen Victoria. From the dais Mr Anthony Clark surveyed his new pupils. There was a hushed anticipation; one of the girls giggled nervously and Mr Clark's eyes sought the sound, but it stopped before he found it.

'It is my unfortunate duty to attempt your education,' he announced. He wasn't joking. Long ago his sense of vocation had been swamped by an intense dislike for the young: now he taught only for the salary.

'It is your no more pleasant duty to submit to this with all the fortitude you can muster,' he went on, looking with distaste at their shining faces.

'What's he saying?' whispered Sean without moving his lips.

'Shh,' said Garrick.

Mr Clark's eyes swivelled quickly and rested on Garrick. He walked slowly down the aisle between the desks and stopped beside him; he took a little of the hair that grew at Garrick's temple between his thumb and his forefinger and jerked it upwards. Garrick squeaked and Mr Clark returned slowly to his dais.

'We will now proceed. Standard Ones kindly open your spelling books at page one. Standard Twos turn to page fifteen . . .' He went on allocating their work.

'Did he hurt you?' breathed Sean. Garrick nodded almost imperceptibly and Sean conceived an immediate and intense hatred for the man. He stared at him.

Mr Clark was a little over thirty years old – thin, and his tight three-piece suit emphasized this fact. He had a pale face made sad by his drooping moustache, and his nose was upturned to such a degree that his nostrils were exposed; they pointed out of his face like the muzzle of a double-barrelled shotgun. He lifted his head from the list he held in his hand and aimed his nostrils straight at Sean. For a second they stared at each other.

'Trouble,' thought Mr Clark; he could pick them unerringly. 'Break him before he gets out of control.'

'You, boy, what's your name?'

Sean turned elaborately and looked over his shoulder. When he turned back there was a little colour in Mr Clark's cheeks. 'Stand up.'

'Who, me?'

'Yes, you.'

Sean stood.

'What's your name?'

'Courtney.'

'Sir!'

'Courtney, sir.'

They looked at each other. Mr Clark waited for Sean to drop his eyes but he didn't.

'Big trouble, much bigger than I thought,' he decided and said aloud, 'All right, sit down.'

There was an almost audible relaxation of tension in the room. Sean could sense the respect of the others around him; they were proud of the way he had carried it off. He felt a touch on his shoulder. It was Anna, the seat behind him was as close as she could sit to him. Ordinarily her presumption would have annoyed him, but now that small touch on his shoulder added to his glow of self-satisfaction.

An hour passed slowly for Sean. He drew a picture of a rifle in the margin of his spelling book then rubbed it out carefully; he watched Garrick for a while until his brother's absorption with his work irritated him.

'Swot,' he whispered, but Garrick ignored him.

Sean was bored. He shifted restlessly in his seat and looked at the back of Karl's neck – there was a ripe pimple on it. He picked up his ruler to prod it. Before he could do so Karl lifted his hand as if to scratch his shoulder but there was a scrap of paper between his fingers. Sean put down the ruler and surreptitiously reached for the note. He held it in his lap, on it was written one word.

'Mosquitoes.'

Sean grinned. Sean's imitation of a mosquito was one of the many reasons why the previous schoolmaster had resigned. For six months old Lizard had believed that there were mosquitoes in the room – then for the next six months he had known there were not. He had tried every ruse he could think of to catch the culprit, and in the end it had got him. Every time the monotonous hum began the tic in the corner of his mouth became more noticeable.

Now Sean cleared his throat and started to hum. Instantly the room was tense with suppressed laughter. Every head, including Sean's, was bent studiously over a book. Mr Clark's hand hesitated in writing on the blackboard but then went on again evenly.

It was a clever imitation; by lowering and raising the volume Sean gave the effect of an insect moving about the room. A slight trembling at his throat was the only sign that he was responsible.

Mr Clark finished writing and turned to face the room. Sean did not make the mistake of stopping, he allowed the mosquito to fly a little longer before settling.

Mr Clark left his dais and walked down the row of desks furthest from Sean. Once or twice he paused to check the work of one of his pupils. He reached the back of the room and moved across to Sean's row. He stopped at Anna's desk.

'It is unnecessary to loop your L's like that,' he told her. 'Let me show you.' He took her pencil and wrote, 'You see what I mean. To show off when writing is as bad as showing off in your everyday behaviour.'

He handed her back her pencil and then pivoting on one foot he hit Sean a mighty crack across the side of the head with his open hand. Sean's head was knocked sideways and the sound of the blow was very loud in the quiet room.

'There was a mosquito sitting on your ear,' said Mr Clark.

– 11 –

In the following two years Sean and Garrick made the change from child to young manhood. It was like riding a strong current, being swept with speed along the river of life.

There were parts of the river that flowed steadily:

Ada was one of these. Always understanding, with the ability to give her understanding expression, unchanging in her love for her husband and the family she had taken as her own.

Waite was another. A little more grey in his hair but big as ever in body, laugh and fortune.

There were parts of the river that ran faster:

Garrick's reliance on Sean. He needed him more strongly each month that passed, for Sean was his shield. If Sean was not there to protect him when he was threatened, then he used his final refuge: he crawled back into himself, into the warm dark mists of his mind.

They went to steal peaches: the twins, Karl, Dennis and two others. There was a thick hedge around Mr Pye's orchard and the peaches that grew on the other side of it were as big as a man's fist. They were sweet as honey but tasted even sweeter when taken on the plunder account. You reached the orchard through a plantation of wattle trees.

'Don't take too many off one tree!' Sean ordered. 'Old Pye will notice it as sure as anything.'

They came to the hedge and Sean found the hole.

'Garry, you stay here and keep cats for us. If anyone comes give a whistle.' Garrick tried not to show his relief, he had no stomach for the expedition.

Sean went on. 'We'll pass the peaches out to you – and don't eat any until we're finished.'

'Why doesn't he come with us?' asked Karl.

''Cause he can't run, that's why. If he gets caught they'll know who the rest of us are for sure and we'll all get it.'

Karl was satisfied. Sean went down on his hands and knees and crawled into the hole in the hedge and one at a time the others followed him until Garrick was left alone.

He stood close to the hedge, drawing comfort from its protecting bulk. The minutes dragged by and Garrick fidgeted nervously – they were taking an awfully long time.

Suddenly there were voices, someone was coming through the plantation towards him. Panic beat up inside him and he shrank back into the hedge, trying to hide; the idea of giving a warning never even entered his head.

The voices were closer and then through the trees he recognized Ronny Pye: with him were two of his friends. Each of them was armed with a slingshot and they walked with their heads thrown back, searching the trees for birds.

For a time it seemed they would not notice Garrick in the hedge; but then, when they had almost passed, Ronny turned his head and saw him. They stared at each other, ten paces apart, Garrick crouched against the hedge and Ronny's expression of surprise slowly changing to one of cunning. He looked around quickly, to make sure that Sean was not there.

'It's old Hobble-dee-hoy,' he announced and his friends came back and stood on each side of him.

'What're you doing, Peg-leg?'

'Rats got your tongue, Peg-leg?'

'No, termites got his leg!' – laughter aimed to hurt.

'Talk to us, Peg-leg.' Ronny Pye had ears that stood out on each side of his head like a pair of fans. He was small for his age which made him vicious and his hair was ginger.

'Come on. Talk to us, Peg-leg.'

Garrick moistened his lips with his tongue, already there were tears in his eyes.

'Hey, Ronny, make him walk for us, like this.' One of the others gave a graphic imitation of Garrick's limp. Again laughter, louder now, more confident and they closed in on him. 'Show us how you walk.'

Garrick swung his head from side to side searching for an escape.

'Your brother's not here,' crowed Ronny. 'No good looking for him, Peg-leg.'

He caught a hold of Garrick's shirt and pulled him out of the hedge.

'Show us how you walk.'

Garrick plucked ineffectually at Ronny's hand.

'Leave me, I'll tell Sean. I'll tell Sean unless you leave me.'

'All right, I'll leave you,' agreed Ronny and with both hands shoved him in the chest. 'Don't come my way – go that way!' Garrick stumbled backwards.

One of the others was ready for him. 'Don't come my way – go that way!' and pushed him in the back. They formed a ring around him and kept him staggering between them.

'Go that way!'

'Go that way!'

The tears were streaked down his cheeks now. 'Please, please stop.'

'Please, please,' they mimicked him.

Then, with a rush of relief, Garrick felt the fluttering start behind his eyes – their faces dimmed, he hardly felt their hands upon him. He fell and his face hit the ground, but there was no pain. Two of them stooped over him to lift him, and there was dirt mixed with the tears on his cheeks.

Sean came through the hedge behind them; the front of his shirt bulged with peaches. For a second he crouched on his hands and knees while he took in what was happening, then he came out of his crouch at a run. Ronny heard him, dropped Garrick and turned.

'You've been pinching Pa's peaches,' he shouted. 'I'll tell—'

Sean's fist hit him on the nose and he sat down. Sean swung towards the other two but they were already running, he chased them a few paces and then came back for Ronny, but he was too late. Ronny was dodging away between the trees holding his face and his nose was bleeding onto his shirt.

'Are you all right, Garry?' Sean knelt beside him, trying to wipe the dirt off his face with a grubby handkerchief. Sean helped him to his feet, and Garrick stood swaying slightly with his eyes open but a remote and vacant smile on his lips.

There were landmarks along the course of the river. Some of them small as a pile of rocks in shallow water:

Waite Courtney looked at Sean across the breakfast table at Theunis Kraal. The fork-load of egg and grilled gammon stopped on the way to his mouth.

'Turn your face towards the window,' he commanded suspiciously. Sean obeyed. 'What the hell is that on your face?'

'What?' Sean ran his hand over his cheek.

'When did you last bath?'

'Don't be silly, my dear.' Ada touched his leg under the table. 'It isn't dirt – it's whiskers.'

'Whiskers, are they?' Waite peered closely at Sean and started to grin, he opened his mouth to speak and Ada knew instantly that he was going to make a joke – one of those ponderous jokes of his, as subtle as an enraged dinosaur, that would wound Sean deep in his half-formed manhood. Quickly she cut in, 'I think you should buy him a razor, don't you, Waite?'

Waite lost the thread of his joke, he grunted and put the egg into his mouth.

'I don't want to cut them,' said Sean and flushed scarlet.

'They'll grow quicker if you shave them a bit at first,' Ada told him.

Across the table from her Garrick fingered his jowls wistfully.

Some of the landmarks were big as headlands:

Waite fetched them from school at the beginning of the December holidays. In the confusion of loading their cases onto the buggy and shouting farewells to Fräulein and to their friends, some of whom they would not see for another six weeks, the twins did not notice that Waite was acting strangely.

It was only later when the horses were heading for home at twice their normal speed that Sean asked, 'What's the hurry, Pa?'

'You'll see,' said Waite, and both Garrick and Sean looked at him with sudden interest. It had been an idle question of Sean's but Waite's answer had them immediately intrigued. Waite grinned at the bombardment of questions but he kept his answers vague. He was enjoying himself. By the time they reached Theunis Kraal the twins were in a frenzy of curiosity.

Waite pulled the horses up in front of the house and one of the grooms ran to take the reins. Ada was waiting on the veranda and Sean jumped down and ran up the steps to her. He kissed her quickly. 'What's happening?' he pleaded. 'Pa won't tell us but we know it's something.'

Garrick hurried up the steps also. 'Go on, tell us.' He caught hold of her arm and tugged it.

'I don't know what you're talking about,' Ada laughed. 'You'd better ask your father again.'

Waite climbed up after them, put one arm around Ada's waist and squeezed her.

'I don't know where they got this idea from,' said Waite, 'but why not tell them to go and have a look in their bedroom? They might as well have their Christmas presents a bit earlier this year.'

Sean beat Garrick to the lounge and was far in the lead by the time he reached the door of their bedroom.

'Wait for me,' called Garrick desperately. 'Please wait for me.'

Sean stopped in the doorway.

'Jesus Christ,' he whispered – they were the strongest words he knew. Garrick came up behind him and together they stared at the pair of leather cases that lay on the table in the middle of the room – long flat cases, heavy polished leather with the corners bound in brass.

'Rifles!' said Sean. He walked slowly to the table as though he were stalking the cases, expecting them at any moment to vanish.

'Look!' Sean reached out to touch with one finger the

gold lettering stamped into the lid of the nearest case. 'Our names on them even.'

He sprung the locks and lifted the lid. In a nest of green baize, perfumed with gun oil, glistened a poem in steel and wood.

'Jesus Christ,' said Sean again. Then he looked over his shoulder at Garrick. 'Aren't you going to open yours?'

Garrick limped up to the table trying to hide his disappointment: he had wanted a set of Dickens so badly.

In the river there were whirlpools:

The last week of the Christmas holidays and Garrick was in bed with one of his colds. Waite Courtney had gone to Pietermaritzburg for a meeting of the Beef Growers' Association and there was very little work to do on the farm that day. After Sean had dosed the sick cattle in the sanatorium paddock and ridden an inspection around the south section he returned to the homestead and spent an hour talking to the stableboys, then he drifted up to the house. Garry was asleep and Ada was in the dairy making butter. He asked for and got an early lunch from Joseph and ate it standing in the kitchen. While he ate he thought over the problem of how to fill the afternoon. He weighed the alternatives carefully. Take the rifle and try for duiker along the edge of the escarpment or ride to the pools above the White Falls and fish for eels. He was still undecided after he had finished eating so he crossed the yard and looked into the cool dimness of the dairy.

Ada smiled at him across the churn. 'Hello, Sean, I suppose you want your lunch.'

'Joseph gave it to me already, thanks, Ma.'

'Joseph has already given it to me,' Ada corrected mildly. Sean repeated it after her and sniffed the dairy smell – he liked the cheesy warmth of new butter and the tang of the cow dung smeared on the earth floor.

'What are you going to do this afternoon?'

'I came to ask you if you wanted venison or eels – I don't know if I want to go fishing or shooting.'

'Eels would be nice – we could jelly them and have them for dinner tomorrow when your father comes home.'

'I'll get you a bucket full.'

He saddled the pony, hung his tin of worms on the saddle and with his pole over his shoulder rode towards Ladyburg. He crossed the Baboon Stroom bridge and turned off the road to follow the stream up to the falls. As he skirted the wattle plantation below the Van Essens' place he realized he had made a mistake in picking this route. Anna, with her skirts held up to her knees, came pelting out from among the trees. Sean kicked the pony into a trot and looked straight ahead.

'Sean – hey, Sean.'

She was ahead of him, running to intercept him; there was no chance of evading her so he stopped the pony.

'Hello, Sean.' She was panting and her face was flushed.

'Hello,' he gruffed.

'Where are you going?'

'There and back to see how far it is.'

'You're going fishing – may I come with you?' She smiled appealingly. Her teeth were small and white.

'No, you talk too much; you'll frighten the fish.'

He started the pony.

'Please, I'll be quiet; honest I will.' She was running next to him.

'No.' He flicked the reins and pulled away from her. He rode for a hundred yards then looked round and she was still following with her black hair streaming out behind her. He stopped the pony and she caught up with him.

'I knew you'd stop,' she told him through her gasps.

'Will you go home? I don't want you following me.'

'I'll be quiet as anything – honest I will.'

He knew she'd follow him right up to the top of the escarpment and he gave in. 'All right, but if you say a word, just one single word, I'll send you home.'

'I promise – help me up, please.'

He dragged her onto the pony's rump and she sat sideways with her arms round his waist. They climbed the escarpment. The path ran close beside the White Falls and they could feel the spray blowing off them fine as mist. Anna kept her promise until she was sure they'd gone too far for Sean to send her back alone. She started talking again. When she wanted an answer from him, which wasn't very often, she squeezed his waist and Sean grunted. Sean knee-haltered the pony, and left him among the trees above the pools. He hid his saddle and bridle in an ant-bear hole and they walked down through the reeds to the water. Anna ran ahead of him and when he came out on to the sandbank she was throwing pebbles into the pool.

'Hey, stop that! You'll frighten the fish,' Sean shouted.

'Oh. I'm sorry. I forgot.'

She sat down and wriggled her bare toes into the sand. Sean baited his hook and lobbed it out into the green water – the current drifted his float in a wide circle under the far bank and they both watched it solemnly.

'It doesn't seem as though there are any fish here,' Anna said.

'You've got to be patient – you can't expect to catch one right away.'

Anna drew patterns in the sand with her toes and five minutes passed slowly. 'Sean—'

'Ssh!'

Another five minutes.

'Fishing's a silly old thing.'

'Nobody asked you to come,' Sean told her.

'It's hot here!' Sean didn't answer.

The high reed beds shut out any breeze and the white sand threw the sun's heat back at them. Anna stood up and wandered restlessly across the sand to the edge of the reeds. She picked a handful of the long spear-shaped leaves and plaited them together.

'I'm bored,' she announced.

'Well, go home then.'

'And I'm hot.'

Sean pulled his line in, inspected the worms and cast them out again. Anna stuck her tongue out at his back.

'Let's have a swim,' she suggested.

Sean ignored her. He stuck the butt of his rod into the sand, pulled his hat down to shield his eyes from the glare and leaned back on his elbows with his legs stretched out in front of him. He could hear the sand crunching as she moved and then there was another silence. He started to worry about what she was doing, but if he looked around it would be a show of weakness.

'Girls!' he thought bitterly.

There was the sound of running feet just behind him. He sat up quickly and started to turn. Her white body flashed past him and hit the water, with a smack like a rising trout. Sean jumped up. 'Hey, what're you doing?'

'I'm swimming,' laughed Anna, waist-deep in green water, with her hair slicked wetly down her shoulders and over her breasts. Sean looked at those breasts, white as the flesh of an apple and nippled in dark pink, almost red. Anna dropped onto her back and kicked the water white.

'*Voet sak*, little fishes! Scat, little fishes,' she gurgled.

'Hey, you mustn't do that,' Sean said half-heartedly. He wanted her to stand up again, those breasts gave him a strange tight feeling in his stomach, but Anna knelt with the water up to her chin. He could see them through the water. He wanted her to stand up.

'It's lovely! Why don't you come in?' She rolled on her stomach and ducked her head under the water; the twin ovals of her bottom broke the surface and Sean's stomach tightened again.

'Are you coming in?' she demanded, rubbing the water out of her eyes with both hands. Sean stood bewildered – within a few seconds his feelings towards her had undergone a major revolution. He wanted very much to be in the water with all those mysterious white bulges – but he was shy.

'You're scared! Come on, I give you guts to come in.' She teased him. The challenge pricked him.

'I'm not scared.'

'Well, come on then.'

He hesitated a few seconds longer, then he threw off his hat and unbuttoned his shirt. He turned his back on her while he dropped his pants then spun round and dived into the pool, thankful for the cover it gave him. His head came out and Anna pushed it under again. He groped and caught her legs, straightened up and threw her on her back. He dragged her towards the shallows, where the water wouldn't cover her. She was thrashing her arms to keep her head out and screaming delightedly. Sean's heels snagged a rock and he fell, letting go of her; before he could recover she had leapt on him and straddled his back. He could have thrown her off, but he liked the feel of her flesh on his – warm through the cool water, slippery with wetness. She picked up a handful of sand and rubbed it into his hair. Sean struggled gently. She threw her arms round his neck and he could feel the whole length of her body along his back. The tightness in his stomach moved up into his chest and he wanted to hold her. He rolled over and reached for her but she twisted out of his hands and dived back into the deep again. Sean splashed after her but she kept out of his reach, laughing at him.

At last they faced each other, still chin deep, and Sean was getting angry. He wanted to hold her. She saw the change of his mood and she waded to the bank, walked to his clothes and picked up his shirt. She dried her face on it, standing naked and unashamed – she had too many brothers for modesty. Sean watched the way her breasts changed shape as she lifted her arms, he looked at the lines of her body and saw that her once skinny legs had filled out; her thighs touched each other all the way up to the base of her belly and there she wore the dark triangular badge of womanhood. She spread the shirt out on the sand and sat down upon it, then she looked at him.

'Are you coming out?'

He came out awkwardly, covering himself with his hands. Anna moved over on the shirt. 'You can sit down, if you like.'

He sat hurriedly and drew his knees up under his chin. He watched her from the corner of his eye. There were little goose-pimples round her nipples from the cold water. She was aware that he was watching her and she pulled back her shoulders, enjoying it. Sean felt bewildered again – she was so clearly in control now. Before she had been someone to growl at but now she was giving the orders and he was obeying.

'You've got hairs on your chest,' Anna said, turning to look at him. Sparse and silky though they were, Sean was glad that he had them. He straightened out his legs.

'And you're much bigger there than Frikkie.' Sean tried to pull up his knees again but she put her hand on his leg and stopped him.

'Can I touch you?'

Sean tried to speak but his throat had closed and no sound came through it. Anna did not wait for an answer.

'Oh, look! It's getting all cheeky – just like Caribou's.'

Caribou was Mr Van Essen's stallion.

'I always know when Pa is going to let Caribou service a mare, he tells me to go and visit Aunt Lettie. I just hide in the plantation. You can see the paddock jolly well from the plantation.'

Anna's hand was soft and restless, Sean could think of nothing else.

'Do you know that people service, just like horses do?' she asked.

Sean nodded, he had attended the biology classes conducted by Messrs Daffel and Company in the school latrines. They were quiet for a while, then Anna whispered.

'Sean, would you service me?'

'I don't know how,' croaked Sean.

'I bet horses don't either the first time, nor people for that matter,' Anna said. 'We could find out.'

They rode home in the early evening, Anna sitting up behind Sean, her arms tight round his waist and the side of her face pressed between his shoulders. He dropped her at the back of the plantation.

'I'll see you at school on Monday,' she said and turned to go.

'Anna—'

'Yes?'

'Is it still sore?'

'No,' and then, after a moment's thought, 'it feels nice.'

She turned and ran into the wattle trees.

Sean rode slowly home. He was empty inside; it was a sad feeling and it puzzled him.

'Where are the fish?' asked Ada.

'They weren't biting.'

'Not even one?'

Sean shook his head and crossed the kitchen.

'Sean.'

'Yes, Ma.'

'Is something wrong?'

'No' – quick denial – 'No, I'm fine.' He slipped into the passage.

Garrick was sitting up in bed. The skin around his nostrils was inflamed and chapped; he lowered the book he was reading and smiled at Sean as he came into the room. Sean went to his own bed and sat on it.

'Where have you been?' Garrick's voice was thick with cold.

'Up at the pools above the falls.'

'Fishing?'

Sean didn't answer, he leaned forward on the bed with his elbows on his knees. 'I met Anna, she came with me.'

Garrick's interest quickened at the mention of her name and he watched Sean's face. Sean still had that slightly puzzled expression.

'Garry,' he hesitated; he had to talk about it. 'Garry, I screwed Anna.'

Garrick drew in his breath with a small hiss. He went very pale, only his nose was still red and sore-looking.

'I mean,' Sean spoke slowly as though he were trying to explain it to himself, 'I mean really screwed her, just like we've talked about. Just like . . .' He made a helpless gesture with his hands, unable to find the words. Then he lay back on the bed.

'Did she let you?' Garrick's voice was almost a whisper.

'She asked me to,' Sean said. 'It was slippery – sort of warm and slippery.'

And then later, long after the lamp was out and they were both in bed, Sean heard Garrick's soft movements in the darkness. He listened for a while until he was certain.

'Garry!' He accused him loudly.

'I wasn't, I wasn't.'

'You know what Pa told us. Your teeth will fall out and you'll go mad.'

'I wasn't, I wasn't.' Garrick's voice was choked with his cold and his tears.

'I heard you,' said Sean.

'I was just scratching my leg. Honestly, honestly, I was.'

And at the end the river plunged over the last waterfall and swept them into the sea of manhood.

Mr Clark had not been able to break Sean. He had provoked instead a bitter contest in which he knew himself to be slowly losing ground, and now he was afraid of Sean. He no longer made Sean stand, for Sean was as tall as he was. The contest had been on for two years; they had explored each other's weaknesses and knew how to exploit them.

Mr Clark could not bear the sound of anyone sniffing; perhaps subconsciously he took it as mockery of his own deformed nose. Sean had a repertoire that varied from a barely audible connoisseur testing-the-bouquet-of-brandy sniff to a loud hawking in the back of his throat.

'Sorry, sir, I can't help it. I've got a bit of a cold.'

But then, to even the score, Mr Clark had realized that Sean was vulnerable through Garrick. Hurt Garrick even a little and you were inflicting almost unbearable agony on Sean.

It had been a bad week for Mr Clark. His liver, weakened by persistent bouts of malaria, had been troubling him. He had suffered with a bilious headache for three days now; there had been unpleasantness with the Town Council about the terms on which his contract was to be renewed; Sean had been in good sniffing form the day before and Mr Clark had had about as much as he was prepared to take.

He came into the schoolroom and took his place on the dais; he let his eyes move slowly over his pupils until they came to Sean.

'Just let him start,' thought Mr Clark. 'Just let him start today and I'll kill him.'

The seating had been rearranged in the last two years. Sean and Garrick had been separated and Garrick was now at the front of the room where Mr Clark could reach him easily. Sean was near the back.

'English Readers,' said Mr Clark. 'Standard Ones turn to page five. Standard Twos turn to—'

Garrick sniffed wetly, hayfever again.

Mr Clark shut his book with a snap.

'Damn you!' he said softly, and then, his voice rising, 'Damn you!' Now he was shaking with rage, the edges of his nostrils were white and flared open.

He came down from the dais to Garrick's desk. 'Damn you! Damn you – you bloody little cripple,' he screamed and hit Garrick across the face with his open hand. Garrick cupped both hands over his cheek and stared at him.

'You dirty little swine,' Mr Clark mouthed at him. 'Now you're starting it too.'

He caught a handful of Garrick's hair and pulled his head down so that his forehead hit the top of the desk. 'I'll teach you. By God, I'll teach you.'

'I'll show you.' Bump.

'I'll teach you.' Bump.

It took Sean that long to reach them. He grabbed Mr Clark's arm and pulled him backwards. 'Leave him alone! He didn't do anything!'

Mr Clark saw Sean's face in front of him – he was past all reason – the face that had tormented him for two long years. He bunched his fist and lashed out at it.

Sean staggered back from the blow, the sting of it made

his eyes water. For a second he lay sprawled across one of the desks, watching Clark and then he growled.

The sound sobered Clark, he backed away but only two paces before Sean was on him. Hitting with both hands, grunting with each punch, Sean drove him against the blackboard. Clark tried to break away but Sean caught the collar of his shirt and dragged him back – the collar tore half loose in his hand and Sean hit him again. Clark slid down the wall until he was sitting against it and Sean stood panting over him.

'Get out,' said Clark. His teeth were stained pink by the blood in his mouth and a little of it spilled out onto his lips. His collar stood up at a jaunty angle under one ear.

There was no sound in the room except Sean's breathing.

'Get out,' said Clark again and the anger drained out of Sean, leaving him trembling with reaction. He walked to the door.

'You too,' Clark pointed at Garrick. 'Get out and don't come back!'

'Come on, Garry,' said Sean.

Garrick stood up from his desk and limped across to Sean and together they went out into the school yard.

'What are we going to do now?' There was a big red lump on Garrick's forehead.

'I suppose we'd better go home.'

'What about our things?' asked Garrick.

'We can't carry all that – we'll have to send for them later. Come on.'

They walked out through the town and along the road to the farm. They had almost reached the bridge on the Baboon Stroom before either of them spoke again.

'What do you reckon Pa will do?' asked Garrick. He was only putting into words the problem that had occupied them both since they left the school.

'Well, whatever he does, it was worth it.' Sean grinned. 'Did you see me clobber him, hey? Smackeroo – right in the chops.'

'You shouldn't have done it, Sean. Pa's going to kill us. Me too and I didn't do anything.'

'You sniffed,' Sean reminded him.

They reached the bridge and leaned over the parapet side by side to watch the water.

'How's your leg?' asked Sean.

'It's sore – I think we should rest a bit.'

'All right, if you say so,' Sean agreed.

There was a long silence, then, 'I wish you hadn't done it, Sean.'

'Well, wishing isn't going to help. Old Nose-Holes is as punched up as he'll ever be and all we can do is think of something to tell Pa.'

'He hit me,' said Garrick. 'He might have killed me.'

'Yes,' agreed Sean righteously, 'and he hit me too.'

They thought about it for a while.

'Perhaps we should just go away,' suggested Garrick.

'You mean without telling Pa?' The idea had attraction.

'Yeah, we could go to sea or something,' Garrick brightened.

'You'd get seasick, you even get sick in a train.'

Once more they applied their minds to the problem. Then Sean looked at Garrick, Garrick looked at Sean and as though by agreement they straightened up and started off once more for Theunis Kraal.

Ada was in front of the house. She had on a wide-brimmed straw hat that kept her face in shadow and over one arm she carried a basket of flowers. Busy with her garden, she didn't notice them until they were halfway across the lawn and when she did she stood motionless. She was steeling herself, trying to get her emotions under control; from experience she had learned to expect the worst from her stepsons and be thankful when it wasn't as bad as that.

As they came towards her they lost momentum and finally halted like a pair of clockwork toys running down.

'Hello,' said Ada.

'Hello,' they answered her together.

Garrick fumbled in his pocket, drew out a handkerchief and blew his nose. Sean stared up at the steep Dutch-gabled roof of Theunis Kraal as though he had never seen it before.

'Yes?' Ada kept her voice calm.

'Mr Clark said we were to go home,' announced Garrick.

'Why?' Ada's calm was starting to crack.

'Well—' Garrick glanced at Sean for support. Sean's attention was still riveted on the roof.

'Well . . . You see Sean sort of punched him in the head until he fell down. I didn't do anything.'

Ada moaned softly, 'Oh, no!' She took a deep breath. 'All right. Start at the beginning and give me the whole story.'

They told it in relays, a garbled rush of words, interrupting each other and arguing over the details. When they had finished Ada said, 'You better go to your room. Your father is working in the home section today and he'll be back for his lunch soon. I'll try and prepare him a little.'

The room had the cheery atmosphere of a condemned cell.

'How much do you reckon he'll give us?' asked Garrick.

'I reckon until he gets tired, then he'll rest and give us some more,' Sean answered.

They heard Waite's horse come into the yard. He said something to the stable boy and they heard him laugh; the kitchen door slammed and there was half a minute of suspense before they heard Waite roar. Garrick jumped nervously.

For another ten minutes they could hear Waite and Ada

talking in the kitchen, the alternate rumble and soothing murmur. Then the tap of Ada's feet along the passage and she came into the room.

'Your father wants to see you – he's in the study.'

Waite stood in front of the fireplace. His beard was powdered with dust and his forehead as corrugated as a ploughed land with the force of his scowl.

'Come in,' he bellowed when Sean knocked and they filed in and stood in front of him. Waite slapped his riding-whip against his leg and the dust puffed out of his breeches.

'Come here,' he said to Garrick and took a handful of his hair. He twisted Garrick's face up and looked at the bruise on his forehead.

'Hmm,' he said. He let go of Garrick's hair and it stood up in a tuft. He threw the riding-whip on the stinkwood desk.

'Come here,' he said to Sean. 'Hold out your hands – no, palms down.'

The skin on both hands was broken and one knuckle was swollen and puffy looking.

'Hmm,' he said again. He turned to the shelf beside the fireplace, took a pipe out of the rack and filled it from the stone jar of tobacco.

'You're a pair of bloody fools,' he said, 'but I'll take a chance and start you on five shillings a week all found. Go and get your lunch . . . we've got work to do this afternoon.'

They stared at him a moment in disbelief and then back towards the door.

'Sean.' Sean stopped, he knew it was too good to be true. 'Where did you hit him?'

'All over, Pa, anywhere I could reach.'

'That's no good,' Waite said. 'You must go for the side of his head – here,' he tapped the point of his jaw with his pipe, 'and keep your fists closed tight or you'll break every finger in your hands before you're much older.'

'Yes, Pa.'

The door closed softly behind him and Waite allowed himself to grin.

'They've had enough book learning anyway,' he said aloud and struck a match to his pipe; when it was drawing evenly he blew out smoke.

'Christ, I wish I could have watched it. That little penpusher will know better than to tangle with my boy again.'

– 12 –

Now Sean had a course along which to race. He was born to run and Waite Courtney led him out of the stall in which he had fretted and gave him his lead. Sean ran, unsure of the prize, unsure of the distance; yet he ran with joy, he ran with all his strength.

Before dawn, standing with his father and Garrick in the kitchen, drinking coffee with hands cupped around the mug, Sean felt excitement for each coming day.

'Sean, take Zama and N'duti with you and make sure there are no strays in the thick stuff along the river.'

'I'll only take one herdboy, Pa, you'll need N'duti at the dipping tank.'

'All right, then. Try and meet us back at the tank before midday, we've got to push through a thousand head today.'

Sean gulped the remains of his coffee and buttoned his jacket. 'I'll get going then.'

A groom held his horse at the kitchen door. Sean slid his rifle into the scabbard and went up into the saddle without putting his foot into the steel; he lifted a hand and grinned at Waite, then he swung the horse and rode across the yard. The morning was still dark and cold. Waite watched him from the doorway.

'So goddamned sure of himself,' thought Waite. Yet he had the son he had hoped for and he was proud.

'What you want me to do, Pa?' Garrick asked beside him.

'Well, there are those heifers in the sick paddock—'

Waite stopped. 'No. You'd better come with me, Garry.'

Sean worked in the early morning when the sunlight was tinted as a stage effect, all golden and gay, and the shadows were long and black. He worked in the midday sun and sweated in the heat; in the rain; in the mist that swirled down grey and damp from the plateau; in the short African twilight, and came home in the dark. He loved every minute of it.

He learned to know cattle. Not by name, for only the trek oxen were named, but by their size and colour and markings, so that by running his eye over one of the herds he knew which animals were missing.

'Zama, the old cow with the crooked horn. Where is she?'

'Nkosi,' no longer the diminutive Nkosizana – little lord.

'Nkosi, yesterday I took her to the sick paddock, she has the worm in her eye.'

He learned to recognize disease almost before it started. The way a beast moved and held its head. He learned the treatment for them. Screw worm – kerosene poured into the wound until the maggots fell out like a shower of rice. Ophthalmia – rinse the eye with permanganate. Anthrax and quarter-evil – a bullet and a bonfire for the carcass.

He delivered his first calf among the acacia trees on the bank of the Tugela; he did it alone with his sleeves rolled up above the elbows and the soapy feel of the slime on his hands. Afterwards, while the mother licked it and it staggered at each stroke of the tongue, Sean felt a choking sensation in his throat.

All this was not enough to burn up his energy. He played while he worked.

Practising his horsemanship: swinging from the saddle and running beside his horse, up again and over the other side, standing on the saddle at full gallop and then opening his legs and smacking down on his backside – his feet finding the stirrups without groping.

Practising with his rifle until he could hit a running jackal at a hundred and fifty paces, cutting the fox-terrier-sized body in half with the heavy bullet.

Then there was much of Garrick's work to do also.

'I don't feel very well, Sean.'

'What's wrong?'

'My leg's sore, you know how it chafes if I ride too much.'

'Why don't you go home, then?'

'Pa says I've got to fix the fence round the Number Three dip tank.' Garrick leaned forward on his horse to rub his leg, giving a brave little smile.

'You fixed it last week,' Sean protested.

'Yes – but the wires sort of came loose again.' There was always a strange impermanency about any repairs that Garrick effected.

'Have you got the wire cutters?' and Garrick produced them with alacrity from his saddle bag.

'I'll do it,' said Sean.

'Hell, man, thanks a lot,' and then a second's hesitation. 'You won't tell Pa, will you?'

'No – you can't help it if your leg's sore,' and Garrick rode home, sneaked through to his bedroom and escaped with Jim Hawkins into the pages of *Treasure Island.*

From this work came a new emotion for Sean. When the rain brought the grass out in green and filled the shallow pans on the plateau with water it was no longer simply a sign that the birdnesting season had begun and that the fishing in the Baboon Stroom would improve – now it meant that they could take cattle up from the valley, it meant that there would be fat on the herds they drove into the sale pens at Ladyburg, it meant that another winter had ended and again the land was rich with life and the promise of life. This new emotion extended to the cattle also. It was a strong, almost savage feeling of possession.

It was in the late afternoon. Sean was sitting on his horse among trees, looking out across open vleiland at the small herd that was strung out before him. They were feeding, heads down, tails flicking lazily. Between Sean and the main body of cattle was a calf – it was three days old, still pale-beige in colour and unsure of its legs. It was trying them out, running clumsy circles in the short grass. From the herd a cow lowed and the calf stopped dead and stood with its legs splayed awkwardly under it and its ears up. Sean grinned and picked up the reins from his horse's neck; it was time to start back for the homestead.

At that moment he saw the lammergeyer: it had already begun its stoop at the calf, dropping big and dark brown from the sky, wings cocked back and its talons reaching for the strike. The wind rustled against it with the speed of its dive.

Sean sat paralysed and watched. The eagle hit the calf and Sean heard bone break, sharp as the snap of a dry stick, and then the calf was down in the grass struggling feebly with the eagle crouched on top of it.

For a second longer Sean sat, dazed with the speed at which it had happened. Then hatred came on him. It came with a violence that twisted his stomach. He hit his horse with his heels and it jumped forward. He drove it at the eagle and as he rode he screamed at it, a high-pitched formless sound, an animal expression of hate.

The eagle turned its head, looking at him sideways with one eye. It opened its great yellow beak and answered his scream, then it loosed its claws from the calf and launched itself into the air. Its wings flogged heavily and it moved low along the ground, gaining speed, lifting, drawing away from Sean.

Sean pulled his rifle from the scabbard and hauled his horse back onto its haunches. He threw himself out of the saddle and levered open the breech of the rifle.

The eagle was fifty yards ahead of him rising fast now. Sean slipped a cartridge into the breech, closed it and brought the rifle up in one continuous movement.

It was a difficult shot. Moving away from him and rising, the beat of its wings jerking its body. Sean fired. The rifle jumped back into his shoulder and the gunsmoke whipped away on the wind, so he could watch the bullet connect.

The eagle collapsed in the air. It burst like a pillow in a puff of feathers and fell with its six-feet-long wings fluttering limply. Before it hit the ground Sean was running.

It was dead when he reached it, but he reversed his rifle: holding it by the muzzle, he swung the butt down from above his head onto its body. At the third blow the butt of his rifle broke off, but he kept on hitting. He was sobbing with fury.

When he stopped and stood panting the sweat was running down his face and his body was trembling. The eagle was a squashy mess of broken flesh and feathers.

The calf was still alive. The rifle was jammed. Sean knelt beside it with tears of anger burning his eyes and killed it with his hunting-knife.

– 13 –

So strong was this new feeling that Sean could hate even Garrick. He did not hate for long, though. Sean's anger and his hatred were quick things, with flames like those of a fire in dry grass: hot and high but soon burnt out and afterwards the ashes dead with no smouldering.

Waite was away when it happened. For three consecutive years Waite Courtney had been nominated for the chairmanship of the Beef Growers' Association and each time he had stood down. He was human enough to want the prestige the office carried with it, but he was also sensible to the fact that his farm would suffer from his frequent absences. Sean and Garrick had been working for two years when the annual election of office bearers came around again.

The night before Waite left for the meeting in Pietermaritzburg he spoke to Ada. 'I had a letter from Bernard last week, my dear.' He was standing before the mirror in their bedroom trimming his beard. 'They insist that I stand for the chair this year.'

'Very wise of them,' said Ada. 'They'd have the best man if you did.'

Waite frowned with concentration as he snipped at his whiskers. She believed so unquestioningly in him that he seldom doubted himself. Now looking at his face in the mirror he wondered how much of his success was owed to Ada's backing.

'You can do it, Waite.' Not a challenge, not a question, but a calm statement of fact. When she said it he believed it.

He laid the scissors down on the chest of drawers and turned to her. She sat cross-legged on the bed in a white nightgown, her hair was down in a dark mass around her shoulders. 'I think Sean can look after things here,' she said, and then quickly, 'and of course Garry.'

'Sean's learning fast,' Waite agreed.

'Are you going to take the job?'

Waite hesitated. 'Yes,' he nodded and Ada smiled.

'Come here.' She held out her hands to him.

Sean drove Waite and Ada to the station at Ladyburg: at the last minute Waite had insisted that she go with him, for he wanted her to be there to share it with him.

Sean put their luggage into the coach and waited while they talked with the small group of cattlemen who were going up to the meeting. The whistle blew and the travellers scattered to their compartments. Ada kissed Sean and climbed up. Waite stayed a second longer on the platform.

'Sean, if you need any help go across to Mr Erasmus at Lion Kop. I'll be back on Thursday.'

'I won't need any help, Pa.'

Waite's mouth hardened. 'Then you must be God, he's the only one who never needs help,' Waite said harshly. 'Don't be a bloody fool – if you run into trouble ask Erasmus.'

He climbed up after Ada. The train jerked, gathered speed and ran out towards the escarpment. Sean watched it dwindle, then he walked back to the buggy. He was master of Theunis Kraal and he liked the feeling. The small crowd on the platform was dispersing and out of it came Anna.

'Hello, Sean.' She had on a green cotton dress that was faded with washing, her feet were bare. She smiled with her small white teeth and watched his face.

'Hello, Anna.'

'Aren't you going up to Pietermaritzburg?'

'No, I've got to look after the farm.'

'Oh!'

They waited in silence, uncomfortable before so many people. Sean coughed and scratched the side of his nose.

'Anna, come on. We've got to get home.' One of her brothers called from in front of the ticket office and Anna leaned towards Sean.

'Will I see you on Sunday?' she whispered.

'I'll come if I can. But I don't know – I've got to look after the farm.'

'Please try, Sean.' Her face was earnest. 'I'll be waiting for you, I'll take some lunch and wait all day. Please come, even if it's only for a little while.'

'All right, I'll come.'

'Promise?'

'Promise.'

She smiled with relief. 'I'll wait for you on the path above the waterfall.'

She turned and ran to join her family and Sean drove back to Theunis Kraal. Garrick was lying on his bed reading.

'I thought Pa told you to get on with the branding of those new cattle we bought on Wednesday.'

Garrick laid down his book and sat up. 'I told Zama to keep them in the kraal until you got back.'

'Pa told you to get on with it. You can't keep them there all day without feed or water.'

'I hate branding,' muttered Garrick. 'I hate it when they moo like that as you burn them, and I hate the stink of burning hair and skin – it gives me a headache.'

'Well someone's got to do it. I can't, I've got to go down and mix new dip into the tanks for tomorrow.' Sean was losing his temper. 'Hell, Garry, why are you always so damn helpless?'

'I can't help it, I can't help it if I've only got one leg.' Garrick was close to tears again. The reference to his leg had the desired effect – Sean's temper steadied instantly.

'I'm sorry.' Sean smiled his irresistible smile. 'I tell you what. I'll do the branding – you fix the tanks. Get the drums of dip loaded onto the Scotch cart, take a couple of the stable boys with you to help. Here are the keys of the storeroom.' He tossed the bunch onto the bed beside Garrick. 'You should be finished before dark.'

At the door he turned.

'Garry, don't forget to do all six tanks – not just the ones near the house.'

So Garrick loaded six drums of dip onto the Scotch cart and went off down the hill. He was home well before dark. The front of his breeches was stained with the dark, tarry chemical and some of it had soaked into the leather of his single riding-boot. As he came out of the kitchen into the passage Sean shouted from the study, 'Hey, Garry, did you finish them?'

Garrick was startled. Waite's study was a sacred place, the inner sanctum of Theunis Kraal. Even Ada knocked before going into it and the twins went there only to receive punishment. Garrick limped along the passage and pushed open the door.

Sean sat with his boots on top of the desk and his ankles neatly crossed. He leaned back in the swivel chair.

'Pa will kill you,' Garrick's voice was shaky.

'Pa's in Pietermaritzburg,' said Sean.

Garrick stood in the doorway and looked around the room. It was the first time he had really seen it. On every previous visit he had been too preoccupied with the violence to come and the only item in the room he had studied closely was the seat of the big leather easy chair as he bent over the arm of it and exposed his backside to the sjambok.

Now he looked at the room. The walls were panelled to the ceiling, the wood was dark yellow and polished. The ceiling was fancy plaster, in a pattern of oak leaves. A single lamp hung from the centre of it on a brass chain. You could walk into the fireplace of brown chipped stone and there were logs laid ready for the match.

Pipes and tobacco jar on the ledge beside the fireplace, guns in a rack along one wall, a bookcase of green and maroon leather bound volumes: encyclopaedias, dictionaries, books on travel and farming, but no fiction. There was an oil painting of Ada on the wall opposite the desk, the artist had captured a little of her serenity: she wore a white dress and carried her hat in her hand. A magnificent set of Cape buffalo horns above the fireplace dominated the room with their great crenellated bosses and wide sweep to the tips.

It was a man's room, with loose dog-hairs on the leopard-skin rugs, and the presence of the man strongly there – it even smelled of Waite. It was as distinctively his as the tweed coat and Terai hat that hung behind the door.

Next to where Sean sat the cabinet was open and a bottle of brandy stood on top of it. Sean had a goblet in his hand.

'You're drinking Pa's brandy,' Garrick accused.

'It's not bad.' Sean lifted the glass and inspected the liquid; he took a careful sip and held it in his mouth, preparing himself to swallow. Garrick watched him with awe and Sean tried not to blink as it went down his throat.

'Would you like some?'

Garrick shook his head and the fumes came up Sean's nose and his eyes ran.

'Pa will kill you!' said Garrick again.

'Sit down,' ordered Sean, his voice husky from the brandy. 'I want to work out a plan for the time Pa's away.'

Garrick advanced on the armchair, but before he reached it he changed his mind – the associations were too painful. He went to the sofa instead and sat on the edge.

'Tomorrow,' Sean held up one finger, 'we'll dip all the

cattle in the home section. I've told Zama to start bringing them early – you did do the tanks, didn't you?'

Garrick nodded and Sean went on.

'On Saturday,' Sean held up his second finger, 'we'll burn fire breaks along the top of the escarpment. The grass is dry as hell up there. You take one gang and start near the falls, I'll ride down to the other end, near Fredericks Kloof. On Sunday . . .' Sean said and then paused. On Sunday Anna.

'I want to go to church on Sunday,' said Garrick quickly.

'That's fine,' agreed Sean. 'You go to church.'

'Are you going to come?'

'No,' said Sean.

Garrick looked down at the leopard-skin rugs that covered the floor – he didn't try to persuade Sean for Anna would be at the service. Perhaps afterwards, if Sean wasn't there to distract her, he could drive her home in the buggy. He started a day dream and wasn't listening as Sean went on talking.

In the morning it was full daylight by the time Sean reached the dip tank. He pushed a small herd of stragglers before him and they came out through the trees and stirrup high grass into the wide area of trampled earth around the tank. Garrick had started running cattle through the dip and there were about ten head already in the draining kraal at the far end, standing wet and miserable, their bodies dark with dip.

Sean drove his herd through the gates of the entrance kraal into the solid pack of brown bodies that were already there. N'duti slid the bars of the gate back into place to hold them.

'I see you, Nkosi.'

'I see you, N'duti. Plenty of work today!'

'Plenty,' agreed N'duti, 'always plenty of work.'

Sean rode around the kraal and tied his horse beneath

one of the trees, then walked across to the tank. Garrick was standing by the parapet and leaning against one of the columns that supported the roof.

'Hello, Garry, how's it going?'

'Fine.'

Sean leaned over the parapet next to Garry. The tank was twenty feet long and eight wide, the surface of the liquid was below ground level. Around the tank was a low wall and over it a roof of thatch to prevent rain diluting the contents.

The herdboys drove the cattle up to the edge and each beast hesitated on the brink.

'E'yapi, E'yapi,' screamed the herdboys and the push of bodies behind it forced it to jump. If one was stubborn, Zama leaned over the railing of the kraal, grabbed its tail and bit it.

Each beast jumped with its nose held high and its forefeet gathered up under its chest; it disappeared completely under the oil black surface and came up again swimming frantically along the tank until its hooves touched the sloping bottom at the far end and it could lumber up into the draining kraal.

'Keep them moving, Zama,' shouted Sean.

Zama grinned at him and bit with big white teeth into a reluctant tail.

The ox was a heavy animal and it splashed a drop up onto Sean's cheek as he leaned over the wall. Sean did not bother to wipe it off, he went on watching.

'Well, if we don't get top prices for this lot at the next sale then the buyers don't know good cattle,' he said to Garry.

'They're all right,' agreed Garry.

'All right? They're the fattest oxen in the district.' Sean was about to enlarge on the theme, but suddenly he was aware of discomfort – the drop of dip was burning his cheek.

He wiped it off with his finger and held it to his nose; the smell of it stung his nostrils. For a second he stared at it stupidly and the spot on his cheek burned like fire.

He looked up quickly. The cattle in the draining kraal were milling restlessly and as he looked one of them staggered sideways and bumped against the railing.

'Zama!' shouted Sean, and the Zulu looked up. 'Stop them. For God's sake don't let any more through.'

There was another ox poised on the edge. Sean snatched off his hat and jumped up onto the wall, he beat the ox in the face with his hat trying to drive it back, but it sprang out into the tank. Sean caught hold of the railing and stepped into the space it had left on the edge of the tank.

'Stop them,' he shouted. 'Get the bars in, don't let any more through.'

He spread his arms across the entrance, holding onto the railing on each side, kicking at the faces of the cattle in front of him.

'Hurry, damn you, get the bars in,' he shouted. The oxen pressed towards him, a wall of horned heads. Pushed forward by those behind and held back by Sean they started to panic; one of them tried to jump over the railing. As it swung its head its horn raked Sean's chest, up across the ribs, ripping his shirt.

Behind him Sean felt the wooden bars being dropped into place, blocking the entrance to the tank, and then Zama's hands on his arm pulling him up out of the confusion of horns and hooves. Two of the herdboys helped him over the railing and Sean shrugged their hands off as soon as he was on the ground.

'Come on,' he ordered and ran to his horse.

'Nkosi, you are bleeding.'

Blood had splotched the front of Sean's shirt but he felt no pain. The cattle that had been through the dip were now in terrible distress. They charged about the kraal, bellowing pitifully; one of them fell and when it got to its feet again its legs were shaking so that it could barely stand.

'The river,' shouted Sean, 'get them down to the river. Try and wash it off. Zama, open the gate.'

The Baboon Stroom was a mile away. One of the oxen died before they could get them out of the kraal, another ten before they reached the river. They died in convulsions, with their bodies shuddering and their eyes turned back into their heads.

Sean drove those that remained down the bank into the river. The water was clear and as each beast went into it, the dip washed off in a dark brown cloud.

'Stand here, Zama. Don't let them come out.'

Sean swam his horse to the far bank and turned back the oxen that were trying to climb it.

'Nkosi – one is drowning,' called N'duti and Sean looked across the river. A young ox was in convulsions in the shallows: its head was under water and its feet thrashed the surface.

Sean slid off his horse and waded out to it. The water was up to his armpits. He tried to hold its head out and drag it to the bank.

'Help me, N'duti,' he shouted, and the Zulu came into the river. It was a hopeless task: each time the ox lunged it pulled them both under with it. By the time they got the ox to the bank it was dead.

Sean sat in the mud beside the body of the ox: he was exhausted and his lungs ached with the water he had breathed.

'Bring them out, Zama,' he gasped. The survivors were standing in the shallows or swimming in aimless circles. 'How many?' asked Sean. 'How many are dead?'

'Two more while you were in the water. Altogether thirteen, Nkosi.'

'Where's my horse?'

'It ran, and I let it go. It will be back at the house.'

Sean nodded.

'Bring them up to the sick paddock. We must watch them for a few days.'

Sean stood up and started walking back towards the dip tank. Garrick was gone, and the main herd was still in the kraal. Sean opened the gate and turned them loose. He felt better by then, and as his strength returned with it came his anger and his hatred. He started along the track towards the homestead. His boots squelched as he walked and he hated Garrick more strongly with each step. Garrick had mixed the dip. Garrick had killed his cattle and Sean hated him.

As Sean came up the slope below the house he saw Garrick standing in the yard. Garrick saw him also; he disappeared into the kitchen and Sean started to run. He went in through the kitchen door and nearly knocked down one of the servants.

'Garrick,' shouted Sean. 'Damn it – where are you?'

He searched the house; once quickly and then again thoroughly. Garrick was gone, but the window of their bedroom was open and there was a dusty boot print on the sill. Garrick had gone over it.

'You bloody coward,' howled Sean and scrambled out after him. He stood a second, with his head swinging from side to side and his fists opening and closing.

'I'll find out,' he howled again. 'I'll find you wherever you're hiding.'

He started across the yard towards the stables and halfway there he saw the door of the dairy was closed. When he tried it he found it was locked from inside. Sean backed away from it and then charged it with his shoulder – the lock burst and the door flew open. Sean skidded across the room and came up against the far wall. Garrick was trying to climb out of the window, but it was small and high up. Sean caught him by the seat of his pants and pulled him down.

'Whatcha do to the dip, hey? Whatcha do to it?' He shouted in Garrick's face.

'I didn't mean to. I didn't know it'd kill them.'

'Tell me what you did.' Sean had hold of the front of his shirt and was dragging him towards the door.

'I didn't do anything. Honest I didn't know.'

'I'm going to hammer you anyway, so you might as well tell me.'

'Please, Sean, I didn't know.'

Sean jammed Garrick against the doorway and held him there with his left hand – his right hand he drew back with the fist bunched.

'No, Sean. Please, no.'

And suddenly the anger was gone from Sean, his hands sank back to his sides.

'All right – just tell me what you did,' he said coldly. His anger was gone but not his hatred.

'I was tired and it was getting late and my leg was hurting,' whispered Garrick, 'and there were still four more tanks to do, and I knew you'd check that all the drums were empty, and it was so late . . . and . . .'

'And?'

'And so I emptied all the dip into the one tank . . . but I didn't know it would kill them, truly I didn't.'

Sean turned away from him and started walking slowly back towards the house. Garrick stumbled after him.

'I'm sorry, Sean, honest I'm sorry. I didn't know that . . .'

Sean walked ahead of him into the kitchen and slammed the door in his face. He went through into Waite's study. From the bookshelf he lifted down the heavy leather-covered stock register and carried it to the desk. He opened the book, picked up a pen and dipped it. For a moment he stared at the page and then in the 'deaths' column he wrote the number *13* and after it the words 'dip poisoning'. He pressed down so hard with the pen that the nib cut the paper.

It took Sean and the herdboys all the rest of that day and the next to bale out the tank, refill it with clean water and mix in fresh dip. He saw Garrick only at meals and they didn't speak.

The next day was Sunday. Garrick went into town early, for the church service started at eight o'clock. When he had gone Sean began his preparations. He shaved – leaning close to the mirror and handling the cut-throat gingerly, shaping his side burns and clearing the hair from the rest of his face until his skin was smooth and fresh-looking. Then he went through to the master-bedroom and helped himself to a generous portion of his father's brilliantine, taking care to screw the lid back on the bottle and replace it exactly as he had found it. He rubbed the brilliantine into his hair and sniffed its perfume appreciatively. He combed his hair over his forehead, parted it down the centre and polished it into a gloss with Waite's silver-backed brushes. Then a clean white shirt, breeches worn only once before, boots as shiny as his hair – and Sean was ready.

The clock on the mantelpiece in the lounge assured him that he was well ahead of time. To be exact, he was two hours early. Eight o'clock now: church didn't end until nine and it would be another hour before Anna could escape from under the eyes of her family and reach the rendezvous above the falls. He settled down to wait. He read the latest copy of the *Natal Farmer*. He had read it three times before for it was a month old, and now even the excellent article on 'Stomach parasites in Cattle and Sheep' had lost much of its punch. Sean's attention wandered – he thought about the day ahead and felt the familiar movement within his breeches. This necessitated a rearrangement for the breeches were tight fitting. Then fantasy palled; Sean was a doer not a thinker, and he went through to the kitchen to solicit a cup of coffee from Joseph. When he had finished it, there was still half an hour to go.

'The hell with it,' said Sean and shouted for his horse. He climbed the escarpment, letting his horse move diagonally up the slope and at the top he dismounted and let it blow. Today he could see the course of the Tugela river out across the plain – it was a belt of dark green. He could count the roofs of the houses in Ladyburg and the church spire, copper clad, shone in the sunlight like a beacon fire.

He mounted again and rode along the edge of the plateau until he reached the Baboon Stroom above the falls. He followed it back and forded it at a shallow place, lifting his feet up on the saddle in front of him to keep his boots dry. He off-saddled next to the pools and knee-haltered his horse, then he followed the path until it dropped over the edge of the plateau into the thick forest that surrounded the falls. It was cool and damp in the forest with moss growing on the trees, for the roof of leaves and creepers shut out the sun. There was a bottle-bird in the undergrowth.

'Glug, glug, glug,' it said, like water poured from a bottle, and its call was almost drowned in the ceaseless thunder of the falls.

Sean spread his handkerchief on a rock beside the path, sat down on it and waited. Within five minutes he was fidgeting impatiently – within half an hour he was grumbling aloud.

'I'll count to five hundred . . . If she hasn't come by then I'm not going to wait.'

He counted and when he reached the promised figure he stopped and peered anxiously down the path. There was no sign of Anna.

'I'm not going to sit here all day,' he announced and made no effort to stand up. A fat yellow caterpillar caught his eye; it was on the trunk of a tree farther down the slope. He picked up a pebble and threw it. It bounced off the tree an inch above the caterpillar.

'Close,' Sean encouraged himself and stooped for another stone. After a while he had exhausted the supply of pebbles around his feet and the caterpillar was still moving leisurely up the trunk. Sean was forced to go out on a foraging expedition for more pebbles. He came back with both hands full and once more took up his position on the rock. He piled the pebbles between his feet and reopened the bombardment. He aimed each throw with the utmost concentration and with his third pebble he hit squarely and the caterpillar popped in a spurt of green juice. Sean felt cheated. He looked around for a new target and instead found Anna standing beside him.

'Hello, Sean.' She had on a pink dress. She carried her shoes in one hand and a small basket in the other. 'I brought some lunch for us.'

'What took you so long?' Sean stood up and wiped his hands on his breeches. 'I thought you weren't coming.'

'I'm sorry – everything went wrong.'

There was an awkward pause and Anna flushed slightly as Sean looked at her. Then she turned and started up the path. 'Come on – I'll race you to the top.'

She ran fast on bare feet, holding her skirts up to her knees and she was out in the sunshine before Sean caught her. He put his arms around her from behind and they fell together into the grass beside the path. They lay holding each other, laughing and panting at the same time.

'The service went on and on – I thought it would never finish,' said Anna, 'and afterwards—'

Before she could finish Sean covered her mouth with his and immediately her arms came up around his neck. They kissed with the tension building up steadily between them until Anna was moaning softly and moving her body against his. Sean released her mouth and moved his lips down across her cheek to her neck.

'Oh, Sean, it's been so long. It's been a whole week.'

'I know.'

'I've missed you so – I thought about you every day.'

Sean had his face pressed into her neck, he didn't answer.

'Did you miss me, Sean?'

'Hmm,' Sean murmured and lifted his mouth to take the lobe of her ear between his teeth.

'Did you think about me while you were working?'

'Hmm.'

'Tell me properly, Sean, say it properly.'

'I missed you, Anna, I thought about you all the time,' lied Sean and kissed her on the mouth. She clung to him and Sean's hand went down, right down to her knee and then up again under her clothes. Anna caught his wrist and held his hand away. 'No, Sean, just kiss me.'

Sean waited until her grip relaxed and then tried again, but this time she twisted away from him and sat up. 'Sometimes I think that's all you want to do.'

Sean felt his temper coming up, but he had the good sense to check it.

'That's not true, Anna. It's just that I haven't seen you for so long and I've missed you so much.'

She softened immediately and reached out to touch his cheek. 'Oh, Sean, I'm sorry. I don't mind really, it's just that – oh, I don't know.' She scrambled to her feet and picked up the basket. 'Come on, let's go on to the pools.'

They had a special place. It was walled in by the reeds and shaded by a big tree that grew on the bank above; the sand was washed clean and white. Sean spread his saddle blanket for them to sit on. They could hear the river, close by but hidden, and the reeds rustled and nodded their fluffy heads with each breath of the wind.

' – and I couldn't get rid of him,' Anna chattered as she knelt on the blanket and unpacked the basket. 'He just sat there and every time I said something he blushed and wriggled on his seat. In the end I just told him, "I'm sorry, Garry, I have to go!"'

Sean scowled. The mention of Garrick had reminded him of the dip; he hadn't forgiven him yet.

'And then when I got into the house I found that Pa and Frikkie were fighting. Ma was in tears and the other kids were locked in the bedroom.'

'Who won?' asked Sean with interest.

'They weren't really fighting – they were just shouting at each other. They were both drunk.'

Sean was always slightly shocked at Anna's casual reference to her family's drinking habits. Everybody knew about Mr Van Essen and his two eldest boys but Anna didn't have to talk about it. Once Sean had tried to correct her. 'You shouldn't say things like that about your Pa. You should respect him.'

And Anna had looked at him calmly and asked, 'Why?' which was a difficult question. But now she changed the subject.

'Do you want to eat yet?'

'No,' said Sean and reached for her. She fought back, shrieking demurely until Sean held her down and kissed her. Then she lay quietly, answering his kisses.

'If you stop me now I'm going to get mad,' whispered Sean and deliberately unfastened the top button of her dress. She watched his face with solemn eyes and her hands stayed on his shoulders until he had undone her blouse down to the waist and then with her fingers she traced the bold black curves of his eyebrows.

'No, Sean, I won't stop you. I want to as well, I want to as much as you do.'

There was so much to discover and each thing was

strange and wonderful and they were the first to find it. The way the muscles stood out down the side of his chest beneath his arms and yet left a place where she could see the outline of his ribs. The texture of her skin, smooth and white with the faint blue suggestion of veins beneath. The deep hollow down the centre of his back – pressing her fingers into it she could feel his spine. The down on her cheeks, so pale and fine he could see it only in the sunlight. The way their lips felt against each other and the tiny flutter of tongues between. The smell of their bodies, one milky warm and the other musky and vigorous. The hair that covered his chest and grew thicker under his arms, and hers: startlingly dark against white skin, a small silky nest of it. Each time there was something new to find and greet with soft sounds of delight.

Now, kneeling before her as she lay with her head thrown back and her arms half-raised to receive him, Sean suddenly bowed his head and touched her with his mouth. The taste of her was clean as the taste of the sea.

Her eyes flew open. 'Sean, no, you mustn't – oh no, you mustn't.' There were lips within lips and a bud as softly resilient as a tiny green grape. Sean found it with the tip of his tongue.

'Oh, Sean, you can't do that. Please, please, please.' And her hands were in the thick hair at the back of his head holding him there.

'I can't stand it any more, come over me . . . quickly, quickly, Sean.'

Filling like a sail in a hurricane, swollen and hard and tight, stretched beyond its limit until it burst and was blown to shreds in the wind and was gone. Everything gone. The wind and the sail, the tension and the wanting, all gone. There was left only the great nothingness which is peace. Perhaps a kind of death; perhaps death is like that. But, like death, not an ending – for even death contains the seeds of resurrection. So they came back from peace to a new beginning, slowly at first and then faster until they were two people again. Two people on a blanket among reeds with the sunlight white on the sand about them.

'Each time it's better and better – isn't it, Sean?'

'Ah!' Sean stretched, arching his back and spreading his arms.

'Sean, you do love me, don't you?'

'Sure. Sure I love you.'

'I think you must love me to have done' – she hesitated – 'to do what you did.'

'I just said so, didn't I?' Sean's attention wandered to the basket. He selected an apple and polished it on the blanket.

'Tell me properly. Hold me tight and tell me.'

'Hell, Anna, how many times have I got to say it?' Sean bit into the apple. 'Did you bring any of your Ma's shortbread?'

It was coming on night when Sean got back to Theunis Kraal. He turned his horse over to one of the grooms and went into the house. His body tingled from the sun, and he felt the emptiness and sadness of after-love, but it was a good sadness, like the sadness of old memories.

Garrick was in the dining-room, eating alone. Sean walked into the room and Garrick looked up nervously.

'Hello, Garry.' Sean smiled at him and Garrick was momentarily dazzled by it. Sean sat down in the chair beside him and punched him lightly on the arm.

'Have you left any for me?' His hatred was gone.

'There's plenty,' Garrick nodded eagerly. 'Try some of the potatoes, they're jolly good.'

– 14 –

'They say the Governor sent for your Pa while he was in Pietermaritzburg. Had him alone for nearly two hours.' Stephen Erasmus took the pipe out of his mouth and spat down onto the railway lines. In his brown homespun and *veldschoen* he did not look like a rich cattleman. 'Well, we don't need a prophet to tell us what it was about, do we?'

'No, sir,' Sean agreed vaguely. The train was late and Sean wasn't listening. He had an entry in the stock register to explain to his father and he was mentally rehearsing his speech.

'*Ja*, we know what it's about all right.' Old Erasmus put the pipe back between his teeth and spoke around it. 'It's been two weeks now since the British Agent was recalled from Cetewayo's kraal at Gingindhlovu. *Liewe Here*! in the old days we'd have called out the Commando long ago.' He packed his pipe, pushing down onto the glowing tobacco with a calloused forefinger. Sean noticed that the finger was twisted and scarred by the trigger-guards of a hundred heavy rifles.

'You've never been on commando have you, *Jong*?'

'No, sir.'

'About time you did then,' said Erasmus, 'about bledy time.'

Up on the escarpment the train whistled and Sean started guiltily.

'There she is.' Erasmus stood up from the bench on which they were sitting and the station master came out from his office with a rolled red flag in his hand. Sean felt his stomach sink slowly until it stopped somewhere just above his knees.

The train ran in past them, whooshing steam and brakes whining. The single passenger coach stopped precisely opposite the wooden platform. Erasmus came forward and took Waite's hand.

'*Goeie More*, Steff.'

'*More*, Waite. They tell me you're the new chairman now. Well done, man.'

'Thanks. Did you get my telegram?' Waite spoke in Afrikaans.

'*Ja*. I got it. I told the others, we'll all be out at Theunis Kraal tomorrow.'

'Good,' Waite nodded. 'You'll stay for lunch, of course. We've got a lot to talk about.'

'Is it what I think it is?' Erasmus grinned wickedly. The tobacco had stained his beard yellow around his mouth and his face was brown and wrinkled.

'I'll tell you all about it tomorrow, Steff.' Waite winked at him, 'But in the meantime you'd better get that old muzzle-loader of yours out of moth-balls.'

They laughed, one deep down and the other a rusty old laugh.

'Grab the bags, Sean. Let's get home.' Waite took Ada's arm and they walked with Erasmus to the buggy. Ada had on a new dress, blue with leg o'mutton sleeves and a picture hat; she looked lovely but a little worried as she listened to them talking. It's strange how women can never face the prospect of war with the same boyish enthusiasm as their men.

'Sean!' Waite Courtney's roar carried clearly from his study along the corridor and through the closed door of the sitting-room. Ada dropped her knitting into her lap and her features set into an expression of unnatural calm. Sean stood up from his chair.

'You should have told him earlier,' Garrick said in a small voice. 'You should have told him during lunch.'

'I didn't get a chance.'

'Sean!' Another blast from the study.

'What's happened now?' asked Ada quietly.

'It's nothing, Ma. Don't worry about it.'

Sean crossed to the door.

'Sean,' Garrick's stricken voice, 'Sean, you won't – I mean you don't have to tell—' He stopped and sat hunched in his chair, his eyes full of desperate appeal.

'It's all right, Garry, I'll fix it.'

Waite Courtney stood over the desk. Between his clenched fists the stock register lay open. He looked up as Sean came in and closed the door.

'What's this?' He prodded the page with a huge square-tipped finger. Sean opened his mouth and then closed it again.

'Come on. I'm listening.'

'Well, Pa—'

'Well, Pa – be buggered. Just tell me how you've managed to massacre half the cattle on this farm in a little over a week?'

'It's not half the cattle – it's only thirteen.' Sean was stung by the exaggeration.

'Only thirteen,' bellowed Waite, '*only* thirteen. God Almighty, shall I tell you how much that is in cash? Shall I tell you how much that is in hard work and time and worry?'

'I know, Pa.'

'You know,' Waite was panting. 'Yes, you know everything. There's nothing anyone can tell you, is there? Not even how to kill thirteen head of prime oxen.'

'Pa—'

'Don't Pa me, by Jesus.' Waite slammed the heavy book closed. 'Just explain to me how you managed it. What's "dip poisoning"? What the bloody hell is "dip poisoning"?

Did you give it to them to drink? Did you stick it up their arses?'

'The dip was too strong,' said Sean.

'And why was the dip too strong? How much did you put in?'

Sean took a deep breath. 'I put in four drums.'

There was silence and then Waite asked softly, '*How much?*'

'Four drums.'

'Are you mad? Are you raving bloody mad?'

'I didn't think it would harm them.' His carefully rehearsed speech forgotten, Sean unconsciously repeated the words he had heard from Garrick. 'It was getting late and my leg was—' Sean bit the sentence off and Waite stared at him, then the confusion cleared from his face.

'Garry!' he said.

'No,' shouted Sean. 'It wasn't him, I did it.'

'You're lying to me.' Waite came round from behind the desk. There was a note of disbelief in his voice. To his knowledge it was the first time it had ever happened. He stared at Sean and then his anger was back more violently than before. He had forgotten the oxen – it was the lie that concerned him now. 'By Christ, I'll teach you to tell the truth.' He snatched up his sjambok from the desk.

'Don't hit me, Pa,' Sean warned him, backing away. Waite threw up the sjambok and swung it down overarm. It hissed softly and Sean twisted away from it, but the tip of the lash caught his shoulder. Sean gasped at the pain and lifted his hand to it.

'You lying little bastard!' shouted Waite and swung the whip sideways as though he were scything wheat, and this time it curled around Sean's chest under his uplifted arm. It split his shirt like a razor cut and the cloth fell away to expose the red ridged welt across his ribs and around his back.

'Here's some more!' Waite lifted the sjambok again and as he stood with his arm thrown back and his body turned off balance he knew he had made a mistake. Sean was no longer clutching the whip marks; his hands were held low and his fists were bunched. At the corners his eyebrows were lifted, giving an expression of satanical fury to his face. He was pale and his lips were drawn back tight, showing his teeth. His eyes, no longer blue but burning black, were on a level with Waite's.

'He's coming for me.' Waite's surprise slowed his reflexes, he couldn't bring his whip-arm down before Sean was on him. Sean hit him, standing solidly on both feet, bringing the full weight of his body into the punch, hurling it into the middle of Waite's exposed chest.

Heart punched, strength oozing out of him, Waite staggered back against the desk. The sjambok fell out of his hand and Sean went after him. Waite had the sensation of being a beetle in a saucer of treacle: he could see and think but he could barely move. He saw Sean take three quick paces forward, saw his right hand cocked like a loaded rifle, saw it aimed at his defenceless face.

In that instant, while his body moved in slow motion but his mind raced, the scales of paternal blindness dropped from Waite Courtney's eyes and he realized that he was fighting a man who matched him in strength and height, and who was his superior in speed. His only advantage lay in the experience he had gathered in forty years of brawling.

Sean threw his punch: it had all the power of the first one and Waite knew that he could not survive that in his face – and yet he could not move to avoid it. He dropped his chin onto his chest and took Sean's fist on the top of his head. The force of it flung him backwards over the desk, but as it hit he heard the brittle crackle of Sean's fingers breaking.

Waite dragged himself to his knees, using the corner of the desk as a support, and looked at his son. Sean was doubled up with pain, holding his broken hand against his stomach. Waite pulled himself to his feet and sucked in big breaths of air, he felt his strength coming back.

'All right,' he said, 'if you want to fight – then we fight.' He came round the desk, moving slowly, his hands ready, no longer underestimating his man.

'I am going to knock the daylights out of you,' announced Waite. Sean straightened up and looked at him. There was agony in his face now, but the anger was there also. Something surged up inside Waite when he saw it.

He can fight and he's game. Now we'll see if he can take a beating. Rejoicing silently Waite moved in on him, watching Sean's left hand, disregarding the broken right for he knew what pain was in it. He knew that no man could use a hand in that condition.

He shot out his own left hand, measuring with it, trying to draw Sean. Sean side-stepped, moving in past it. Waite was wide open for Sean's right, his broken right, the hand he could not possibly use – and Sean used it with all his strength into Waite's face.

Waite's brain burst into bright colours and darkness, he spun sideways, falling, hitting the leopard-skin rug with his shoulder and sliding with it across the floor into the fireplace. Then in the darkness he felt Sean's hands on him and heard Sean's voice.

'Pa, oh, my God, Pa. Are you all right?'

The darkness cleared a little and he saw Sean's face, the anger gone from it and in its place worry that was almost panic.

'Pa, oh, my God! Please, Pa.'

Waite tried to sit up, but he could not make it. Sean had to help him. He knelt next to Waite holding him, fumbling helplessly with his face, trying to brush the hair back off his forehead, stroking the rumpled beard into place. 'I'm sorry, Pa, truly I'm sorry. Let me help you to the chair.'

Waite sat in the chair and massaged the side of his jaw. Sean hovered over him, his own hand forgotten.

'What you want to do – kill me?' asked Waite ruefully.

'I didn't mean it. I just lost my temper.'

'I noticed,' said Waite, 'I just happened to notice that.'

'Pa – about Garry. You don't have to say anything to him, do you?'

Waite dropped his hand from his face and looked at Sean steadily.

'I'll make a bargain with you,' he said. 'I'll leave Garry out of it if you'll promise me two things. One: You never lie to me again.'

Sean nodded quickly.

'Two: If anybody ever takes a whip to you again you swear to me you'll give him the same as you just gave me.'

Sean started to smile and Waite went on gruffly, 'Now let's have a look at your hand.'

Sean held it out and Waite examined it, moving each finger in turn. Sean winced.

'Sore?' asked Waite. *He hit me with that. Sweet Jesus, I've bred me a wild one.*

'A little.' Sean was white-faced again.

'It's a mess,' said Waite. 'You'd better get into town right away and let Doctor Van have a go at it.'

Sean moved towards the door.

'Hold on.' Sean stopped and Waite pulled himself out of his chair. 'I'll come with you.'

'I'll be all right, Pa, you stay and rest.'

Waite ignored this and walked towards him.

'Really, Pa, I'll be all right on my own.'

'I'm coming with you,' Waite said harshly; and then softly, almost inaudibly, 'I want to, dammit.'

He lifted his arm as though to put it around Sean's shoulders, but before it touched him he let it drop back to his side and together they went out into the corridor.

– 15 –

With two fingers in splints Sean handled his knife awkwardly at lunch the next day, but his appetite was unimpaired. As was only right and fitting he took no part in the conversation except on the rare occasions that a remark was addressed directly to him. But he listened, his jaws chewing steadily and his eyes moving from speaker to speaker. He and Garry sat side by side in a backwater of the luncheon board while the guests were grouped in order of seniority around Waite.

Stephen Erasmus by age and wealth was in the right-hand seat; opposite him Tim Hope-Brown, just as wealthy but ten years younger; below him Gunther Niewenhuizen, Sam Tingle and Simon Rousseau. If you added it all together you could say that Waite Courtney had about a hundred thousand acres of land and half a million sterling sitting around his table. They were brown men – brown clothing, brown boots and big brown, calloused hands. Their faces were brown and battered-looking and now that the meal was in its closing stages their usual reserve was gone and there was a tendency among them to talk all at the same time and to perspire profusely. This was not entirely a consequence of the dozen bottles of good Cape Mossel that Waite had provided nor of the piles of food they had eaten – it was more than that. There was a sense of expectancy among them, an eagerness they were finding it difficult to suppress.

‘Can I tell the servants to clear away, Waite?’ Ada asked from the end of the table.

‘Yes, thank you, my dear. We’ll have coffee in here, please.’

He stood up and fetched a box of cigars from the sideboard and carried it to each of his guests in turn. When the ends were cut and the tips were glowing, every man leaning back in his chair with a recharged glass and a cup of coffee in front of him, Ada slipped out of the room and Waite cleared his throat for silence.

‘Gentlemen.’ They were all watching him. ‘Last Tuesday I spent two hours with the Governor. We discussed the recent developments across the Tugela.’

Waite lifted his glass and sipped at it, then held it by the stem and rolled it between his fingers as he went on.

‘Two weeks ago the British Agent at the Zulu king’s kraal was recalled. Recalled is perhaps the wrong word – the king offered to smear him with honey, and tie him over an ant-hill, an offer that Her Britannic Majesty’s Agent declined with thanks. Shortly thereafter he packed his bags and made for the border.’

There was a small ruffle of laughter.

‘Since then Cetewayo has collected all his herds which were grazing near the Tugela and driven them into the north; he has commanded a buffalo hunt for which he has decided he will need *all* his impis – twenty thousand spears. This hunt is to be held along the banks of the Tugela, where the last buffalo was seen ten years ago.’ Waite sipped at his glass, watching their faces. ‘And he has ordered that all wounded game is to be followed across the border.’

There was a sigh then, a murmur from them. They all knew that this was the traditional Zulu declaration of war.

‘So, man, what are we going to do about it. Must we sit here and wait for them to come and burn us out?’

Erasmus leaned forward watching Waite.

'Sir Bartle Frere met Cetewayo's Indunas a week ago. He has given them an ultimatum. They have until January the eleventh to disband the impis and take the Queen's Agent back into Zululand. In the event that Cetewayo disregards the ultimatum, Lord Chelmsford is to command a punitive column of regulars and militia. The force is being assembled now and will leave Pietermaritzburg within the next ten days. He is to cross the Tugela at Rorke's Drift and engage the impis before they break out. It is intended to end this constant threat to our border and break the Zulu nation for ever as a military power.'

'It's about bledy time,' said Erasmus.

'His Excellency has gazetted me full colonel and ordered me to raise a commando from the Ladyburg district. I have promised him at least forty men fully armed, mounted and provisioned who will be ready to join Chelmsford at the Tugela. Unless any of you object I am appointing you gentlemen as my captains and I know I can rely upon you to help me make good my promise to His Excellency.'

Suddenly Waite dropped his stilted manner and grinned at them. 'You will collect your own pay. It will be in cattle, as usual.'

'How far north has Cetewayo driven his herds?' asked Tim Hope-Brown.

'Not far enough, I'll warrant,' cackled Stephen Erasmus.

'A toast,' said Simon Rousseau jumping to his feet and holding up his glass. 'I give you a toast: the Queen, Lord Chelmsford and the Royal Herds of Zululand.'

They all stood and drank it, and then suddenly embarrassed by their display they sat down again, coughing awkwardly and shuffling their feet,

'All right,' said Waite, 'let's get down to details. Steff, you'll be coming and your two eldest boys?'

'*Ja*, three of us and my brother and his son. Put down five, Erasmus.'

'Good. What about you, Gunther?'

They began the planning. Men, horses and wagons were marshalled on paper; each of the captains was allotted a series of tasks. There was question, answer and argument that filled the hours before the guests left Theunis Kraal. They rode in a bunch, trippling their horses, sitting slack and long-legged in the saddles, moving up the far slope along the road to Ladyburg. Waite and his sons stood on the front step and watched them go.

'Pa—' Garry tried tentatively for Waite's attention.

'Yes, boy?' Waite kept his eyes on the group. Steff Erasmus turned in the saddle and waved his hat above his head, Waite waved back.

'Why do we have to fight them, Pa? If the Governor just sent somebody to talk to them, then we wouldn't have to fight.'

Waite glanced at him, frowning slightly.

'Anything worth having is worth fighting for, Garry. Cetewayo has raised twenty thousand spears to take this from us—' Waite swept his arm in a circle that took in the whole of Theunis Kraal. 'I think it's worth fighting for – don't you, Sean?'

'You bet,' Sean nodded eagerly.

'But couldn't we just make a treaty with them?' Garry persisted.

'Another cross on a piece of paper.' Waite spoke with fierce disdain. 'They found one like that on Piet Retrief's body – hell of a lot of good it did him.'

Waite walked back into the house with his sons following him.

He lowered himself into his armchair, stretched his legs out in front of him and smiled at Ada. 'Damn good lunch, my dear.' He clasped his hands over his stomach, belched involuntarily and was immediately contrite. 'I beg your pardon – it just slipped out.'

Ada bent her head over her sewing to hide her smile.

'We've got a lot to do in the next few days.' He turned his attention back to his sons. 'We'll take one mule wagon and a pair of horses each. Now about ammunition . . .'

'But, Pa, couldn't we just – ?' Garry started again.

'Shut up,' said Waite, and Garry subsided miserably into one of the other chairs.

'I've been thinking,' announced Sean.

'Not you as well,' growled Waite. 'Damn it to hell, here's your chance to win your own cattle and . . .'

'That's just what I've been thinking,' Sean cut in. 'Everybody will have more cattle than they know what to do with. The prices will drop way down.'

'They will at first,' admitted Waite, 'but in a year or two they'll climb back again.'

'Shouldn't we sell now? Sell everything except the bulls and breeding cows, then after the war we'll be able to buy back at half the price.'

For a moment Waite sat stunned and then slowly his expression changed.

'My God, I never thought of that.'

'And Pa,' Sean was twisting his hands together in his enthusiasm, 'we'll need more land. When we bring the herds back across the Tugela there won't be enough grazing to go round. Mr Pye has called the mortgages on Mount Sinai and Mahoba's Kloof. He's not using the land. Couldn't we lease them from him now before everybody starts looking for grazing?'

'We had a lot to do before you started thinking,' said Waite softly, 'but now we've really got to work.'

He searched his pockets, found his pipe and while he filled it with tobacco he looked at Sean. He tried to keep his face neutral but the pride kept showing.

'You keep thinking like that and you'll be a rich man one day.' Waite could not know how true his prophecy would prove – the time was still remote when Sean could drop the purchase price of Theunis Kraal across a gaming table, and laugh at the loss.

– 16 –

The Commando was moving out on New Year's Day. New Year's Eve was set down for a double celebration: 'Welcome 1879', and 'God speed the Ladyburg Mounted Rifles'. The whole district was coming into town for the *braaivleis* and dancing that was being held in the square. Feast the warriors – laugh, dance and sing, then form them up and march them out to war.

Sean and Garry rode in early. Ada and Waite were to follow later in the afternoon. It was one of those bright days of a Natal summer: no wind and no clouds, the kind of day when the dust from a wagon hangs heavy in the air. They crossed the Baboon Stroom and from the farther ridge looked down across the town and saw the wagon dust on every road leading into Ladyburg.

'Look at them come,' said Sean; he screwed up his eyes against the glare and stared at the north road. 'That will be the Erasmus wagon. Karl will be with them.'

The wagons looked like beads on a string.

'That's the Petersens',' said Garry, 'or the Niewehuisens'.'

'Come on,' shouted Sean, and slapped the free end of his reins across his horse's neck. They galloped down the road. The horses they rode were big glossy animals, with their manes cropped like English hunters.

They passed a wagon. There were two girls sitting beside mama on the box seat, the Petersen sisters. Dennis Petersen and his father were riding ahead of the wagon.

Sean whooped as he raced past the wagon and the girls laughed and shouted something that was lost in the wind.

'Come on, Dennis,' howled Sean as he swept past the two sedately trotting outriders. Dennis's horse reared and then settled in to run, chasing Sean. Garry trailed them both.

They reached the crossroads, lying flat along their horses' necks, pumping the reins like jockeys. The Erasmus wagon was trundling down to meet them.

'Karl,' Sean called as he held his horse a little to stand in the stirrups. 'Karl. Come on, man, catch a wayo, Cetewayo!'

They rode into Ladyburg in a bunch. They were all flush-faced and laughing, excited and happy at the prospect of dancing and killing.

The town was crowded, its streets congested with wagons and horses and men and women and girls and dogs and servants.

'I've got to stop at Pye's store,' said Karl, 'come with me – it won't take long.'

They hitched their horses and went into the store; Sean, Dennis and Karl walked noisily and talked aloud. They were men, big sun-burned raw-boned men, muscled from hard work, but uncertain of the fact that they were men. Therefore, walk with a swagger and laugh too loud, swear when Pa isn't listening and no one will know you have your doubts.

'What are you going to buy, Karl?'

'Boots.'

'That'll take all day – you'll have to try them on. We'll miss half the fun.'

'There'll be nothing doing for another couple hours,' protested Karl. 'Wait for me, you chaps.'

Karl sitting on the counter, trying boots on his large feet, was not a spectacle that could hold Sean's interest for long. He drifted away amongst the piles of merchandise that cluttered Pye's store. There were stacks of pick handles, piles of blankets, bins of sugar and salt and flour, shelves of groceries and clothing, overcoats and women's dresses and hurricane-lamps and saddles hanging from the roof, and all of it was permeated by the peculiar smell of a general dealer's store: a mixture of paraffin, soap and new cloth.

Pigeon to its coop, iron to magnet . . . Sean's feet led him to the rack of rifles against the far wall of the room. He lifted down one of the Lee Metford carbines and worked the action; he stroked the wood with his fingertips, then he weighed it in his hands to feel the balance and finally brought it up to his shoulder.

'Hello, Sean.' His ritual interrupted, Sean looked up at the shy voice.

'It's Strawberry Pie,' he said smiling. 'How's school?'

'I've left school now. I left last term.'

Audrey Pye had the family colouring but with a subtle difference – instead of carrot her hair was smoked copper with glints in it. She was not a pretty girl, her face was too broad and flat, but she had that rare skin that too seldom goes with red hair: creamy unfreckled purity.

'Do you want to buy anything, Sean?'

Sean placed the carbine back in the rack.

'Just looking,' he said. 'Are you working in the store now?'

'Yes.' She dropped her eyes from Sean's scrutiny. It was a year since he'd last seen her. A lot can change in a year; she now had that within her blouse which proved she was no longer a child. Sean eyed it appreciatively and she glanced up and saw the direction of his eyes; the cream of her skin clouded red. She turned quickly towards the trays of fruit.

'Would you like a peach?'

'Thanks,' said Sean and took one.

'How's Anna?' asked Audrey.

'Why ask me?' Sean frowned.

'You're her beau, aren't you?'

'Who told you that?' Sean's frown became a scowl.

'Everybody knows that.'

'Well, everybody's wrong.' Sean was irritated by the suggestion that he was one of Anna's possessions. 'I'm nobody's beau.'

'Oh!' Audrey was silent a moment, then, 'I suppose Anna will be at the dance tonight?'

'Most probably.' Sean bit into the furry golden peach and studied Audrey. 'Are you going, Strawberry Pie?'

'No,' Audrey answered wistfully. 'Pa won't let me.'

How old was she? Sean made a quick calculation . . . three years younger than he was. That made her sixteen. Suddenly Sean was sorry she wouldn't be at the dance.

'That's a pity,' he said. 'We could have had some fun.' Linking them together, with the plural 'we', Sean threw her into confusion again. She said the first words she could think of, 'Do you like the peach?'

'Hmm.'

'It's from our orchard.'

'I thought I recognized the flavour.' Sean grinned and Audrey laughed. Her mouth was wide and friendly when she laughed. 'I knew you used to pinch them. Pa knew it was you. He used to say he'd set a mantrap in that hole in the hedge.'

'I didn't know he'd found that hole – we used to cover it up each time.'

'Oh, yes,' Audrey assured him, 'we knew about it all the time. It's still there. Some nights when I can't sleep I climb out of my bedroom window and go down through the orchard, through the hedge into the wattle plantation. It's so dark and quiet in the plantation at night – scary, but I like it.'

'You know something,' Sean spoke thoughtfully. 'If you couldn't sleep tonight and came down to the hedge at ten o'clock, you might catch me pinching peaches again.'

It took a few seconds for Audrey to realize what he had said. Then the colour flew up her face again and she tried to speak but no words came. She turned with a swirl of skirt and darted away among the shelves. Sean bit the last of the flesh off the peach pip and dropped it on the floor. He was smiling as he walked across to join the others.

'Hell's teeth, Karl, how much longer are you going to be?'

– 17 –

There were fifty or more wagons outspanned around the perimeter of the square but the centre was left open, and here the braaivleis pits were burning, the flames already sinking to form glowing beds. Trestle-tables stood in two lines near the fires and the women worked at them cutting meat and boerwors, buttering bread, arranging platoons of pickle bottles, piling the food on trays and sweetening the evening with their voices and laughter.

In a level place a huge buck-sail was spread for the dancing and at each corner a lantern hung on a pole. The band was tuning with squeaks from the fiddles and preliminary asthma from the single concertina.

The men gathered in knots amongst the wagons or squatted beside the braaivleis pits, and here and there a jug pointed its base briefly at the sky.

'I don't like to be difficult, Waite,' Petersen came across to where Waite was standing with his captains, 'but I see you've put Dennis in Gunther's troop.'

'That's right.' Waite offered him the jug and Petersen took it and wiped the neck with his sleeve.

'It's not you, Gunther,' Petersen smiled at Gunther Niewehuisen, 'but I would be much happier if I could have Dennis in the same troop as myself. Keep an eye on him, you know.'

They all looked at Waite to hear what he would say. 'None of the boys are riding with their fathers. We've purposely arranged it that way. Sorry, Dave.'

'Why?'

Waite Courtney looked away, over the wagons at the furious red sunset that hung above the escarpment. 'This isn't going to be a bushbuck shoot, Dave. You may find that you'll be called upon to make decisions that will be easier for you if you're not making them about your own son.'

There was a murmur of agreement and Steff Erasmus took his pipe out of his mouth and spat into the fire. 'There are some things it is not pretty for a man to see. They are too hard for him to forget. He should not see his son kill his first man, also he should not see his son die.'

They were silent then, knowing this truth. They had not spoken of it before because too much talk softens a man's stomach, but they knew death and understood what Steff had said. One by one their heads turned until they were all staring across the square at the gathering of youngsters beyond the fires. Dennis Petersen said something but they could not catch the words and his companions laughed.

'In order to live a man must occasionally kill,' said Waite, 'but when he kills too young, he loses something . . . a respect for life: he makes it cheap. It is the same with a woman, a man should never have his first woman until he understands about it. Otherwise that too becomes cheap.'

'I had my first when I was fifteen,' said Tim Hope-Brown.

'I can't say it made them any cheaper; in fact I've known them to be bloody expensive.'

Waite's big boom led the laughter.

'I know your old man pays you a pound a week but what about us, Sean?' protested Dennis. 'We aren't all millionaires.'

'All right, then,' Sean agreed, 'five shillings in the pool. Winner takes the lot.'

'Five bob is reasonable,' Karl opined, 'but let's get the rules clear so there's no argument afterwards.'

'Kills only, woundings don't count,' said Sean.

'And they have to be witnessed,' insisted Frikkie Van Essen. He was older than the others; his eyes were already a little bloodshot for he had made a start on the evening's drinking.

'All right, dead Zulus only and a witness to each kill. The highest score takes the pool.' Sean looked around the circle of faces for their assent. Garry was hanging back on the fringe. 'Garry will be banker. Come on, Garry, hold out your hat.'

They paid the money into Garrick's hat and he counted it.

'Two pounds – from eight of us. That's correct.'

'Hell, the winner will be able to buy his own farm.'

They laughed.

'I've got a couple of bottles of smoke hidden in my saddle bags,' Frikkie said. 'Let's go and try them.'

The hands of the clock on the church tower showed quarter before ten. There were silver-edged clouds around the moon, and the night had cooled. Rich meaty smelling steam from the cooking pits drifted across the dancers, fiddles sawed and the concertina bawled the beat, dancers danced and the watchers clapped in time and called encouragement to them. Someone whooped like a Highlander in the feverish pattern of movement, in the fever of fun. Dam the dribble of minutes with laughter, hold the hour, lay siege against the dawn!

'Where are you going, Sean?'

'I'll be back just now.'

'But where are you going?'

'Do you want me to tell you, Anna, do you really want to know?'

'Oh, I see. Don't be long. I'll wait for you by the band.'

'Dance with Karl.'

'No, I'll wait for you, Sean. Please don't be long. We've got such a little time left.'

Sean slipped through the circle of wagons. He kept in the tree shadow along the sidewalk, round the side of Pye's store and down the lane, running now, jumped the ditch and through the barbed wire fence. It was dark in the plantation and quiet as she had said; dead leaves rustled and a twig popped under his feet. Something ran in the darkness, scurry of small feet. Sean's stomach flopped over: nerves, only a rabbit. He came to the hedge and searched for the hole, missed it and turned back, found it and through into the orchard. He stood with his back against the wall of vegetation and waited. The trees were moon grey and black below. He could see the roof of the house beyond them. He knew she'd come, of course. He had told her to.

The church clock chimed the hour and then later the single stroke of the quarter hour. Angry now, damn her! He went up through the orchard, cautiously staying in shadow. There was a light in one of the side windows, he could see it spilling out into a yellow square on the lawn. He circled the house softly.

She was at the window with the lamp behind her. Her face was dark but lamplight lit the edges of her hair into a coppery halo. There was something of yearning in her attitude, leaning forward over the sill. He could see the outline of her shoulders through the white cloth of her gown.

Sean whistled, pitching it low to reach her only, and she started at the sound. A second longer she stared out from light into the dark and then she shook her head, slowly and regretfully from side to side. She closed the curtains and through them Sean saw her shadow move away. The lamp went out.

Sean went back through the orchard and the plantation. He was trembling with anger. From the lane he heard the music in the square and he quickened his pace. He turned the corner and saw the lights and movement.

'Silly little fool,' he said out loud, anger still there but something else as well. Affection? Respect?

'Where have you been? I've waited nearly an hour.' Possessive Anna.

'There and back to see how far it is.'

'Funny! Sean Courtney, where have you been?'

'Do you want to dance?'

'No.'

'All right, don't then.'

Karl and some of the others were standing by the cooking pits. Sean started for them.

'Sean, Sean, I'm sorry.' Penitent Anna. 'I'd love to dance, please.'

They danced, jostled by other dancers, but neither of them spoke until the band stopped to wipe their brows and wet dry throats.

'I've got something for you, Sean.'

'What is it?'

'Come, I'll show you.'

She led him from the light among the wagons and

stopped by a pile of saddles and blankets. She knelt and opened one of the blankets and stood up again with the coat in her hands.

'I made it for you. I hope you like it.'

Sean took it from her. It was sheepskin, tanned and polished, stitched with love, the inside wool bleached snowy white.

'It's beautiful,' Sean said. He recognized the labour that had gone into it. It made him feel guilty: gifts always made him feel guilty.

'Thank you very much.'

'Try it on, Sean.'

Warm, snug at the waist, room to move in the shoulders; it enhanced his considerable bulk. Anna stood close to him, arranging the collar.

'You look nice in it,' she said. Smug pleasure of the giver.

He kissed her and the mood changed. She held him tight around the neck. 'Oh, Sean, I wish you weren't going.'

'Let's say goodbye properly.'

'Where?'

'My wagon.'

'What about your parents?'

'They've gone back to the farm. Pa's coming in tomorrow morning. Garry and I are sleeping here.'

'No, Sean, there are too many people. We can't.'

'You don't want to,' Sean whispered. 'It's a pity because it might be the last time ever.'

'What do you mean?' She was suddenly still and small in his arms.

'I'm going away tomorrow. You know what might happen?'

'No. Don't talk like that. Don't even think it.'

'It's true.'

'No, Sean, don't. Please don't.'

Sean smiled in the darkness. So easy, so very easy.

'Let's go to my wagon.' He took her hand.

– 18 –

Breakfast in the dark, cooking fires around the square, voices quiet, men standing with their wives, holding the small children in farewell. The horses saddled, rifles in the scabbards and blanket rolls behind, four wagons drawn up in the centre of the square with the mules in the traces.

'Pa should be here any minute. It's nearly five o'clock,' said Garry.

'They're all waiting for him,' agreed Sean. He shrugged at the weight of the bandolier strapped over his shoulder.

'Mr Niewehuizen has made me one of the wagon drivers.'

'I know,' said Sean. 'Can you handle it?'

'I think so.'

Jane Petersen came towards them.

'Hello, Jane. Is your brother ready yet?'

'Nearly. He's just saddling up.'

She stopped in front of Sean and shyly held out a scrap of green-and-yellow silk.

'I've made you a cockade for your hat, Sean.'

'Thanks, Jane. Won't you put it on for me?' She pinned up the brim of Sean's hat; he took it back from her and set it at a jaunty angle on his head.

'I look like a general now,' he said and she laughed at him. 'How about a goodbye kiss, Jane?'

'You're terrible,' said little Jane and went away quickly, blushing. Not so little, Sean noticed. There were so many of them you hardly knew where to start.

'Here's Pa,' announced Garry, as Waite Courtney rode into the square.

'Come on,' said Sean and untied his horse. From all around the square, men were leading out their horses.

'See you later,' said Garry and limped off towards one of the waiting mule wagons.

Waite rode at the head of the column. Four troops of fifteen men in double file, four wagons behind them, and then the loose horses driven by black servants.

They moved out across the square, through the litter of the night's festivities, and into the main street. The women watched them in silence, standing motionless with the children gathered around them. These women had seen men ride out before against the tribes; they did not cheer for they too were wise in the ways of death, they had learned that there is no room for glory in the grave.

Anna waved to Sean. He did not see her for his horse was skittish and he was past her before he had it under control. She let her hand drop back to her side and watched him go. He wore the skeepskin coat.

Sean did see the coppery flash and the swiftly-blown kiss from the upstairs window of Pye's store. He saw it because he was looking for it. He forgot his injured pride sufficiently to grin and wave his hat.

Then they were out of the town, and at last even the small boys and dogs that ran beside them fell back and the column trotted out along the road to Zululand.

The sun came up and dried the dew. The dust rose from under the hooves and drifted out at an angle from the road. The column lost its rigidity as men spurred ahead or dropped back to ride with their friends. They rode in groups and straggles, relaxed and cheerfully chatting, as informal as a party out for a day's shooting. Each man had taken to the field in the clothing he considered most suitable. Steff

Erasmus wore his church suit, but he was the most formally attired of the group. They had only one standard item of uniform among them: this was the green-and-yellow cockade. However, even here there was scope for individual taste: some wore them on their hats, some on their sleeves and others on their chests. They were farmers, not fighting men, but their rifle scabbards were battered with use, their bandoliers worn with easy familiarity and the wood of their gun butts was polished from the caress of their hands.

It was middle afternoon before they reached the Tugela.

'My God, look at that!' whistled Sean. 'I've never seen so many people in one place in my life before.'

'They say there are four thousand,' said Karl.

'I know there are four thousand.' Sean ran his eyes over the camp. 'But I didn't know four thousand was that many.'

The column was riding down the last slope to Rorke's Drift. The river was muddy brown and wide, rippling over the shallows of the crossing place. The banks were open and grassy with a cluster of stone-walled buildings on the near side. In a quarter-mile radius around the buildings Lord Chelmsford's army was encamped. The tents were laid out in meticulous lines, row upon row with the horses picketed between them. The wagons were marshalled by the Drift, five hundred at least, and the whole area swarmed with men.

The Ladyburg Mounted Rifles, in a solid bunch that overflowed the road behind their Colonel, came down to the perimeter of the camp and found their passage blocked by a sergeant in a dress coat and with a fixed bayonet.

'And who be you, may I ask?'

'Colonel Courtney – and a detachment of the Ladyburg Mounted Rifles.'

'What's that? Didn't catch it.'

Waite Courtney stood in his stirrups and turned to face his men.

'Hold on there, gentlemen. We can't all talk at once.'

The hubbub of conversation and comment behind him faded and this time the sergeant heard him.

'Ho! Beg your pardon, sir. I'll call the orderly officer.'

The orderly officer was an aristocrat and a gentleman. He came and looked at them. 'Colonel Courtney?' There was a note of disbelief in his voice.

'Hello,' said Waite with a friendly smile. 'I hope we are not too late for the fun.'

'No, I don't believe you are.' The officer's eyes fastened on Steff Erasmus. Steff lifted his top hat politely. '*More, Meneer*.' The bandoliers of ammunition looked a little out of place slung across his black frockcoat.

The officer tore his eyes away from him. 'You have your own tents, Colonel?'

'Yes, we've got everything we need.'

'I'll get the sergeant here to show you where to make camp.'

'Thank you,' said Waite.

The officer turned to the sergeant. So carried away was he that he took the man by the arm. 'Put them far away. Put them on the other side of the Engineers—' he whispered frantically. 'If the General sees this lot . . .' He shuddered, but in a genteel fashion.

– 19 –

Garrick first became conscious of the smell. Thinking about it served as a rallying point for his attention and he could start to creep out of the hiding-place in his mind. For Garrick, these returns to reality were always accompanied by a feeling of light-headedness and a heightening of the senses. Colours were vivid, skin sensitive to the touch, tastes and smells sharp and clear.

He lay on a straw mattress. The sun was bright, but he was in shade. He lay on the veranda of the stone-walled hospital above Rorke's Drift. He thought about the smell that had brought him back. It was a blending of corruption and sweat and dung, the smell of ripped bowels and congealing blood.

He recognized it as the smell of death. Then his vision came into focus and he saw the dead. They were piled along the wall of the yard where the cross-fire from the store and the hospital had caught them; they were scattered between the buildings, and the burial squads were busy loading them onto the wagons. They were lying down the slope to the Drift, they were in the water and on the far bank. Dead Zulus, with their weapons and shields strewn about them. Hundreds of them, Garrick thought with astonishment: no, thousands of them.

Then he was aware that there were two smells; but both of them were the smells of death. There was the stink of the black, balloon-bellied corpses swelling in the sun and there was the smell from his own body and the bodies of the men about him, the same smell of pain and putrefaction but mixed with the heaviness of disinfectant. Death wearing antiseptic – the way an unclean girl tries to cover her menstrual odour.

Garrick looked at the men around him. They lay in a long row down the veranda, each on his own mattress. Some were dying and many were not but on all of them the bandages were stained with blood and iodine. Garrick looked at his own body. His left arm was strapped across his bare chest and he felt the ache start beating within him, slow and steady as a funeral drum. There were bandages around his head. I'm wounded – again he was astonished. How? But how?

'You've come back to us, Cocky,' said a cheerful cockney from beside him. 'We thought you'd gone clean bonkers.'

Garrick turned his head and looked at the speaker; he was a small monkey-faced man in a pair of flannel underpants and a mummy suit of bandages.

'Doc said it was shock. He said you'd come out of it soon enough.' The little man raised his voice, 'Hey, Doc, the hero is completely mentos again.' The doctor came quickly, tired-looking, dark under the eyes, old with overwork.

'You'll do,' he said, having groped and prodded. 'Get some rest. They're sending you back home tomorrow.' He moved away for there were many wounded, but then he stopped and looked back. He smiled briefly at Garrick. 'I doubt it will ease the pain at all but you've been recommended for the Victoria Cross. The General endorsed your citation yesterday. I think you'll get it.' Garrick stared at the doctor as memory came back patchily.

'There was fighting,' Garrick said.

'You're bloody well tooting there was!' the little man beside him guffawed.

'Sean!' said Garrick. 'My brother! What happened to my brother?' There was silence then and Garrick saw the quick shadow of regret in the doctor's eyes. Garrick struggled into a sitting position.

'And my Pa. What happened to my father?'

'I'm sorry,' said the doctor with simplicity, 'I'm afraid they were both killed.'

Garrick lay on his mattress and looked down at the Drift. They were clearing the corpses out of the shallows now, splashing as they dragged them to the bank. He remembered the splashing as Chelmsford's army had crossed. Sean and his father had been among the scouts who had led the column, three troops of the Ladyburg Mounted Rifles and sixty men of the Natal Police. Chelmsford had used these men who knew the country over which the initial advance was to be made.

Garrick had watched them go with relief. He could

hardly believe the good fortune that had granted him a squirting dysentery the day before the ultimatum expired and the army crossed the Tugela.

'The lucky bastards,' protested one of the other sick as they watched them go. Garrick was without envy: he did not want to go to war, he was content to wait here with thirty other sick men and a garrison of sixty more to hold the Drift while Chelmsford took his army into Zululand.

Garrick had watched the scouts fan out from the Drift and disappear into the rolling grassland, and the main body of men and wagons follow them until they too had crawled like a python into the distance and left a well-worn road behind them through the grass.

He remembered the slow slide of days while they waited at the Drift. He remembered grumbling with the others when they were made to fortify the store and the hospital with bags and biscuit tins filled with sand. He remembered the boredom.

Then, his stomach tightening, he remembered the messenger.

'Horseman coming.' Garrick had seen him first. Recovered from his dysentery he was doing sentry duty above the Drift.

'The General's left his toothbrush behind, sent someone back for it,' said his companion. Neither of them stood up. They watched the speck coming across the plain towards the river.

'Coming fast,' said Garrick. 'You'd better go and call the Captain.'

'I suppose so,' agreed the other sentry. He trotted up the slope to the store and Garrick stood up and walked down to the edge of the river. His peg sank deep into the mud.

'Captain says to send him up to the store when he gets here.' Garrick's companion came back and stood beside him.

'Something funny about the way he's riding,' said Garrick, 'he looks tired.'

'He must be drunk. He's falling about in the saddle like it's Saturday night.'

Garrick gasped suddenly, 'He's bleeding, he's wounded.'

The horse plunged into the Drift and the rider fell forward onto its neck; the side of his shirt was shiny black with blood, his face was pale with pain and dust. They caught his horse as it came out of the water and the rider tried to shout but his voice was a croak. 'In the name of God prepare yourselves. The Column's been surrounded and wiped out. They're coming – the whole black howling pack of them. They'll be here before nightfall.'

'My brother,' said Garrick. 'What happened to my brother?'

'Dead,' said the man. 'Dead, they're all dead.' He slid sideways off his horse.

They came, the impis of Zulu in the formation of the bull, the great black bull whose head and loins filled the plain and whose horns circled left and right across the river to surround them. The bull stamped with twenty thousand feet and sang with ten thousand throats until its voice was the sound of the sea on a stormy day. The sunlight reflected brightly from the spear blades as it came singing to the Tugela.

'Look! Those in front are wearing the helmets of the Hussars,' one of the watchers in the hospital exclaimed. 'They've been looting Chelmsford's dead. There's one wearing a dress coat and some are carrying carbines.'

It was hot in the hospital for the roof was corrugated-iron and the windows were blocked with sandbags. The rifle slits let in little air. The men stood at the slits, some in pyjamas, some stripped to the waist and sweating in the heat.

'It's true then, the Column has been massacred.'

'That's enough talking. Stand to your posts and keep your mouths shut.'

The impis of Zulu crossed the Tugela on a front five hundred yards wide. They churned the surface to white with their crossing.

'My God! Oh, my God!' whispered Garrick as he watched them come. 'We haven't got a chance, there are so many of them.'

'Shut up. Damn you,' snapped the sergeant at the Gatling machine-gun beside him and Garry covered his mouth with his hand.

'—Grabbed O'Riley by the neck
Shoved his head in a pail of water
Rammed that pistol up his—'

sang one of the malaria cases in delirium and somebody else laughed, shrill hysteria in the sound.

'Here they come!'

'Load!'

The metallic clashing of rifle mechanism. 'Hold your fire, men. Fire on command only.'

The voice of the bull changed from a deep sonorous chant to the shrill ululation of the charge – high-pitched frenzy of the blood squeal.

'Steady, men. Steady. Hold it. Hold your fire.'

'Oh, my God!' whispered Garrick softly, watching them come back up the slope. 'Oh, my God! – please don't let me die.'

'Ready!'

The van had reached the wall of the hospital yard. Their plumed head-dresses were the frothy crest of a black wave as they came over the wall.

'Aim!'

Sixty rifles lifted and held, aimed into the press of bodies.

'Fire!'

Thunder, then the strike of bullets into flesh, a sound as though a handful of gravel had been flung into a puddle of mud. The ranks reeled from the blow. The clustered barrels of the Gatling machine-gun jump – jump – jumped as they swung, cutting them down so they fell upon each other, thick along the wall. The stench of burnt black powder was painful to breathe.

'Load!'

The bullet-ravaged ranks were re-forming as those from behind came forward into the gaps.

'Aim!'

They were coming again, solid black and screaming halfway across the yard.

'Fire!'

Garrick sobbed in the shade of the veranda and pressed the fingers of his right hand into his eye sockets to squeeze out the memory.

'What's the trouble, Cocky?' The Cockney rolled painfully onto his side and looked at Garrick.

'Nothing!' said Garrick quickly. 'Nothing!'

'Coming back to you, is it?'

'What happened? I can only remember pieces of it.'

'What happened!' The man echoed his question, 'What didn't happen!'

'The doctor said—' Garrick looked up quickly. 'He said the General had endorsed my citation. That means Chelmsford's alive. My brother and my father – they must be alive as well!'

'No such luck, Cocky. The Doc's taken a fancy to you – you with one leg doing what you did – so he made inquiries about your folk. It's no use.'

'Why?' asked Garrick desperately. 'Surely if Chelmsford's alive they must be too?'

The little man shook his head. 'Chelmsford's made a

base camp at a place called Isandhlwana. He left a garrison there with all the wagons and supplies. He took a flying column out to raid, but the Zulus circled around him and attacked the base camp, then they came on here to the Drift. As you know, we held them for two days until Chelmsford's flying column came to help us.'

'My folk – what happened to them?'

'Your father was at the Isandhlwana camp. He didn't escape. Your brother was with Chelmsford's column but he was cut off and killed in one of the skirmishes before the main battle.'

'Sean dead?' Garrick shook his head. 'No, it's not possible. They couldn't have killed him.'

'You'd be surprised how easily they did it,' said the Cockney. 'A few inches of blade in the right place is enough for the best of them.'

'But not Sean – you didn't know him. You couldn't understand.'

'He's dead, Cocky. Him and your Pa and seven hundred others. The wonder is we aren't too.' The man wriggled into a more comfortable position on his mattress. 'The General made a speech about our defence here. Finest feat of arms in the annals of British courage – or something like that.'

He winked at Garrick. 'Fifteen citations for the old V.C. – you's one of them. I ask you, Cocky, isn't that something? What's your girl friend going to do when you come home with a mucking great gong clanking around on your chest, hey?'

He stared at Garrick and saw the tears oozing in oily lines down his cheeks.

'Come on, Cock. You're a bloody hero.' He looked away from Garrick's grief. 'Do you remember that part – do you remember what you did?'

'No,' Garrick's voice was husky. *Sean. You can't leave me alone. What am I going to do, now that you're gone?*

'I was next to you. I saw it all. I'll tell you about it,' said the Cockney.

As he talked so the events came back and fitted into sequence in Garrick's mind.

'It was on the second day, we'd held off twenty-three charges.'

Twenty-three, was it as many as that? Garrick had lost count; it might have been but a single surging horror. Even now he could taste the fear in the back of his throat and smell it rancid in his own sweat.

'Then they piled wood against the hospital wall and set fire to it.' Zulus coming across the yard carrying bundles of faggots, falling to the rifles, others picking up the bundles and bringing them closer until they too died and yet others came to take their place. Then flames pale yellow in the sunlight, a dead Zulu lying on the bonfire his face charring, and the smell of him mingled with the smoke.

'We knocked a hole in the back wall and started to move the sick and wounded out through it and across to the store.'

The boy with the assegai through his spine had shrieked like a girl as they lifted him.

'Them bloody savages came again as soon as they saw we were pulling out. They came from that side.' He pointed with his bandaged arm, 'Where the chaps in the store couldn't reach them, and there was only you and I and a couple of others at the loopholes – everyone else was carrying the wounded.'

There had been a Zulu with the blue heron feathers of an Induna in his head-dress. He had led the charge. His shield was dried oxhide dappled black and white, and at his wrists and ankles were bunches of war rattles. Garrick had fired at the instant the Zulu half-turned to beckon to his warriors – the bullet sliced across the tensed muscles of his belly and unzipped it like a purse. The Zulu went down on his hands and knees with his entrails bulging out in a pink and purple mass.

'They reached the door of the hospital and we couldn't fire on them from the angle of the windows.'

The wounded Zulu started to crawl towards Garrick, his mouth moving and his eyes fastened on Garrick's face. He still had his assegai in his hand. The other Zulus were beating at the door and one of them ran his spear blade through a crack in the woodwork and lifted the bar. The door was open.

Garrick watched the Zulu crawling towards him through the dust with his pink wet bowels swinging like a pendulum under him. The sweat was running down Garrick's cheeks and dripping off the end of his chin, his lips were trembling. He lifted his rifle and aimed into the Zulu's face. He could not fire.

'That's when you moved, Cocky. I saw the bar lifted out of its brackets and I knew that in the next second there'd be a mob of them in through the door and we'd stand no chance against their spears at close range.'

Garrick let go his rifle and it rattled on the concrete floor. He turned away from the window. He could not watch that crippled, crawling thing. He wanted to run, to hide. That was it – to hide. He felt the fluttering start behind his eyes, and his sight began to grey.

'You were nearest to the door. You did the only thing that could have saved us. Though I know I wouldn't have had the guts to do it.'

The floor was covered with cartridge cases – brass cylinders shiny and treacherous under foot. Garrick stumbled; as he fell he put out his arm.

'Christ,' the little Cockney shuddered, 'to put your arm into the brackets like that – I wouldn't have done it.'

Garrick felt his arm snap as the mob of Zulus threw themselves against the door. He hung there staring at his twisted arm, watching the door tremble and shake as they beat against it. There was no pain and after a while everything was grey and warm and safe.

'We fired through the door until we had cleared them away from the other side. Then we were able to get your arm free, but you were out cold. Been that way ever since.'

Garrick stared out across the river. He wondered if they had buried Sean or left him in the grass for the birds.

Lying on his side Garrick drew his legs up against his chest, his body was curled. Once as a brutal small boy he had cracked the shell of a hermit crab. Its soft fat abdomen was so vulnerable that its vitals showed through the transparent skin. It curled its body into the same defensive attitude.

'I'll reckon you'll get your gong,' said the Cockney.

'Yes,' said Garrick. He didn't want it. He wanted Sean back.

– 20 –

Doctor Van Rooyen gave Ada Courtney his arm as she stepped down from the buggy. In fifty years he had not obtained immunity from other people's sorrow. He had learned only to conceal it: no trace of it in his eyes, or his mouth, or his lined and whiskered face.

'He's well, Ada. They did a good job on his arm: that is, for military surgeons. It will set straight.'

'When did they arrive?' asked Ada.

'About four hours ago. They sent all the Ladyburg wounded back in two wagons.'

Ada nodded, and he looked at her with the professional shield of indifference, hiding the shock he felt at the change in her appearance. Her skin was as dry and lifeless as the petals of a pressed flower, her mouth had set determinedly against her grief and her widow's weeds had doubled her age.

'He's waiting for you inside.' They walked up the steps of the church and the small crowd opened to let them pass. There were subdued greetings for Ada and the usual funereal platitudes. There were other women there wearing black, with swollen eyes.

Ada and the doctor went into the cool gloom of the church. The pews had been pushed against the wall to make room for the mattresses. Women were moving about between them and men lay on them.

'I'm keeping the bad ones here, where I can watch them,' the doctor told her. 'There's Garry.'

Garrick stood up from the bench on which he was sitting. His arm was slung awkwardly across his chest. He limped forward to meet them, his peg tapped loudly on the stone floor.

'Ma, I'm—' he stopped. 'Sean and Pa—'

'I've come to take you home, Garry.' Ada spoke quickly, flinching at the sound of those two names.

'They can't just let them lie out there, they should—'

'Please, Garry. Let's go home,' said Ada. 'We can talk about it later.'

'We are all very proud of Garry,' said the doctor.

'Yes,' said Ada. 'Please, let's go home, Garry.' She could feel it there just below the surface and she held it in: so much sorrow confined in so small a place. She turned back towards the door, she mustn't let them see it. She mustn't cry here in front of them, she must get back to Theunis Kraal.

Willing hands carried Garrick's bags out to the buggy

and Ada took the reins. Neither of them spoke again until they crossed the ridge and looked down at the homestead.

'You're the master of Theunis Kraal now, Garry,' said Ada softly and Garrick stirred uneasily on the seat beside her. He didn't want it, he didn't want the medal. He wanted Sean.

– 21 –

'I hope you don't mind me coming,' said Anna, 'but I had to talk to you.'

'No. I'm glad you did. Truly I'm glad,' Garrick assured her earnestly. 'It's so good to see you again, Anna. It feels like forever since we left.'

'I know, and so much – so much has happened. My Pa and yours. And – and Sean.' She stopped. 'Oh, Garry, I just can't believe it yet. They've told me and told me but I can't believe it. He was so – so alive.'

'Yes,' said Garrick, 'he was so alive.'

'He talked about dying the night before he left. I hadn't even thought about it until then.' Anna shook her head in disbelief, 'And I never dreamed it could happen to him. Oh, Garry, what am I going to do?'

Garrick turned and looked at Anna. The Anna he loved, Sean's Anna. But Sean was dead. He felt an idea move within him, not yet formed in words, but real enough to cause a sick spasm of conscience. He shied away from it.

'Oh, Garry. What can I do?'

She was asking for help, the appeal was apparent in her voice. Her father killed at Isandhlwana, her elder brothers still with Chelmsford at Tugela, her mother and the three small children to feed. How blind of him not to see it!

'Anna, can I help you? Just tell me.'

'No, Garry. I don't think anyone can.'

'If it's money—' He hesitated discreetly. 'I'm a rich man now. Pa left the whole of Theunis Kraal to Sean and I, and Sean isn't—' She looked at him without answering.

'I can lend you some to tide you over—' blushed Garrick, 'as much as you need.'

She went on staring at him while her mind adjusted itself. Garrick master of Theunis Kraal, he was rich, twice as rich as Sean would have been. And Sean was dead.

'Please, Anna. Let me help you. I want to, really I do.'

He loved her, it was pathetically obvious – and Sean was dead.

'You will let me, Anna?'

She thought of hunger and bare feet, dresses washed until you could see through them when you held them to the light, petticoats patched and cobbled. And always the fear, the uncertainty you must live with when you are poor. Garry was rich and alive, Sean was dead.

'Please tell me you will.' Garrick leaned forward and took her arm, he gripped it fiercely in his agitation and she looked into his face. You could see the resemblance, she thought, but Sean had strength where here there was softness and uncertainty. The colour was wrong also, pale sand and paler blue instead of brutal black and indigo. It was as though an artist had taken a portrait and with a few subtle strokes had altered its meaning completely so as to make it into an entirely different picture. She did not want to think about his leg.

'It's sweet of you, Garry,' she said, 'but we've got a little in the bank and the plot is free of debt. We've got the horses; we can sell them if we have to.'

'What is it then? Please tell me.'

She knew then what she was going to do. She could not lie to him – it was too late for that. She would have to tell him, but she knew that the truth would not make any difference to him. Well, perhaps a little – but not enough to prevent her getting what she wanted. She wanted to be rich, and she wanted a father for the child she carried within her.

'Garry, I'm going to have a baby.'

Garrick's chin jerked up and his breathing jammed and then started again.

'A baby?'

'Yes, Garrick. I'm pregnant.'

'Whose? Sean's?'

'Yes, Garry. I'm going to have Sean's baby.'

'How do you know, are you sure?'

'I'm sure.'

Garrick pulled himself out of his chair and limped across the veranda. He stopped against the railing and gripped it with his good hand; the other was still in the sling. His back was turned to Anna and he stared out across the lawns of Theunis Kraal to the lightly-forested slope beyond.

Sean's baby. The idea bewildered him. He knew that Sean and Anna did that together. Sean had told him and Garrick had not resented it. He was jealous, but only a little, for Sean had let him share in it by telling him and so some of it had belonged to him also. But a baby. Sean's baby.

Slowly the full implication came to him. Sean's baby would be a living part of his brother, the part that had not been cut down by the Zulu blades. He had not completely lost Sean. Anna – she must have a father for her child, it was unthinkable that she could go another month without marrying. He could have both of them, everything he loved in one package. Sean and Anna. She must marry him, she had no other choice. Triumph surged up within him and he turned to her.

'What will you do, Anna?' He felt sure of her now. 'Sean's dead. What will you do?'

'I don't know.'

'You can't have the baby. It would be a bastard.' He saw her wince at the word. He felt very certain of her.

'I'll have to go away – to Port Natal.' She spoke without expression in her voice. Looking calmly at him, knowing what he would say, 'I'll leave soon,' she said, 'I'll be all right. I'll find some way out.'

Garrick watched her face as she spoke. Her head was small on shoulders wide for a girl, her chin was pointed, her teeth were slightly crooked but white – she was very pretty despite the catlike set of her eyes.

'I love you, Anna,' he said. 'You know that, don't you?'

She nodded slowly and her hair moved darkly on her shoulders. The cat eyes softened contentedly. 'Yes, I know, Garry.'

'Will you marry me?' He said it breathlessly.

'You don't mind? You don't mind about Sean's baby?' she said, knowing he did not.

'I love you, Anna.' He came towards her clumsily and she looked up at his face. She did not want to think about the leg.

'I love you, nothing else matters.' He reached for her and she let him hold her.

'Will you marry me, Anna?' He was trembling.

'Yes.' Her hands were quiescent on his shoulders. He sobbed softly and her expression changed to one of distaste. She made the beginnings of a movement to push him away but stopped herself.

'My darling, you won't regret it. I swear you won't,' he whispered.

'We must do it quickly, Garry.'

'Yes. I'll go into town this afternoon and speak to Padre—'

'No! Not here in Ladyburg,' Anna cut in sharply. 'People will have too much to say. I couldn't stand it.'

'We'll go up to Pietermaritzburg,' Garrick acquiesced.

'When, Garry?'

'As soon as you like.'

'Tomorrow,' she said. 'We'll go tomorrow.'

– 22 –

The Cathedral in Pietermaritzburg stands on Church Street. Grey stone with a bell-tower and iron railings between the street and the lawns. Pigeons strut puff-chested on the grass.

Anna and Garrick went up the paved path and into the semi-dark of the Cathedral. The stained glass window had the sun behind it, making the interior glow weirdly with colour. Because they were both nervous they held hands as they stood in the aisle.

'There's no one here,' whispered Garrick.

'There must be,' Anna whispered back. 'Try through that door there.'

'What shall I say?'

'Just tell him we want to get married.'

Garrick hesitated.

'Go on.' Anna still whispered, pushing him gently towards the door of the vestry.

'You come with me,' said Garrick. 'I don't know what to say.'

The priest was a thin man with steel-rimmed spectacles. He looked over the top of them at the nervous pair in the doorway and shut the book on the desk in front of him.

'We want to get married,' Garrick said and blushed crimson.

'Well,' said the priest drily, 'you have the right address. Come in.'

He was surprised at their haste and they argued a little,

then he sent Garrick down to the Magistrates' Court for a special licence. He married them, but the ceremony was hollow and unreal. The drone of the priest's voice was almost lost in the immense cavern of the Cathedral as they stood small and awed before him. Two old ladies who came in to pray stayed on gleefully to witness for them, and afterwards they both kissed Anna and the priest shook Garrick's hand. Then they went out again into the sunlight. The pigeons still strutted on the lawn and a mule wagon rattled down Church Street with the coloured driver singing and cracking his whip. It was as though nothing had happened.

'We're married,' said Garrick doubtfully.

'Yes,' agreed Anna, but she sounded as though she didn't believe it either.

They walked back to the hotel side by side. They didn't talk or touch each other. Their luggage had been taken up to their room and the horses had been stabled. Garrick signed the register and the clerk grinned at him.

'I've put you in Number Twelve, sir, it's our honeymoon suite.' One of his eyelids drooped slightly and Garrick stammered in confusion.

After dinner, an excellent dinner, Anna went up to the room and Garrick sat on in the lounge drinking coffee. It was almost an hour later that he mustered the courage to follow her. He crossed the drawing-room of their suite, hesitated at the bedroom door then went in. Anna was in bed. She had pulled the bedclothes up to her chin and she looked at him with her inscrutable cat's eyes.

'I've put your nightshirt in the bathroom, on the table,' she said.

'Thank you,' said Garrick. He stumbled against a chair as he crossed the room. He closed the door behind him, undressed quickly and leaning naked over the basin splashed water onto his face; then he dried and pulled the nightshirt over his head. He went back into the bedroom: Anna lay with her face turned away from him. Her hair was loose on the pillow, shining in the lamplight.

Garrick sat on the edge of the chair. He lifted the hem of his nightshirt above his knee and unfastened the straps of his leg, laid the peg carefully beside the chair and massaged the stump with both hands. It felt stiff. He heard the bed creak softly and he looked up. Anna was watching him, staring at his leg. Hurriedly Garrick pulled down his nightshirt to cover the protruding, slightly enlarged end with its folded line of scar-tissue. He stood up, balancing, and then hopped one-legged across to the bed. He was blushing again.

He lifted the edge of the blankets and slipped into the bed and Anna jerked violently away from him.

'Don't touch me,' she said hoarsely.

'Anna. Please don't be scared.'

'I'm pregnant, you mustn't touch me.'

'I won't. I swear I won't.'

She was breathing hard, making no attempt to hide her revulsion.

'Do you want me to sleep in the drawing-room, Anna? I will if you say so.'

'Yes,' she said, 'I want you to.'

He gathered his dressing-gown from the chair and stooping picked up his leg. He hopped to the door and turned back to face her. She was watching him still.

'I'm sorry, Anna, I didn't mean to frighten you.' She did not answer him and he went on.

'I love you. I swear I love you more than anything in the world. I wouldn't hurt you, you know that, don't you? You know I wouldn't hurt you?'

Still she did not answer and he made a small gesture of

appeal, the wooden leg clutched in his hand and the tears starting to fill his eyes. 'Anna. I'd kill myself rather than frighten you!'

He went quickly through the door and closed it behind him. Anna scrambled out of the bed and with her nightdress flurrying around her legs she ran across the room to the door and turned the key in the lock.

– 23 –

In the morning Garrick was bewildered to find Anna in a mood of girlish gaiety. She had a green ribbon in her hair and her green frock was faded but pretty. She chattered happily through breakfast and while they were having their coffee she leaned across the table and touched Garrick's hand. 'What shall we do today, Garry?'

Garrick looked surprised, he hadn't thought that far ahead. 'I suppose we'd better catch the afternoon train back to Ladyburg,' he said.

'Oh, Garry,' Anna pouted effectively. 'Don't you love me enough to give me a honeymoon?'

'I suppose—' Garrick hesitated and then, 'of course, I didn't think of it.' He grinned excitedly. 'Where can we go?'

'We could take the mail boat down the coast to Capetown,' Anna suggested.

'Yes!' Garrick adopted the idea immediately. 'It'll be fun.'

'But, Garry—' Anna's eagerness faded. 'I only have two old dresses with me.' She touched her clothes. Garrick sobered also while he grappled with this new problem. Then he found the solution.

'We'll buy you some more!'

'Oh, Garry, could we? Could we really?'

'We'll buy you all you can use, more than you can use. Come on, finish your coffee and we'll go into town and see what they have.'

'I'm finished.' Anna stood up from the table ready to go.

– 24 –

They had a stateroom on the *Dunottar Castle* from Port Natal to Capetown. There were other young people aboard. Anna, in her elegant new clothing and sparkling with excitement, formed the centrepiece of a gay little group that played deck games, dined, danced and flirted as the mailboat drove south through the sunny, golden days of early autumn.

At first Garrick was content to stay unobtrusively close to Anna. He was there to hold her coat, fetch a book or carry a rug. He watched her fondly, revelling in her success, hardly jealous when she almost disappeared behind a palisade of attentive young men, not resenting the sofa which formed his uncomfortable bed in the drawing-room of their suite.

Then gradually there came a realization among their travelling companions that Garrick was paying for most of the refreshments and other little expenses that came up each day. They became aware of him and of the fact that he appeared to be the richest of the group. From there it needed only a small adjustment to their thinking to admit Garrick to the circle. The men addressed remarks directly at him and some of the other girls flirted with him openly and sent him on small errands. Garrick was at once overjoyed and appalled by these attentions, for he could not cope with the lightning exchange of banter that flickered around him and left him stammering and blushing. Then Garrick found how easy it really was.

'Have a dram, old chap?'

'No, really. I don't, you know.'

'Nonsense, everybody does. Steward, bring my friend here a whisky.'

'Really, no really I won't.'

And of course Garrick did. It tasted foul and he spilt a little on Anna's evening dress; while he wiped it up with his handkerchief she whispered a barbed reprimand and then laughed gaily at a joke from the moustached gentleman on her right. Garrick shrank miserably back in his chair and forced down the rest of the whisky. Then slowly and exquisitely the glow came upon him, starting deep down inside him and spreading out warmly to the very tips of his fingers.

'Have another one, Mr Courtney?'

'Yes, thanks. I'll have the same again, but I think it's my round.' He had the next drink. They were sitting in deck-chairs on the upper deck in the shelter of the superstructure, there was a moon and the night was warm. Someone was talking about Chelmsford's Zulu campaign.

'You're wrong on that point,' Garrick said clearly. There was a small silence.

'I beg your pardon!' the speaker glanced at him with surprise. Garrick leaned forward easily in his chair and began talking. There was a stiffness at first but he made a witticism and two of the women laughed. Garrick's voice strengthened. He gave a quick and deep-sighted résumé of the causes and effects of the war. One of the men asked a question. It was a sharp one but Garrick saw the essence of it and answered neatly. It was all very clear and he found the words without effort.

'You must have been there,' one of the girls hazarded.

'My husband was at Rorke's Drift,' said Anna quietly, looking at him as though he were a stranger. 'Lord Chelmsford has cited him for the award of the Victoria Cross. We are waiting to hear from London.'

The party was silent again, but with new respect.

'I think it's my round, Mr Courtney. Yours is whisky, isn't it?'

'Thank you.'

The dry musty taste of the whisky was less offensive this time; he sipped it thoughtfully and found that there was a faint sweetness in the dry.

As they went down to their staterooms later that night Garrick put his arm around Anna's waist.

'What fun you were tonight!' she said.

'Only a reflection of your charm, my darling, I am your mirror.' He kissed her cheek and she pulled away, but not violently.

'You're a tease, Garry Courtney.'

Garrick slept on his back on the sofa with a smile on his face and no dreams, but in the morning his skin felt tight and dry and there was a small ache behind his eyes. He went through to the bathroom and cleaned his teeth; it helped a little but the ache behind his eyes was still there. He went back to the drawing-room and rang for the cabin steward.

'Good morning, sir.'

'Can you bring me a whisky and soda?' Garry asked hesitantly.

'Certainly, sir.'

Garry did not put the soda into it but drank it neat, like medicine. Then afterwards miraculously the glow was there again, warming him. He had hardly dared to hope for it.

He went through to Anna's cabin. She was rosy with sleep, her hair a joyous tangle on the pillow.

'Good morning, my darling.' Garrick stooped over her and kissed her, and his hand moved to cover one of her breasts through the silk of her gown.

'Garry, you naughty boy.' She slapped his wrist, but jokingly.

There was another honeymoon couple aboard returning to their farm near Capetown – seventy-five acres of the finest vines on the whole of the Cape Peninsula, the man's own words. Anna and Garrick were forced by sheer persistence to accept their invitation to stay with them.

Peter and Jane Hugo were a delightful pair. Very much in love, rich enough, popular and in demand with Capetown society. With them Anna and Garrick spent an enchanted six weeks.

They went racing at Milnerton.

They swam at Muizenberg in the warm Indian Ocean. They picnicked at Clifton and ate crayfish, fresh caught and grilled over open coals. They rode to hounds with the Cape Hunt and caught two jackals after a wild day's riding over the Hottentots' Holland. They dined at the Fort and Anna danced with the Governor.

They went shopping in the bazaars that were filled with treasures and curiosities from India and the Orient. Whatever Anna wanted she was given. Garry bought himself something as well – a silver flask, beautifully worked and set with cornelians. It fitted into the inside pocket of his coat without showing a bulge. With its help Garrick was able to keep pace with the rest of the company.

Then the time came for them to leave. The last night there were only the four of them for dinner and it was sad with the regret of present parting, but happy with the memory of shared laughter.

Jane Hugo cried a little when she kissed Anna goodnight. Garry and Peter lingered on downstairs until the bottle was finished and then they walked upstairs together and shook hands outside Garry's bedroom. Peter spoke gruffly. 'Sorry to see you two go. We've got used to having you round. I'll wake you early and we can go out for a last early morning ride before the boat leaves.'

Garry changed quietly in the bathroom and went through to the bedroom. His peg made no sound on the heavily carpeted floor. He crossed to his own bed and sat down to unstrap his peg.

'Garry,' Anna whispered.

'Hullo, I thought you were asleep.'

There was a stirring and Anna's hand came out from under the bedclothes, held towards him in invitation.

'I was waiting to say goodnight to you.'

Garry crossed to her bed, suddenly awkward again.

'Sit down for a minute,' said Anna and he perched on the edge of her bed. 'Garry, you don't know how much I've enjoyed these last weeks. They've been the happiest days of my whole life. Thank you so much, my husband.'

She reached up and touched his cheek. She looked small and warm curled up in the bed.

'Kiss me goodnight, Garry.'

He leaned forward to touch her forehead with his lips but she moved quickly and took it full on her mouth.

'You can come in, if you like,' she whispered, her mouth still against his. She opened the bedclothes with one hand.

So Garry came to her when the bed was warm, and the wine still sang a little in her head and she was ready in the peculiar passion of early pregnancy. It should have been so wonderfully good.

Impatient now, ready to lead him, she reached down to touch and then stilled into surprised disbelief. Where there should have been hardness, male and arrogant, there was slackness and uncertainty.

Anna started to laugh. Not even the shotgun blast had hurt as deeply as that laugh.

'Get out,' she said through the cruel laughter. 'Go to your own bed.'

– 25 –

Anna and Garrick had been married two full months when they came back to Theunis Kraal. Garrick's arm was out of plaster, Peter Hugo's doctor had fixed that for him.

They took the road that by-passed the village and crossed the Baboon Stroom bridge. At the top of the rise Garry pulled the horses to a halt and they looked out across the farm.

'I can't understand why Ma moved into town,' said Garrick. 'She didn't have to do that. There's plenty of room for everybody at Theunis Kraal.'

Anna sat silently and contentedly beside him. She had been relieved when Ada had written to them at Port Natal after they had telegraphed her the news of their marriage. Young as she was Anna was woman enough to recognize the fact that Ada had never liked her. Oh, she was sweet enough when they met, but Anna found those big dark eyes of hers disconcerting. They looked too deep and she knew they found the things she was trying to hide.

'We'll have to go and see her as soon as we can. She must come back to the farm – after all Theunis Kraal is her home too,' Garrick went on. Anna moved slightly in her seat, *let her stay in the house in Ladyburg, let her rot there*, but her voice was mild as she answered, 'Theunis Kraal belongs to you now, Garry, and I'm your wife. Perhaps your stepmother knows what's best.' Anna touched his arm and smiled at him, 'Anyway we'll talk about it some other time. Let's get home now, it's been a long drive and I'm very tired.'

Immediately concerned, Garrick turned to her. 'I'm terribly sorry, my dear. How thoughtless of me.' He touched the horses with the whip and they went down the slope towards the homestead.

The lawns of Theunis Kraal were green and there were cannas in bloom, red and pink and yellow.

It's beautiful, thought Anna, *and it's mine. I'm not poor any more.* She looked at the gabled roof and the heavy yellow wood shutters on the windows as the carriage rolled up the drive.

There was a man standing in the shade of the veranda. Anna and Garrick saw him at the same time. He was tall with shoulders as wide and square as the crosstree of a gallows. He stepped out of the shadow and came down the front steps into the sunlight. He was smiling with white teeth in a brown burnt face; it was the old irresistible smile.

'Sean,' whispered Anna.

– 26 –

Sean really noticed him for the first time when they stopped to water the horses. They had left Chelmsford's Column the previous noon to scout towards the north-east. It was a tiny patrol – four mounted white men and a half-a-dozen Nongaai, the loyal Native troops from Natal.

He took the reins from Sean's hands. 'I will hold your horse while you drink.' His voice had a resonance to it and Sean's interest quickened. He looked at the man's face and liked it immediately. The whites of the eyes had no yellow in them and the nose was more Arabic than negroid. His colour was dark amber and his skin shone with oil.

Sean nodded. There is no word in the Zulu language for 'thank you', just as there are no words for 'I am sorry'.

Sean knelt beside the stream and drank. The water tasted sweet for he was thirsty; when he stood again there were damp patches on his knees and water dripping from his chin.

He looked at the man who was holding his horse. He wore only a small kilt of civet-cat tails: no rattles nor cloak, no head-dress. His shield was black rawhide and he carried two short stabbing spears.

'How are you called?' Sean asked, noticing the breadth of the man's chest and the way his belly muscles stood out like the static ripples on a windswept beach.

'Mbejane.' Rhinoceros.

'For your horn?' The man chuckled with delight, his masculine vanity tickled.

'How are you called, Nkosi?'

'Sean Courtney.'

Mbejane's lips formed the name silently and then he shook his head.

'It is a difficult name.' He never said Sean's name – not once in all the years that were to follow.

'Mount up,' called Steff Erasmus. 'Let's get moving.'

They swung up onto the horses, gathered the reins and loosened the rifles in the scabbards. The Nongaai who had been stretched out resting on the bank stood up.

'Come on,' said Steff. He splashed through the stream. His horse gathered itself and bounded up the far bank and they followed him. They moved in line abreast across the grassland, sitting loose and relaxed in their saddles, the horses trippling smoothly.

At Sean's right stirrup ran the big Zulu, his long extended stride easily pacing Sean's horse. Once in a while Sean dropped his eyes from the horizon and looked down at Mbejane; it was a strangely comforting feeling to have him there.

They camped that night in a shallow valley of grass.

There were no cooking fires; they ate biltong for supper, the black strips of dried salt meat, and washed it down with cold water.

'We're wasting our time. There hasn't been a sign of Zulu in two days' riding,' grumbled Bester Klein, one of the troopers.

'I say we should turn back and rejoin the Column. We're getting farther and farther away from the centre of things – we're going to miss the fun when it starts.'

Steff Erasmus wrapped his blanket more closely about his shoulders: the night's first chill was on them.

'Fun, is it?' He spat expertly into the darkness. 'Let them have the fun, if we find the cattle.'

'Don't you mind missing the fighting?'

'Look, you, I've hunted bushmen in the Karroo and the Kalahari, I've fought Xhosas and Fingoes along the Fish river, I went into the mountains after Moshesh and his Basutos. Matabele, Zulu, Bechuana – I've had fun with all of them. Now four or five hundred head of prime cattle will be payment enough for any fun we miss.' Steff lay back and adjusted his saddle behind his head. 'Anyway what makes you think there won't be guards on the herds when we find them. You'll get your fun – I promise you.'

'How do you know they've got the cattle up here?' insisted Sean.

'They're here,' said Steff, 'and we'll find them.' He turned his head towards Sean. 'You've got the first watch, keep your eyes open.' He tilted his top hat forward over his face, groped with his right hand to make sure his rifle lay beside him and then spoke from under the hat, 'Goodnight.' The others settled down into their blankets: fully-dressed, boots on, guns at hand. Sean moved out into the darkness to check the Nongaai pickets.

There was no moon, but the stars were fat and close to earth; they lit the land so that the four grazing horses were dark blobs against the pale grass. Sean circled the camp and found two of his sentries awake and attentive. He had posted Mbejane on the north side and now he went there. Fifty yards in front of him he picked up the shape of the small bush beside which he had left Mbejane. Suddenly Sean smiled and sank down onto his hands and knees, he cradled his rifle across the crooks of his elbows and began his stalk. Moving flat along the ground silently, slowly he closed in on the bush. Ten paces from it he stopped and lifted his head, careful to keep the movement inchingly slow. He stared, trying to find the shape of the Zulu among the scraggy branches and bunches of leaves. The point of a stabbing spear pricked him below the ear in the soft of his neck behind the jaw bone. Sean froze but his eyes rolled sideways and in the starlight he saw Mbejane kneeling over him holding the spear.

'Does the Nkosi seek me?' asked Mbejane solemnly, but there was laughter deep down in his voice. Sean sat up and rubbed the place where the spear had stung him.

'Only a night ape sees in the dark,' Sean protested.

'And only a fresh caught catfish flops on its belly,' chuckled Mbejane.

'You are Zulu,' Sean stated, recognizing the arrogance, although he had known immediately from the man's face and body that he was not one of the bastard Natal tribes who spoke the Zulu language but were no more Zulu than a tabby-cat is a leopard.

'Of Chaka's blood,' agreed Mbejane, reverence in his voice as he said the old king's name.

'And now you carry the spear against Cetewayo, your king?'

'My king?' The laughter was gone from Mbejane's voice. 'My king?' he repeated scornfully.

There was silence and Sean waited. Out in the darkness

a jackal barked twice and one of the horses whickered softly.

'There was another who should have been king, but he died with a sharpened stick thrust up into the secret opening of his body, until it pierced his gut and touched his heart. That man was my father,' said Mbejane. He stood up and went back into the shelter of the bush and Sean followed him. They squatted side by side, silent but watchful. The jackal cried again up above the camp and Mbejane's head turned towards the sound.

'Some jackals have two legs,' he whispered thoughtfully. Sean felt the tingle along his forearms.

'Zulus?' he asked. Mbejane shrugged, a small movement in the darkness.

'Even if it is, they will not come for us in the night. In the dawn, yes, but never in the night.' Mbejane shifted the spear in his lap. 'The old one with the tall hat and grey beard understands this. Years have made him wise, that's why he sleeps so sweetly now but mounts up and moves in the darkness before each dawn.'

Sean relaxed slightly. He glanced sideways at Mbejane.

'The old one thinks that some of the herds are hidden near here.'

'Years have made him wise,' repeated Mbejane. 'Tomorrow we will find the land more broken, there are hills and thick thorn bush. The cattle will be hidden among them.'

'Do you think we'll find them?'

'Cattle are difficult to hide from a man who knows where to look.'

'Will there be many guards with the herds?'

'I hope so,' answered Mbejane, his voice a purr. His hand crept to the shaft of his assegai and caressed it. 'I hope there will be very many.'

'You would kill your own people, your brothers, your cousins?' asked Sean.

'I would kill them as they killed my father.' Mbejane's voice was savage now. 'They are not my people. I have no people. I have no brothers – I have nothing.'

Silence settled between them again, but slowly the ugliness of Mbejane's mood evaporated and in its place came a sense of companionship. Each of them felt comforted by the other's presence. They sat on into the night.

– 27 –

Mbejane reminded Sean of Tinker working a bird, he had the same half-crouched gait and the same air of complete absorption. The white men sat their horses in silence watching him. The sun was well up already and Sean unbuttoned his sheepskin coat and pulled it off. He strapped it onto the blanket roll behind him.

Mbejane had moved out about fifty yards from them and now he was working slowly back towards them. He stopped and minutely inspected a wet pat of cow dung.

'*Hierdie Kaffir verstaan wat hy doen*,' opined Steff Erasmus approvingly, but no one else spoke. Bester Klein fidgeted with the hammer of his carbine; his red face was already sweaty in the rising heat.

Mbejane had proved right, they were in hilly country. Not the smoothly rounded hills of Natal but hills with rocky crests, deeply gullied and ravined between. There was thorn forest and euphorbia covering the sides of the hills with a lattice work of reptile grey trunks, and the grass was coarse and tall.

'I could use a drink,' said Frikkie Van Essen and wiped his knuckles across his lips.

'Chee peep, chee peep,' a barbet called stridently in the

branches of the kaffir boom tree under which they waited. Sean looked up; the bird was brown and red among the scarlet flowers which covered the tree.

'How many?' asked Steff and Mbejane came to stand at his horse's head.

'Fifty – no more,' he answered.

'When?'

'Yesterday, after the heat of the day they moved slowly down the valley. They were grazing. They cannot be more than half an hour's ride ahead of us.'

Steff nodded. Fifty head only, but there would be more.

'How many men with them?'

Mbejane clucked his tongue disgustedly. 'Two *umfaans*.' He pointed with his spear at a dusty place where the print of a half grown boy's bare foot showed clearly. 'There are no men.'

'Good,' said Steff. 'Follow them.'

'They told us that if we found anything we must go back and report,' protested Bester Klein quickly. 'They said we shouldn't start anything on our own.'

Steff turned in his saddle. 'Are you frightened of two *umfaans*?' he asked coldly.

'I'm not frightened of anything, it's just what they told us.' Klein flushed redder in his already red face.

'I know what they told us, thank you,' said Steff. 'I'm not going to start anything, we're just going to have a look.'

'I know you,' burst out Klein. 'If you see cattle you'll go mad for them. All of you, you're greedy for cattle like some men are for drink. Once you see them you won't stop.' Klein was a railway ganger.

Steff turned away from him. 'Come on, let's go.'

They rode out of the shade of the kaffir boom tree into the sunlight, Klein muttering softly to himself and Mbejane leading them down the valley.

The floor of the valley sloped gradually and on each side

of them the ground rose steep and rocky. They travelled quickly with Mbejane and the other Nongaai thrown out as a screen and the horsemen cantering in a line with their stirrups almost touching.

Sean levered open the breech of his rifle and drew out the cartridge. He changed it for another from the bandolier across his chest.

'Fifty head is only ten apiece,' complained Frikkie.

'That's a hundred quid – as much as you earn in six months.' Sean laughed with excitement and Frikkie laughed with him.

'You two keep your mouths shut and your eyes open.' Steff's voice was phlegmatic, but he couldn't stop the excitement from sparkling in his eyes.

'I knew you were going to raid,' sulked Klein. 'I knew it, sure as fate.'

'You shut up also,' said Steff and grinned at Sean.

They rode for ten minutes; then Steff called softly to the Nongaai and the patrol halted. No one spoke and every man stood with his head alert and his ears straining.

'Nothing,' said Steff at last. 'How close are we?'

'Very close,' Mbejane answered. 'We should have heard them from here.'

Mbejane's exquisitely muscled body was shiny with sweat and the pride of his stance set him apart from the other Nongaai. There was a restrained eagerness about him, for the excitement was infectious.

'All right, follow them,' said Steff. Mbejane settled the rawhide shield securely on his shoulder and started forward again.

Twice more they stopped to listen and each time Sean and Frikkie were more restless and impatient.

'Sit still,' snapped Steff. 'How can we hear anything with you moving about?'

Sean opened his mouth, but before he could answer they

all heard an ox low mournfully ahead of them among the trees.

'That's it!'

'We've got them!'

'Come on!'

'No, wait!' Steff ordered. 'Sean, take my farlookers and climb up that tree. Tell me what you can see.'

'We're wasting time,' argued Sean. 'We should—'

'We should learn to do as we're damn well told,' said Steff. 'Get up that tree.'

With the binoculars slung around his neck, Sean clambered upwards until he sat high in a crotch of two branches. He reached out and broke off a twig which obscured his vision, then exclaimed immediately, 'There they are, right ahead of us!'

'How many?' Steff called up to him.

'A small herd – two herdboys with them.'

'Are they among the trees?'

'No,' said Sean, 'they're in the open. Looks like a patch of swamp.'

'Make sure there aren't any other Zulus with them.'

'No—' Sean started to answer but Steff cut him short.

'Use the glasses, dammit. They'll be hiding if they're there.'

Sean brought up the glasses and focused them. The cattle were fat and sleek skinned, big horned and bodies dappled black on white. A cloud of white tick-birds hovered over them. The two herdboys were completely naked, youngsters with the thin legs and the disproportionately large genitals of the Africans. Sean turned the glasses slowly back and forth searching the patch of swamp and the surrounding bush. At last he lowered them.

'Only the two herdboys,' he said.

'Come down then,' Steff told him.

The herdboys fled as soon as the patrol rode out into the

open. They disappeared among the fever trees on the far side of the swamp.

'Let them go,' laughed Steff. 'The poor little buggers are going to be in enough trouble as it is.'

He spurred his horse forward into the vivid green patch of swamp grass. It was lush: thick and tall enough to reach his saddle.

The others followed him in with the mud squelching and sucking at the hooves of the horses. They could see the backs of the cattle showing above the grass a hundred yards ahead of them. The tick-birds circled squawking.

'Sean, you and Frikkie cut around to the left—' Steff spoke over his shoulder and before he could finish the grass around them was full of Zulus, at least a hundred of them in full war dress.

'Ambush!' yelled Steff. 'Don't try and fight, too many of them. Get out!' and they dragged him off his horse.

Horses panicked in the mud, whinnying as they reared. The bang of Klein's rifle was almost drowned in the triumphant roar of the warriors. Mbejane jumped to catch the bridle of Sean's horse; he dragged its head around.

'Ride, Nkosi, quickly. Do not wait.'

Klein was dead, an assegai in his throat and the blood bursting brightly from the corners of his mouth as he fell backwards.

'Hold on to my stirrup leather.' Sean felt surprisingly calm. A Zulu came at him from the side; Sean held his rifle across his lap and fired with the muzzle almost in the man's face. It cut the top off his head. Sean ejected the cartridge case and reloaded.

'Ride, Nkosi!' Mbejane shouted again. He had made no effort to obey Sean: his shield held high he barged into two of the attackers and knocked them down into the mud. His assegai rose and fell, rose and fell.

'*Ngi Dhla*,' howled Mbejane. 'I have eaten.' Fighting

madness on him, he jumped over the bodies and charged. A man stood to meet him and Mbejane hooked the edge of his shield under his and jerked it aside, exposing the man's left flank to his blade.

'*Ngi Dhla*,' Mbejane howled again.

He had torn an opening in the ring of attackers and Sean rode for it, his horse churning heavily through the mud. A Zulu caught at his reins and Sean fired with his muzzle touching the man's chest. The Zulu screamed.

'Mbejane,' shouted Sean. 'Take my stirrup!'

Frikkie Van Essen was finished; his horse was down and Zulus swarmed over him with red spears.

Leaning out of the saddle Sean circled Mbejane's waist with his arm and plucked him out of the mud. He struggled wildly but Sean held him. The ground firmed under his horse's hooves, they were moving faster. Another Zulu stood in their way with his assegai ready. With Mbejane kicking indignantly under one arm and his empty rifle in his other hand Sean was helpless to defend himself. He shouted an obscenity at the Zulu as he rode down on him. The Zulu dodged to one side and darted in again. Sean felt the sting of the blade across his shin and then the shock as it went on into his horse's chest. They were through, out of the swamp and into the trees.

Sean's horse carried him another mile before it fell. The assegai had gone in deep. It fell heavily but Sean was able to kick his feet out of the irons and jump clear. He and Mbejane stood looking down at the carcass – both of them were panting.

'Can you run in those boots?' asked Mbejane urgently.

'Yes.' They were light *veldschoen*.

'Those breeches will hold your legs.' Mbejane knelt swiftly and with his assegai cut away the cloth until Sean's legs were bare from the thighs down. He stood up again and listened for the first sounds of pursuit. Nothing.

'Leave your rifle, it is too heavy. Leave your hat and your bandolier.'

'I must take my rifle,' protested Sean.

'Take it then,' Mbejane flashed impatiently. 'Take it and die. If you carry that they'll catch you before noon.'

Sean hesitated a second longer and then he changed his grip, holding the rifle by the barrel like an axe. He swung it against the trunk of the nearest tree. The butt shattered and he threw it from him.

'Now we must go,' said Mbejane.

Sean glanced quickly across at his dead horse, the leather thongs held his sheepskin coat onto the saddle. All Anna's hard work wasted, he thought wryly. Then following Mbejane he started to run.

The first hour was bad; Sean had difficulty matching his step to that of Mbejane. He ran with his body tensed and soon had a stabbing stitch in his side. Mbejane saw his pain and they stopped for a few minutes while Mbejane showed him how to relax it away. Then they went on with Sean running smoothly. Another hour went by and Sean had found his second wind.

'How long will it take us to get back to the main army?' grunted Sean.

'Two days perhaps . . . don't talk,' answered Mbejane.

The land changed slowly about them as they ran. The hills not so steep and jagged, the forest thinned and again they were into the rolling grassland.

'It seems we are not being followed.' It was half an hour since Sean had last spoken.

'Perhaps,' Mbejane was non-committal. 'It is too soon yet to tell.'

They ran on side by side, in step so their feet slapped in unison on the hard-baked earth.

'Christ, I'm thirsty,' said Sean.

'No water,' said Mbejane, 'but we'll stop to rest a while at the top of the next rise.'

They looked back from the crest. Sean's shirt was soaked with sweat and he was breathing deeply but easily.

'No one following us,' Sean's voice was relieved. 'We can slow down a bit now.'

Mbejane did not answer. He also was sweating heavily but the way he moved and held his head showed he was not yet beginning to tire. He carried his shield on his shoulder and the blade of the assegai in his other hand was caked with black, dry blood. He stared out along the way they had come for fully five minutes before he growled angrily and pointed with his assegai.

'There! Close to that clump of trees. Can you see them?'

'Oh, hell!' Sean saw them: about four miles behind, on the edge of the forest where it thinned out, a black pencil line drawn on the brown parchment of grassland. But the line was moving.

'How many of them?' asked Sean.

'Fifty,' hazarded Mbejane. 'Too many.'

'I wish I had brought my rifle,' muttered Sean.

'If you had they would be much closer now – and one gun against fifty—' Mbejane left it unfinished.

'All right, let's get going again,' said Sean.

'We must rest a little longer. This is the last time we can stop before nightfall.'

Their breathing had slowed. Sean took stock of himself: he was aching a little in the legs, but it would be hours yet before he was really tired. He hawked a glob of the thick gummy saliva out of his throat and spat it into the grass. He wanted a drink but knew that would be fatal folly.

'Ah!' exclaimed Mbejane. 'They have seen us.'

'How do you know?' asked Sean.

'Look, they are sending out their chasers.' From the head

of the line a trio of specks had detached themselves and were drawing ahead.

'What do you mean?' Sean scratched the side of his nose uneasily. For the first time he was feeling the fear of the hunted – vulnerable, unarmed, with the pack closing in.

'They are sending their best runners ahead to force us beyond our strength. They know that if they push us hard enough – even though they break their own wind while they do it – we will fall easily to the others that follow.'

'Good God.' Sean was now truly alarmed. 'What are we going to do about it?'

'For every trick, there is a trick,' said Mbejane. 'But now we have rested enough, let us go.'

Sean took off down the hill like a startled duiker, but Mbejane pulled him up sharply.

'That is what they want. Run as before.' And once again they fell into the steady lope, swinging long-legged and relaxed.

'They're closer,' said Sean when they reached the top of the next hill. Three specks were now well ahead of the others.

'Yes.' Mbejane's voice was expressionless. They went over the crest and down the other side, the slap-slap-slap of their feet together and their breathing an unaltering rhythm: suck blow, suck blow.

There was a tiny stream in the bottom of the valley, clean water rippling over white sand. Sean jumped it with only a single longing glance and they started up the far slope. They were just short of the crest when behind them they heard a thin distant shout. He and Mbejane looked round. On the top of the hill they had just left, only a half a mile away, were the three Zulu runners, and as Sean watched they plunged down the slope towards him with their tall feather head-dresses bobbing and their leopard-tail kilts swirling about their legs. They had thrown aside their shields, but each man carried an assegai.

'Look at their legs,' exulted Mbejane. Sean saw that they ran with the slack, blundering steps of exhaustion.

'They are finished, they have run too hard.' Mbejane laughed. 'Now we must show them how afraid we are: we must run like the wind, run as though a hundred Tokoloshe* breathe on our necks.'

It was only twenty paces to the crest of the slope and they pelted panic-stricken up and over the top. But the instant they were out of sight Mbejane caught Sean's arm and held him.

'Get down,' he whispered. They sank into the grass and then crawled back on their stomachs until they lay just below the crest.

Mbejane held his assegai pointed forward, his legs were gathered up under him and his lips were drawn back in a half grin.

Sean searched in the grass and found a rock the size of an orange. It fitted neatly into his right hand.

They heard the Zulus coming, their horny bare feet pounding up the hill and then their breathing, hoarse hissing gasps, closer and closer until suddenly they came up over the crest. Their momentum carried them down to where Sean and Mbejane stood up out of the grass to meet them. Their fatigue-grey faces crumbled into expressions of complete disbelief; they had expected to find their quarry half a mile ahead of them. Mbejane killed one with his assegai, the man did not even lift his arms to parry the thrust; the point came out between his shoulders.

Sean hurled the rock into the face of another. It made a sound like a ripe pumpkin dropped on a stone floor; he fell backwards with his assegai spinning from his hand.

* A chimera of Zulu mythology.

The third man turned to run and Mbejane landed heavily on his back, bore him down and then sat astride his chest, pushed his chin back and cut his throat.

Sean looked down at the man he had hit; he had lost his head-dress and his face had changed shape. His jaw hung lopsided, he was still moving feebly.

I have killed three men today, thought Sean, *and it was so easy*.

Without emotion he watched Mbejane come across to his victim. Mbejane stooped over him and the man made a small gasping sound then lay still. Mbejane straightened up and looked at Sean.

'Now they cannot catch us before dark.'

'And only a night ape can see in the dark,' said Sean. Remembering the joke, Mbejane smiled; the smile made his face younger. He picked up a bunch of dry grass and wiped his hands on it.

The night came only just in time to save them. Sean had run all day and at last his body was stiffening in protest; his breathing wheezed painfully and he had no moisture left to sweat with.

'A little longer, just a little longer.' Mbejane whispered encouragement beside him.

The pack was spread out, the stronger runners pressing a scant mile behind them and the others dwindling back into the distance.

'The sun is going; soon you can rest.' Mbejane reached out and touched his shoulder; strangely, Sean drew strength from that brief physical contact. His legs steadied slightly and he stumbled less frequently as they went down the next slope. Swollen and red, the sun lowered itself below the land and the valleys were full of shadow.

'Soon now, very soon.' Mbejane's voice was almost crooning. He looked back: the figures of the nearest Zulu were indistinct. Sean's ankle twisted under him and he fell heavily; he felt the earth graze the skin from his cheek and he lay on his chest with his head down.

'Get up,' Mbejane's voice was desperate. Sean vomited painfully, a cupful of bitter bile.

'Get up.' Mbejane's hands were on him, dragging him to his knees.

'Stand up or die here,' threatened Mbejane. He took a handful of Sean's hair and twisted it mercilessly. Tears of pain ran into Sean's eyes and he swore and lashed out at Mbejane.

'Get up,' goaded Mbejane and Sean heaved to his feet.

'Run,' said Mbejane, half-pushing him and Sean's legs began to move mechanically under him. Mbejane looked back once more. The nearest Zulu was very close but almost merged into the fading twilight. They ran on, Mbejane steadying Sean when he staggered, Sean grunting in his throat with each step, his mouth hanging open, sucking air across a swollen tongue.

Then quickly, in the sudden African transition from day to night, all colour was gone from the land and the darkness shut down in a close circle about them. Mbejane's eyes flicked restlessly back and forth, picking up shapes in the gloom, judging the intensity of the light. Sean reeled unseeing beside him.

'We will try now,' decided Mbejane aloud. He checked Sean's run and turned him right at an acute angle on their original track, now they were heading back towards the hunters at a tangent that would take them close past them but out of sight in the darkness.

They slowed to a walk, Mbejane holding Sean's arm across his shoulders to steady him, carrying his assegai ready in his other hand. Sean walked dully, his head hanging.

They heard the leading pursuers passing fifty paces away in the darkness and a voice called in Zulu, 'Can you see them?'

'*Aibo*!' Negative answered another.

'Spread out, they may try to turn in the dark.'

'*Yeh-bo*!' Affirmative.

Then the voices were passed and silence and night closed about them once more. Mbejane made Sean keep walking. A little bit of moon came up and gave them light and they kept going with Mbejane gradually working back onto a course towards the southeast. They came to a stream at last with trees along its bank. Sean drank with difficulty, for his throat was swollen and sore. Afterwards they curled together for warmth on the carpet of leaves beneath the trees and they slept.

– 28 –

They found Chelmsford's last camp on the following afternoon: the neat lines of black camp fires and the flattened areas where the tents had stood, the stakes which had held the horse pickets and the piles of empty bully-beef tins and five-pound biscuit tins.

'They left two days ago,' said Mbejane.

Sean nodded, not doubting the correctness of this. 'Which way did they go?'

'Back towards the main camp at Isandhlwana.'

Sean looked puzzled.

'I wonder why they did that.'

Mbejane shrugged. 'They went in haste – the horsemen galloped ahead of the infantry.'

'We'll follow them,' said Sean.

The spoor was a wide road for a thousand men had passed along it and the wagons and gun carriages had left deep ruts.

They slept hungry and cold beside the spoor and the

next morning there was frost in the low places when they started out.

A little before noon they saw the granite dome of Isandhlwana standing out against the sky and unconsciously they quickened their pace. Isandhlwana, the Hill of the Little Hand. Sean was limping for his boot had rubbed the skin from one heel. His hair was thick and matted with sweat and his face was plastered with dust.

'Even army bully beef is going to taste good,' said Sean in English, and Mbejane did not answer for he did not understand, but he was looking ahead with a vaguely worried frown on his face.

'Nkosi, we have seen no one for two days' march. It comes to me that we should have met patrols from the camp before now.'

'We might have missed them,' said Sean without much interest, but Mbejane shook his head. In silence they went on. The hill was closer now so they could make out the detail of ledge and fissure that covered the dome in a lacework pattern.

'No smoke from the camp,' said Mbejane. He lifted his eyes and started visibly.

'What is it?' Sean felt the first tingle of alarm.

'*N'yoni*,' said Mbejane softly and Sean saw them. A dark pall, turning like a wheel slowly, high above the hill of Isandhlwana, still so far off that they could not distinguish the individual birds: only a shadow, a thin dark shadow in the sky. Watching it Sean was suddenly cold in the hot noonday sun. He started to run.

There was movement below them on the plain. The torn canvas of an overturned wagon flapped like a wounded bird, the scurry and scuffle of the jackals and higher up the slope of the kopje the hunch-shouldered trot of a hyena.

'Oh, my God!' whispered Sean. Mbejane leaned on his

spear; his face was calm and withdrawn but his eyes moved slowly over the field.

'Are they dead? Are they all dead?' The question required no answer. He could see the dead men in the grass, thick about the wagons and then scattered more thinly back up the slope. They looked very small and inconsequential. Mbejane stood quietly waiting. A big black kolbes vulture planed across their front, the feathers in its wing-tips flated like the fingers of a spread hand. Its legs dropped, touched and it hopped heavily to rest among the dead, a swift transformation from beautiful flight to obscene crouching repose. It bobbed its head, ruffled its feathers and waddled to dip its beak over a corpse that wore the green Hunting Tartan of the Gordons.

'Where is Chelmsford? Was he caught here also?'

Mbejane shook his head. 'He came too late.'

Mbejane pointed with his spear at the wide spoor that skirted the battlefield and crossed the shoulder of Isandhlwana towards the Tugela. 'He has gone back to the river. He has not stopped even to bury his dead.'

Sean and Mbejane walked down towards the field. On the outskirts they picked their way through the debris of Zulu weapons and shields; there was rust forming on the blades of the assegais. The grass was flattened and stained where the dead had lain, but the Zulu dead were gone – sure sign of victory.

They came to the English lines. Sean gagged when he saw what had been done to them. They lay piled upon each other, faces already black, and each one of them had been disembowelled. The flies crawled in their empty stomach cavities.

'Why do they do that?' he asked. 'Why do they have to hack them up like that?'

He walked on heavily past the wagons. Cases of food and drink had been smashed open and scattered in the grass, clothing and paper and cartridge cases lay strewn around the dead, but the rifles were gone. The smell of putrefaction was so thick that it coated his throat and tongue like castor oil.

'I must find Pa,' Sean spoke quietly in almost a conversational tone. Mbejane walked a dozen paces behind him. They came to the lines where the Volunteers had camped. The tents had been slashed to tatters and trampled into the dust. The horses had been stabbed while still tethered to their picket lines; they were massively bloated. Sean recognized Gypsy, his father's mare. He crossed to her.

'Hello, girl,' he said. The birds had taken her eyes out; she lay on her side, her stomach so swollen that it was as high as Sean's waist. He walked around her. The first of the Ladyburg men lay just beyond. He recognized all fifteen of them although the birds had been at them also. They lay in a rough circle, facing outwards. Then he found a sparse trail of corpses leading up towards the shoulder of the mountain. He followed the attempt that the Volunteers had made to fight their way back towards the Tugela and it was like following a paper chase. Along the trail, thick on each side of it, were the marks where the Zulus had fallen.

'At least twenty of them for every one of us,' whispered Sean, with a tiny flicker of pride. He climbed on up and at the top of the shoulder, close under the sheer rock cliff of Isandhlwana, he found his father.

There were four of them, the last four: Waite Courtney, Tim Hope-Brown, Hans and Nile Erasmus. They lay close together. Waite was on his back with his arms spread open, the birds had taken his face away down to the bone, but they had left his beard and it stirred gently on his chest as the wind touched it. The flies, big metallic green flies, crawled thick as swarming bees in the open pit of his belly.

Sean sat down beside his father. He picked up a discarded felt hat that lay beside him and covered his terribly mutilated face. There was a green-and-yellow silk cockade on the hat, strangely gay in the presence of so much death. The flies buzzed sullenly and some came to settle on Sean's face and lips. He brushed them away.

'You know this man?' asked Mbejane.

'My father,' said Sean, without looking up.

'You too.' Compassion and understanding in his voice, Mbejane turned away and left them alone.

'I have nothing,' Mbejane had said. Now Sean also had nothing. There was hollowness: no anger, no sorrow, no ache, no reality even. Staring down at this broken thing, Sean could not make himself believe that this was a man. Meat only; the man had gone.

Later Mbejane came back. He had cut a sheet of canvas from one of the unburned wagons and they wrapped Waite in it. They dug his grave. It was hard work for the soil was thick with rock and shale. They laid Waite in the grave, with his arms still widespread in *rigor mortis* beneath the canvas for Sean could not bring himself to break them. They covered him gently and piled rocks upon the place. They stood together at the head of the grave.

'Well, Pa – ' Sean's voice sounded unnatural. He could not make himself believe he was talking to his father.

'Well, Pa – ' he started again, mumbling self-consciously. 'I'd like to say thanks for everything you've done for me.' He stopped and cleared his throat. 'I reckon you know I'll look after Ma and the farm as best I can – and Garry also.' His voice trailed away once more and he turned to Mbejane.

'There is nothing to say.' Sean's voice was surprised, hurt almost.

'No,' agreed Mbejane. 'There is nothing to say.'

For a few minutes longer Sean stood struggling to grapple with the enormity of death, trying to grasp the utter finality of it, then he turned away and started walking towards the

Tugela. Mbejane walked a little to one side and a pace behind him. *It will be dark before we reach the river*, thought Sean. He was very tired and he limped from his blistered heel.

– 29 –

'Not much farther,' said Dennis Petersen.

'No,' Sean grunted. He was irritated at the statement of the obvious; when you come out of Mahoba's Kloof and have the Baboon Stroom next to the road on your left hand, then it is five miles to Ladyburg. As Dennis had said: not much farther.

Dennis coughed in the dust. 'That first beer is going to turn to steam in my throat.'

'I think we can ride ahead now.' Sean wiped at his face, smearing the dust. 'Mbejane and the other servants can bring them in the rest of the way.'

'I was going to suggest it.' Dennis was obviously relieved. They had almost a thousand head of cattle crowding the road ahead of them and raising dust for them to breathe. It had been two days' drive from Rorke's Drift where the Commando had disbanded.

'We'll hold them in the sale pens tonight and send them out tomorrow morning – I'll tell Mbejane.'

Sean clapped his heels into his horse and swung across to where the big Zulu trotted at the heels of the herd. A few minutes' talk and then Sean signalled to Dennis. They circled out on each side of the herd and met again on the road ahead of it.

'They've lost a bit of condition,' grumbled Dennis looking back.

'Bound to,' said Sean. 'We've pushed them hard for two days.'

A thousand head of cattle, five men's share of Cetewayo's herds – Dennis and his father, Waite, Sean and Garrick – for even dead men drew a full share.

'How far ahead of the others do you reckon we are?' asked Dennis.

'Dunno,' said Sean. It wasn't important and any answer would be only a guess: pointless question is just as irritating as obvious statement. It suddenly occurred to Sean that but a few months previously a question like that would have started a discussion and argument that might have lasted half an hour. What did that mean? It meant that he had changed. Having answered his own question, Sean grinned sardonically.

'What're you laughing at?' asked Dennis.

'I was just thinking that a lot has changed in the last few months.'

'*Ja*,' said Dennis and then silence except for the broken beat of their hooves. 'It's going to seem funny without Pa,' Dennis said wistfully. Mr Petersen had been at Isandhlwana. 'It's going to seem funny being just Ma, the girls and me on the farm.'

They didn't speak again for a while. They were thinking back across the brief months and the events that had changed their lives.

Neither of them yet twenty years of age, but already head of his family, a holder of land and cattle, initiated into grief and a killer of men. Sean was older now with new lines in his face, and the beard he wore was square and spade-shaped. They had ridden with the Commandos who had burned and plundered to avenge Isandhlwana. At Ulundi they had sat their horses behind the ranks of Chelmsford's infantry in the hot sun, quietly waiting as Cetewayo massed his impis and sent them across open ground to overwhelm the frail square of men. They had waited through the din of the regular, unhurried volleys and watched the great black bull of Zulu tearing itself to shreds against the square. Then at the end the ranks of infantry had opened and they had ridden out, two thousand horsemen strong, to smash for ever the power of the Zulu empire. They had chased and hunted until the darkness had stopped them and they had not kept score of the kill.

'There's the church steeple,' said Dennis.

Sean came back slowly out of the past. They were at Ladyburg.

'Is your stepmother out at Theunis Kraal?' asked Dennis.

'No, she's moved into town – the cottage on Protea Street.'

'I suppose she doesn't want to be in the way now that Anna and Garry are married,' said Dennis.

Sean frowned quickly.

'How do you like old Garry getting Anna?' Dennis chuckled and shook his head. 'I reckon you could have got twenty-to-one odds he didn't have a chance.'

Sean's frown became a scowl. Garry had made him look such a damn fool – Sean hadn't finished with Anna.

'Have you heard from them yet? When are they coming home?'

'The last time we heard was from Pietermaritzburg; they sent a wire to Ma just to say they were married. She got it a couple of days before I arrived home from Isandhlwana. That was two months ago; as far as I know we haven't heard since.'

'I suppose Garry's so firmly settled on the nest they'll have to prise him off with a crowbar.' Dennis chuckled again, lewdly. Sean had a sudden and shockingly vivid mental picture of Garry on top of Anna; her knees were up high, her head was thrown back and her eyes were closed; she was making that little mewing sound.

'Shut up, you dirty bastard,' snarled Sean.

Dennis blinked. 'Sorry, I was only joking.'

'Don't joke about my family, he's my brother.'

'And she was your girl, hey?' murmured Dennis.

'Do you want a punch?'

'Cool down, man, I was joking.'

'I don't like that kind of joke, see?'

'All right. All right. Cool down.'

'It's dirty, that's dirty talk.' Sean was trying desperately to shut out the picture of Anna; she was in wild orgasm, her hands pleading at the small of Garrick's back.

'Jesus, since when have you become a saint?' asked Dennis and, urging his horse into a gallop, drew ahead of Sean; he kept going along the main street towards the hotel. Sean considered calling him back, but finally let him go.

Sean turned right into a shady side street. The cottage was the third house down. Waite had purchased it three years before as an investment. It was a charming little place, set among trees in a small green garden with flowers: thatched, whitewashed and surrounded by a wooden picket fence. Sean hitched his horse at the gate and went up the path.

There were two women in the sitting-room when he pushed the door open. They both stood up, surprise instantly becoming delight as they recognized him. It warmed him inside to see it – it's good to be welcome.

'Oh Sean, we weren't expecting you.' Ada came quickly to him. He kissed her and saw that sorrow had left its marks on her. He felt vaguely guilty that Waite's death had not wrought so obvious a change in him. He held her away at arm's length.

'You're beautiful,' he said. She was thin. Her eyes were too big for her face and the grief was in them like shadows in the forest, but she smiled and laughed at him.

'We thought you'd be back on Friday. I'm so glad you've come earlier.'

Sean looked past Ada.

'Hello, Strawberry Pie.' She was hovering impatiently for his attention.

'Hello, Sean.' She flushed a little with his eyes on her, but she did not drop hers.

'You look older,' she said, hardly noticing the dust that caked his skin, powdered his hair and eyelashes, and reddened his eyes.

'You've just forgotten what I look like,' he said, turning back to Ada.

'No, I'd never do that,' whispered Audrey so softly that neither of them heard her. She felt swollen up inside her chest.

'Sit down, Sean.' Ada led him to the big armchair across from the fireplace. There was a daguerreotype of Waite on the mantel.

'I'll get you a cup of tea.'

'How about a beer, Ma?' Sean sank into the chair.

'Of course – I'll get it.'

'No.' Audrey flew across the room towards the kitchen. 'I'll get it.'

'They're in the pantry, Audrey,' Ada called after her, and then to Sean, 'She's such a sweet child.'

'Look again,' Sean smiled. 'She's no child.'

'I wish Garry—' Ada cut herself short.

'What do you wish?' Sean prompted her. She was quiet for a moment, wishing that Garrick could have found a girl like Audrey instead of –

'Nothing,' she said to Sean and came to sit near him.

'Have you heard from Garry again?' asked Sean.

'No. Not yet, but Mr Pye says he had a cheque come through the bank – cashed in Capetown.'

'Capetown?' Sean raised a dusty eyebrow. 'Our boy's living life to the hilt.'

'Yes,' said Ada, remembering the size of that cheque. 'He is.'

Audrey came back into the room: she had a large bottle and a glass on a tray. She crossed to Sean's chair. Sean touched the bottle; it was cold.

'Quickly, wench,' Sean encouraged her. 'I'm dying of thirst.'

The first glass emptied in three swallows. Audrey poured again and, with the replenished glass in his fist, Sean settled back comfortably in the chair.

'Now,' said Ada, 'tell us all about it.'

In the warmth of their welcome – his muscles aching pleasantly, the glass in his hand – it was good to talk. He had not realized that there was so much to tell. At the first hint of slackening in his flow of speech either Ada or Audrey was ready with a question to keep him going.

'Oh, my goodness,' gasped Audrey at last. 'It's nearly dark outside, I must go.'

'Sean,' Ada stood up. 'Will you see that she gets home safely?'

They walked side by side in the half darkness, under the flamboyants. They walked in silence until Audrey spoke.

'Sean, were you in love with Anna?' She blurted out the question and Sean experienced his standard reaction: quick anger. He opened his mouth to blast her, then checked. It was a nice question. Had he been in love with Anna? He thought about it now for the first time, phrasing the question with care that he might answer it with truth. He felt a sudden rush of relief and he was smiling when he told her.

'No, Strawberry Pie, no, I was never in love with Anna.' The tone of his voice was right, he wasn't lying. She walked on happily beside him.

'Don't bother to come up to the house.' She noticed for the first time his stained and dirty clothing that might embarrass him in front of her parents. She wanted it to be right from the start.

'I'll watch you till you get to the door,' said Sean.

'I suppose you'll be going out to Theunis Kraal tomorrow?' she asked.

'First thing in the morning,' Sean assured her. 'There's a hell of a lot of work to do.'

'But you'll be coming to the store?'

'Yes,' said Sean and the way he looked at her made her blush and hate her redhead's skin which betrayed her so easily. She went quickly up the path and then stopped and looked back.

'Sean, please don't call me Strawberry Pie any more.'

Sean chuckled. 'All right, Audrey, I'll try to remember.'

– 30 –

Six weeks had gone since his return from the Zulu Campaign, Sean reflected, six weeks that had passed in a blur of speed. He sipped coffee from a mug the size of a German beer *stein*, sitting in the centre of his bed with his nightshirt hitched up to his waist and his legs crossed in comfortable Buddha fashion. The coffee was hot; he sipped noisily and then exhaled steam from his mouth.

The last six weeks had been full – too full for brooding grief or regret, although in the evenings, when he sat in the study with Waite's memory all about him, the ache was still there.

The days seemed to pass before they had fairly begun. There were three farms now: Theunis Kraal and the other two rented from old man Pye. He had stocked them with the looted cattle and the purchases he had made since his return. The price of prime beef had dropped to a new low, with nearly a hundred thousand cattle brought back from Zululand and Sean could afford to be selective in his buying. He could also afford to wait while the price climbed up again.

Sean swung his legs off the bed and walked across the room to the washstand. He poured water from the jug into the basin and tested it tentatively with one finger. It was so cold it stung. He stood hesitating in his ridiculously feminine nightshirt, with dark chest hairs curling out above the elaborately embroidered front. Then he mustered his courage and plunged his face into the basin; he scooped water with both hands and poured it over the back of his neck, massaged it into his hair with hooked fingers and emerged at last blowing heavily with water dripping down onto his nightshirt. He towelled, stripped off the damp garment and stood naked peering out of the window. It had lightened enough for him to make out the smoky swirl of drizzle and mist beyond the pane.

'A hell of a day,' he grumbled aloud, but his tone was deceptive. He felt excitement for this day; he was fresh and sharp-edged, hungry for breakfast, ready to go for there was work to do.

He dressed, hopping on one leg as he got into his breeches, stuffing in the tails of his shirt and then sitting on the bed to pull on his boots. Now he was thinking about Audrey – he must try and get into town tomorrow to see her.

Sean had decided on matrimony. He had three good reasons. He had found that it was easier to get into the Bank of England's vaults than to get under Audrey's petticoats without marrying her. When Sean wanted something no price was too high to pay.

Living at Theunis Kraal with Garry and Anna, Sean had decided that it would be pleasant to have his own woman to cook for him, mend his clothes and listen to his stories, for Sean was feeling a little left out.

The third consideration, by no means the least significant, was Audrey's connections with the local bank. She was one of the very few weaknesses in old man Pye's armour. He might even weigh in with Mahoba's Kloof Farm as a wedding present, though even the optimist in Sean realized that this hope was extravagant. Pye and his money were not easily parted.

Yes, Sean decided, he would have to find time to get into town and tell Audrey – in Sean's mind it wasn't a question of asking her. Sean brushed his hair, combed his beard, winked at himself in the mirror and went out into the passage. He could smell breakfast cooking and his mouth started to water.

Anna was in the kitchen. Her face was flushed from the heat of the stove.

'What's for breakfast, little sister?'

She turned to him, quickly brushing the hair off her forehead with the back of her hand.

'I'm not your sister,' she said. 'I wish you wouldn't call me that.'

'Where's Garry?' Sean asked as though he had not heard her protest.

'He's not up yet.'

'The poor boy's exhausted, no doubt.' Sean grinned at her and she turned away in confusion. Sean looked at her bottom without desire. Strange that Anna being Garry's wife should kill his appetite for her. Even the memory of what they had done before was vaguely obscene, incestuous.

'You're getting fat,' he said noticing the new heaviness of her body. She ducked her head but did not answer and Sean went on, 'I'll have four eggs, please, and tell Joseph not to dry them out completely.'

Sean went through into the dining-room and Garry came in through the side door at the same moment. His face was still vacant from sleep. Sean got a whiff of his breath; it smelled of stale liquor.

'Good morning, Romeo,' said Sean and Garry grinned sheepishly. His eyes were bloodshot and he hadn't shaved.

'Hello, Sean. How did you sleep?'

'Beautifully, thank you. I take it that you did also.' Sean sat down and spooned porridge from the tureen.

'Have some?' he asked Garry.

'Thanks.' Sean passed him the plate. He noticed how Garry's hand shook. *I'll have to talk to him about letting up on the bottle a trifle.*

'Hell, I'm hungry.' They talked the jerky, disconnected conversation of the breakfast table. Anna came through and joined them. Joseph brought the coffee.

'Have you told Sean yet, Garry?' Anna spoke suddenly, clearly and with decision.

'No.' Garry was taken by surprise, he spluttered his coffee.

'Told me what?' Sean asked. They were silent and Garrick fluttered his hand nervously. This was the moment he had been dreading – what if Sean guessed, what if he knew it was his baby and took them away, Anna and the baby, took them away and left Garry with nothing. Haunted by wild unreasonable fears, Garrick stared fixedly across the table at his brother.

'Tell him, Garry,' commanded Anna.

'Anna's going to have a baby,' he said. He watched Sean's face, saw the surprise change slowly to delight, felt Sean's arm close round his shoulders in a painful hug, almost crushing him.

'That's great,' Sean exulted, 'that's wonderful. We'll have the house full of kids in no time if you keep that up, Garry. I'm proud of you.'

Grinning stupidly with relief Garrick watched Sean hug Anna more gently and kiss her forehead.

'Well done, Anna, make sure it's a boy. We need cheap labour around here.'

He hasn't guessed, thought Garrick, *he doesn't know and it will be mine. No one can take it away from me now.*

That day they worked in the south section. They stayed together, Garry laughing in happy confusion at Sean's banter. It was delightful to have Sean give him so much attention. They finished early; for once Sean was in no mood for work.

'My reproductive brother, every barrel loaded with buck-shot.' Sean leaned across and punched Garry's shoulder. 'Let's knock it off and go into town. We can have a few quick ones to celebrate at the hotel and then go and tell Ada.'

Sean stood up in the stirrup and yelled above the moo and mill of the herd.

'Mbejane, bring those ten sick ones up to the house and don't forget that tomorrow we are going to fetch cattle from the sale pens.'

Mbejane waved in acknowledgement and Sean turned back to Garrick.

'Come on, let's get the hell out of here.'

They rode side by side, globules of moisture covering their oilskins and shining on Sean's beard. It was still cold and the escarpment was hidden in the wet mist.

'It's real brandy-drinking weather,' said Sean and Garrick did not answer. He was frightened again. He didn't want to tell Ada. She would guess. She guessed everything, she would know it was Sean's child. You couldn't lie to her.

The horses' hooves plopped wetly in the mud. They reached the spot where the road forked and climbed over the ridge to Ladyburg.

'Ada's going to love being a grandma,' chuckled Sean, and at that moment his horse stumbled slightly, broke its gait and started favouring its near fore. Sean dismounted, lifted the hoof and saw the splinter driven deep into the frog.

'Damn it to hell,' he swore. He bent his head, gripped the hilt of the splinter with his teeth and drew it out.

'Well, we can't go into Ladyburg now, that leg will be sore for days.' Garry was relieved; it put off the time when he must tell Ada.

'Your horse isn't lame. Off you go, man, give her my love.' Sean looked up at him.

'We can tell her some other time. Let's get back home,' Garry demurred.

'Go on, Garry, it's your baby. Go and tell her.'

Garrick argued until he saw Sean's temper rising, then with a sigh of resignation he went and Sean led his own horse back to Theunis Kraal. Now that he was walking the oilskin was uncomfortably hot and heavy, Sean took it off and slung it over the saddle.

Anna was standing on the *stoep* as he came up to the homestead.

'Where's Garry?' she called.

'Don't worry. He's gone into town to see Ada. He'll be back by supper-time.'

One of the stable boys came to take Sean's horse. They talked together and then Sean stooped to lift the injured hoof. His breeches tightened across his buttocks and enhanced the long moulded taper of his legs. Anna looked at him. He straightened up and his shoulders were wide beneath the damp white linen of his shirt. He smiled at her as he came up the steps of the *stoep*. The rain had made his beard curl and he looked like a mischievous pirate.

'You must take better care of yourself now.' He put his hand on her upper arm to lead her inside. 'You can't stand around in the cold any more.' They went in through the glass doors. Anna looked up at him, the top of her head on a level with his shoulder.

'You're a damn fine woman, Anna, and I'm sure you're going to make a fine baby.' It was a mistake, for as he said it his eyes softened and his face turned down towards her. He let his arm drop around her shoulders.

'Sean!' She said his name as though it were an exclamation of pain. She moved quickly, fiercely within the circle of his arm, her body flattened itself against his and her hands went up to catch in the thick hair at the back of his head. She pulled his face down and her mouth opened warm and wet across his lips, her back arched and thrust her thighs against his legs. She moaned softly as she kissed him. For startled seconds Sean stood imprisoned in her embrace, then he tore his face away.

'Are you mad?' He tried to push her from him, but she fought her way back through his fending hands. She locked her arms around him and pressed her face against his chest.

'I love you. Please, please. I love you. Just let me hold you, that's all. I just want to hold you.' Her voice was muffled by the damp cloth of his shirt. She was shivering.

'Get away from me.' Roughly Sean broke her hold and almost threw her backwards onto the couch beside the fireplace.

'You're Garry's wife now, and you'll soon be the mother of his child. Keep your hot little body for him.' Sean stood back from her with his anger starting to mount.

'But I love you, Sean. Oh, my God, if I could only make you understand how I've suffered, living here with you and not being able to touch you even.'

Sean strode across to where she sat. 'Listen to me.' His voice was harsh. 'I don't want you. I never loved you, but now I could no more touch you than I could go with my own mother.' She could see the revulsion in his face. 'You're Garry's wife; if ever again you look at another man I'll kill you.'

He lifted his hands, holding them with the fingers crooked ready. 'I'll kill you with my bare hands.'

His face was close to hers. She could not bear the

expression in his eyes: she lashed out at him. He pulled back in time to save his eyes, but her nails gouged bloody lines across his cheek and down the side of his nose. He caught her wrists and held her while a thin trickle of blood dribbled down into his beard. She twisted in his hands, jerking her body from side to side, and she screamed at him.

'You swine, you dirty, dirty swine. Garry's wife, you say. Garry's baby, you say.' She threw her head back and laughed wildly through her screaming. 'Now I'll tell you the truth. What I have within me you gave me. It's yours! Not Garry's!' Sean let go her wrists and backed away from her.

'It can't be,' he whispered, 'you must be lying.' She followed him.

'Don't you remember how you said goodbye to me before you went to war? Don't you remember that night in the wagon? Don't you remember – don't you? Don't you?' She was talking quietly now, using her words to wound him.

'That was months ago. It can't be true,' Sean stammered, still moving away from her.

'Three and a half months,' she told him. 'Your brother's baby will be a little early, don't you think? But lots of people have premature babies—' Her voice droned on steadily, she was shivering uncontrollably now and her face was ghostly pale. Sean could stand it no longer.

'Leave me, leave me alone. I've got to think. I didn't know.' He brushed past her and went out into the passage. She heard the door of Waite's study slam shut and she stood still in the centre of the floor. Gradually her panting came under control and the storm surf of her anger abated to expose the black reefs of hatred beneath. She crossed the floor, went down the passage and into her own bedroom. She stood in front of the mirror and looked at herself.

'I hate him.' Her lips formed the words in the mirror. Her face was still pale. 'There's one thing I can take from him. Garry's mine now, not his.'

She pulled the pins from her hair and let them drop onto the floor; her hair fell down her back. She shook it onto her shoulders then lifted her hands and tangled it into confusion. Her teeth closed on her own lips, she bit until she tasted blood.

'Oh, God, I hate him, I hate him,' she whispered through the pain. Her hands came down onto the front of her dress. She tore it open, then in the mirror looked without interest at the round bosses of her nipples that were already darkening with the promise of fruition. She kicked off her shoes.

'I hate him.' She stooped and her hands went up under her skirts into the petticoats. She loosened her pantaloons and stepped out of them; she held them across her chest to tear them, then threw them next to the bed. She swept her arm across the top of her dressing-table: one of the bowls hit the floor and burst with a splash of face-powder and there was the sudden pungent reek of spilled perfume. She crossed to the bed and dropped onto it. She lifted her knees and her petticoats fell back like the petals of a flower: her white legs and lower body were the stamen.

Just before nightfall there was a shy knock on her door.

'What is it?' she asked.

'The Nkosikazi has not told me what I should cook for dinner.' Old Joseph's voice was raised respectfully.

'There will be no dinner tonight. You and all the servants may go.'

'Very well, Nkosikazi.'

Garrick came home in the dark. He had been drinking; she heard him stagger as he crossed the *stoep*, and his voice slur as he called.

'Hallo. Where's everybody? Anna! Anna! I'm back.' Silence for a while as he lit one of the lamps and then the hurried thump, thump of his peg along the passage and his voice again edged with alarm.

'Anna, Anna, where are you?'

He pushed the door open and stood with the lamp in his hand. Anna rolled away from the light, pressing her face into the pillow and hunching her shoulders. She heard him set the lamp down on the dressing-table, felt his hands pulling down her skirts to cover her nakedness, then gently turn her to face him. She looked into his face and saw the uncomprehending horror in it.

'My darling, oh Anna, my darling, what's happened?' He started at her broken lips and her breasts. Bewildered he turned his head and looked at the bottles on the floor, at her torn pantaloons. His face hardened and came back to her.

'Are you hurt?' She shook her head.

'Who? Tell me who did it.' She turned away from him again, hiding her face.

'My darling, my poor darling. Who was it – one of the servants?'

'No,' her voice stifled with shame.

'Please tell me, Anna. What happened?'

She sat up quickly and threw her arms about him, holding him hard so her lips were near his ear. 'You know, Garry. You know who did it.'

'No, I swear I don't, please tell me.'

Anna drew her breath in deep, held it a second then breathed it out. 'Sean!'

Garrick's body convulsed in her arms, she heard him grunt as though he had been hit. Then he spoke. 'This too. Now this too.'

He loosened her hands from his neck and pushed her gently down onto the pillows. He crossed to the cupboard, opened one of the drawers and took out Waite's service pistol.

He's going to kill Sean, she thought. Garrick went out of the room without looking at her again. She waited with her hands clenched at her sides and her whole body stretched tightly. When the shot came at last it was surprisingly muted and unwarlike. Her body relaxed, her hands opened and she began to cry softly.

– 31 –

Garry limped down the passage. The pistol was heavy and the checkered grip rough in his hand. There was light showing under the study door at the end of the passage. It was unlocked. Garrick went in.

Sean sat with his elbows on the desk and his face in his hands but he looked up as Garrick came in through the door. The scratches had already dried black across his cheek, but the flesh around them was red and inflamed. He looked at the pistol in Garrick's hand.

'She has told you.' There was no question or expression in his voice.

'Yes.'

'I hoped that she wouldn't,' said Sean. 'I wanted her to spare you that at least.'

'Spare me?' Garrick asked. 'What about her? Did you think of her?'

Sean did not answer, instead he shrugged and laid back tiredly in his chair.

'I never realized before what a merciless swine you are,' choked Garrick. 'I have come to kill you.'

'Yes.' Sean watched the pistol come up. Garrick was holding it with both hands, his sandy hair hung forward onto his forehead.

'My poor Garry,' Sean said softly and immediately the pistol started to shake. It sank until Garrick held it, still with both hands between his knees. He crouched over it, blubbering – chewing at his lips to stop himself. Sean started out of his chair to go to him, but Garrick recoiled against the door-jamb.

'Keep away from me,' he yelled, 'don't touch me.' He threw the pistol, the sharp edge of the hammer cut across Sean's forehead, jerking his head back. The pistol glanced off and hit the wall behind him. It fired and the bullet splintered the panelled woodwork.

'We're finished,' Garrick screamed. 'We're finished for ever.' He groped wildly for the door and stumbled out into the passage, through the kitchens into the rain. He fell many times as the grass caught his peg, but each time he scrambled up and kept running. He sobbed with each step in the utter darkness of the night.

At last the growl of the rain-engorged Baboon Stroom blocked his way. He stood on the bank with the drizzle blowing into his face.

'Why me, why always me?' He screamed his agony into the darkness. Then with a rush of relief as strong as the torrent in the river-bed below him he felt the moth flutter its wings behind his eyes. The warmth and the greyness closed about him and he sank down onto his knees in the mud.

– 32 –

Sean took very little with him: his bedroll, a rifle and a spare horse. Twice in the darkness he lost the path to Mbejane's kraal but each time his horse found it again. Mbejane had built his big grass beehive hut well away from the quarters of the other servants, for he was Zulu of royal blood. When at last Sean came to it there were a few minutes of sleepy stirring and muttering within before Mbejane, with a blanket draped around his shoulders and an old paraffin lamp in his hand, came out to Sean's shouts.

'What is it, Nkosi?'

'I am going, Mbejane.'

'Where to?'

'Wherever the roads lead. Will you follow?'

'I will get my spears,' said Mbejane.

Old man Pye was still in his office behind the bank when they reached Ladyburg. He was counting the sovereigns and stacking them in neat golden piles and his hands were as gentle on them as a man's hands on the body of the woman he loves, but he reached quickly for the open drawer at his side as Sean shouldered the door open.

'You don't need that,' said Sean and Pye lifted his hand guiltily off the pistol.

'Good gracious! I didn't recognize you, my boy.'

'How much have I got credited to my account?' Sean cut through the pleasantries.

'This isn't banking hours, you know.'

'Look here, Mr Pye, I'm in a hurry. How much have I got?'

Pye climbed out of his chair and crossed to the big iron safe. Shielding it with his body he tumbled the combination and swung open the door. He brought the ledger across to the desk.

'Carter – Cloete – Courtney,' he muttered as he turned the pages. 'Ah – Ada – Garrick – Sean. Here we are. Twelve hundred and ninety-six pounds eight and eight pence; of course, there are last month's accounts at the store still unpaid.'

'Call it twelve hundred then,' said Sean. 'I want it now and while you are counting it you can give me pen and paper.'

'Help yourself, there on the desk.'

Sean sat at the desk, pushed the piles of gold out of his way, dipped the pen and wrote. When he had finished he looked up at old Pye.

'Witness that, please.'

Pye took the paper and read it through. His face went limp with surprise.

'You're giving your half share of Theunis Kraal and all the cattle to your brother's first born!' he exploded.

'That's right, please witness it.'

'You must be mad,' protested Pye. 'That's a fortune you're giving away. Think what you're doing – think of your future. I had hoped that you and Audrey—' He stopped himself and went on. 'Don't be a fool, man.'

'Please witness it, Mr Pye,' said Sean and, muttering under his breath, Pye signed quickly.

'Thank you.' Sean folded the document, slipped it into an envelope and sealed it. He put it away inside his coat.

'Where's the money?' he asked.

Pye pushed a canvas bag across to him. His expression was one of disgust; he wanted no truck with fools.

'Count it,' he said.

'I'll take your word for it,' said Sean and signed the receipt.

Sean rode out past the sale-pens and up the escarpment along the road to Pietermaritzburg. Mbejane trotted at his stirrup leading the spare horse. They stopped at the top of the escarpment. The wind had blown the clouds open and the starlight came through. They could see the town below them with here and there a lighted window.

I should have said goodbye to Ada, Sean thought. He looked down the valley towards Theunis Kraal. He could see no light. He touched the letter in the inside pocket of his coat.

'I'll post it to Garry from Pietermaritzburg,' he spoke aloud.

'Nkosi?' asked Mbejane.

'I said, "It's a long road, let us begin."'

'Yes,' agreed Mbejane. 'Let us begin.'

– II –

Witwatersrand

– 1 –

They turned north from Pietermaritzburg and climbed steadily up across bleak grassland towards the mountains. On the third day they saw the Drakensberg, jagged and black as the teeth of an ancient shark along the skyline.

It was cold; wrapped in his kaross Mbejane trailed far behind Sean. They had exchanged perhaps two dozen words since they left Pietermaritzburg for Sean had his thoughts and they were evil company. Mbejane was keeping discreetly out of his way. Mbejane felt no resentment, for a man who had just left his home and his cattle was entitled to brood. Mbejane was with sadness himself – he had left a fat woman in his bed to follow Sean.

Mbejane unplugged his small gourd snuff-box, picked a pinch and sniffed it delicately. He looked up at the mountains. The snows upon them were turning pink in the sunset and in a little while now they would make camp, and then again perhaps they would not. It made no difference.

Sean rode on after dark. The road crossed another fold in the veld and they saw the lights in the valley below.

'Dundee,' Sean thought without interest. He made no effort to hasten his horse but let it amble down towards the town. Now he could smell the smoke from the coal mine, tarry and thick in the back of his throat. They entered the main street. The town seemed deserted in the cold. Sean did not intend stopping – he would camp on the far side;

but when he reached the hotel he hesitated. There was warmth in there and laughter and the sound of men's voices and he was suddenly aware that his fingers were stiff with cold.

'Mbejane, take my horse. Find a place to camp beyond the town and make a fire so I won't miss you in the dark.'

Sean climbed down and walked into the bar. The room was full, miners most of them – he could see the grey coal dust etched into their skins. They looked at him incuriously as he crossed to the counter and ordered a brandy. He drank it slowly, making no attempt to join the loud talk around him.

The drunk was a short man but built like Table Mountain, low, square and solid. He had to stand on tiptoe to put his arm around Sean's neck.

'Have a drink with me, *Boetie*.' His breath smelt sour and old.

'No thanks.' Sean was in no mood for drunks.

'Come on, come on,' the drunk insisted; he staggered and Sean's drink slopped onto the counter.

'Leave me alone.' Sean shrugged the arm away.

'You've got something against me?'

'No. I just feel like drinking alone.'

'You don't like my face, maybe?' The drunk held it close to Sean's. Sean didn't like it.

'Push off, there's a good fellow.'

The drunk slapped the counter.

'Charlie, give this big ape a drink. Make it a double. If he don't drink it, I ram it down his throat.'

Sean ignored the proffered glass. He swallowed what remained in his own and turned for the door. The drunk threw the brandy in his face. The spirit burned his eyes and he hit the man in the stomach. As his head came down Sean hit him again – in the face. The drunk spun sideways, fell and lay bleeding from his nose.

'What you hit him for?' Another miner was helping the drunk into a sitting position.

'It wouldn't cost you nothing to have a drink with him.' Sean felt the hostility in the room; he was the outsider.

'This boy is looking for trouble.'

'He's a tough monkey. We know how to handle tough monkeys.'

'Come on, let's sort this bastard out.'

Sean had hit the man as a reflex action. He was sorry now, but his guilt evaporated as he saw them gathering against him. Gone too was his mood of depression and in its place was a sense of relief. This was what he needed.

There were six of them moving in on him in a pack. Six was a fairly well-rounded number. One of them had a bottle in his hand and Sean started to smile. They were talking loudly, spreading courage and waiting for one of their fellows to start it.

Sean saw movement out of the side of his eye and jumped back to cover it with his hands ready.

'Steady on there,' a very English voice soothed him. 'I have come to offer my services. It seems to me you have adversaries and to spare.' The speaker had stood up from one of the tables behind Sean. He was tall, with a gauntly ravaged face and an immaculate grey suit.

'I want them all,' said Sean.

'Damned unsporting.' The newcomer shook his head. 'I'll buy the three gentlemen on the left if your price is reasonable.'

'Take two as a gift and consider yourself lucky.' Sean grinned at him and the man grinned back. They had almost forgotten the impending action in the pleasure of meeting.

'Very decent of you. May I introduce myself – Dufford Charleywood.' He shifted the light cane into his left hand and extended his right to Sean.

'Sean Courtney.' Sean accepted the hand.

'Are you bastards going to fight or what?' protested one of the miners impatiently.

'We are, dear boy, we are,' said Duff and moved lightly as a dancer towards him, swinging the cane. Thin as it was it made a noise like a well-hit baseball along the man's head.

'Then there were five,' said Duff. He flicked the cane and, weighted with lead, it made a most satisfactory swish. Like a swordsman he lunged into the throat of the second miner. The man lay on the floor and made a strangling noise.

'The rest are yours, Mr Courtney,' said Duff regretfully.

Sean dived in low, spreading his arms to scoop up all four pairs of legs at once. He sat up in the pile of bodies and started punching and kicking.

'Messy, very messy,' murmured Duff disapprovingly. The yelps and thuds gradually petered into silence and Sean stood up. His lip was bleeding and the lapel was torn off his jacket.

'Drink?' asked Duff.

'Brandy, please.' Sean smiled at the elegant figure against the bar. 'I won't refuse another drink this evening.'

They took the glasses to Duff's table, stepping over the bodies as they went.

'Mud in your eye!'

'Down the old red lane!'

Then they studied each other with frank interest, ignoring the clearing up operations being conducted around them.

'You are travelling?' asked Duff.

'Yes, are you?'

'No such luck. I am in the permanent employ of Dundee Collieries Ltd.'

'You work here?' Sean looked incredulous for Duff was a peacock among pigeons.

'Assistant Engineer,' nodded Duff. 'But not for long; the taste of coal-dust sticks in my craw.'

'May I suggest something to wash it out?'

'A splendid idea,' agreed Duff.

Sean brought the drinks to the table.

'Where are you headed?' asked Duff.

'I was facing north when I started,' shrugged Sean, 'I just kept going that way.'

'Where did you start from?'

'South.' Sean answered abruptly.

'Sorry, I didn't mean to pry.' Duff smiled. 'Yours is brandy, isn't it?'

The barman came round from behind the counter and crossed to their table.

'Hello, Charlie,' Duff greeted him. 'I take it you require compensation for the damage to your fittings and furniture?'

'Don't worry about it, Mr Charleywood. Not often we have a good barney like that. We don't mind the odd table and chair as long as it's worth watching. Have it on the house.'

'That's extremely good of you.'

'That's not what I came across for, Mr Charleywood. I've got something I'd like you to take a look at, you being a mining chap and all. Could you spare a minute, sir?'

'Come on, Sean. Let's see what Charlie's got for us. My guess is it's a beautiful woman.'

'It's not actually, sir,' said Charlie seriously and led the way through into the back room. Charlie reached up and took a lump of rock down from one of the shelves. He held it out to Duff. 'What do you make of that?'

Duff took it and weighed it in his hand, then peered closely at it. It was glassy grey, blotched with white and dark-red and divided by a broad black stripe.

'Some sort of conglomerate.' Duff spoke without enthusiasm. 'What's the mystery?'

'Friend of mine brought it down from Kruger's Republic on the other side of the mountains. He says it's gold bearing. They've made a big strike at a place called Witwatersrand just outside Pretoria. Of course, I don't put much store by these rumours 'cos you hear them all the time: diamonds and gold, gold and diamonds.'

Charlie laughed and wiped his hands on his apron.

'Anyway my friend says the Boers are selling mining licences to them as want to dig for the stuff. Thought I'd just get you to have a look.'

'I'll take this with me, Charlie, and pan it in the morning. Right now my friend and I are drinking.'

– 2 –

Sean opened his eyes the next morning to find the sun burning in through the window above his bed. He closed them again hurriedly and tried to remember where he was. There was a pain in his head that distracted him and a noise. The noise was a regular croaking rattle; it sounded as though someone was dying. Sean opened his eyes and turned his head slowly. Someone was in the bed across the room. Sean groped for a boot and threw it; there was a snort and Duff's head came up. For a second he regarded Sean through eyes as red as a winter sunset and then he subsided gently back into the blankets.

'Keep it down to a bellow,' whispered Sean. 'You are in the presence of grave illness.'

A long time later a servant brought coffee.

'Send word to my office that I am sick,' commanded Duff.

'I have done so.' The servant clearly understood his master. He went on, 'There is one outside who seeks the other Nkosi.' He glanced at Sean. 'He is greatly worried.'

'Mbejane. Tell him to wait,' said Sean.

They drank coffee in silence, sitting on the edge of their beds.

'How did I get here?' asked Sean.

'Laddie, if you don't know, then nobody does.' Duff stood up and crossed the room to find fresh clothing. He was naked and Sean saw that although he was slim as a boy his body was finely muscled.

'My God, what does Charlie put in his liquor?' complained Duff as he picked up his jacket.

He found the lump of rock in the pocket, brought it out and tossed it onto the packing-case that served as a table. He regarded it sourly as he finished dressing, then he went to the great pile of bachelor debris that filled one corner of the room. He scratched around and came out with a steel pestle-and-mortar and a battered black gold pan.

'I feel very old this morning,' he said as he started to crush the rock to powder in the mortar. He poured the powder into the pan, carried it out to the corrugated iron water tank beside the front door and filled the pan from the tap.

Sean followed him and they sat together on the front step. Duff worked the pan, using a practised dip and swing that set the contents spinning like a whirlpool and slopped a little over the front lip with each turn. He filled it again with clean water.

Suddenly Sean felt Duff stiffen beside him. He glanced at his face and saw that his hangover had gone; his lips were shut in a thin line and his bloodshot eyes were fastened on the pan.

Sean looked down and saw the gleam through the water, like the flash of a trout's belly as it turns to take the fly. He felt the excitement prickle up his arms and lift the hair on his neck.

Quickly Duff splashed fresh water into the pan; three

more turns and he flicked it out again. They sat still, not speaking, staring at the golden tail curved round the bottom of the pan.

'How much money have you got?' Duff asked without looking up.

'Little over a thousand.'

'As much as that. Excellent! I can raise about five hundred but I'll throw in my mining experience. Equal partners – do you agree?'

'Yes.'

'Then why are we sitting here? I'm going down to the bank. Meet me on the edge of town in half an hour.'

'What about your job?' Sean asked.

'I hate the smell of coal – the hell with my job.'

'What about Charlie?'

'Charlie is a poisoner – the hell with Charlie.'

– 3 –

They camped that night in the mouth of the pass with the mountains standing up before them. They had pushed the pace all that afternoon and the horses were tired – they turned their tails to the wind and cropped at the dry winter grass.

Mbejane built a fire in the shelter of a red stone outcrop and they huddled beside it brewing coffee, trying to keep out of the snow-cold wind, but it came down off the mountains and blew a plume of sparks from the fire. They ate; then Mbejane curled up beside the fire, pulled his kaross over his head and did not move again until morning.

'How far is it to this place?' Sean asked.

'I don't know,' Duff admitted. 'We'll go up through the pass tomorrow – fifty or sixty miles through the mountains

– and then we'll be out into the high veld. Perhaps another week's riding after that.'

'Are we chasing rainbows?' Sean poured more coffee into the mugs.

'I'll tell you when we get there.' Duff picked up his mug and cupped his hands around it. 'One thing's certain – that sample was stinking with gold. If there's much of that stuff around somebody's going to get rich.'

'Us, perhaps?'

'I've been on gold stampedes before. The first ones in make the killings. We might find the ground for fifty miles around as thick with claim pegs as quills on a porcupine's back.' Duff sipped noisily at his coffee. 'But we've got money – that's our ace in the hole. If we peg a proposition we've got capital to work it. If we're too late we can buy claims from the brokers. If we can't, well, there're other ways of getting gold than grubbing for it – a store, a saloon, a transport business, take your pick.'

Duff flicked the coffee grounds out of his mug. 'With money in your pocket you're somebody; without it anyone can kick you in the teeth.' He took a long black cheroot out of his top pocket and offered it to Sean. Sean shook his head and Duff bit the tip from the cheroot and spat it into the fire. He picked up a burning twig and lit it, sucking with content.

'Where did you learn mining, Duff?'

'Canada.' The wind whipped the smoke away from his mouth as Duff exhaled.

'You've been around?'

'I have, laddie. It's too damn cold to sleep; we'll talk instead. For a guinea I'll tell you the story of my life.'

'Tell me first, I'll see if it's worth it!' Sean pulled the blanket up around his shoulders and waited.

'Your credit is good,' agreed Duff. He paused dramatically.

'I was born thirty-one years ago, fourth and youngest son to the sixteenth Baron Roxby – that is, not counting the others who never made it to puberty.'

'Blue blood,' said Sean.

'Of course, just look at my nose. But please don't interrupt. Very early in the game my father, the sixteenth Baron, dispelled with a horsewhip any natural affection we may have owed him. Like Henry the Eighth he preferred children in the abstract. We kept out of his way and that suited everybody admirably. A sort of armed truce.

'Dear father had two great passions in life: horses and women. During his sixty-two glorious years he acquired a fine collection of both. My fifteen-year-old cousin, a comely wench as I recall, was his last and unattained ambition. He took her riding every day and fingered her most outrageously as he helped her in and out of the saddle. She told me about it with giggles.

'However father's horse, a commendably moral creature, cut short the pursuit by kicking father on the head, presumably in the middle of one of these touching scenes. Poor father was never the same again. In fact so much was he altered by this experience that two days later, to the doleful clangour of bells and a collective sigh of relief from his sons and his neighbours who owned daughters, they buried him.'

Dufford leaned forward and prodded the fire.

'It was all very sad. I or any of my brothers could have told father that not only was my cousin comely but she had the family sporting instincts developed to a remarkable degree. After all who should know better than we? We were her cousins and you know how cousins will be cousins. Anyway father never found out and to this day I feel guilty – I should have told him. He would have died happier . . . Do I bore you?'

'No, go on. I've had half a guinea's worth already,' Sean laughed.

'Father's untimely decease made no miraculous changes in my life. The seventeenth Baron, brother Tom, once he had the title was every bit as tight-fisted and unpleasant as father had been. There I was at nineteen on an allowance too small to enable me to pursue the family hobbies, gathering mould in a grim old castle forty miles from London, with the development of my sensitive soul being inhibited by the undiluted company of my barbaric brothers.

'I left with three months' advance allowance clutched in my sweaty palm and the farewells of my brothers ringing in my ears. The most sentimental of these was "don't bother to write".

'Everybody was going to Canada: it seemed like a good idea so I went too. I made money and spent it. I made women and spent them also, but the cold got to me in the end.'

Duff's cheroot had died; he re-lit it and looked at Sean.

'It was so cold you couldn't urinate without getting frostbite on your equipment, so I began to think of lands tropical, of white beaches and sun, of exotic fruits and even more exotic maidens. The peculiar circumstances that finally decided me to leave are painful to recall and we will not dwell upon them. I left, to say the least, under a cloud. So here you see me freezing slowly to death, with a bearded ruffian for company and not an exotic maiden within a day's ride.'

'A stirring tale – well told,' applauded Sean.

'One story deserves another – let's hear your tale of woe.'

Sean's smile slid off his face. 'Born and bred here in Natal. Left home a week or so ago, also in painful circumstances.'

'A woman?' asked Duff with deep compassion.

'A woman,' agreed Sean.

'The sweet bitches,' sighed Duff. 'How I love them.'

– 4 –

The pass ran like a twisted gut through the Drakensberg. The mountains stood up sheer and black on each side of them, so they rode in shadow and saw the sun only for a few hours in the middle of the day. Then the mountains dropped away and they were out into the open.

Open was the word for the high veld. It stretched away flat and empty, grass and brown grass dwindling to a distant meeting with the pale empty sky. But the loneliness could not blunt the edge of their excitement: each mile covered, each successive camp along the ribbon road ground it sharper until at last they saw the name in writing for the first time. Forlorn as a scarecrow in a ploughed land the signpost pointed right and said, 'Pretoria', pointed left and said, 'Witwatersrand'.

'The Ridge of White Waters,' whispered Sean. It had a ring to it that name – a ring like a hundred millions in gold.

'We're not the first,' muttered Duff. The left-hand fork of the road was deeply scored by the passage of many wagons.

'No time to worry about that.' Sean had the gold sickness on him now. 'There's a little speed left in these mokes – let's use it.'

It came up on the horizon as a low line above the emptiness, a ridge of hills like a hundred others they had crossed. They went up it and from the top looked down.

Two ridges ran side by side, north and south, four miles or so apart. In the shallow valley between they could see the flash of the sun off the swamp pools that gave the hills their name.

'Look at them,' groaned Sean.

The tents and wagons were scattered along the length of the valley and in between them the prospect trenches were raw wounds through the grass. The trenches were concentrated along a line down the centre of the valley.

'That's the strike of the reef,' said Duff, 'and we're too late – it's all pegged!'

'How do you know?' protested Sean.

'Use your eyes, laddie. It's all gone.'

'There might be some they've overlooked.'

'These boys overlook nothing. Let's go down and I'll show you.' Duff prodded his horse and they started down. He spoke over his shoulder to Sean. 'Look up there near that stream – they aren't wasting time. They've got a mill going already. It's a four-stamp rig by the looks of it.'

They rode into one of the larger encampments of tents and wagons; there were women at work around the fires and the smell of food brought saliva jetting from under Sean's tongue. There were men also, sitting among the wagons waiting for their suppers.

'I'm going to ask some of these characters what's going on here,' said Sean. He climbed down off his horse and tossed the reins to Mbejane. Duff watched him with a wry grin as he tried in succession to engage three different men in conversation. Each time Sean's victim avoided his eyes, mumbled vaguely and withdrew. Sean finally gave up and came back to the horses.

'What's wrong with me?' he asked plaintively. 'Have I got a contagious clap?'

Duff chuckled. 'They've got gold sickness,' he said.

'You're a potential rival. You could die of thirst and not one of them would spit on you, lest it gave you strength to crawl out and peg something they hadn't noticed.'

He sobered. 'We're wasting time. There's an hour left before dark, let's go and have a look for ourselves.'

They trotted out towards the area of mauled earth. Men were working pick and shovel in the trenches, some of them lean and tough-looking with a dozen natives working beside them; others fat from an office stool, sweating and gritting teeth against the pain of blistered palms, their faces and arms burnt angry red by the sun. All of them greeted Sean and Duff with the same suspicious hostility.

They rode slowly towards the north and every hundred yards with sickening regularity they came across a claim peg with a cairn of stones around its foot and the scrap of canvas nailed to it. Printed in crude capitals on the canvas was the owner's name and his licence number.

Many of the claims were as yet untouched and on these Duff dismounted and searched in the grass, picking up pieces of rock and peering at them before discarding them again. Then once more they moved on with sinking spirits and increasing exhaustion. They camped after dark on the open windy ridge and while the coffee brewed they talked.

'We're too late.' Sean scowled into the fire.

'We've got money, laddie, just remember that. Most of these gentlemen are broke – they are living on hope, not beef and potatoes. Look at their faces and you'll see despair starting to show. It takes capital to work reef gold: you need machinery and money for wages, you have to pipe in water and pile rock, you need wagons and time.'

'Money's no good without a claim to work,' brooded Sean.

'Stay with me, laddie. Have you noticed how many of these claims haven't been touched yet? They belong to speculators and my guess is that they are for sale. In the next few weeks you'll see the men sorted out from the boys—'

'I feel like packing up. This isn't what I expected.'

'You're tired. Sleep well tonight and tomorrow we'll see how far this reef runs – then we'll start some scheming.'

Duff lit one of his cheroots and sucked on it: in the firelight his face was as gaunt as a Red Indian's. They sat on in silence for a while, then Sean spoke.

'What's that noise?' It was a dull tom-tom beat in the darkness.

'You'll get used to that if you stay around here much longer,' said Duff. 'It's the stamps on that mill we saw from the high ground. It's a mile or so farther up the valley; we'll pass it in the morning.'

They were on the move again before the sun was up and they came to the mill in the morning's uncertain light. The mill crouched black and ugly on the smooth curve of the ridge, defiant as a quixotic monster. Its jaws thumped sullenly as it chewed the rock; it snorted steam and screeched metallically.

'I didn't realize it was so big,' said Sean.

'It's big all right,' agreed Duff, 'and they cost money, they don't give them away. Not many men around here can afford a set-up like that.'

There were men moving around the mill, tending its needs, feeding it rock and fussing about the copper tables over which its gold-laden faeces poured. One of the men came forward to offer them the usual hospitality. 'This is private ground. We don't want sightseers around here – keep on going.'

He was a dapper little man with a round brown face and a derby hat pulled down to his ears. His moustache bristled like the whiskers of a fox terrier.

'Listen, Francois, you miserable bloody earthworm, if you talk to me like that I'll push your face around the back of your head,' Duff told him, and the dapper one blinked uncertainly and came closer, peering up at them.

'Who are you? Do I know you?'

Duff pushed his hat back so the man could see his face.

'Duff!' crowed the little man delightedly. 'It's old Duff.' He bounced forward to take Duff's hand as he dismounted. Sean watched the orgy of reunion with amusement. It lasted until Duff managed to bring it under control and lead the little Afrikander across to make the introduction.

'Sean, this is Francois du Toit. He's an old friend of mine from the Kimberley diamond fields.'

Francois greeted Sean and then relapsed once more into the excited chorus of '*Gott*, it's good to see you, old Duff.' He pounded Duff's back despite the nimble footwork that Duff was using to spoil his aim. Another few minutes of this passed before Francois composed himself to make his first coherent statement.

'Listen, old Duff, I'm just in the middle of cleaning the amalgam tables. You and your friend go down to my tent. I'll be with you in half an hour, tell my servant to make you some breakfast. I won't be long, man. *Gott*, man, it's good to see you.'

'An old lover of yours?' asked Sean when they were alone.

Duff laughed. 'We were on the diamond fields together. I did him a favour once – pulled him out of a caving drive when the rock fall had broken his legs. He's a good little guy and meeting him here is the proverbial answer to a prayer. What he can't tell us about this goldfield no one else can.'

Francois came bustling into the tent well under the promised half hour and during breakfast Sean was an outsider in a conversation where every exchange began, 'Do you remember – ?' or 'What happened to old so and so?'

Then, when the plates were empty and the coffee mugs

filled, Duff asked, 'So, what are you doing here, Franz? Is this your own outfit?'

'No, I'm still with the Company.'

'Not that whoreson Hradsky?' Duff registered mock alarm. 'Tha – tha that's ta – ta – terrible,' he imitated a stutter.

'Cut it out, Duff.' Francois looked nervous. 'Don't do that, you want me to lose my job?'

Duff turned to Sean with an explanation. 'Norman Hradsky and God are equals, but in this part of the world God takes his orders from Hradsky.'

'Cut it out, Duff.' Francois was deeply shocked but Duff went on imperturbably.

'The organization through which Hradsky exercises his divine powers is referred to with reverently bated breath as "The Company". In actual fact its full and resounding title is The South African Mining and Lands Company. Do you get the picture?'

Sean nodded smiling and Duff added as an afterthought, 'Hradsky is a bastard and he stutters.'

It was too much for Francois. He leaned across and caught Duff's arm. 'Please, man. My servant understands English, cut it out, Duff.'

'So the Company has started on these fields, hey? Well, well, it must be pretty big,' mused Duff and Francois followed with relief onto safer ground.

'It is! You just wait and see, it's going to make the diamond fields look like a church bazaar!'

'Tell me about it,' said Duff.

'They call it the Rotten Reef or the Banket or the Heidelberg Reef – but in fact there are three reefs, not one. They run side by side like layers in a sandwich cake.'

'All three have pay gold?' Duff shot the question and Francois shook his head. There was a light in his eyes; he was happy talking gold and mining.

'No – you can forget about the outer reef, just traces there. Then there's the Main Reef. That's a bit better, it's as much as six feet thick in places and giving good values, but it's patchy.'

Francois leaned eagerly across the table; in his excitement his thick Afrikaans accent was very noticeable.

'The bottom reef is the winner, we call it the Leader Reef. It's only a few inches thick and some places it fades out altogether, but it's rich. There's gold in it like plums in a pudding. It's rich, Duff, I'm telling you that you won't believe it until you see it!'

'I'll believe you,' said Duff. 'Now tell me where I can get some of this Leader Reef for myself.'

Francois sobered instantly, a shutter dropped over his eyes and hid the light that had shone there a moment before.

'It's gone. It's all gone,' he said defensively. 'It's all been pegged, you've come too late.'

'Well, that's that,' said Duff and a big silence settled on the gathering. Francois fidgeted on his stool, chewing at the ends of his moustache and scowling into his mug. Duff and Sean waited quietly; it was obvious that Francois was wrestling with himself, two loyalties tearing him down the middle. Once he opened his mouth and then closed it again; he blew on his coffee to cool it and the heat came off it in steam.

'Have you got any money?' He fired the question with startling violence.

'Yes,' said Duff.

'Mr Hradsky has gone down to Capetown to raise money. He has a list of a hundred and forty claims that he will buy when he gets back.' Francois paused guiltily. 'I'm only telling you this because of what I owe you.'

'Yes, I know.' Duff spoke softly. Francois took an audible breath and went on.

‘On the top of Mr Hradsky’s list is a block of claims that belongs to a woman. She is willing to sell and they are the most likely-looking propositions on the whole field.’

‘Yes?’ Duff encouraged him.

‘This woman has started an eating-house about two miles from here on the banks of the Natal Spruit. Her name is Mrs Rautenbach, she serves good food. You could go and have a meal there.’

‘Thanks, Francois.’

‘I owed it to you,’ Francois said gruffly, then his mood changed quickly and he chuckled. ‘You’ll like her, Duff, she’s a lot of woman.’

Sean and Duff went to eat lunch at Mrs Rautenbach’s. It was an unpainted corrugated-iron building on a wooden frame and the sign above the veranda said in letters of red and gold ‘Candy’s Hotel. High-class cuisine. Free toilet facilities. No drunks or horses admitted. Proprietor Mrs Candella Rautenbach.’

They washed off the dust in the enamel basin which stood on the veranda, dried themselves on the free towel and combed in the free mirror on the wall.

‘How do I look?’ asked Duff.

‘Ravishing,’ said Sean, ‘but you don’t smell so good. When did you last bath?’

They went into the dining-room and found it almost full, but there was an empty table against the far wall. The room was hot and thick with pipe smoke and the smell of cabbage. Dusty, bearded men laughed and shouted or ate silently and hungrily. They crossed the room to the table and a coloured waitress came to them.

‘Yes?’ she asked. Her dress was damp at the armpits.

‘May we have the menu?’

The girl looked at Duff with faint amusement. ‘Today we got steak and mashed potatoes with pudding afterwards.’

‘We’ll have it,’ Duff agreed.

'You sure as hell won't get nothing else,' the girl assured him and trotted back to the kitchen.

'The service is good,' Duff enthused. 'We can only hope that the food and the proprietress are of the same high standard.'

The meat was tough but well flavoured and the coffee was strong and sweet. They ate with appreciation until Sean, who was facing the kitchen, stopped his fork on its way to his mouth. A hush was on the room.

'Here she is,' he said.

Candy Rautenbach was a tall and bright, shiny blonde and her skin was Nordic flawlessness as yet unspoiled by the sun. She filled the front of her blouse and the back of her skirt with a pleasant abundance. She was well aware of and yet not disconcerted by the fact that every eye in the room was on one of those areas. She carried a ladle which she twitched threateningly at the first hand that reached out to pinch her rump, the hand withdrew and Candy smiled sweetly and moved on among the tables. She stopped occasionally to chat with her customers and it was clear that many of these lonely men came here not only to eat. They watched her avidly, grinning with pleasure when she spoke to them. She reached their table and Sean and Duff stood up. Candy blinked with surprise.

'Sit down, please.' The small courtesy had touched her. 'You are new here?'

'We got in yesterday,' Duff smiled at her. 'And the way you cook a steak makes me feel as though I were home again.'

'Where are you from?' Candy looked at the two of them with perhaps just a shade more than professional interest.

'We've come up from Natal to have a look around. This is Mr Courtney – he is interested in new investments and he thought that these goldfields might provide an outlet for some of his capital.'

Sean just managed to stop his jaw dropping open and then quickly assumed the slightly superior air of a big financier as Duff went on.

'My name is Charleywood. I am Mr Courtney's mining adviser.'

'Pleased to meet you. I am Candy Rautenbach.' She was impressed.

'Won't you join us for a few minutes, Mrs Rautenbach?' Duff drew back a chair for her and Candy hesitated.

'I have to check up in the kitchen – perhaps later.'

'Do you always lie so smoothly?' Sean spoke with admiration when Candy had gone.

'I spoke no untruths,' Duff defended himself.

'No, but the way you tell the truth! How the hell am I going to play up to the role you have created for me?'

'You'll learn to live with it, don't worry. Just look wise and keep your mouth shut,' Duff advised. 'What do you think of her anyway?'

'Toothsome,' said Sean.

'Decidedly palatable,' agreed Duff.

When Candy came back Duff kept the conversation light and general for a while, but when Candy started asking some sharp questions it was immediately apparent that her knowledge of geology and mining was well above average and Duff remarked on it.

'Yes, my husband was in the game. I picked it up from him.' She reached into one of the pockets of her blue and white checked skirt and brought out a small handful of rock samples. She put them down in front of Duff. 'Can you name those?' she asked. It was the direct test, she was asking him to prove himself.

'Kimberlite. Serpentine. Feldspar.' Duff reeled them off and Candy relaxed visibly.

'As it happens I have a number of claims pegged along the Heidelberg Reef. Perhaps Mr Courtney would care to have a look at them. Actually, I am negotiating at the moment with The South African Mining and Lands Company who are very interested.'

Sean made his solitary but valuable contribution to the conversation. 'Ah yes,' he nodded sagely. 'Good old Norman.'

Candy was shaken – not many men used Hradsky's Christian name. 'Will tomorrow morning be convenient?' she asked.

– 5 –

That afternoon they bought a tent from a disillusioned hopeful who had thrown up his job on the Natal Railways to make the pilgrimage to Witwatersrand and now needed money to get home. They pitched it near the Hotel and went down to the Natal Spruit to take a long overdue bath. That night they held a mild celebration on the half bottle of brandy that Duff produced from his saddlebag and the next morning Candy took them out to the claims. She had twenty of them pegged right along the Banket. She led them to a spot where the reef outcropped.

'I'll leave you two to look around. If you're interested we can talk about it when you come to the Hotel. I've got to get back now, there'll be hungry mouths to feed.'

Duff escorted Candy to her horse, giving her his arm across the rough ground and helping her into the saddle in a manner he must have learned from his father. He watched her ride away then came back to Sean. He was elated.

'Tread lightly, Mr Courtney, walk with reverence for beneath your feet lies our fortune.'

They went over the ground, Sean like a friendly bloodhound and Duff cruising with the restless circling of a tiger shark. They inspected the claim notices, paced out the boundaries and filled their pockets with chips of rock, then they rode back to their tent and Duff brought out his pestle, mortar and pan. They took them down to the bank of the Natal Spruit and all afternoon crushed the rock and worked the pan. When they had tested the last sample Duff gave his judgement.

'Well, there's gold – and I'd say it's payable gold. It's not nearly as rich as the one we panned at Dundee but that must have been a selected piece of the Leader Reef!' He paused and looked seriously at Sean. 'I think it's worth a try. If the Leader Reef is there we'll find it and in the meantime we won't lose money by working the main reef.'

Sean picked up a pebble and tossed it into the stream in front of him. He was learning for the first time the alternate thrill and depression of gold sickness when one minute you rode the lightning and the next you dropped abruptly into the depths. The yellow tails in the pan had looked pathetically thin and undernourished to him.

'Supposing you're right and supposing we talk Candy into selling her claims, how do we go about it? That four-stamp mill looked a devilishly complicated and expensive bit of machinery to me, not the kind of thing you can buy over the counter in every general dealer's store.'

Duff punched his shoulder and smiled lopsidedly at him. 'You've got your Uncle Duff looking after you. Candy will sell her claims – she trembles when I touch her, a day or two more and she'll be eating out of my hand. As for the mill . . . When I came out to this country I fell in with a rich Cape farmer whose lifelong ambition had been to have his own gold mine. He selected a ridge which in his undisputed wisdom as a grower of grapes he considered to be an ideal place for his mine. He hired me to run it for him, purchased a mill of the latest and most expensive vintage and prepared himself to flood the market with gold.

After six months when we had processed vast quantities of assorted quartz, schist and earth and recovered sufficient gold to fit into a mouse's ear without touching the sides, my patron's enthusiasm was somewhat dampened and he dispensed with my invaluable services and closed the circus down. I left for the diamond fields and as far as I know the machinery is still lying there waiting for the first buyer with a couple of hundred pounds to come and pick it up.' Duff stood up and they walked back towards the tent. 'However, first things first. Do you agree that I should continue the negotiations with Mrs Rautenbach?'

'I suppose so.' Sean was feeling more cheerful again. 'But are you sure your interest in Mrs Rautenbach is strictly line of duty?'

Duff was shocked. 'Don't think for a minute that my intentions are anything but to further the interests of our partnership. You can't believe that my animal appetite plays any part in what I intend doing?'

'No, of course not,' Sean assured him. 'I hope you can force yourself to go through with it.'

Duff laughed. 'While we are on the subject I think this is as good a time as any for you to develop a stomach ailment and retire to your lonely bed. From now on until we've got the agreement signed your boyish charm will be of no great value in the proceedings. I'll tell Candy that you've given me authority to act on your behalf.'

Duff combed his curls, put on the clothes that Mbejane had washed for him and disappeared in the direction of Candy's Hotel. Time passed slowly for Sean; he sat and chatted with Mbejane, drank a little coffee and when the sun went down retired to his tent. He read one of Duff's books by the light of the hurricane lamp but could not concentrate on it; his mind kept straying to thoughts of blonde hair. When someone scratched on the canvas door he leapt up with a confused hope that Candy had decided to come and deal with him direct. It was the coloured girl from the Hotel, her crinkly black hair at odds with what he had been thinking.

'Madame says she's sorry to hear about your sickness and to tell you to have two spoons of this,' she told him and offered Sean the bottle of castor oil.

'Tell your mistress, thank you very much.'

Sean accepted the medicine and started to close the tent flap again.

'Madame told me to stay and make sure that you took two full spoons – I have to take the bottle back and show her how much you've had.'

Sean's stomach cringed. He looked at the coloured girl standing resolute in the doorway, determined to carry out her instructions. He thought of poor Duff doing his duty like a man – he could do no less. He swallowed down the thick clinging oil with his eyes closed then went back to his book. He slept uneasily, starting up occasionally to look at the empty bed across the tent. The medicine drove him out into the cold at half past two in the morning. Mbejane was curled up next to the fire and Sean scowled at him. His regular contented snoring seemed a calculated mockery. A jackal yelped miserably up on the ridge, expressing Sean's feelings exactly, and the night wind fanned his bare buttocks.

Duff came home in the dawning. Sean was wide awake.

'Well, what happened?' he demanded.

Duff yawned. 'At one stage I began to doubt whether I was man enough. However, it worked out to the satisfaction of all concerned. What a woman!' He pulled off his shirt and Sean saw the scratches across his back.

'Did she give you any castor oil?' Sean asked bitterly.

'I'm sorry about that.' Duff smiled at him sympathetically. 'I tried to dissuade her – truly I did. She's a very motherly person. Most concerned about your stomach.'

'You still haven't answered my question. Did you make any progress with the claims?'

'Oh that—' Duff pulled the blankets up under his chin. 'We disposed of that early on in the proceedings. She'll take a down payment of ten pounds each on them and give us an option to buy the lot at any time during the next two years for ten thousand. We arranged that over dinner. The rest of the time was devoted, in a manner of speaking, to shaking hands over the deal. Tomorrow afternoon – or rather this afternoon – you and I'll ride across to Pretoria and get a lawyer to write up an agreement for her to sign. But right now I need some sleep. Wake me at lunch time. Goodnight, laddie.'

Duff and Sean brought the agreement back from Pretoria the following evening. It was an impressive four-page document full of 'in so much as' and 'party of the first part'. Candy led them to her bedroom and they sat around anxiously while she read it through twice.

She looked up at last and said, 'That seems all right – but there is just one other thing.' Sean's heart sank and even Duff's smile was strained. It had all been too easy so far.

Candy hesitated and Sean saw with faint surprise that she was blushing. It was a pleasant thing to see the peach of her cheeks turning to ripe apple and they watched it with interest, their tension lessening perceptibly. 'I want the mine named after me.'

They nearly shouted with relief.

'An excellent idea! How about the Rautenbach Reef Mine?'

Candy shook her head. 'I'd rather not be reminded of him – we'll leave him out of it.'

'Very well – let's call it the Candy Deep. A little premature, I suppose, as we are still at ground level, but pessimism never pays,' suggested Duff.

'Yes, that's lovely,' Candy enthused, flushing again but this time with pleasure. She scrawled her name across the bottom of the document while Sean fired out the cork of the champagne which Duff had bought in Pretoria. They clinked glasses and Duff gave the toast 'To Candy and the Candy Deep – may one grow sweeter and the other deeper with each passing day.'

– 6 –

'We'll need labour, about ten natives to start with. That'll be your problem,' Duff told Sean. It was the following morning and they were eating breakfast in front of the tent. Sean nodded but didn't try to answer until he had swallowed his mouthful of bacon.

'I'll get Mbejane onto that right away. He'll be able to get us Zulus, even if he has to drive them here with a spear at their backs.'

'Good – in the meantime you and I'll ride back to Pretoria again to buy the basic equipment. Picks, shovels, dynamite and the like.' Duff wiped his mouth and filled his coffee cup. 'I'll show you how to start moving the overburden and stacking the ore in a dump. We'll pick a site for the mill and then I'll leave you to get on with it while I head south for the Cape to see my farmer friend. God and the weather permitting ours will be the second mill working on these fields.'

They brought their purchases back from Pretoria in a small ox wagon. Mbejane had done his work well. There were a dozen Zulus lined up for Sean's approval next to the tent with Mbejane standing guard over them like a cheerful sheepdog. Sean walked down the line, stopping to ask each man his name and joke with him in his own language. He came to the last in the line. 'How are you called?'

'My name is Hlubi, Nkosi.'

Sean pointed at the man's well-rounded paunch bulging out above his loincloth.

'If you come to work for me, we'll soon have you delivered of your child.'

They burst out in delighted laughter and Sean smiled at them affectionately: proud simple people, tall and big-muscled, completely defenceless against a well-timed jest. Through his mind flashed the picture of a hill in Zululand, a battlefield below it and the flies crawling in the pit of an empty stomach. He shut the picture out quickly and shouted above their laughter.

'So be it then – sixpence a day and all the food you can eat. Will you sign on to work for me?'

They chorused their assent and climbed up onto the back of the wagon. Sean and Duff took them out to the Candy Deep and they laughed and chattered like children going on a picnic.

It took another week for Duff to instruct Sean in the use of dynamite, to explain how he wanted the first trenches dug and to mark out the site for the mill and the dump. They moved the tent up to the mine and worked twelve hours every day. At night they rode down to Candy's Hotel to eat a full meal and then Sean rode home alone. He was so tired by evening that he hardly envied Duff the comfort of Candy's bedroom; instead he found himself admiring Duff's stamina. Each morning he looked for signs of fatigue in his partner but, although his face was lean and gaunt as ever, his eyes were just as clear and his lopsided smile just as cheerful.

'How you do it beats me,' Sean told him the day they finished marking out the mill site.

Duff winked at him. 'Years of practice, laddie, but between you and me the ride down to the Cape will be a welcome rest.'

'When are you going?' Sean asked.

'Quite frankly I think that every day I stay on here increases the risk of someone else getting in before us. Mining machinery is going to be at a premium from now on. You have got things well in hand now . . . What do you say?'

'I was starting to think along the same lines,' Sean agreed. They walked back to the tent and sat down in the camp chairs, from where they could look down the length of the valley. The week before about two dozen wagons had been outspanned around Candy's Hotel, but now there were at least two hundred and from where they sat they could count another eight or nine encampments, some even larger than the one around Candy's place. Wood and iron buildings were beginning to replace the canvas tents and the whole veld was criss-crossed with rough roads along which mounted men and wagons moved without apparent purpose.

The restless movement, the dust clouds raised by the passage of men and beasts, and the occasional deep crump, crump of dynamite firing in the workings along the Banket – all heightened the air of excitement, of almost breathless expectancy that hung over the whole goldfield.

'I'll leave at first light tomorrow,' Duff decided. 'Ten days' riding to the railhead at Colesberg and another four days by train will get me there. With luck I'll be back in under two months.' He wriggled round in his chair and looked directly at Sean. 'After paying Candy her two hundred pounds and with what I spent in Pretoria I've only got about a hundred and fifty left. Once I get to Paarl I'll have to pay out three or four hundred for the mill, then I'll need to hire twenty or thirty wagons to bring it up here – say eight hundred pounds altogether to be on the safe side.'

Sean looked at him. He had known this man a few short weeks. Eight hundred was the average man's earnings for three years. Africa was a big land, a man could disappear easily. Sean loosened his belt and dropped it onto the table; he unbuttoned the money pouch.

'Give me a hand to count it out,' he told Duff.

'Thanks,' said Duff and he was not talking about the money. With trust asked for so simply and given so spontaneously the last reservations in their friendship shrivelled and died.

– 7 –

When Duff had gone Sean drove himself and his men without mercy. They stripped the overburden off the Reef and exposed it across the whole length of the Candy claims, then they broke it up and started stacking it next to the mill site. The dump grew bigger with every twelve-hour day worked. There was still no trace of the Leader Reef but Sean found little time to worry about that. At night he climbed into bed and slept away his fatigue until another morning called him back to the workings. On Sundays he rode across to Francois's tent and they talked mining and medicines. Francois had an enormous chest of patent medicines and a book titled *The Home Physician*. His health was his hobby and he was treating himself for three major ailments simultaneously. Although he was occasionally unfaithful, his true love was sugar diabetes. The page in *The Home Physician* which covered this subject was limp and grubby from the touch of his fingers. He could recite the symptoms from memory and he had all of them. His other favourite was tuberculosis of the bone; this moved around his body with alarming rapidity taking only a week to leave his hip and reach his wrist. Despite his failing health, however, he was an expert on mining and Sean picked his brain shamelessly. Francois's sugar diabetes did not prevent him from sharing a bottle of brandy with Sean on Sunday evenings. Sean kept away from Candy's Hotel – that shiny blonde hair and peach skin would have been too much temptation. He couldn't trust himself not to wreck his new friendship with Duff by another importunate affair, so instead he sweated away his energy in the trenches of the Candy Deep.

Every morning he set his Zulus a task for the day, always just a little more than the day before. They sang as they worked and it was very seldom that the task was not complete by nightfall. The days blurred into each other and turned to weeks which quadrupled like breeding amoebae and became months. Sean began to imagine Duff giving the Capetown girls a whirl with his eight hundred pounds. One evening he rode south for miles along the Cape road, stopping to question every traveller he met and when he finally gave up and returned to the goldfields he went straight to one of the canteens to look for a fight. He found a big, yellow-haired German miner to oblige him. They went outside and for an hour they battered each other beneath a crisp Transvaal night sky surrounded by a ring of delighted spectators. Then he and the German went back into the canteen, shook each other's bleeding hands, drank a vow of friendship together and Sean returned to the Candy Deep with his devil exorcized for the time being.

The next afternoon Sean was working near the north boundary of the claims; at this point they had burrowed down about fifteen feet to keep contact with the reef. Sean had just finished marking the shot holes for the next blast and the Zulus were standing around him taking snuff and spitting on their hands before attacking the rock once more.

'Mush, you shag-eared villains. What's going on here, a trade union meeting?' The familiar voice came from above their heads. Duff was looking down at them. Sean scrambled straight up the side of the trench and seized him in a bear hug. Duff was thinner, his jowls covered with a pale stubble and his curly hair white with dust. When the fury of greeting had subsided a little Sean demanded, 'Well, where's the present you went to fetch me?'

Duff laughed. 'Not far behind, all twenty-five wagons full of it.'

'You got it then?' Sean roared.

'You're damn right I did! Come with me and I'll show you.'

Duff's convoy was strung out four miles across the veld, most of the wagons double-teamed against the enormous weight of the machinery. Duff pointed to a rust-streaked cylinder that completely filled one of the leading wagons.

'That is my particular cross, seven tons of the most spiteful, stubborn and evil boiler in the world. If it's broken the wagon axle once it's broken it a dozen times since we left Colesberg, not to mention the two occasions on which it capsized itself – once right in the middle of a river.'

They rode along the line of wagons.

'Good God! I didn't realize there'd be so much.' Sean shook his head dubiously. 'Are you sure you know how it all fits together?'

'Leave it to your Uncle Duff. Of course, it's going to need a bit of work done on it, after all it's been lying out in the open for a couple of years. Some of it was rusted up solid, but the judicious use of grease, new paint and the Charleywood brain will see the Candy Deep plant breaking rock and spitting out gold within a month.' Duff broke off and waved to a horseman coming towards them. 'This is the transport contractor. Frikkie Malan – Mr Courtney, my partner.'

The contractor pulled up next to them and acknowledged the introduction. He wiped the dust off his face with the sleeve of his shirt.

'*Gott*, man, Mr Charleywood, I don't mind telling you

that this is the hardest money I've ever worked for. Nothing personal – but I'll be *vragtig* glad to see the last of this load.'

– 8 –

Duff was wrong; it took much longer than a month. The rust had eaten deep into parts of the machinery and each bolt they twisted open was red with the scaly cancer. They worked the usual twelve-hour day chipping and scraping, filing and greasing, knuckles knocked raw against steel and palms wet and red where the blisters had burst. Then one day suddenly and miraculously they were finished. Along the ridge of the Candy Deep, neat and sweet smelling in its new paint, thick with yellow grease and waiting only to be fitted together, lay the dismembered mill.

'How long has it taken us so far?' Duff asked.

'It seems like a hundred years.'

'Is that all?' Duff feigned surprise. 'Then I declare a holiday – two days of meditation.'

'You meditate, brother – I'm going to do some carousing.'

'That's an excellent alternative – let's go!'

They started at Candy's place but she threw them out after the third fight so they moved on. There were a dozen places to drink at and they tried them all. Others were celebrating, because the day before old Kruger, the President of the Republic, had given official recognition to the goldfields. This had the sole effect of diverting the payments for mining licences from the pockets of the farmers who owned the land into the Government coffers. No one worried about that, except possibly the farmers. Rather it was an excuse for a party. The canteens were packed with swearing, sweating men. Duff and Sean drank with them.

The Crown and Anchor boards were doing a steady business in every bar and the men who crowded around them were the new population of the goldfields. Diggers bare to the waist and caked with dirt, salesmen with loud clothes and louder voices selling everything from dynamite to dysentery cure, an evangelist peddling salvation, gamblers mining pockets, gentlemen trying to keep the tobacco juice off their boots, boys new-flown from home and wishing themselves back, Boers bearded and drab-suited, drinking little but watching with inscrutable eyes the invaders of their land. Then there were the others, the clerks and farmers, the rogues and contractors listening greedily to the talk of gold.

The coloured girl, Martha, came to find Sean and Duff on the afternoon of the second day. They were in a mud-brick and thatch hut called The Tavern of the Bright Angels. Duff was doing a solo exhibition of the Dashing White Sergeant partnered by a chair; Sean and the fifty or so other customers were beating the rhythm on the bar counter with glasses and empty bottles.

Martha skittered across to Sean, slapping at the hands that tried to dive up her skirts and squealing sharply every time her bottom was pinched. She arrived at Sean's side flushed and breathless.

'Madame says you must come quickly – there's big trouble,' she gasped and started to run the gauntlet back to the door. Someone flipped up her dress behind and a concerted masculine roar approved the fact that she wore nothing under the petticoats.

Duff was so engrossed in his dancing that Sean had to carry him bodily out of the bar and dip his head in the horse trough outside before he could gain his attention.

'What the hell did you do that for?' spluttered Duff and swung a round-arm punch at Sean's head. Sean ducked under it and caught him about the body to save him falling on his back.

'Candy wants us – she says there's big trouble.'

Duff thought about that for a few seconds, frowning with concentration, then he threw back his head and sang to the tune of 'London's Burning',

> 'Candy wants us – Candy wants us
> We don't want Candy, we want brandy.'

He broke out of Sean's grip and headed back for the bar. Sean caught him again and pointed him in the direction of the Hotel. Candy was in her bedroom. She looked at the two of them as they swayed arm-in-arm in the doorway.

'Did you enjoy your debauch?' she asked sweetly. Duff mumbled and tried to straighten his coat. Sean tried to steady him as his feet danced an involuntary sideways jig.

'What happened to your eye?' she asked Sean and he fingered it tenderly; it was puffed and blue. Candy didn't wait for an answer but went on, still sweetly:

'Well, if you two beauties want to own a mine by tomorrow you'd better sober up.'

They stared at her and Sean spoke deliberately but nevertheless indistinctly.

'Why, what's the matter?'

'They're going to jump the claims, that's the matter. This new proclamation of a State goldfield has given the drifters the excuse they've been waiting for. About a hundred of them have formed a syndicate. They claim that the old titles aren't legal any more; they are going to pull out the pegs and put in their own.'

Duff walked without a stagger across to the washbasin beside Candy's bed; he splashed his face, towelled it vigorously then stooped and kissed her. 'Thanks, my sweet.'

'Duff, please be careful,' Candy called after them.

'Let's see if we can't hire a few mercenaries,' Sean suggested.

'Good idea, we'll try and find a few sober characters – there should be some in Candy's dining-room.'

They made a short detour on their way back to the mine and stopped at Francois's tent; it was dark by then and Francois came out in a freshly ironed nightshirt. He raised an eyebrow when he saw the five heavily armed men with Sean and Duff.

'You going hunting?' he asked.

Duff told him quickly and Francois was hopping with agitation before he had finished.

'Steal my claims, the thunders, the stinking thunders!' He rushed into his tent and came out again with a double-barrelled shotgun.

'We'll see, man, we'll see how they look full of buckshot.'

'Francois, listen to me,' Sean shouted him down. 'We don't know which claims they'll go to first. Get your men ready and if you hear shooting our way come and give us a hand – we'll do the same for you.'

'*Ja, ja*, we'll come all right – the dirty thunders.' His nightshirt flapping around his legs Francois trotted off to call his men.

Mbejane and the other Zulus were cooking dinner, squatting round the three-legged pot. Sean rode up to them.

'Get your spears,' he told them. They ran for their huts and almost immediately came crowding back.

'Nkosi, where's the fight?' they pleaded, food forgotten.

'Come on, I'll show you.'

They placed the hired gunmen amongst the mill machinery from where they could cover the track which led up to the mine. The Zulus they hid in one of the prospect trenches. If it developed into a hand-to-hand fight the syndicate was in for a surprise. Duff and Sean walked a little way down the slope to make sure their defenders were all concealed.

'How much dynamite have we got?' Sean asked thoughtfully. Duff stared at him a second, then he grinned.

'Sufficient, I'd say. You're full of bright ideas this evening.' He led the way back to the shed which they used as a storeroom.

In the middle of the track a few hundred yards down the slope they buried a full case of explosive and placed an old tin can on top of it to mark the spot. They went back to the shed and spent an hour making grenades out of bundles of dynamite sticks, each with a detonator and a very short fuse. Then they settled down huddled into their sheepskin coats, rifles in their laps and waited.

They could see the lights of the encampments straggled down the valley and hear an occasional faint burst of singing from the canteens, but the moonlit road up to the mine remained deserted. Sean and Duff sat side by side with their backs against the newly painted boiler.

'How did Candy find out about this, I wonder?' Sean asked.

'She knows everything. That hotel of hers is the centre of this goldfield and she keeps her ears open.'

They relapsed into silence again while Sean formed his next question.

'She's quite a girl – our Candy.'

'Yes,' agreed Duff.

'Are you going to marry her, Duff?'

'Good God!' Duff straightened up as though someone had stuck a knife into him. 'You going mad, laddie, or else that was a joke in the worst possible taste.'

'She dotes on you and from what I've seen you're fairly well disposed towards her.' Sean was relieved at Duff's quick rejection of the idea. He was jealous, but not of the woman.

'Yes, we've got a common interest, that I won't deny –

but marriage!' Duff shivered slightly, not altogether from the cold. 'Only a fool makes the same mistake twice.'

Sean turned to him with surprise. 'You've been married before?' he asked.

'With a vengeance. She was half Spanish and the rest Norwegian, a smoking bubbly mixture of cold fire and hot ice.' Duff's voice went dreamy. 'The memory has cooled sufficiently for me to think of it with a tinge of regret.'

'What happened?'

'I left her.'

'Why?'

'We only did two things well together and one of them was fight. If I close my eyes I can still see the way she used to pout with those lovely lips and bring them close to my ear before she hissed out a particularly foul word, then – hey ho! back to bed for the reconciliation.'

'Perhaps you made the wrong choice. You look around, you'll see millions of happily married people.'

'Name me one,' challenged Duff and the silence lengthened as Sean thought.

Then Duff went on, 'There's only one good reason for marriage, and that's children.'

'And companionship – that's another good reason.'

'Companionship from a woman?' Duff cut in incredulously. 'Like perfume from garlic. They're incapable of it. I suppose it's the training they get from their mothers, who are after all women themselves, but how can you be friends with someone who suspicions every little move you make, who takes your every action and weighs it on the balance of he loves me, he loves me not?' Duff shook his head unhappily. 'How long can a friendship last when it needs an hourly declaration of love to nourish it? The catechism of matrimony, "Do you love me, darling?" "Yes, darling, of course I do, my sweet." It's got to sound convincing every time otherwise tears.'

Sean chuckled.

'All right, it's funny – it's hilarious until you have to live with it,' Duff mourned. 'Have you ever tried to talk to a woman about anything other than love? The same things that interest you leave them cold. It comes as a shock the first time you try talking sense to them and suddenly you realize that their attention is not with you – they get a slightly fixed look in their eyes and you know they are thinking about that new dress or whether to invite Mrs Van der Hum to the party, so you stop talking and that's another mistake. That's a sign; marriage is full of signs that only a wife can read.'

'I hold no brief for matrimony, Duff, but aren't you being a little unfair, judging everything by your own unfortunate experience?'

'Select any woman, slap a ring on her third finger and she becomes a wife. First she takes you into her warm, soft body, which is pleasant, and then she tries to take you into her warm, soft mind, which is not so pleasant. She does not share, she possesses – she clings and she smothers. The relation of man to woman is uninteresting in that it conforms to an inescapable pattern, nature has made it so for the very good reason that it requires us to reproduce; but in order to obtain that result every love, Romeo and Juliet, Bonaparte and Josephine not excepted, must lead up to the co-performance of a simple biological function. It's such a small thing – such a short-lived, trivial little experience. Apart from that man and woman think differently, feel differently and are interested in different things. Would you call that companionship?'

'No, but is that a true picture? Is that all there is between them?' Sean asked.

'You'll find out one day. Nature in her preoccupation with reproduction has planted in the mind of man a barricade; it has sealed him off from the advice and experience of his fellowmen, inoculated him against it. When your time comes you'll go to the gallows with a song on your lips.'

'You frighten me.'

'It's the sameness of it all that depresses me – the goddamn monotony of it.' Duff shifted his seat restlessly then settled back against the boiler. The interesting relationships are those in which sex the leveller takes no hand – brothers, enemies, master and servant, father and son, man and man.'

'Homosexuals?'

'No, that's merely sex out of step and you're back to the original trouble. When a man takes a friend he does it not from an uncontrollable compulsion but in his own free choice. Every friendship is different, ends differently or goes on for ever. No chains bind it, no ritual or written contract. There is no question of forsaking all others, no obligation to talk about it – mouth it up and gloat on it the whole time.' Duff stood up stiffly. 'It's one of the good things in life. How late is it?'

Sean pulled out his watch and tilted its face to catch the moonlight. 'After midnight – it doesn't look as if they're coming.'

'They'll come – there's gold here, another uncontrollable compulsion. They'll come. The question is when.'

The lights along the valley faded out one by one, the deep singsong voices of the Zulus in the prospect trench stilled and a small cold wind came up and moved the grass along the ridge of the Candy Deep. Sitting together, sometimes drowsing, sometimes talking quietly, they waited the night away. The sky paled, then pinked prettily. A dog barked over near Hospital Hill and another joined it. Sean stood up and stretched, he glanced down the valley towards Ferrieras Camp and saw them. A black moving blot of horsemen, overflowing the road, lifting no dust from the dew-damp earth, spreading out to cross the Natal Spruit then bunching together on the near bank before coming on.

'Mr Charleywood, we have company.'

Duff jumped up.

'They might miss us and go on to the Jack and Whistle first.'

'We'll see which road they take when they come to the fork. In the meantime let's get ready. Mbejane,' shouted Sean and the black head popped out of the trench.

'Nkosi?'

'Are you awake? They are coming.'

The blackness parted in a white smile. 'We are awake.'

'Then get down and stay down until I give the word.'

The five mercenaries were lying belly down in the grass, each with a newly-opened packet of cartridges at his elbow. Sean hurried back to Duff and they crouched behind the boiler.

'The tin can shows up clearly from here. Do you think you can hit it?'

'With my eyes closed,' said Sean.

The horsemen reached the fork and turned without hesitation towards the Candy Deep, quickening their paces as they came up the ridge. Sean rested his rifle across the top of the boiler and picked up the speck of silver in his sights.

'What's the legal position, Duff?' he asked out of the corner of his mouth.

'They've just crossed our boundary – they are now officially trespassers,' Duff pronounced solemnly.

One of the leading horses kicked over the tin can and Sean fired at the spot on which it had stood. The shot was indecently loud in the quiet morning and every head in the syndicate lifted with alarm towards the ridge, then the ground beneath them jumped up in a brown cloud to meet the sky. When the dust cleared there was a struggling tangle of downed horses and men. The screams carried clearly up to the crest of the ridge.

'My God,' breathed Sean, appalled at the destruction.

'Shall we let them have it, boss?' called one of the hired men.

'No,' Duff answered him quickly. 'They've had enough.'

The flight started, riderless horses, mounted men and others on foot were scattering back down the valley. Sean was relieved to see that they left only half a dozen men and a few horses lying in the road.

'Well, that's the easiest fiver you've ever earned,' Duff told one of the mercenaries. 'I think you can go home now and have some breakfast.'

'Wait, Duff.' Sean pointed. The survivors of the explosion had reached the road junction again and there they were being stopped by two men on horseback.

'Those two are trying to rally them.'

'Let's change their minds, they're still within rifle range.'

'They are not on our property any more,' disagreed Sean. 'Do you want to wear a rope?'

They watched while those of the syndicate who had had enough fighting for one day disappeared down the road to the camps and the rest coagulated into a solid mass at the crossroad.

'We should have shot them up properly while we had the chance,' grumbled one of the mercenaries uneasily. 'Now they'll come back – look at that bastard talking to them like a Dutch uncle.'

They left their horses and spread out, then they started moving cautiously back up the slope. They hesitated just below the line of boundary pegs then ran forward, tearing up the pegs as they came.

'All together, gentlemen, if you please,' called Duff

politely and the seven rifles fired. The range was long and the thirty or so attackers ran doubled up and dodging. The bullets had little effect at first, but as the distance shortened men started falling. There was a shallow donga running diagonally down the slope and as each of the attackers reached it he jumped down into it and from its safety started a heated reply to the fire of Sean's men. Bullets spanged off the machinery, leaving bright scars where they struck.

Mbejane's Zulus were adding their voices to the confusion.

'Let us go down to them now, Nkosi.'

'They are close – let us go.'

'Quiet down, you madmen, you'd not go a hundred paces against those rifles,' Sean snarled impatiently.

'Sean, cover me,' whispered Duff. 'I'm going to sneak round the back of the ridge, rush them from the side and lob a few sticks of dynamite into that donga.'

Sean caught his arm, his fingers dug into it so that Duff winced.

'You take one step and I'll break a rifle butt over your head – you're as bad as those Blacks. Now keep shooting and let me think.' Sean peered over the top of the boiler but ducked again as a bullet rang loudly against it, inches from his ear. He stared at the new paint in front of his nose, put his shoulder against it; the boiler rocked slightly. He looked up and Duff was watching him.

'We'll walk down together and lob that dynamite,' Sean told him. 'Mbejane and his bloodthirsty heathens will roll the boiler in front of us. These other gentlemen will cover us, we'll do this thing in style.'

Sean called the Zulus out of the trench and explained to them. They chorused their approval of the scheme and jostled each other to find a place to push against the boiler.

Sean and Duff filled the front of their shirts with the dynamite grenades and lit a short length of tarred rope each.

Sean nodded to Mbejane.

'Where are the children of Zulu?' sang Mbejane, shrilling his voice in the ancient rhetorical question.

'Here,' answered his warriors braced ready against the boiler.

'Where are the spears of Zulu?'

'Here.'

'How bright are the spears of Zulu?'

'Brighter than the Sun.'

'How hungry are the spears of Zulu?'

'Hungrier than the locust.'

'Then let us take them to the feeding.'

'*Yeh-bo*.' Explosive assent and the boiler revolved slowly to the thrust of black shoulders.

'*Yeh-bo*.' Another reluctant revolution.

'*Yeh-bo*.' It moved more readily.

'*Yeh-bo*.' Gravity caught it. Ponderously it bumped down the slope and they ran behind it. The fire from the donga doubled its volume, rattling like hail against the huge metal cylinder. The singing of the Zulus changed its tone also; the deep-voiced chanting quickened, climbed excitedly, and became the blood trill. That insane, horrible squealing made Sean's skin crawl, tickled his spine with the ghost fingers of memory, but it inflamed him also. His mouth opened and he squealed with them. He touched the first grenade with the burning rope then flung it in a high spluttering sparking arc. It burst in the air above the donga. He threw again. Crump, crump. Duff was using his explosive as well. The boiler crashed over the lip of the donga and came to rest in a cloud of dust; the Zulus followed it in, spreading out, still shrieking, and now their assegais were busy. The white men broke, clawed frantically out of the ravine and fled, the Zulus hacking at them as they ran.

When Francois arrived with fifty armed diggers following him the fight was over.

'Take your boys down to the camps. Comb them out carefully. We want every one of those that got away,' Duff told him. 'It's about time we had a little law and order on this field.'

'How will we pick out the ones that were in on it?' asked Francois.

'By their white faces and the sweat on their shirts you will know them,' Duff answered.

Francois and his men went, leaving Sean and Duff to clean up the battlefield. It was a messy job – the stabbing spears had made it so. They destroyed those horses that the blast had left still half alive and they gleaned more than a dozen corpses from the donga and the slope below it. Two of them were Zulus. The wounded, and there were many, they packed into a wagon and took them down to Candy's Hotel.

It was early afternoon by the time they arrived. They threaded the wagon through the crowd and stopped it in front of the Hotel. It seemed the entire population of the goldfield was there, packed around the small open space in which Francois was holding his prisoners.

Francois was almost hysterical with excitement. He was sweeping the shotgun around in dangerous circles as he harangued the crowd. Then he darted back to prod one of the prisoners with the twin muzzles.

'You thunders,' he screamed. 'Steal our claims – hey – steal our claims.'

At that moment he caught sight of Duff and Sean bringing the wagon through the press.

'Duff, Duff. We got them. We got the whole lot of

them.' The crowd backed respectfully away from the menace of that circling shotgun and Sean flinched as it pointed directly at him for a second.

'So I see, Francois,' Duff assured him. 'In fact, I have seldom seen anyone more completely had.'

Francois's prisoners were swathed in ropes; they could move only their heads and as additional security a digger with a loaded rifle stood over each of them. Duff climbed down off the wagon.

'Don't you think you should slacken those ropes a little?' Duff asked dubiously.

'And have them escape?' Francois was indignant.

'Do you think they'd get very far?'

'No, I don't suppose so.'

'Well, another half hour and they'll all have gangrene – look at that one's hand already, a beautiful shade of blue.'

Reluctantly Francois conceded and told his men to untie them.

Duff pushed his way through the crowd and climbed the steps of the Hotel. From there he held up his hands for silence.

'There have been a lot of men killed today – we don't want it to happen again. One way we can prevent it is to make sure that this lot get what they deserve.' Cheers were led by Francois.

'But we must do it properly. I suggest we elect a committee to deal with this affair and with any other problems that crop up on these fields. Say ten members and a chairman.'

More cheers.

'Call it the Diggers' Committee,' shouted someone and the crowd took up the name enthusiastically.

'All right, the Diggers' Committee it is. Now we want a chairman, any suggestions?'

'Mr Charleywood,' shouted Francois.

'Yes, Duff – he'll do.'

'Yes, Duff Charleywood.'

'Any other suggestions?'

'No,' roared the crowd.

'Thank you, gentlemen.' Duff smiled at them. 'I am sensible of the honour. Now, ten members.'

'Jock and Trevor Heyns.'

'Karl Lochtkamper.'

'Francois du Toit.'

'Sean Courtney.'

There were fifty nominations. Duff baulked at counting votes so the committee was elected by applause. He called the names one at a time and judged the strength of the response to each. Sean and Francois were among those elected. Chairs and a table were brought out onto the veranda and Duff took his seat. With a water-jug he hammered for silence, declared the first session of the Diggers' Committee open and then immediately fined three members of the crowd ten pounds each for discharging firearms during a meeting – gross contempt of Committee. The fines were paid and a proper air of solemnity achieved.

'I'll ask Mr Courtney to open the case for the prosecution.'

Sean stood up and gave a brief description of the morning's battle, ending, 'You were there, Your Honour, so you know all about it anyway.'

'So I was,' agreed Duff. 'Thank you, Mr Courtney. I think that was a very fair picture you presented. Now,' he looked at the prisoners, 'who speaks for you?'

There was a minute of shuffling and whispering, then one of them was pushed forward. He pulled off his hat and blushed purple.

'Your Worship,' he began, then stopped, wriggling with embarrassment.

'Your Worship.'

'You've said that already.'

'I don't rightly know where to begin, Mr Charleywood – I mean Your Honour, sir.'

Duff looked at the prisoners again.

'Perhaps you'd like to reconsider your choice.'

Their first champion was withdrawn in disgrace and a fresh one sent forward to face the Committee. He had more fire.

'You bastards got no right to do this to us,' he started and Duff promptly fined him ten pounds. His next attempt was more polite.

'Your Honour, you can't do this to us. We had our rights, you know, that new proclamation and all, I mean, them old titles wasn't legal no more now, was they? We just came along as peaceful as you please, the old titles not being legal, we got a right to do what we done. Then you bastards, I mean Your Honour, dynamited us and like we had a right to protect ourselves, I mean after all, didn't we, sir?'

'A brilliant defence most ably conducted. Your fellows should be grateful to you,' Duff complimented him, then turned to his Committee. 'Well now, how say you merry gentlemen. Guilty or not guilty?'

'Guilty.' They spoke together and Francois added for emphasis, 'The dirty thunders.'

'We will now consider sentence.'

'String them up,' shouted someone and instantly the mood changed. The mob growled: an ugly sound.

'I'm a carpenter, I'll whip you up a handsome set of gallows in no time at all.'

'Don't waste good wood on them. Use a tree.'

'Get the ropes.'

'String them up.'

The crowd surged in, lynch mad. Sean snatched Francois's shotgun and jumped up onto the table.

'So help me God, I'll shoot the first one of you that

touches them before this court says so.' They checked and Sean pressed his advantage. 'At this range I can't miss. Come on, try me – there's two loads of buckshot in here. Someone will get cut in half.' They fell back still muttering.

'Perhaps you've forgotten, but there's a police force in this country and there's a law against killing. Hang them today and it'll be your turn tomorrow.'

'You're right, Mr Courtney, it'll be cruel, heartless murder. That it will,' wailed the spokesman.

'Shut up, you bloody fool,' Duff snarled at him and someone in the crowd laughed. The laughter caught on and Duff sighed silently with relief. That had been very close.

'Give them the old tar and feathers.'

Duff grinned. 'Now you're talking sense. Who's got a few barrels of tar for sale?' He looked round. 'What, no offers? Then we'll have to think of something else.'

'I've got ten drums of red paint – thirty shillings each, good imported brand.' Duff recognized the speaker as a trader who had opened a general dealer's store down at Ferrieras Camp.

'Mr Tarry suggests paint. What about it?'

'No, it comes off too easily – that's no good.'

'I'll let you have it cheap – twenty-five shillings a drum.'

'No – stick your ruddy paint,' the crowd booed him.

'Give them a twist on Satan's Roulette Wheel,' shouted another voice, and the crowd clamoured agreement.

'That's it – give them the wheel.'

'Round and round and round she goes – where she stops nobody knows,' roared a black-bearded digger from the roof of the shanty across the road. The crowd howled.

Sean watched Duff's expression – the smile had gone. He was weighing it up. If he stopped them again they might lose all patience and risk the shotgun. He couldn't chance it.

'All right. If that's what you want.' He faced the terrified cluster of prisoners. 'The sentence of this court is that you play roulette with the devil for one hour and that you then leave this goldfield – if we catch you back here again you'll get another hour of it. The wounded are excused the first half of the sentence. I think they've had enough. Mr du Toit will supervise the punishment.'

'We'd prefer the paint, Mr Charleywood,' pleaded the spokesman again.

'I bet you would,' said Duff softly, but the crowd was carrying them away already, out towards the open veld beyond the Hotel. Most of them had staked claims of their own and they didn't like claim jumpers. Sean climbed down off the table.

'Let's go and have a drink,' Duff said to him.

'Aren't you going to watch?' asked Sean.

'I've seen it done once before down in the Cape. That was enough.'

'What do they do?'

'Go and have a look, I'll be waiting for you at the Bright Angels. I'll be surprised if you stay the full hour.'

By the time Sean joined the crowd most of the wagons had been gathered from the camps and drawn up in a line. Men swarmed round them fitting jacks under the axles to lift the big back wheels clear of the ground. Then the prisoners were hustled forward – one to each wheel. Eager hands lifted them and held them while their wrists and ankles were lashed to the rim of the wheel with the hub in the middle of their backs and their arms and legs spread-eagled like stranded starfish. Francois hurried along the line checking the ropes and placing four diggers at each wheel, two to start it and another two to take over when those were tired. He reached the end, came back to the centre again, pulled his watch from his pocket, checked the time, then shouted.

'All right – turn them, *kerels*.'

The wheels started moving, slowly at first then faster as they built up momentum. The bodies strapped to them blurred with the speed.

'Round and round and round she goes – round and round and round she goes,' chanted the crowd gleefully.

Within minutes there was a burst of laughter from the end of the line of wagons. Someone had started vomiting, it sprayed from him like yellow sparks from a catherine wheel. Then another and another joined in. Sean could hear them retching and gasping as the centrifugal force flung the vomit up against the back of their throats and out of their noses. He waited a few more minutes but when their bowels started to empty he turned away gagging and headed for the Bright Angel.

'Did you enjoy it?' asked Duff.

'Give me a brandy,' answered Sean.

– 9 –

With the Diggers' Committee dispensing rough justice a semblance of order came to the camps. President Kruger wanted no part in policing the nest of ruffians and cut-throats which was growing up just outside his Capital and he contented himself with placing his spies among them and leaving them to work out their own salvation. After all, the field was far from proved and the chances were that in another year the veld would again be as deserted as it had been nine months before. He could afford to wait; in the meantime the Diggers' Committee had his tacit sanction.

While the ants worked, cutting down into the reef with pick and with dynamite, the grasshoppers waited in the bars and shanties. So far only the Jack and Whistle mill was turning out gold, and only Hradsky and Francois du Toit knew how much gold was coming out of it. Hradsky was still in Capetown crusading for capital and Francois spoke to no one, not even to Duff, about the mill's productivity.

The rumours flew like sand in a whirlwind. One day it seemed that the reef had pinched out fifty feet below the surface, and the next the canteens buzzed with the news that the Heyns brothers had gone down a hundred feet and were pulling out nuggets the size of musket balls. Nobody knew but everybody was prepared to guess.

Up at the Candy Deep, Duff and Sean worked on relentlessly. The mill took shape on its concrete platform, its jaws open for the first bite at the rock. The boiler was swung up onto its cradle by twenty sweating, singing Zulus. The copper tables were fitted up ready to be smeared with quicksilver. There was no time to worry about the reef nor the dwindling store of money in Sean's cash belt. They worked and they slept – there was nothing else. Duff took to sharing Sean's tent up on the ridge and Candy had her featherbed to herself again.

On the twentieth of November they fired the boiler for the first time. Tired and horny-handed, their bodies lean and tempered hard with toil, they stood together and watched the needle creek up round the pressure gauge until it touched the red line at the top.

Duff grunted. 'Well, at least we've got power now.' Then he punched Sean's shoulder. 'What the hell are you standing here for – do you think this is a Sunday School picnic? There's work to do, laddie.'

On the second of December they fed the mill its first meal and watched the powdered rock flow across the amalgam tables. Sean threw his arm round Duff's neck in an affectionate half-Nelson, Duff hit him in the stomach and pulled his hat down over his eyes, they drank a glass of brandy each at supper and laughed a little but that was all. They were too tired to celebrate. From now on one of them must be in constant attendance on that iron monster. Duff took the first night shift and when Sean went up to the mill next morning he found him weaving on his feet, his eyes sunk deep in dark sockets.

'By my reckoning we've run ten tons of rock through her. Time to clean the tables and see just how much gold we've picked up.'

'You go and get some sleep,' said Sean and Duff ignored him.

'Mbejane, bring a couple of your savages here, we're going to change the tables.'

'Listen, Duff, it can wait an hour or two. Go and get your head down.'

'Please stop drivelling – you're as bad as a wife.'

Sean shrugged. 'Have it your own way, show me how you do it then.'

They switched the flow of powdered rock onto the second table that was standing ready; then with a broad bladed spatula Duff scraped the mercury off the copper top of the first table, collecting it in a ball the size of a coconut.

'The mercury picks up the tiny particles of gold,' he explained to Sean as he worked, 'and lets the grains of rock wash across the table and fall off into the dump. Of course it doesn't collect it all, some of it goes to waste.'

'How do you get the gold out again?'

'You put the whole lot in a retort and boil off the mercury – the gold stays behind.'

'Hell of a waste of mercury, isn't it?'

'No, you catch it as it condenses and use it again. Come on, I'll show you.'

Duff carried the ball of amalgam down to the shed, placed it in the retort and lit the blow-lamp. With the heat on it the ball dissolved and started to bubble. Silently they stared at it. The level in the retort fell.

'Where's the gold?' Sean asked at last.

'Oh, shut up,' Duff snapped impatiently, and then, repentant, 'Sorry, laddie, I feel a bit jaded this morning.'

The last of the mercury steamed off and there it was, glowing bright, molten yellow. A drop of gold the size of a pea. Duff shut off the blow-lamp and neither of them spoke for a while. Then Sean asked, 'Is that all?'

'That, my friend, is all,' agreed Duff wearily. 'What do you want to do with it – fill a tooth?'

He turned towards the door with a droop to his whole body.

'Keep the mill running, we might as well go down with our colours flying.'

– 10 –

It was a miserable Christmas dinner. They ate it at Candy's Hotel. They had credit there. She gave Duff a gold signet ring and Sean a box of cigars. Sean had never smoked before but now the sting of it in his lungs gave him a certain masochistic pleasure. The dining-room roared with men's voices and cutlery clatter, the air was thick with the smell of food and tobacco smoke while in one corner – marooned on a little island of gloom – sat Sean, Duff and Candy.

Once Sean lifted his glass at Duff and spoke like an undertaker's clerk. 'Happy Christmas.'

Duff's lips twitched back in a dead man's grin. 'And the same to you.'

They drank. Then Duff roused himself to speak. 'Tell me again – how much have we got left? I like to hear you say it; you have a beautiful voice, you should have played Shakespeare.'

'Three pounds and sixteen shillings.'

'Yes, yes, you got it just right that time – three pounds

and sixteen shillings – now to really make me feel Christmassy, tell me how much we owe.'

'Have another drink.' Sean changed the subject.

'Yes, I think I will, thank you.'

'Oh please, you two, let's just forget about it for today,' pleaded Candy. 'I planned for it to be such a nice party – look, there's Francois! Hey, Francois – over here!'

The dapper du Toit bustled across to their table.

'Happy Christmas, kerels, let me buy you a drink.'

'It's nice to see you.' Candy gave him a kiss. 'How are you? You're looking fine.'

Francois sobered instantly. 'It's funny you should say that, Candy. As a matter of fact I'm a bit worried.' He tapped his chest and sank down into an empty chair. 'My heart, you know, I've been waiting for it to happen, and then yesterday I was up at the mill, just standing there, you understand, when suddenly it was as though a vice was squeezing my chest. I couldn't breathe – well, not very well anyway. Naturally I hurried back to my tent and looked it up. Page eighty-three. Under "Diseases of the Heart".' He shook his head sadly. 'It's very worrying. You know I wasn't a well man before, but now this.'

'Oh, no,' wailed Candy. 'I can't stand it – not you too.'

'I'm sorry, have I said something wrong?'

'Just in keeping with the festive spirit at this table.' She pointed at Duff and Sean. 'Look at their happy faces – if you'll excuse me I'm going to check up in the kitchen.' She went.

'What's wrong, old Duff?'

Duff flashed his death's head grin across the table at Sean.

'The man wants to know what's wrong – tell him.'

'Three pounds sixteen shillings,' said Sean and Francois looked puzzled.

'I don't understand.'

'He means we're broke – flat broke.'

'*Gott*, I'm sorry to hear that, Duff, I thought you were going good. I've heard the mill running all this month, I thought you'd be rich by now.'

'The mill's been running all right and we've recovered enough gold to block a flea's backside.'

'But why, man? You are working the Leader Reef, aren't you?'

'I'm beginning to think this Leader Reef of yours is a bedtime story.'

Francois peered into his glass thoughtfully.

'How deep are you?'

'We've got one incline shaft down about fifty feet.'

'No sign of the Leader?' Duff shook his head and Francois went on.

'You know when I first spoke to you a lot of what I said was just guessing.'

Duff nodded.

'Well, I know a bit more about it now. What I am going to tell you is for you alone – I'll lose my job if it gets out, you understand?'

Duff nodded again.

'So far the Leader Reef has only been found at two places. We've got it on the Jack and Whistle and I know the Heyns brothers have struck it on the Cousin Jock Mine. Let me draw it for you.' He picked up a knife and drew in the gravy on the bottom of Sean's plate. 'This is the Main Reef running fairly straight. Here I am, here is the Cousin Jock and here you are in between us. Both of us have found the Leader and you haven't. My guess is it's there all right – you just don't know where to look.

'At the far end of the Jack and Whistle claims the Main Reef and the Leader are running side by side two feet apart but by the time they reach the boundary nearest to the Candy Deep they've opened up to seventy feet apart. Now on the boundary of the Cousin Jock they're back to fifty feet apart. To me it seems that the two reefs form the shape of a long bow, like this.' He drew it in. 'The Main Reef is the string and the Leader Reef is the wood. I'm telling you, Duff, if you cut a trench at right-angles to the Main Reef you'll find it – and when you do you can buy me a drink.'

They listened gravely and when Francois finished Duff leaned back in his chair. 'If we'd known this a month ago! Now how are we going to raise the money to cut this new trench and still keep the mill running?'

'We could sell some of our equipment,' suggested Sean.

'We need it, every scrap of it, and besides if we sold one spade the creditors would be on us like a pack of wolves, howling for their money.'

'I'd make you a loan if I had it – but with what Mr Hradsky pays me—' Francois shrugged. 'You'll need about two hundred pounds. I haven't got it.'

Candy came back to the table in time to hear Francois's last remark.

'What's this all about?'

'Can I tell her, Francois?'

'If you think it will do any good.'

Candy listened, then thought for a moment. 'Well, I've just bought ten plots of ground in Johannesburg, this new Government village down the valley, so I'm short myself. But I could let you have fifty pounds if that would help.'

'I've never borrowed money from a lady before – it'll be a new experience. Candy, I love you.'

'I wish you meant that,' said Candy, but luckily for Duff his hearing failed him completely just as Candy spoke. He went on hurriedly.

'We'll need another hundred and fifty or so – let's hear your suggestions, gentlemen.'

There was a long silence, then Duff started to smile and he was looking at Sean.

'Don't tell me, let me guess.' Sean forestalled him. 'You're going to put me out to stud?'

'Close – but not quite right. How are you feeling, laddie?'

'Thank you, I'm all right.'

'Strong?'

'Yes.'

'Brave?'

'Come on, Duff, let's have it. I don't like that look in your eye.'

Duff pulled a notebook out of his pocket and wrote in it with a stump of pencil. Then he tore out the page and handed it to Sean. 'We'll have posters like this put up in every canteen on the goldfields.'

Sean read it:

ON NEW YEAR'S DAY MR SEAN COURTNEY HEAVY-WEIGHT CHAMPION OF THE TRANSVAAL REPUBLIC WILL STAND TO MEET ALL COMERS IN FRONT OF CANDY'S HOTEL FOR

A PURSE OF FIFTY POUNDS ASIDE.

Spectators' Fee, 2s. All Welcome.

Candy was reading it over his shoulder. She squeaked.

'That's wonderful. I'll have to hire extra waiters to serve drinks and I'll run a buffet luncheon. I suppose I could charge two shillings a head?'

'I'll fix the posters,' Francois was not to be outdone, 'and I'll send a couple of my chaps down to put up a ring.'

'We'll close the mill down until New Year – Sean will have to get a lot of rest. We'll put him on light training only. No drinking, of course, and plenty of sleep,' said Duff.

'It's all arranged then, is it?' asked Sean. 'All I've got to do is go in there and get beaten to a pulp?'

'We're doing this for you, laddie, so that you can be rich and famous.'

'Thank you, thank you very much.'

'You like to fight, don't you?'

'When I'm in the mood.'

'Don't worry, I'll think up some dirty names to call you – get you worked up in no time.'

– 11 –

'How are you feeling?' Duff asked for the sixth time that morning.

'No change since five minutes ago,' Sean reassured him.

Duff pulled out his watch, stared at it, held it to his ear and looked surprised that it was still ticking.

'We've got the challengers lined up on the veranda. I've told Candy to serve them free drinks – as much as they want. Every minute we can wait here gives them a little longer to take on a load of alcohol. Francois is collecting the gate money in my valise; as you win each bout the stakes will go into it as well. I've got Mbejane stationed at the mouth of the alley beside the Hotel. If there's a riot one of us will throw the bag to him and he'll head for the long grass.'

Sean was stretched out on Candy's bed with his hands behind his head. He laughed. 'I can find no fault with your planning. Now for pity's sake calm down, man. You're making me nervous.'

The door burst open and Duff leapt out of his chair at the crash. It was Francois, he stood in the doorway holding his chest.

'My heart,' he panted. 'This is doing my heart no good.'

'What's happening outside?' Duff demanded.

'We've collected over fifty pounds gate money already.

There's a mob up on the roof that haven't paid, but every time I go near them they throw bottles at me.'

Francois cocked his head on one side. 'Listen to them.' The noise of the crowd was barely softened by the flimsy walls of the Hotel. 'They won't wait much longer – you'd better come out before they start looking for you.'

Sean stood up. 'I'm ready.'

Francois hesitated.

'Duff, you remember Fernandes, that Portuguese from Kimberley?'

'Oh no!' Duff anticipated him. 'Don't tell me he's here.'

Francois nodded. 'I didn't want to alarm you but some of the local boys clubbed in and telegraphed south for him. He arrived on the express coach half an hour ago. I had hoped he wasn't going to make it in time, but—' He shrugged.

Duff looked at Sean sadly.

'Bad luck, laddie.'

Francois tried to soften the blow. 'I told him it was first come first served. He's sixth in the line so Sean will be able to make a couple of hundred quid anyway – then we can always say he's had enough and close the contest.'

Sean was listening with interest. 'This Fernandes is dangerous?'

'They were thinking of him when they invented that word,' Duff told him.

'Let's go and have a look at him.'

Sean led the way out of Candy's room and down the passage.

'Did you get hold of a scale to weigh them with?' Duff asked Francois as they hurried after Sean.

'No, there's not one on the fields that goes over a hundred and fifty pounds – but I have Gideon Barnard outside.'

'How does that help us?'

'He's a cattle dealer – all his life he's been judging animals on the hoof. He'll give us the weights to within a few pounds.'

Duff chuckled. 'That'll have to do then. Besides I doubt we'll be claiming any world titles.'

Then they were out on the veranda blinking in the brightness of the sun and the thunder of the crowd.

'Which is the Portuguese?' whispered Sean – he needn't have asked. The man stood out like a gorilla in a cage of monkeys. A shaggy coating of hair began on his shoulders and continued down his back and chest, completely hiding his nipples and exaggerating the bulge of his enormous belly.

The crowd opened a path for Sean and Duff and they walked along it to the ring. Hands slapped Sean's back but the well-wishes were drowned in the churning sea of sound. Jock Heyns was the referee – he helped Sean through the ropes and ran his hands over his pockets.

'Just checking,' he apologized. 'We don't want any scrap iron in the ring.' Then he beckoned to a tall, brown-faced fellow who was leaning on the ropes chewing tobacco.

'This is Mr Barnard our weighing steward. Well, what do you say, Gideon?'

The steward hosed a little juice from the side of his mouth.

'Two hundred and ten.'

'Thank you.' Jock held up his hands and after a few minutes was rewarded with a comparative silence.

'Ladies and Gentlemen.'

'Who you talking to, Guvnor?'

'We are privileged to have with us today – Mr Sean Courtney.'

'Wake up, *Boet*, he's been with us for months.'

'The heavyweight champion of the Republic.'

'Why not make it the world, cock, he's got just as much right to that title.'

'Who will fight six bouts—'

'If it lasts that long.'

' – for his title and a purse of fifty pounds each.'

Sustained cheering.

'The first challenger – at two hundred and ten pounds – Mr Anthony—'

'Hold on,' Sean shouted, 'who says he's first?'

Jock Heyns had taken a deep breath to bellow the name. He let it escape with a hiss. 'It was arranged by Mr du Toit.'

'If I fight them, then I pick them – I want the Port . . .'

Duff's hand whipped over Sean's mouth and his whisper was desperate. 'Don't be a bloody fool – take the easy ones first. Use your head – we aren't doing this for fun, we're trying to finance a mine, remember?'

Sean clawed Duff's hand off his mouth. 'I want the Portuguese,' he shouted.

'He's joking,' Duff assured the crowd, then turned on Sean fiercely. 'Are you mad? That dago's a man-eater, we're fifty pounds poorer before you start.'

'I want the Portuguese,' repeated Sean with all the logic of a small boy picking the most expensive toy in the shop.

'Let him have the dago,' shouted the gentlemen on the hotel roof and Jock Heyns eyed them nervously; it was clear that they were about to add a few more bottles to the argument.

'All right,' he agreed hastily. 'The first challenger, at—' he glanced at Barnard and repeated after him, 'two hundred and fifty-five pounds – Mr Felezardo da Silva Fernandes.'

In a storm of hoots and applause the Portuguese waddled down off the veranda and into the ring. Sean had seen Candy at the dining-room window and he waved to her. She blew him a two-handed kiss and at that instant Trevor

Heyns, the timekeeper, hit the bucket which served as a gong and Sean heard Duff's warning shout. Instinctively he started to duck. There was a flash of lightning inside his skull and he found himself sitting in amongst the legs of the first line of spectators.

'The bastard King hit me,' Sean complained loudly. He shook his head and was surprised to find it still attached to his body. Someone poured a glass of beer over him and it steadied him. He felt his anger flaming up through his body.

'Six,' counted Jock Heyns.

The Portuguese was standing at the ropes. 'Come back, Leetle Sheet, I haf some more for you, not half.'

Sean's anger jumped in his throat.

'Seven, eight.'

Sean gathered his legs under him.

'I kiss your mother.' Fernandes puckered his lips and smacked them. 'I love your sister, like this.' He demonstrated graphically.

Sean charged. With the full weight of his run behind it, his fist thudded into the Portuguese's mouth, then the ropes caught Sean and catapulted him back into the crowd once more.

'You weren't even in the ring, how could you hit him?' protested one of the spectators who had broken Sean's fall. He had money on Fernandes.

'Like this!' Sean demonstrated. The man sat down heavily and had nothing further to say. Sean hurdled the ropes. Jock Heyns was halfway through his second count when Sean interrupted him by lifting the reclining Portuguese to his feet, using the tangled bush of his hair as a handle. He balanced the man on his unsteady legs and hit him again.

'One, two, three . . .' resignedly Jock Heyns began his third count, this time he managed to reach ten.

There was a howl of protest from the crowd and Jock Heyns struggled to make himself heard above it.

'Does anyone want to lodge a formal objection?'

It seemed that there were those who did.

'Very well, please step into the ring. I can't accept shouted comments.' Jock's attitude was understandable – he stood to lose a considerable sum if his decision were reversed. But Sean was patrolling the ropes as hungrily as a lion at feeding time. Jock waited a decent interval, then held up Sean's right arm.

'The winner – ten minutes for refreshments before the next bout. Will the keepers please come and fetch their property.' He gestured towards the Portuguese.

'Nice going, laddie, unorthodox perhaps but beautiful to watch.' Duff took Sean's arm and led him to a chair on the veranda.

'Three more to go, then we can call it a day.' He handed Sean a glass.

'What's this?'

'Orange juice.'

'I'd prefer something a little stronger.'

'Later, laddie.'

Duff collected the Portuguese purse and dropped it into the valise while that gentleman was being carried from the ring by his straining sponsors and laid to rest at the far end of the veranda.

Mr Anthony Blair was next. His heart was not in the encounter. He moved prettily enough on his feet but always in the direction best calculated to keep him out of reach of Sean's fists.

'The boy's a natural long-distance champ.'

'Watch it, Courtney, he'll run you to death.'

'Last lap, Blair, once more round the ring and you've done five miles.'

The chase ended when Sean, now sweating gently, herded him in a corner and there dispatched him.

The third challenger had by this time developed a pain in his chest.

'It hurts like you wouldn't believe it,' he announced through gritted teeth.

'Does it sort of gurgle in your lungs as you breathe?' asked Francois.

'Yes, that's it – gurgles like you wouldn't believe it.'

'Pleurisy,' diagnosed du Toit with more than a trace of envy in his voice.

'Is that bad?' the man asked anxiously.

'Yes it is. Page one hundred and sixteen. The treatment is—'

'Then I won't be able to fight. Hell, that's bad luck,' the invalid complained cheerfully.

'It's exceptionally bad luck,' agreed Duff. 'It means you'll have to forfeit your purse money.'

'You wouldn't take advantage of a sick man?'

'Try me,' Duff suggested pleasantly.

The fourth contestant was a German. Big, blond and happy-faced. He stumbled three or four times on his way to the ring, tripped over the ropes and crawled to his corner on hands and knees; once there he was able to regain his feet with a little help from the ring post. Jock went close to him to smell his breath and before he could dodge, the German caught him in a bear hug and led him into the opening steps of a waltz. The crowd loved it and there were no objections when at the end of the dance Jock declared Sean the winner on a technical knockout. More correctly the decision should have gone to Candy who had provided the free drinks.

'We can close down the circus now if you want to, laddie,' Duff told Sean. 'You've made enough to keep the Candy Deep afloat for another couple of months.'

'I haven't had a single good fight out of the lot of them. But I like the looks of this last one. The others were for business; this one I'll have just for the hell of it.'

'You've been magnificent – now you deserve a little fun,' agreed Duff.

'Mr Timothy Curtis. Heavyweight champion of Georgia, U.S.A.' Jock introduced him.

Gideon Barnard put his weight at two hundred and ten pounds, the same as Sean's. Sean shook his hand and from the touch of it knew he was not going to be disappointed.

'Glad to know you.' The American's voice was as soft as his grip was hard.

'Your servant, sir,' said Sean and hit the air where the man's head had been an instant before. He grunted as a fist slogged into his chest under his raised right arm and backed away warily. A soft sigh blew through the crowd and they settled down contentedly. This was what they had come to see.

The red wine was served early; it flew in tiny drops every time a punch was thrown or received. The fight flowed smoothly around the square of trampled grass. The sound of bone on flesh was followed immediately by the growl of the crowd and the seconds between were filled with the hoarse breathing of the two men and the slither, slither of their feet.

'Yaaaa!' Through the tense half silence ripped a roar like that of a mortally wounded foghorn. Sean and the American jumped apart startled, and turned with everyone else to face Candy's Hotel. Fernandes was with them again; his mountain-wide hairiness seemed to fill the whole veranda. He picked up one of Candy's best tables and holding it across his chest tore off two of its legs as though they were the wings of a roasted chicken.

'Francois, the bag!' shouted Sean. Francois snatched it up and threw it high over the heads of the crowd. Sean held his breath as he followed its slow trajectory, then he blew out again with relief as he saw Mbejane field the pass and vanish around the corner of the Hotel.

'Yaaaa!' Fernandes gave tongue again. With a table leg in each hand he charged the crowd that stood between him and Sean; it scattered before him.

'Do you mind if we finish this some other time?' Sean asked the American.

'Of course not. Any time at all. I was just about to leave myself.'

Duff reached through the ropes and caught Sean's arm.

'There's someone looking for you – or had you noticed?'

'It might just be his way of showing friendliness.'

'I wouldn't bet on it – are you coming?'

Fernandes rumbled to a halt, braced himself and threw. The table leg whirred like a rising pheasant an inch over Sean's head, ruffling his hair with the wind of its passage.

'Lead on, Duff.' Sean was uncomfortably conscious of the fact that Fernandes was again in motion towards him, still armed with a long oak, and that three very thin ropes were all that stood between them. The speed that Sean and Duff turned on them made Mr Blair's earlier exhibition seem like that of a man with both legs in plaster. Fernandes, carrying top weight as he was, never looked like catching them.

Francois came up to the Candy Deep just after midday with the news that the Portuguese, after beating three of his sponsors into insensibility, had left on the noon coach back to Kimberley.

Duff uncocked his rifle. 'Thanks, Franz, we were waiting lunch for him. I thought he might call on us.'

'Have you counted the takings?'

'Yes, your commission is in that paper bag on the table.'

'Thanks, man, let's go down and celebrate.'

'You go and have one for us.'

'Hey, Duff, you promised—' Sean started.

'I said later – in three or four weeks' time. Now we've got a little work to do, like digging a trench fifty feet deep and three hundred yards long.'

'We could start first thing tomorrow.'

'You want to be rich, don't you?' asked Duff.

'Sure, but—'

'You want nice things, like English suits, French champagne and—'

'Yes, but—'

'Well, stop arguing, get off your fat arse and come with me.'

– 12 –

The Chinese use firecrackers to keep the demons away. Duff and Sean applied the same principle. They kept the mill running; as long as its clunking carried across the valley to the ears of their creditors all was well. Everyone accepted the fact that they were working a payable reef and left them alone, but the money they fed into the front of the mill had halved its value by the time it came out of the other side in those pathetic little yellow pellets.

In the meantime they cut their trench, tearing into the earth in a race against Settlement Day. They fired dynamite and as the last stones dropped back out of the sky they were in again, coughing with the fumes, to clear the loosened rock and start drilling the next set of holes. It was summer, the days were long, and while it was light they worked. Some evenings they lit the last fuses by lantern light.

Sand fell through the hour-glass faster than they had bargained for, the money dribbled away and on the fifteenth of February Duff shaved himself, changed his shirt and went to see Candy about another loan. Sean watched him walk away down the slope. They had sold the horses a week before, and he said a small prayer – the first for many years.

Duff came back in the late morning. He stood on the edge of the trench and watched Sean tamping in the charges for the next cut. Sean's back was shiny with sweat; each individual muscle standing out in relief, swelling and subsiding as he moved.

'That's the stuff, laddie, keep at it.'

Sean looked up with dust-reddened eyes. 'How much?' he asked.

'Another fifty, and this is the last – or so she threatens.'

Sean's eyes fastened on the package Duff held under his arm.

'What's that?'

He could see the stains seeping through the brown paper and the saliva flooded out from under his tongue.

'Prime beef chops – no mealie meal porridge for lunch today.' Duff grinned at him.

'Meat.' Sean caressed the word. 'Underdone – bleeding a little as you bite it, a trace of garlic, just enough salt.'

'And you beside me, singing in the wilderness,' agreed Duff. 'Cut out the poetry, light those fuses and let's go and eat.'

An hour later they walked side by side along the bottom of their trench, Mbejane and his Zulus crowding behind them. Sean belched. 'Ah, pleasant memory, I'll never be able to look another plate of mealie meal in the face again.'

They reached the end, where the freshly broken earth and rock lay piled. Sean felt the thrill start in his hands, tingle up his arms and squeeze his lungs. Then Duff's fingers were biting into his shoulder; he could feel them trembling.

It looked like a snake, a fat grey python crawling down one wall of the trench, disappearing under the heap of new rubble and out the other side.

Duff moved first, he knelt and picked up a piece of the reef, a big grey mottled lump of it and he kissed it.

'It must be it, hey, Duff? It must be the Leader?'

'It's the end of the rainbow.'

'No more mealie meal,' Sean said softly and Duff laughed. Then Sean laughed. Wildly, crazily, together they howled their triumph.

– 13 –

'Let me hold it again,' said Sean.

Duff passed it across to him.

'Hell, it's heavy.'

'There's nothing heavier,' agreed Duff.

'Must be all of fifty pounds.'

Sean held the bar in two hands, it was the size of a cigar box. 'More!'

'We've retrieved all our losses in two days' working.'

'And some to spare, I'd say.'

Sean placed the gold bar on the table between them. It shone with little yellow smiles in the lantern light and Duff leaned forward and stroked it, its surface felt knobbly from the rough casting.

'I can't keep my hands off it,' he confessed sheepishly.

'I can't either!' Sean reached out to touch it. 'We'll be able to pay Candy out for the claims in another week or two.'

Duff started. 'What did you say?'

'I said we'd be able to pay Candy out.'

'I thought I wasn't hearing things.' Duff patted his arm indulgently. 'Listen to me, laddie, I'll try and put it simply. How long have we got the option on these claims for?'

'Three years.'

'Correct – now the next question. How many people on these fields have any money?'

Sean looked mystified. 'Well, we have now and – and . . .'

'No one else, that is until Hradsky gets back,' Duff finished for him.

'What about the Heyns brothers? They've cut open the Leader Reef.'

'Certainly, but it won't do them any good, not until their machinery arrives from England.'

'Go on!' Sean wasn't quite sure where Duff was leading.

'Instead of paying Candy out now we are going to use this' – he patted the gold bar – 'and all its little brothers to buy up every likely claim we can lay our hands on. For a start there are Doc Sutherland's claims between us and the Jack and Whistle. Then we are going to order a couple of big ten-stamp mills and when those are spilling out gold we'll use it to buy land, finance brick works, engineering shops, transport companies and the rest. I've told you before there are more ways of making gold than digging for it.'

Sean was staring at him silently.

'Have you got a head for heights?' asked Duff.

Sean nodded.

'You're going to need it, because we are going up where the eagles fly – you are about to be a party to the biggest financial killing this country has ever seen.'

Sean lit one of Candy's cigars; his hand was a little unsteady.

'Don't you think it would be best to – well – not try and go too quickly. Hell, Duff, we've only been working the Leader for two days—'

'And we've made a thousand pounds,' Duff interrupted him. 'Listen to me, Sean, all my life I've been waiting for an opportunity like this. We're the first in on this field, it's as wide open as the legs of a whore. We're going to go in and take it.'

The next morning Duff had the good fortune to find Doc Sutherland early enough to talk business with him, before he began the day's drinking. Another hour would have been too late. As it was Doc knocked over his glass and fell out of his chair before he finally signed away twenty-five claims to Sean and Duff. The ink was hardly dry on the agreement before Duff was riding down to Ferrieras Camp to look for Ted Reynecke who held the claims on the other side of the Cousin Jock. Up on the Candy Deep Sean nursed the mill and bit his nails. Within seven days Duff had bought over one hundred claims and committed them to forty thousand pounds in debts.

'Duff, you're going mad.' Sean pleaded with him. 'We'll lose everything again.'

'How much have we pulled out of the Candy Deep so far?'

'Four thousand.'

'Ten per cent of what we owe in ten days – and with a miserable little four-stamp mill at that. Hold on to your hat, laddie, tomorrow I'm going to sign up for the forty claims on the other side of the Jack and Whistle. I would have had them today but that damned Greek is holding out for a thousand pounds apiece. I'll have to give it to him, I suppose.'

Sean clutched his temples.

'Duff – please, man, we're in over our necks already.'

'Stand back, laddie, and watch the wizard work.'

'I'm going to bed – I suppose I'll have to take your shift again in the morning if you're determined to spend tomorrow ruining us.'

'That's not necessary, I've hired that Yankee – Curtis. You know, your sparring partner. It turns out he's a miner and he's willing to work for thirty a month. So you can come to town with me and watch me make you rich. I'm meeting the Greek at Candy's Hotel at nine o'clock.'

– 14 –

At nine o'clock Duff was talking and Sean sat silently on the edge of his chair; at ten the Greek had still not put in an appearance. Duff was moody and Sean was garrulous with relief. At eleven Sean wanted to go back to the mine.

'It's an omen, Duff, God looked down and he saw us sitting here all ready to make a terrible mistake. "No," he said, "I can't let them do it – I'll have the Greek break a leg – I can't let it happen to such nice boys."'

'Why don't you go and join a Trappist monastery?' Duff checked his watch. 'Come on, let's go!'

'Yes, sir!' Sean stood up with alacrity. 'We'll get back in plenty of time to clean the tables before lunch.'

'We're not going home, we're going to look for the Greek.'

'Now listen, Duff.'

'I'll listen later – come on.'

They rode across to the Bright Angels, left the horses outside and walked in together. It was dark in the canteen after the sunshine outside, but even in the gloom a group at one of the tables caught their attention immediately. The Greek sat with his back to them; the line of his parting seemed to be drawn with white chalk and a ruler through the oily black waves of his hair. Sean's eyes switched from him to the two men that sat across the table from him. Jews, there was no mistaking it, but there any similarity ended. The younger one was thin with smooth olive skin drawn tight across the bold bones of his cheeks; his lips were very red and his eyes, fringed with girl's lashes, were toffee-brown and melting. In the chair beside him was a man with a body that had been shaped in wax then held near a hot flame. Shoulders rounded to the verge of deformity drooped down over a pear-shaped body; with difficulty they supported the great Taj Mahal domed head. His hair was styled in the fashion of Friar Tuck, thick only around the ears. But the eyes – the flickering yellow eyes – there was nothing comical about them.

'Hradsky,' hissed Duff, then his expression changed. He smiled as he walked across to the table.

'Hello, Nikky, I thought we had an appointment.'

The Greek twisted quickly in his chair.

'Mr Charleywood, I'm sorry, I was held up.'

'So I see, the woods are full of highwaymen.'

Sean saw the flush start to come up out of Hradsky's collar then sink back again.

'Have you sold?' Duff asked.

The Greek nodded nervously.

'I'm sorry, Mr Charleywood, but Mr Hradsky paid my price and no haggling – cash money, too!'

Duff let his eyes wander across the table.

'Hello, Norman. How's your daughter?'

This time the flush escaped from Hradsky's shirt and flooded over his face. He opened his mouth, his tongue clucked twice, then he closed it again.

Duff smiled, he looked at the younger Jew. 'Say it for him, Max.'

The toffee eyes dropped to the table top. 'Mr Hradsky's daughter is very well.'

'I believe she married soon after my involuntary departure from Kimberley.'

'That is correct.'

'Wise move, Norman, much wiser than having your bully boys run me out of town. That wasn't very nice of you.'

No one spoke.

'We must get together some time and have a chat about old times. Until then, fa – fa – fare ye we – we – well.'

On the way back to the mine Sean asked, 'He's got a daughter? If she looks like him you were lucky to escape.'

'She didn't – she was like a bunch of ripe grapes with the bloom on them.'

'I can hardly credit it.'

'Neither could I. The only conclusion I could reach was that Max did that job for him as well.'

'What's the story about Max?'

'He's the Court Jester. Rumour has it that after Hradsky has finished hanging it out, Max shakes it for him.'

Sean laughed and Duff went on, 'But don't underestimate Hradsky. His stutter is his only weakness and with Max to talk for him he's overcome that. Beneath that monumental skull is a brain as quick and merciless as a guillotine. Now that he's arrived on this goldfield there's going to be some action; we'll have to gallop to keep up with him.'

Sean thought for a few seconds, then, 'Talking about action, Duff, now that we've lost the Greek's claims and won't have to use all our ready money satisfying him, let's give some thought to ordering new machinery to work the claims we have got.'

Duff grinned at him.

'I sent a telegram to London last week. There'll be a pair of brand new ten-stamp mills on the water to us before the end of the month.'

'Good God, why didn't you tell me?'

'You were worried enough as it was – I didn't want to break your heart.'

Sean opened his mouth to blast Duff out of the saddle. Duff winked at him before he could talk and Sean's lips trembled. He felt the laughter in his throat, he tried to stop it but it swamped him.

'How much is it going to cost us?' he howled through his mirth.

'If you ask that question once more, I'll strangle you,' Duff laughed back at him. 'Rest content in the knowledge that if we're going to have enough to honour the bills of lading when those mills arrive at Port Natal, we'll have to run a mountain of Leader Reef through our little rig during the next few weeks.'

'What about the payments on the new claims?'

'That's my department – I'll worry about that.'

And so their partnership crystallized; their relationship was established over the weeks that followed. Duff with his magic tongue and his charming, lopsided grin was the one who negotiated, who poured the oil on the storm waters churned up by impatient creditors. He was the storehouse of mining knowledge which Sean tapped daily, he was the conceiver of schemes, some wild, others brilliant. But his fleeting nervous energy was not designed to bring them to fruition. He lost interest quickly and it was Sean who finally rejected the least likely Charleywood brain children and adopted the others that were more deserving; once he had made himself stepfather to them he reared them as though they were his own. Duff was the theorist, Sean the practician. Sean could see why Duff had never found success before, but at the same time he recognized that without him he would be helpless. He watched with profound admiration the way that Duff used the barely sufficient flow of gold from the Candy Deep to keep the mill running, pay the tradesmen, meet the claim monies as they fell due and still save enough for the new machinery. He was a man juggling with live coals: hold one too long and it burns, let one fall and all fall. And Duff, deep-down-uncertain Duff, had a wall to put his back against. His speech never showed it but his eyes did when he looked at Sean. Sometimes he felt small next to Sean's big body and bigger determination, but it was a good feeling: like being on a friendly mountain.

They put up new buildings around the mill: storerooms, a smelting house and cabins for Sean and Curtis. Duff was sleeping at the Hotel again. The location for the Natives sprawled haphazard down the back slope of the ridge, retreating a little each week as the white mountain of the mine dump grew and pushed it back. The whole valley was changing. Hradsky's new mills arrived and stood up along the ridge, tall and proud until their own dumps dwarfed them. Johannesburg, at first a mere pattern of surveyors' pegs, sucked the scattered encampments onto her grassy chequerboard and arranged them in a semblance of order along her streets.

The Diggers' Committee, its members tired of having to scrape their boots every time they went indoors, decreed public latrines be erected. 'Then, flushed with their own audacity, they built a bridge across the Natal Spruit, purchased a water cart to lay the dust on the streets of Johannesburg and passed a law prohibiting burials within half a mile of the city centre. Sean and Duff as members of the Committee felt it their duty to demonstrate their faith in the goldfield, so they bought twenty-five plots of ground in Johannesburg, five pounds each to be paid within six months. Candy recruited all her customers and in one weekend of frantic effort they razed her Hotel to the ground, packed every plank and sheet of iron onto their wagons, carried it a mile down the valley and re-erected it on her own land in the centre of the township. During the party she gave them on that Sunday night they nearly succeeded in dismantling it for the second time. Each day the roads from Natal and the Cape fed more wagons, more men into the Witwatersrand goldfield. Duff's suggestion that the Diggers' Committee levy a guinea a head from all newcomers to help finance the public works was reluctantly rejected, the general feeling being that if it led to civil rebellion there were more newcomers than Committee members and no one fancied being on the losing side.

One morning, when he came out to the mine, Duff brought a telegram with him. He handed it to Sean without comment. Sean read it. The machinery had arrived.

'Good God, it's three weeks early.'

'They must have had a downhill sea, or a following wind or whatever it is that makes ships go faster,' muttered Duff.

'Have we got enough to pay the bill?' asked Sean.

'No.'

'What are we going to do?'

'I'll go and see the little man at the bank.'

'He'll throw you out in the street.'

'I'll get him to give us a loan on the claims.'

'How the hell are you going to do that – we haven't paid for them yet.'

'That's what you call financial genius. I'll simply point out to him that they're worth five times what we bought them for.' Duff grinned. 'Can you and Curtis carry on here without me for today while I go and arrange it?'

'You arrange it and I'll happily give you a month's holiday.'

When Duff came back that afternoon he carried a paper with him. It had a red wax seal in the bottom corner, across the top it said 'Letter of Credit' and in the middle, standing out boldly from the mass of small print, was a figure that ended in an impressive string of noughts.

'You're a bloody marvel,' said Sean.

'Yes, I am rather, aren't I?' agreed Duff.

– 15 –

The Heyns brothers' machinery was on the same ship. Jock and Duff rode down to Port Natal together, hired a hundred wagons and brought it all back in one load.

'I'll tell you what I'll do with you, Jock, I'll wager you that we get our mills producing before you do. Loser pays for the transport on the whole shipment,' Duff challenged him when they reached Johannesburg where, in Candy's new bar-room, they were washing the dust out of their throats.

'You're on!'

'I'll go further, I'll put up a side bet of five hundred.'

Sean prodded Duff in the ribs.

'Gently, Duff – we can't afford it.' But Jock had already snapped up the bet.

'What do you mean we can't afford it?' whispered Duff. 'We've got nearly fifteen hundred pounds left on the letter of credit.'

Sean shook his head. 'No, we haven't.'

Duff pulled the paper from his inside pocket and tapped Sean's nose with it. 'There – read for yourself.'

Sean took it out of Duff's hand.

'Thanks, old chap, I'll go and pay the man now.'

'What man?'

'The man with the wagons.'

'What wagons?'

'The wagons that you and Jock hired in Port Natal. I've bought them.'

'The hell you say!'

'It was your idea to start a transport business. Just as soon as they've offloaded they'll be on their way again to pick up a shipment of coal from Dundee.'

Duff grinned at him. 'Don't you ever forget an idea? All right, laddie, off you go – we'll just have to win the bet, that's all.'

One of the mills they placed on the Candy Deep, the other on the new claims beyond the Cousin Jock Mine. They hired two gangs from among the unemployed in Johannesburg. Curtis supervised one of them and Sean the other, while Duff darted back and forth keeping an eye on both. Each time he passed the Cousin Jock he spent a few minutes checking Trevor and Jock's progress.

'They've got the edge on us, Sean; their boilers are up and holding pressure already,' he reported fretfully, but the next day he was smiling again.

'They didn't mix enough cement in the platform – it started to crumble as soon as they put the crusher on it. They'll have to cast it again. That set them back three or four days.'

The betting down in the canteens fluctuated sharply with each change of fortune. Francois came up to the Candy Deep one Saturday afternoon. He watched them work, made a suggestion or two, then remarked, 'They're giving three-to-one against you at the Bright Angels; they reckon the Heynses will be finished by next weekend.'

'Go down and put another five hundred pounds on for me,' Duff told him, and Sean shook his head despairingly.

'Don't worry, laddie, we can't lose – that amateur mining engineer, Jock Heyns, has assembled his crusher jaws all arse-about-face. I only noticed it this morning – he's in for a surprise when he tries to start up. He'll have to strip the whole damn rig.'

Duff was right – they brought both their mills into production a comfortable fifteen hours before the Heyns brothers. Jock rode over to see them with his jaw on his chest. 'Congratulations.'

'Thanks, Jock, did you bring your cheque book?'

'That's what I came to talk about. Can you give me a little time?'

'Your credit's good,' Sean assured him, 'come and have a drink and let me sell you some coal.'

'Ah, yes, I heard your wagons arrived back this morning. What price are you charging?'

'Fifteen pounds a hundredweight.'

'Good God. You bloody bandit, I bet it cost you less than five shillings a hundredweight.'

'A man's entitled to a reasonable profit,' protested Sean.

It had been a long hard pull up to the top of the hill but Sean and Duff had arrived at last and from there it was downhill all the way. The money poured in.

The geological freak that had bowed the Leader Reef away from the Main across the Candy Deep claims had, at the same time, enriched it – injected it full of the metal. Francois was there one evening when they put the ball of amalgam into the retort. His eyes bulged as the mercury boiled away; he stared at the gold the way a man watches a naked woman.

'*Gott*! I'm going to have to call you two thunders "Mister" from now on.'

'Have you ever seen richer reef, Francois?' Duff gloated.

Francois shook his head slowly. 'You know my theory about the reef being the bed of an old lake – well this bears it out. The kink in your reef must have been a deep trench along the bottom of the lake. It would have acted as a natural gold trap. Hell, man, what luck. With your eyes closed you have picked the plum out of the pudding. The Jack and Whistle is half as rich as this.'

Their overdraft at the bank dropped like a barometer in a hurricane; the tradesmen started greeting them with a smile; they gave Doc Sutherland a cheque which would have kept even him in whisky for a hundred years. Candy kissed them both when they paid her out in full, plus interest at seven per cent. Then she built herself a new Hotel, double storied, with a crystal chandelier in the dining-room and a magnificent bedroom suite on the second floor done out in maroon and gold. Duff and Sean rented it immediately but with the express understanding that if ever the Queen visited Johannesburg they would allow her to use it. In anticipation Candy called it the Victoria Rooms.

Francois, with a little persuasion, agreed to take over the running of the Candy Deep. He moved his possessions, one chest of clothes and four chests of patent medicines, across from the Jack and Whistle. Timothy Curtis was the manager of the mill on the new claims; they named it the Little Sister Mine. Although not nearly as rich as the Candy Deep it was producing a sweet fortune each month, for Curtis worked as well as he fought.

By the end of August Sean and Duff had no more creditors: the claims were theirs, the mills were theirs and they had money to invest.

'We need an office of our own here in town. We can't run this show from our bedrooms,' complained Sean.

'You're right,' agreed Duff, 'we'll build on that corner plot nearest the market square.' The plan was for a modest little four-room building, but it finally expanded to two stories, stinkwood floors, oak panelling and twenty rooms. What they couldn't use they rented.

'The price of land has trebled in three months,' said Sean, 'and it's still moving.'

'You're right – now's the time to buy,' Duff agreed. 'You're starting to think along the right lines.'

'It was your idea.'

'Was it?' Duff looked surprised.

'Don't you remember your "up where the eagles fly" speech?'

'Don't you forget anything?' asked Duff.

They bought land: one thousand acres at Orange Grove

and another thousand around Hospital Hill. Their transport wagons, now almost four hundred strong, plied in daily from Port Natal and Lourenço Marques. Their brickfields worked twenty-four hours a day, seven days a week, to try to meet the demand for building materials.

It took Sean almost a week to dissuade Duff from building an Opera House but he succeeded and instead they joined most of the other members of the Diggers' Committee in financing a different type of pleasure palace. At Duff's suggestion they called it the Opera House. They recruited the performers not from the great companies of Europe but from the dock areas of Capetown and Port Natal and chose as the conductor a Frenchwoman of vast experience named Blue Bessie after the colour of her hair. The Opera House provided entertainment on two levels. For the members of the Committee and the other emergent rich there was a discreet side entrance, a lavishly furnished lounge where one could buy the finest champagne and discuss the prices on the Kimberley Stock Exchange, and beyond the lounge were a series of tastefully decorated retiring-rooms. For the workers there was a bare corridor to queue in, no choice for your money and a five-minute time limit. In one month the Opera House produced more gold than the Jack and Whistle mine.

By December there were millionaires in Johannesburg: Hradsky, the Heyns brothers, Karl Lochtkamper, Duff Charleywood, Sean Courtney and a dozen others. They owned the mines, the land, the buildings and the city: the aristocracy of the Witwatersrand, knighted with money and crowned with gold.

A week before Christmas, Hradsky, their unacknowledged but undoubted king, called them all to a meeting in one of the private lounges of Candy's Hotel.

'Who the hell does he think he is,' complained Jock Heyns, 'ordering us round like a bunch of kaffirs.'

'*Verdammt Juden*!' agreed Lochtkamper.

But they went, every last man of them, for whatever Hradsky did had the smell of money about it and they could no more resist it than a dog can resist the smell of a bitch in season.

Duff and Sean were the last to arrive and the room was already hazed with cigar smoke and tense with expectation. Hradsky sagged in one of the polished leather armchairs with Max sitting quietly beside him; his eyes flickered when Duff walked in but his expression never changed. When Duff and Sean had found chairs Max stood up. 'Gentlemen, Mr Hradsky has invited you here to consider a proposition.'

They leaned forward slightly in their chairs and there was a glitter in their eyes like hounds close upon the fox.

'From time to time it is necessary for men in your position to find capital to finance further ventures and to consolidate past gains; on the other hand those of us who have money lying idle will be seeking avenues for investment.' Max cleared his throat and looked at them with his sad brown eyes.

'Up to the present there has been no meeting-place for these mutual needs such as exists in the other centres of the financial world. Our nearest approach to it is the Stock Exchange at Kimberley which, I'm sure you will agree, is too far removed to be of practical use to us here at Johannesburg. Mr Hradsky has invited you here to consider the possibility of forming our own Exchange and, if you accept the idea, to elect a chairman and governing body.'

Max sat down and in the silence that followed they took up the idea, each one fitting it into his scheme of thinking, testing it with the question 'How will I benefit?'.

'*Ja*, it's dom fine idea.' Lochtkamper spoke first.

'Yes, it's what we need.'

'Count me in.'

While they schemed and bargained, setting the fees, the

place and the rules, Sean watched their faces. The faces of bitter men, happy men, quiet ones and big bull-roarers but all with one common feature – that greedy glitter in the eyes. It was midnight before they finished.

Max stood up again.

'Gentlemen, Mr Hradsky would like you to join him in a glass of champagne to celebrate the formation of our new enterprise.'

'This I can't believe; the last time he paid for drinks was back in 'sixty,' declared Duff. 'Quickly somebody – find a waiter before he changes his mind.'

Hradsky hooded his eyes to hide the hatred in them.

– 16 –

With its own Stock Exchange and bordel Johannesburg became a city. Even Kruger recognized it; he deposed the Diggers' Committee and sent in his own police force, sold monopolies for essential mining supplies to members of his family and Government, and set about revising his tax laws with special attention to mining profits. Despite Kruger's efforts to behead the gold-laying goose, the city grew, overflowed the original Government plots and spread brawling and blustering out into the surrounding veld.

Sean and Duff grew with it. Their way of life changed swiftly; their visits to the mines fell to a weekly inspection and they left it to their hired men. A steady river of gold poured down from the ridge to their offices on Eloff Street, for the men they hired were the best that money could find.

Their horizons closed in to encompass only the two panelled offices, the Victoria Rooms and the Exchange. Yet within that world Sean found a thrill that he had never dreamed existed. He had been oblivious to it during the first feverish months; he had been so absorbed in laying the foundations that he could spare no energy for enjoying or even noticing it.

Then one day he felt the first voluptuous tickle of it. He had sent to the bank for a land title document he needed, expecting it to be delivered by a junior clerk – but instead the sub-manager and a senior clerk filed respectfully into his office. It was an exquisite physical shock and it gave him a new awareness. He noticed the way men looked at him as he passed them on the street. He realized suddenly that over fifteen hundred human beings depended on him for their livelihood.

There was satisfaction in the way a path cleared for him and Duff as they crossed the floor of the Exchange each morning to take their places in the reserved leather armchairs of the members' lounge. When Duff and he leaned together and talked quietly before the trading began, even the other big fish watched them. Hradsky with his fierce eyes hooded by sleepy lids, Jock and Trevor Heyns, Karl Lochtkamper – any of them would have given a day's production from their mines to overhear those conversations.

'Buy!' said Sean.

'Buy! Buy! Buy!' clamoured the pack and the prices jumped as they hit them, then slumped back as they sucked their money away and put it to work elsewhere.

Then one March morning in 1886 the thrill became so acute it was almost an orgasm. Max left the chair at Norman Hradsky's side and crossed the lounge towards them. He stopped in front of them, lifted his sad eyes off the patterned carpet and almost apologetically proffered a loose sheaf of papers.

'Good morning, Mr Courtney. Good morning, Mr Charleywood. Mr Hradsky has asked me to bring this new share issue to your attention. Perhaps you would be interested in these reports, which are, of course, confidential, but he feels they are worthy of your support.'

You have power when you can force a man who hates you to ask for your favours. After the first advance by Hradsky they worked together often. Hradsky never acknowledged their existence by word or look. Each morning Duff called a cheerful greeting across the full width of the lounge, 'Hello, chatterbox,' or 'Sing for us, Norman.'

Hradsky's eyes would flicker and he would sag a little lower into his chair, but before the bell started the day's trading Max would stand up and come across to them, leaving his master staring into the empty fireplace. A few soft sentences exchanged and Max would walk back to Hradsky's side.

Their combined fortunes were irresistible: in one wild morning's trading alone they added another fifty thousand to their store of pounds.

An untaught boy handles his first rifle like a toy. Sean was twenty-two. The power he held was a more deadly weapon than any rifle, and much sweeter, more satisfying to use. It was a game at first with the Witwatersrand as a chessboard, men and gold for pieces. A word or a signature on a slip of paper would set the gold jingling and the men scampering. The consequences were remote and all that mattered was the score, the score chalked up in black figures on a bank statement. Then in that same March he was made to realize that a man wiped off the board could not be laid back in the box with as much compassion as a carved wooden knight.

Karl Lochtkamper, the German with a big laugh and a happy face, laid himself open. He needed money to develop a new property on the east end of the Rand; he borrowed and signed short-term notes on his loans, certain that he could extend them if necessary. He borrowed secretly from men he thought he could trust. He was vulnerable and the sharks smelt him out.

'Where is Lochtkamper getting his money?' asked Max.

'Do you know?' asked Sean.

'No, but I can guess.'

Then the next day Max came back to them again.

'He has eight notes out. Here is the list,' he whispered sadly. 'Mr Hradsky will buy the ones that have a cross against them. Can you handle the rest?'

'Yes,' said Sean.

They closed on Karl on the last day of the quarter; they called the loans and gave him twenty-four hours to meet them. Karl went to each of the three banks in turn.

'I'm sorry, Mr Lochtkamper, we have loaned over our budget for this quarter.'

'Mr Hradsky is holding your notes – I'm sorry.'

'I'm sorry, Mr Lochtkamper, Mr Charleywood is one of our directors.'

Karl Lochtkamper rode back to the Exchange. He walked across the floor and into the lounge for the last time. He stood in the centre of the big room, his face grey, his voice bitter and broken.

'Let Jesus have this much mercy on you when your time comes. Friends! My friends! Sean, how many times haf we drunk together? And you, Duff, was it yesterday you shook my hand?'

Then he went back across the floor, out through the doors. His suite in the Great North Hotel wasn't fifty yards from the Exchange. In the members' lounge they heard the pistol shot quite clearly.

That night Duff and Sean got drunk together in the Victoria rooms.

'Why did he have to do it? Why did he have to kill himself?'

'He didn't,' answered Duff. 'He was a quitter.'

'If I'd known he was going to do that – my God, if only I'd known.'

'Damn it, man, he took a chance and lost – it's not our fault. He would have done the same to us.'

'I don't like this – it's dirty. Let's get out, Duff.'

'Someone gets knocked down in the rush and you want to cry "enough!"'

'It's different now somehow, it wasn't like this at the start.'

'Yes, and it'll be different in the morning. Come on, laddie, I know what you need.'

'Where are we going?'

'To the Opera House.'

'What will Candy say?'

'Candy doesn't have to know.'

Duff was right; it was different in the morning. There was the usual hurly-burly of work at the office and some tense action at the Exchange. He thought about Karl only once during the day and somehow it didn't seem to matter so much. They sent him a nice wreath.

He had faced the reality of the game he was playing. He had considered the alternative which was to get out with the fortune he had already made; but to do that would mean giving up the power he held. The addiction was already seated too deeply, he could not deny it. So his subconscious opened, sucked in his conscience and swallowed it deep down into its gut. He could feel it struggling there sometimes, but the longer it stayed swallowed the more feeble those struggles became. Duff comforted him: Duff's words were like a gastric juice that helped to digest that lump in the gut and he had not yet learned that what Duff said and what Duff did were not necessarily what Duff believed.

Play the game without mercy, play to win.

– 17 –

Duff stood with his back to the fireplace in Sean's office smoking a cheroot while they waited for the carriage to take them up to the Exchange. The fire behind him silhouetted his slimly tapered legs with the calves encased in polished black leather. He still wore his top coat, for the winter morning was cold. It fell open at his throat to show a diamond that sparkled and glowed in his cravat.

'. . . you get used to a woman somehow,' he was saying. 'I've known Candy four years now and yet it seems I've been with her all my life.'

'She's a fine girl,' Sean agreed absently as he dipped his pen and scribbled his signature on the document in front of him.

'I'm thirty-five now,' Duff went on. 'If I'm ever to have a son of my own . . .'

Sean laid down the pen deliberately and looked up at him; he was starting to grin.

'The man said to me once "They take you into their soft little minds" and again he said "They don't share, they possess". Is this a new tune I hear?'

Duff shifted uneasily from one foot to the other.

'Things change,' he defended himself. 'I'm thirty-five . . .'

'You're repeating yourself,' Sean accused and Duff smiled weakly.

'Well, the truth is . . .'

He never finished the sentence; hooves beat urgently in the street outside and both their faces swung in the direction of the window.

'Big hurry!' said Sean coming quickly to his feet. 'Big trouble!' He crossed to the window. 'It's Curtis, and by his face it's not good news he brings.'

There were voices outside the door raised in agitation and the quick rush of feet, then Timothy Curtis burst into the room without knocking. He wore a miner's overall and splattered gumboots. 'We've hit a mud rush on the ninth level.'

'How bad?' Duff snapped.

'Bad enough – it's flooded right back to number eight.'

'Jesus, that will take two months at least to clear,' Sean exclaimed. 'Does anyone else in town know – have you told anyone?'

'I came straight here – Cronje and five men were up at the face when it blew.'

'Get back there immediately,' ordered Sean, 'but ride quietly, we don't want the whole world to know there's trouble. Don't let a soul off the property. We must have time to sell out.'

'Yes, Mr Courtney.' Curtis hesitated. 'Cronje and five others were hit by the rush. Shall I send word to their wives?'

'Can't you understand English? I don't want a whisper of this to get out before ten o'clock. We've got to have time.'

'But, Mr Courtney—' Curtis was appalled. He stood staring at Sean and Sean felt the sick little stirring of guilt. Six men drowned in treacle-thick mud . . . He made an irresolute gesture with his hands.

'We can't—' He stopped and Duff cut in.

'They're dead now, and they'll be just as dead when we tell their wives at ten o'clock. Get going, Curtis.'

They sold their shares in the Little Sister within an hour of the start of trading and a week later they bought them back at half the price. Two months later the Little Sister was back on full production again.

– 18 –

They split their land at Orange Grove into plots and sold them, all but a hundred acres and on that they started building a house. Into the designing of it they poured their combined energy and imagination. With money Duff seduced the horticulturist of the Capetown Botanical Gardens and brought him up by express coach. They showed him the land.

'Make me a garden,' said Duff.

'The whole hundred acres?'

'Yes.'

'It'll cost a pretty penny.'

'That is no problem.'

The carpets came from Persia, the wood from the Knysna forests and the marble from Italy. On the gates at the entrance to the main drive they engraved the words 'At Xanadu did Kublai Khan a stately pleasure dome decree'. As the gardener had predicted, it all cost a pretty penny. Each afternoon when the Exchange closed they would drive up together and watch the builders at work. One day Candy came with them and they showed it off to her like two small boys.

'This will be the ballroom.' Sean bowed to her. 'May I have the pleasure of this dance?'

'Thank you, sir.' She curtsied, then swept away on his arm across the unsanded boards.

'This will be the staircase,' Duff told her, 'marble – black and white marble – and there on the main landing in a glass case will be Hradsky's head, beautifully mounted with an apple in his mouth.'

They climbed laughing up the rough concrete ramp.

'This is Sean's room – the bed is being made of oak,

thick oak to withstand punishment.' They trooped with linked arms down the passage.

'And this is my room – I was thinking of a solid gold bath but the builder says it's too heavy and Sean says it's too vulgar. Look at that view; from here you can see out across the whole valley. I could lie in bed in the mornings and read the prices on the Exchange floor with a telescope.'

'It's lovely,' Candy said dreamily.

'You like it?'

'Oh, yes.'

'It could be your room too.'

Candy started to blush and then her face tightened with annoyance. 'He was right – you are vulgar.'

She started for the door and Sean fumbled for his cigars to cover his embarrassment. With two quick steps Duff caught her and turned her to face him. 'You sweet idiot, that was a proposal.'

'Let me go.' Near to tears she twisted in his hands. 'I don't think you're funny.'

'Candy – I'm serious. Will you marry me?'

The cigar dropped out of Sean's mouth but he caught it before it hit the ground. Candy was standing very still, her eyes fastened on Duff's face.

'Yes or no – will you marry me?'

She nodded once slowly and then twice very fast.

Duff looked at Sean over his shoulder. 'Leave us, laddie.'

On the way back to town Candy had regained her voice. She chattered happily and Duff answered her with his lopsided grin. Sean hunched morosely in one corner of the carriage. His cigar was burning unevenly and he threw it out of the window.

'You'll let me keep the Victoria rooms, I hope, Candy.'

There was a silence.

'What do you mean?' asked Duff.

'Two's company,' Sean answered.

'Oh, no,' Candy exclaimed.

'It's your house as well.' Duff spoke sharply.

'I give it to you – a wedding present.'

'Oh, shut up,' Duff grinned, 'it's big enough for all of us.'

Candy crossed quickly to Sean's seat and put her hand on his shoulder.

'Please – we've been together a long time. We'd be lonely without you.'

Sean grunted.

'Please!'

'He'll come,' said Duff.

'Please.'

'Oh, well—' Sean frowned ungraciously.

– 19 –

They went racing at Milnerton. Candy with a hat full of ostrich feathers, Sean and Duff with pearl grey toppers and gold heads on their canes.

'You can pay for your wedding gown by putting fifty guineas on Trade Wind! She can't lose—' Duff told Candy.

'What about Mr Hradsky's new filly? I've heard she's a good bet,' Candy asked and Duff frowned.

'You want to go over to the enemy?'

'I thought you and Hradsky were almost partners.' Candy twirled her parasol. 'From the rumours I've heard you work with him all the time.'

Mbejane slowed the carriage as they ran into the crush of pedestrians and coaches outside the Turf Club gates.

'Well you've heard wrong both times. His Sun Dancer will never hold Trade Wind over the distance, she's bred too light in the legs. Frenchified with Huguenot blood; she'll fade within the mile. And as far as Hradsky being our partner, we throw him an occasional bone. Isn't that right, Sean?'

Sean was watching Mbejane's back. The Zulu, in loin clothes only and his spears laid carefully on the boards at his feet, was handling the horses with an easy familiarity. They cocked their ears back to catch his voice, deep and soft, as he talked to them.

'Isn't that right, Sean?' Duff repeated.

'Of course,' agreed Sean vaguely. 'You know – I think I'll get Mbejane a livery. He looks out of place in those skins.'

'Well, some of the other horses from the same stud were stayers. Sun Honey won the Cape Derby twice and Eclipse showed up the English stock in the Metropolitan Handicap last year,' Candy argued.

'Huh,' Duff smiled his superiority, 'well, you can take my word for it that Trade Wind will walk the main race today and he'll be back in his stable before Sun Dancer sees the finishing post.'

'Maroon and gold – the same as our racing colours,' Sean muttered thoughtfully. 'That would go very well with his black skin, perhaps a turban with an ostrich feather in it.'

'What the hell are you talking about?' complained Duff.

'Mbejane's livery.'

They left the carriage in the reserved area and went through to the members' grandstand, Candy sailing prettily between her escorts.

'Well, Duff, we've got the nicest looking woman here today.'

'Thank you.' Candy smiled up at Sean.

'Is that why you keep trying to look down the front of her dress?' challenged Duff.

'You filthy-minded beast.' Sean was shocked.

'Don't deny, it,' Candy teased, 'but I find it very flattering – you're welcome.'

They moved through the throng of butterfly-coloured dresses and stiffly-suited men. A ripple of greetings moved with them.

'Morning, Mr Courtney.' The accent was on the 'Mister'. 'How's your Trade Wind for the big race?'

'Put your pants on him.'

'Hello, Duff, congratulations on your engagement.'

'Thanks, Jock, it's time you took the plunge as well.'

They were rich, they were young, they were handsome and all the world admired them. Sean felt good, with a pretty girl on his arm and a friend walking beside him.

'There's Hradsky – let's go across and engage in a little hog-baiting,' Duff suggested.

'Why do you hate him so much?' Candy asked softly.

'Look at him and answer your own question. Have you ever seen anything more pompous, joyless and unlovable?'

'Oh, leave him alone, Duff, don't spoil the day. Let's go down to the paddock.'

'Come on!' Duff steered them across to where Hradsky and Max were standing alone by the rail of the track.

'Salome, Norman, and peace to you also, Maximilian.' Hradsky nodded and Max murmured sadly; his lashes touched his cheeks as he blinked.

'I noticed you two chatting away and thought I would come across and listen to your stimulating repartee.'

He received no answer and went on. 'I saw your new filly exercising on the practice track yesterday evening and I said to myself, Norman's got a girl friend – that's what it is – he's bought a hack for his lady. But now they tell me you are going to race her. Oh, Norman, I wish you'd consult me before you do these silly things. You're an impetuous little devil at times.'

'Mr Hradsky is confident that Sun Dancer will make a reasonable showing today,' Max murmured.

'I was about to offer you a side bet, but being a naturally

kind-hearted person, I feel it would be taking an unfair advantage.'

A small crowd had gathered round them listening with anticipation. Candy tugged gently at Duff's elbow trying to lead him away.

'I thought five hundred guineas would be acceptable to Norman.' Duff shrugged. 'But let's forget it.'

Hradsky made a fierce little sign with his hands and Max interpreted smoothly. 'Mr Hradsky suggests a thousand.'

'Rash, Norman, extremely rash.' Duff sighed. 'But I suppose I must accommodate you.'

They walked down to the refreshment pavilion. Candy was quiet awhile, then she said, 'An enemy like Mr Hradsky is a luxury that even you two gods can't afford. Why don't you leave him alone?'

'It's a hobby of Duff's,' explained Sean as they found seats at one of the tables. 'Waiter – bring us a bottle of Pol Roger.'

Before the big race they went down to the paddock. A steward opened the wicket gate for them and they passed into the ring of circling horses. A gnome in silk of maroon and gold came to meet them and touched his cap then stood awkwardly, fingering his whip.

'He looks good this morning, sir.' The little man nodded at Trade Wind. There was a dark patch of sweat on the horse's shoulder and he mouthed the snaffle, lifting his feet delicately. Once he snorted and rolled his eyes in mock terror.

'He's got an edge on him, sir, eager kind of – if you follow me.'

'I want you to win, Harry,' said Duff.

'So do I, sir, I'll do my best.'

'There's a thousand guineas for you if you do.'

'A thousand—' the jockey repeated on an outgoing breath.

Duff looked across to where Hradsky and Max were standing talking to their trainer. He caught Hradsky's eye, glanced significantly at Hradsky's honey-coloured filly and shook his head sympathetically.

'Win for me, Harry,' he said softly.

'That I will, sir!'

The groom led the big stallion across to them and Sean flicked the jockey up into the saddle.

'Good luck.'

Harry settled his cap and gathered up the reins; he winked at Sean, his hobgoblin face wrinkling in a grin.

'There's no better luck than a thousand guineas, sir, if you follow me.'

'Come on.' Duff caught Candy's arm. 'Let's get a place at the rail.'

They hustled her out of the paddock and across the members' enclosure. The rail was crowded but a place opened for them respectfully and no one jostled them.

'I can't understand you two,' Candy laughed breathlessly. 'You make an extravagant bet, then you fix it so you can get nothing even if you win.'

'Money's not the problem,' Duff assured her.

'He won that much from me at Klabejas last night,' Sean commented. 'If Trade Wind beats the filly his prize will be the look on Hradsky's face – the loss of a thousand guineas will hurt him like a kick between the legs.'

The horses came parading past, stepping high next to the grooms who held them, then they turned free and cantered back, dancing sideways, throwing their heads, shining in the sunlight like the bright silk upon their backs. They moved away round the curve of the track.

The crowd rustled with excitement, a bookmaker's voice carried over the buzz.

'Twenty-to-one bar two. Sun Dancer at fives. Trade Wind even money.'

Duff showed his teeth as he smiled. 'That's right, you tell the people.'

Candy twisted her gloves nervously and looked up at Sean.

'You there in the grandstand – can you see what they're doing?'

'They're in line now, moving up together – it looks as though they'll get away first time,' Sean told her without taking his binoculars from his eyes. 'Yes, there they go – they're away!'

'Tell me, tell me,' commanded Candy, pounding Sean's shoulder.

'Harry's showing in front already – can you see the filly, Duff?'

'I saw a flash of green in the pack – yes, there she is lying sixth or seventh.'

'What horse is that next to Trade Wind?'

'That's Hamilton's gelding, don't worry about him, he won't last to the turn.'

The frieze of horses, their heads going like hammers and the dust lifting pale and thin behind them, were framed by the guide rail and the white mine dumps beyond them. Like a string of dark beads they moved up the back stretch and then bunched in the straight.

'Trade Wind's still there – I think he's making ground – the gelding's finished and no sign of the filly yet.'

'Yes! There she is, Duff, wide on the outside. She's moving up.'

'Come on, my darling—' Duff half whispered. 'Let's see you foot it now.'

'She's clear of the pack – she's coming up, Duff, she's coming up fast,' Sean warned.

'Come on, Trade Wind, hold her off,' Duff pleaded. 'Keep her there, boy.'

The pounding of the hooves reached them now, a sound

like distant surf, but rising sharply. The colours showed, emerald green above a honey skin and maroon and gold leading on the bay.

'Trade Wind – come on Trade Wind,' shrieked Candy. Her hat flopped over her eyes as she hopped; she ripped it off impatiently and her hair tumbled to her shoulders.

'She's catching him, Duff!'

'Give him the whip, Harry, for Christ's sake – the whip, man.'

The hoof beats crescendoed, thundered up to them, then passed. The filly's nose was at Harry's boot, creeping steadily forward, now level with Trade Wind's heaving shoulder.

'The whip, God damn you,' screamed Duff, 'give him the whip.'

Harry's right arm moved, fast as a mamba – crack, crack; they heard the whip above the howling crowd, above the drumming of hooves and the bay jumped at its sting. Like a pair in harness the two horses swept over the finishing line.

'Who won?' Candy asked as though she were in pain.

'I couldn't see, damn it,' Duff answered.

'Nor could I—' Sean took out his handkerchief and wiped his forehead. 'That didn't do my heart any good – as Francois would say. Have a cigar, Duff.'

'Thanks – I need one.'

Everyone in the crowd was turned to face the board above the judges' box and an uneasy silence held them.

'Why do they take such a long time to make up their minds?' complained Candy. 'I'm so upset that I can only last a minute before I visit the Ladies' Room.'

'The numbers are going up,' shouted Sean.

'Who is it?' Candy jumped to try and see over the heads of the crowd then stopped hurriedly with an expression of alarm on her face.

'Number Sixteen,' bellowed Duff and Sean together, 'it's Trade Wind!'

Sean punched Duff in the chest and Duff leaned over and snapped Sean's cigar in half. Then they caught Candy between them and hugged her. She let out a careful shriek and fought her way out of their arms. 'Excuse me,' she said and fled.

'Let me buy you a drink.' Sean lit the mutilated stump of his cigar.

'No, it's my honour, I insist.' Duff took his arm and they walked with big satisfied grins towards the pavilion. Hradsky was sitting at one of the tables with Max. Duff walked up behind him, lifted his top hat off his head with one hand and with the other ruffled Hradsky's few remaining hairs.

'Never mind, Norman, you can't win all the time.'

Hradsky turned slowly. He retrieved his hat and smoothed back his hair, his eyes glittered yellow.

'He's going to talk,' whispered Duff excitedly.

'I agree with you, Mr Charleywood, you can't win all the time,' said Norman Hradsky. It came out quite clearly with only a small catch on the 'c's' – they were always difficult letters for him. He stood up, put his hat back on his head and walked away.

'I will have a cheque delivered to your office early on Monday morning,' Max told them quietly without taking his eyes off the table. Then he stood up and followed Hradsky.

– 20 –

Sean came through from the bathroom, his beard in wild disorder and a bath-towel round his waist.

> 'The famous Duke of York
> He had ten thousand men
> He marched them up to the top of the hill
> And he marched them down again.'

He sang as he poured bay rum from a cut-glass bottle into his cupped hands and rubbed it into his hair. Duff sat in one of the gilt chairs watching him. Sean combed his hair carefully then smiled at himself in the mirror.

'You magnificent creature,' Sean told his reflection.

'You're getting fat,' Duff grunted.

Sean looked hurt. 'It's muscle.'

'You've got a backside on you like a hippopotamus.'

Sean removed his towel and turned his back to the mirror; he surveyed it over his shoulder.

'I need a heavy hammer to drive a long nail,' he protested.

'Oh, no,' groaned Duff. 'Your wit at this time of the morning is like pork for breakfast, heavy on the stomach.'

Sean took a silk shirt out of his drawer, held it like a toreador's cape, made two passes and swirled it onto his back with a half veronica.

'*Olé*!' applauded Duff wryly. Sean pulled on his trousers and sat to fit his boots.

'You're in a nice mood this morning,' he told Duff.

'I've just come through an emotional hurricane!'

'What's the trouble?'

'Candy wants a church wedding.'

'Is that bad?'

'Well, it's not good.'

'Why?'

'Is your memory so short?'

'Oh, you mean your other wife.'

'That's right, my other wife.'

'Have you told Candy about her?'

'Good God, no.' Duff looked horrified.

'Yes, I see your problem – what about Candy's husband? Doesn't that even the score between you?'

'No, he has gone to his reward.'

'Well, that's convenient. Does anyone else know you're married already?' Duff shook his head.

'What about Francois?'

'No, I never told him.'

'Well, what's your problem – take her down to the church and marry her.'

Duff looked uncomfortable.

'I don't mind marrying a second time in a magistrate's court, it would only be a couple of old Dutchmen I'd be cheating, but to go into a church—' Duff shook his head.

'I'd be the only one who'd know,' said Sean.

'You and the headman.'

'Duff,' Sean beamed at him. 'Duff, my boy, you have scruples – this is amazing!'

Duff squirmed a little in his chair.

'Let me think.' Sean held his forehead dramatically. 'Yes, yes, it's coming to me – that's it.'

'Come on, tell me.' Duff sat on the edge of his chair.

'Go to Candy and tell her it's all fixed, not only are you prepared to marry her in a church but you're even going to build your own church.'

'That's wonderful,' Duff murmured sarcastically, 'that's the way out of my difficulties all right.'

'Let me finish.' Sean started filling his silver cigar case. 'You also tell her that you want a civil ceremony as well – I believe that's what royalty do. Tell her that, it should win her over.'

'I still don't follow you.'

'Then you build your own chapel up at Xanadu – we can find a distinguished-looking character, dress him up in a dog collar and teach him the right words. That keeps Candy happy. Immediately after the service the priest takes the coach for Capetown. You take Candy down to the magistrate's office and that keeps you happy.'

Duff looked stunned then slowly his face broke into a great happy smile. 'Genius – pure inspired genius.'

Sean buttoned his waistcoat. 'Think nothing of it. And now if you'll excuse me I'll go and do some work – one of us has to make sufficient to allow you to indulge these strange fancies of yours.'

Sean shrugged on his coat, picked up his cane and swung it. The gold head gave it a balance like a handmade shotgun. The silk next to his skin and the halo of bay rum round his head made him feel good.

He went down the stairs. Mbejane had the carriage waiting for him in the Hotel yard. The body tilted slightly at Sean's weight and the leather upholstery welcomed him with a yielding softness. He lit his first cigar of the day and Mbejane smiled at him.

'I see you, Nkosi.'

'I see you also, Mbejane, what is that lump on the side of your head?'

'Nkosi, I was a little drunk, otherwise that ape of Basuto would never have touched me with his fighting stick.'

Mbejane rolled the carriage smoothly out of the yard and into the street.

'What were you fighting about?'

Mbejane shrugged. 'Must a man have a reason to fight?'

'It is usual.'

'It is in my memory that there was a woman,' said Mbejane.

'That is also usual – who won this fight?'

'The man bled a little, his friends took him away. The woman, when I left, was smiling in her sleep.'

Sean laughed, then ran his eyes over the undulating plain of Mbejane's bare back. It was definitely not in keeping. He hoped his secretary had remembered to speak to the tailor. They pulled up in front of his offices. One of his clerks hurried down off the veranda and opened the door of the carriage.

'Good morning, Mr Courtney.'

Sean went up the stairs with his clerk running ahead of him like a hunting dog.

'Good morning, Mr Courtney,' another polite chorus from the row of desks in the main office. Sean waved his cane at them and went through into his own office. His portrait leered at him from above the fireplace and he winked at it.

'What have we this morning, Johnson?'

'These requisitions, sir, and the pay cheques, sir, and development reports from the engineers, sir, and . . .'

Johnson was a greasy-haired little man in a greasy-looking alpaca coat; with each 'sir' he made a greasy little bow. He was efficient so Sean hired him, but that didn't mean he liked him.

'You got a stomach ache, Johnson?'

'No, sir.'

'Well, for God's sake, stand up straight, man.'

Johnson shot to attention.

'Now let's have them one at a time.'

Sean dropped into his chair. At this time of the day came the grind. He hated the paper work and so he tackled it with grim concentration, making random checks on the long rows of figures, trying to associate names with faces and querying requisitions that appeared exorbitant until finally he wrote his signature between the last of Johnson's carefully pencilled crosses and threw his pen onto the desk.

'What else is there?'

'Meeting with Mr Maxwell from the Bank at twelve-thirty, sir.'

'And then?'

'The agent for Brooke Bros. at one, and immediately after that Mr MacDougal, sir, then you're expected up at the Candy Deep mine.'

'Thank you, Johnson, I'll be at the Exchange as usual this morning if anything out of the ordinary comes up.'

'Very good, Mr Courtney. Just one other thing.' Johnson pointed at the brown paper parcel on the couch across the room. 'From your tailor.'

'Ah!' Sean smiled. 'Send my servant in here.' He walked across and opened the parcel. Within a few minutes Mbejane filled the doorway.

'Nkosi?'

'Mbejane – your new uniform.' Sean pointed at the clothes laid out on the couch. Mbejane's eyes switched to the gold and maroon finery, his expression suddenly dead.

'Put it on – come on, let's see how you look.'

Mbejane crossed to the couch and picked up the jacket. 'These are for me?'

'Yes, come on, put it on.' Sean laughed.

Mbejane hesitated, then slowly he loosened his loin cloth and let it drop. Sean watched him impatiently as he buttoned on the jacket and pantaloons, then he walked in a critical circle around the Zulu.

'Not bad,' he muttered, and then in Zulu, 'Is it not beautiful?'

Mbejane wriggled his shoulders against the unfamiliar feel of the cloth and said nothing.

'Well, Mbejane, do you like it?'

'When I was a child I went with my father to trade cattle at Port Natal. There was a man who went about the town with a monkey on a chair, the monkey danced and the people laughed and threw money to it. That monkey had such a suit as this. Nkosi, I do not think he was a very happy monkey.'

The smile slipped off Sean's face. 'You would rather wear your skins?'

'What I wear is the dress of a warrior of Zululand.'

There was still no expression on Mbejane's face. Sean opened his mouth to argue with him but before he could speak he lost his temper.

'You'll wear that uniform,' he shouted. 'You'll wear what I tell you to wear and you'll do it with a smile, do you hear me?'

'Nkosi, I hear you.' Mbejane picked up his loin cloth of leopard tails and left the office. When Sean went out to the carriage Mbejane was sitting on the driver's seat in his new livery. All the way to the Exchange his back was stiff with protest and neither of them spoke. Sean glared at the doorman of the Exchange, drank four brandies during the morning, rode back to his office again at noon scowling at Mbejane's still protesting back, shouted at Johnson, snapped at the bank manager, routed the representative from Brooke Bros. and drove out to the Candy Deep in a high old rage. But Mbejane's silence was impenetrable and Sean couldn't re-open the argument without sacrifice of pride. He burst into the new administrative building of the Candy Deep and threw the staff into confusion.

'Where's Mr du Toit?' he roared.

'He's down the Number Three shaft, Mr Courtney.'

'What the hell is he doing down there? He's supposed to be waiting for me here.'

'He didn't expect you for another hour, sir.'

'Well, get me some overalls and a mining helmet, don't just stand there.'

He clapped the tin hat on his head and stamped his heavy gumboots across to the Number Three shaft. The skip dropped him smoothly five hundred feet into the earth and he climbed out at the tenth level.

'Where's Mr du Toit?' he demanded of the shift boss at the lift station.

'He's up at the face, sir.'

The floor of the drive was rough and muddy; his gumboots squelched as he set off down the tunnel. His carbide lamp lit the uneven rock walls with a flat white light and he felt himself starting to sweat. Two natives pushing a cocopan back along the railway lines forced him to flatten himself against one wall to allow them to pass and while he waited he felt inside his overalls for his cigar case. As he pulled it out it slipped from his hand and plunked into the mud. The cocopan was gone by that time so he stooped to pick up the case. His ear came within an inch of the wall and a puzzled expression replaced his frown of annoyance. The rock was squeaking. He laid his ear against it. It sounded like someone grinding his teeth. He listened to it for a while trying to guess the cause; it wasn't the echo of shovels or drills, it wasn't water. He walked another thirty yards or so down the drive and listened again. Not so loud here but now the grinding noise was punctuated with an occasional metallic snap like the breaking of a knife blade. Strange; very strange; he had never heard anything like it before. He walked on down the drive, his bad mood lost in his preoccupation with this new problem. Before he reached the face he met Francois.

'Hello, Mr Courtney.' Sean had long since given up

trying to stop Francois calling him that. '*Gott*, I'm sorry I wasn't there to meet you. I thought you were coming at three.'

'That's all right, Francois, how are you?'

'My rheumatism's been giving me blazes, Mr Courtney, but otherwise I'm all right. How's Mr Charleywood?'

'He's fine.' Sean couldn't restrain his curiosity any longer. 'Tell me something, Franz, just now I put my ear against the wall of the drive and I heard an odd noise, I couldn't make out what it was.'

'What kind of noise?'

'A sort of grinding, like – like . . .' Sean searched for words to describe it, 'like two pieces of glass being rubbed together.'

Francois's eyes flew wide open and then began to bulge, the colour of his face changed to grey and he caught Sean's arm.

'Where?'

'Back along the drive.'

The breath jammed in Francois's throat and he struggled to speak through it, shaking Sean's arm desperately.

'Cave-in!' he croaked. 'Cave-in, man!'

He started to run but Sean grabbed him. Francois struggled wildly.

'Francois, how many men up at the face?'

'Cave-in.' Francois's voice was now hysterically shrill. 'Cave-in.' He broke Sean's grip and raced away towards the lift station, the mud flying from his gumboots. His terror infected Sean and he ran a dozen paces after Francois before he stopped himself. For precious seconds he wavered with fear slithering round like a reptile in his stomach; go back to call the others and perhaps die with them or follow Francois and live. Then the fear in his belly found a mate, a thing just as slimy and cold; its name was shame, and shame it was that drove him back towards the face. There were five blacks and a white man there, bare-chested and shiny with sweat in the heat. Sean shouted those two words at them and they reacted the way bathers do when someone on the beach shouts 'shark'. The same moment of paralysed horror, then the panic. They came stampeding back along the tunnel. Sean ran with them, the mud sucked at his heavy boots and his legs were weak with easy living and riding in carriages. One by one the others passed him.

'Wait for me,' he wanted to scream. 'Wait for me.' He slipped on the greasy footing, scraping his shoulder on the rough wall as he fell, and dragged himself up again, mud plastered in his beard, the blood humming in his ears. Alone now he blundered on down the tunnel. With a crack like a rifle shot one of the thick shoring timbers broke under the pressure of the moving rock and dust smoked from the roof of the tunnel in front of him. He staggered on and all around him the earth was talking, groaning, protesting, with little muffled shrieks. The timbers joined in again, crackling and snapping, and as slowly as a theatre curtain the rock sagged down from above him. The tunnel was thick with dust that smothered the beam of his lamp and rasped his throat. He knew then that he wasn't going to make it but he ran on with the loose rock starting to fall about him. A lump hit his mining helmet and jarred him so that he nearly fell. Blinded by the swirling dust fog he crashed at full run into the abandoned cocopan that blocked the tunnel, he sprawled over the metal body of the trolley with his thighs bruised from the collision.

'Now I'm finished,' he thought, but instinctively he pulled himself up and started to grope his way around the cocopan to continue his flight. With a roar the tunnel in front of him collapsed. He dropped on his knees and crawled between the wheels of the cocopan, wriggling under the sturdy steel body just an instant before the roof above him collapsed also. The noise of the fall around him seemed to last for ever, but then it was over and the rustling and grating of the rock as it settled down was almost silence in comparison. His lamp was lost and the darkness pressed as heavily on him as the earth squeezed down on his tiny shelter. The air was solid with dust and he coughed; he coughed until his chest ached and he tasted salty blood in his mouth. There was hardly room to move, the steel body of the trolley was six inches above him, but he struggled until he managed to open the front of his overalls and tear a piece off the tail of his shirt. He held the silk like a surgical mask across his mouth and nose. It strained the dust out of the air so he could breathe. The dust settled; his coughing slowed and finally stopped. He felt surprise that he was still alive and cautiously he started exploring. He tried to straighten out his legs but his feet touched rock. He felt with his hands, six inches of head room and perhaps twelve inches on either side, warm mud underneath him and rock and steel all around. He took off his helmet and used it as a pillow. He was in a steel coffin buried five hundred feet deep. He felt the first flutter of panic. 'Keep your mind busy, think of something, think of anything but the rock around you, count your assets,' he told himself. He started to search his pockets, moving with difficulty in the cramped space.

'One silver cigar case with two Havanas.' He laid it down next to him.

'One box of matches, wet.' He placed it on top of the case.

'One pocket watch.'

'One handkerchief, Irish linen, monogrammed.'

'One comb, tortoiseshell – a man is judged by his appearance.' He started to comb his beard but found immediately that though this occupied his hands it left his mind free. He put the comb down next to his matches.

'Twenty-five pounds in gold sovereigns—' He counted

them carefully, 'yes, twenty-five. I shall order a bottle of good champagne.' The dust was chalky in his mouth so he went on hurriedly, 'And a Malay girl from the Opera. No, why be mean – ten Malay girls. I'll have them dance for me, that'll pass the time. I'll promise them a sovereign each to bolster their enthusiasm.'

He continued the search, but there was nothing else. 'Gumboots, socks, well-cut trousers, shirt torn I'm afraid, overalls, a tin hat, and that's all.'

With his possessions laid out carefully beside him and his cell explored he had to start thinking. First he thought about his thirst. The mud in which he lay was too thick to yield water. He tried straining it through his shirt without success, and then he thought about air. It seemed quite fresh and he decided that sufficient was filtering in from the loosely packed rock around him to keep him alive.

To keep him alive – alive until the thirst killed. Until he died curled up like a foetus in the warm womb of the earth. He laughed, a worm in a dark warm womb. He laughed again and recognized it as the beginnings of panic, he thrust his fist into his mouth to stop himself, biting down hard on his knuckles. It was very quiet, the rock had stopped moving.

'How long will it take? Tell me, Doctor. How long have I got?'

'Well, you are sweating. You'll lose moisture quite rapidly. I'd say about four days,' he answered himself.

'What about hunger, Doctor?'

'Oh, no, don't worry about that, you'll be hungry, of course, but the thirst will kill you.'

'And typhoid, or is it typhus, I can never remember. What about that, Doctor?'

'If there were dead men trapped in here with you there'd be a good chance, but you're alone, you know.'

'Do you think I'll go mad, Doctor, not immediately, of course, but in a few days?'

'Yes, you'll go mad.'

'I've never been mad before, not that I know of anyway, but I think it will help to go mad now, don't you?'

'If you mean, will it make it easier, well, I don't know.'

'Ah! now you're being obscure – but I follow you. You mean in that sleep of madness what dreams will come? You mean, will madness be more real than reality? You mean, will dying mad be worse than dying thirsty? But then I may beat the madness. This cocopan might buckle under the strain, after all there must be thousands of tons of rock bearing down on it. That's quite clever, you know, Doctor; as a medical man you should appreciate it. Mother Earth was saved but, alas, the child was stillborn, she bore down too hard.' Sean had spoken aloud, and now he felt foolish. He picked up a piece of stone and tapped the cocopan with it.

'It sounds firm enough. A most pleasing noise, really.' He beat harder on the metal body – one, two, three, one, two, three – then dropped the stone. Soft as an echo, distant as the moon, he heard his taps repeated. His whole body stiffened at the sound, and he started to shiver with excitement. He snatched up the stone: three times he rapped, and three times the answer came back to him.

'They heard me, sweet merciful Christ, they heard me.' He laughed breathlessly. 'Dear Mother Earth, don't bear down, please don't bear down. Just be patient. Wait a few days and by Caesarean they'll take this child out of your womb.'

Mbejane waited until Sean disappeared down the Number Three shaft before he took off his new jacket. He folded it carefully on the driver's seat next to him. He sat and enjoyed the feel of the sun on his skin for a while, then he climbed off the carriage and went to the horses. He took them one at a time to the trough for water then returned them to their harnesses, buckling them in loosely. He picked up his spears from the footboard and moved across to a patch of short grass next to the administrative building. He sat down and went to work on the blade, humming softly to himself as he honed. At last he ran an expert thumb along each edge, grunted, shaved a few hairs off his forearm, smiled contentedly and laid his spears beside him in the grass. He lay back and the sun warmed him to sleep.

The shouting woke him. He sat up and automatically checked the height of the sun. He had slept an hour or more. Duff was shouting and Francois, mud-splattered and frightened-looking, was answering him. They were standing together in front of the administrative building. Duff's horse was sweating. Mbejane stood up and went across to them; he listened closely, trying to understand their staccato voices. They went too fast for him, but something was wrong, that much he knew.

'It's caved in almost to the Number Ten lift station,' Francois said.

'You left him in there,' accused Duff.

'I thought he was following me, but he turned back.'

'What for – why did he turn back?'

'To call the others—'

'Have you started clearing the drive?'

'No, I was waiting for you.'

'You stupid bloody idiot, he might be alive in there . . . every minute is vital.'

'But he hasn't a chance, Mr Charleywood, he must be dead.'

'Shut up, damn you.'

Duff swung away from him and started running towards

the shaft. There was a crowd gathered beneath the high steel structure of the head gear, and suddenly Mbejane knew it was Sean. He caught up with Duff before he reached the shaft.

'Is it the Nkosi?'

'Yes.'

'What has happened?'

'The rock has fallen on him.'

Mbejane pushed his way into the skip next to Duff and neither of them spoke again until they reached the tenth level. They went down the drive, only a short way before they reached the end. There were men there with crowbars and shovels standing undecided, waiting for orders, and Mbejane shouldered a path through them. He and Duff stood together in front of the new wall of broken rock that sealed the tunnel, and the silence went on and on. Then Duff turned on the white shift-boss.

'Were you at the face?'

'Yes.'

'He went back to call you, didn't he?'

'Yes.'

'And you left him there?'

The man couldn't look at Duff.

'I thought he was following us,' he muttered.

'You thought only of your own miserable skin,' Duff told him, 'you filthy little coward, you slimy yellow bastard, you . . .'

Mbejane caught Duff's arm and Duff stopped his tirade. They all heard it then – clink, clink, clink.

'It's him – it must be him,' whispered Duff, 'he's alive!' He snatched a crowbar from one of the natives and knocked against the side of the tunnel. They waited, their breathing the only sound, until the answer came back to them louder and sharper than before. Mbejane took the crowbar out of Duff's hands. He thrust it into a crack in the rock jam and his back muscles bunched as he heaved. The bar bent like a liquorice stick, he threw it away and went at the stone with his bare hands.

'You!' Duff snapped at the shift-boss. 'We'll need timber to shore up as we clear the fall – get it.' He turned to the natives. 'Four of you working on the face at one time – the rest of you carry the stone away as we loosen it.'

'Do you want any dynamite?' asked the shift-boss.

'And bring the rock down a second time? Use your brains, man. Go and get that timber and call Mr du Toit while you're at the surface.'

In four hours they cleared fifteen feet of tunnel, breaking the larger slabs of stone with sledge hammers and prising the pieces out of the jam. Duff's body ached and his hands were raw. He had to rest. He walked slowly back to the lift station and there he found blankets and a huge dish of soup.

'Where did this come from?'

'Candy's Hotel, sir. Half Johannesburg is waiting at the head of the shaft.'

Duff huddled into a blanket and drank a little of the soup. 'Where's du Toit?'

'I couldn't find him, sir.'

Up at the face Mbejane worked on. The first four natives came back to rest and fresh men took their place. Mbejane led them, grunting an order occasionally but otherwise reserving his strength for the assault on the rock. For an hour Duff rested and when he returned to the head of the tunnel Mbejane was still there. Duff watched him curl his arms round a piece of stone the size of a beer keg, brace his legs and tear the stone out of the jam. Earth and loose rock followed it, burying Mbejane's legs to the knees, and Duff jumped forward to help him.

Another two hours and Duff had to rest again. This time he led Mbejane back with him, gave him a blanket and made him drink a little soup. They sat next to each other with their backs against the wall of the tunnel and blankets over their shoulders. The shift-boss came to Duff.

'Mrs Rautenbach sent this down for you, sir.'

It was a half-bottle of brandy.

'Tell her, thank you.' Duff pulled the cork with his teeth and swallowed twice. It brought the tears into his eyes – he offered the bottle to Mbejane.

'It is not fitting,' Mbejane demurred.

'Drink.'

Mbejane drank, wiped the mouth of the bottle carefully on his blanket and handed it back. Duff took another swallow and offered it again but Mbejane shook his head.

'A little of that is strength, too much is weakness. There is work to do now.'

Duff corked the bottle.

'How long before we reach him?' asked Mbejane.

'Another day, maybe two.'

'A man can die in two days,' mused the Zulu.

'Not one with a body like a bull and a temper like a devil,' Duff assured him. Mbejane smiled and Duff went on groping for his words in Zulu.

'You love him, Mbejane?'

'Love is a woman's word.'

Mbejane inspected one of his thumbs; the nail was torn loose, standing up like a tombstone; he took it between his teeth, pulled it off and spat it onto the floor of the drive. Duff shuddered as he watched.

'Those baboons will not work unless they are driven.' Mbejane stood up. 'Are you rested?'

'Yes,' lied Duff, and they went back to the face.

Sean lay in the mud with his head on the hard pillow of the helmet. The darkness was as solid as the rock around him. He tried to imagine where the one ended and the other began – by doing that he could stop himself feeling his thirst so strongly. He could hear the ring of hammer on stone and the rattle of rock falling free but it never seemed to come any closer. The whole side of his body was stiff and sore but he could not turn over, his knees caught on the cocopan every time he tried and the air in his little cave was starting to taste stale – his head ached. He moved again, restlessly, and his hand brushed the small pile of sovereigns. He struck at them, scattering them into the mud. They were the bait that had led him into this trap. Now he would give them, and all the millions of others, for just the feel of the wind in his beard and the sun in his face. The darkness clung to him, thick and cloying as black treacle; it seemed to fill his nose, his throat and eyes, smothering him. He groped and found the matchbox. For a few seconds of light he would burn up most of the precious oxygen in his cave and call it fair exchange – but the box was sodden. He struck match after match but the wet heads crumbled without a spark and he threw them away and clenched his eyelids to keep the darkness out. Bright colours formed in front of his closed eyes, moving and rearranging themselves until suddenly and very clearly they formed a picture of Garrick's face. He hadn't thought about his family for months, he had been too busy reaping the golden harvest, but now memories crowded back. There were so many things he had forgotten. Everything else had become unimportant when compared with power and gold – even lives, men's lives, had meant nothing. But now it was his own life, teetering on the edge of the black cliff.

The sound of the sledge-hammers broke into his thoughts again. There were men on the other side of the blocked tunnel trying to save him, working their way into the treacherous rock pile which might collapse again at any minute. People were more valuable than the poisonous metal, the little gold discs that lay smugly beside him in the mud while men struggled to save him.

He thought of Garry, crippled by his careless shotgun, father to the bastard he had sired, of Ada whom he had left without a word of goodbye, of Karl Lochtkamper with the pistol in his hand and half his head splattered across the floor of his bedroom, of other nameless men dead or broken because of him.

Sean ran his tongue across his lips and listened to the hammers; he was certain they were nearer now.

'If I get out of here, it'll be different. I swear it.'

Mbejane rested for four hours in the next thirty-six. Duff watched the flesh melt off him in sweat. He was killing himself. Duff was worn out; he could no longer work with his hands but he was directing the teams who were shoring up the reclaimed tunnel. By the second evening they had cleared a hundred feet of the drive. Duff paced it out and when he reached the face he spoke to Mbejane.

'How long since you last signalled to him?'

Mbejane stepped back with a sledge-hammer in his tattered hands; its shaft was sticky and brown with blood.

'An hour ago and even then it sounded as though there were but the length of a spear between us.'

Duff took a crowbar from one of the other natives and tapped the rock. The answer came immediately.

'He's hitting something made of iron,' Duff said. 'It sounds as though he's only a few feet away. Mbejane, let these other men take over. If you wish you can stay and watch but you must rest again now.'

For answer Mbejane lifted the hammer and swung it against the face. The rock he hit cracked and two of the natives stepped up and levered it loose with their crowbars. At the back of the hole it left in the wall they could see the corner of the cocopan. Everyone stared at it, then Duff shouted.

'Sean, Sean, can you hear me?'

'Stop talking and get me out of here.' Sean's voice was hoarse with thirst and dust, and muffled by the rock.

'He's under the cocopan.'

'It's him.'

'Nkosi, are you all right?'

'We've found him.'

The shouts were picked up by the men working behind them in the drive and passed back to those waiting at the lift station.

'They've found him – he's all right – they've found him.'

Duff and Mbejane jumped forward together, their exhaustion completely forgotten. They cleared the last few lumps of rock and with their shoulders touching knelt and peered under the cocopan.

'Nkosi, I see you.'

'I see you also, Mbejane, what took you so long?'

'Nkosi, there were a few small stones in the way.'

Mbejane reached under the cocopan and with his hands under Sean's armpits pulled him out.

'What a hell of a place you chose to go to ground in, laddie. How are you feeling?'

'Give me some water and I'll be all right.'

'Water – bring water,' shouted Duff.

Sean gulped it, trying to drink the whole mug in one mouthful. He coughed and it shot out of his nose.

'Easy, laddie, easy.' Duff thumped his back. Sean drank the next mugful more slowly and finished panting from the effort.

'That was good.'

'Come on, we've got a doctor waiting up on top.' Duff draped a blanket over his shoulders. Mbejane picked Sean up across his chest.

'Put me down, damn you, I haven't forgotten how to walk.'

Mbejane set him down gently, but his legs buckled like those of a man just out of bed from a long illness and he clutched at Mbejane's arm. Mbejane picked him up again and carried him down to the lift station. They rode up in the skip into the open.

'The moon's shining. And the stars – my God, they're beautiful.' There was wonder in Sean's voice; he sucked the night air into his lungs but it was too rich for him and he started coughing again. There were people waiting at the head of the shaft and they crowded round them as they stepped out of the skip.

'How is he?'

'Are you all right, Sean?'

'Doc Symmonds is waiting in the office.'

'Quickly, Mbejane,' said Duff, 'get him out of the cold.'

One on either side of him they hurried Sean across to the administrative building and laid him on the couch in Francois's office. Symmonds checked him over, looked down his throat and felt his pulse.

'Have you got a closed carriage here?'

'Yes,' Duff answered.

'Well, wrap him up warmly and get him home to bed. With the dust and bad air he's been breathing there's serious danger of pneumonia. I'll come down with you and give him a sedative.'

'I won't need one, Doc,' Sean grinned at him.

'I think I know what's best for you, Mr Courtney.' Doctor Symmonds was a young man. He was the fashionable doctor among the rich of Johannesburg and he took it very seriously.

'Now if you please, we'll get you to your hotel.' He started to pack his instruments back into his valise.

'You're the doctor,' Sean agreed, 'but before we go will

you have a look at my servant's hands, they're in a hell of a mess. There's hardly any meat left on them.'

Doctor Symmonds did not look up from what he was doing. 'I have no Kaffir practice, Mr Courtney, I'm sure you'll find some other doctor to attend to him when we get back to town.'

Sean sat up slowly, he let the blankets slip off his shoulders. He walked across to Doctor Symmonds and held him by the throat against the wall. The doctor had a fine pair of waxed moustaches and Sean took one of them between the thumb and forefinger of his free hand: he plucked it out like feathers from the carcass of a dead fowl and Doctor Symmonds squealed.

'Starting now, Doctor, you have a Kaffir practice,' Sean told him. He pulled the handkerchief out of Symmonds' top pocket and dabbed at the little drops of blood on the doctor's bare upper lip.

'Be a good fellow – see to my servant.'

– 21 –

When Sean woke the next morning the hands of the grandfather clock across the bedroom pointed at the top of their dial. Candy was in the room opening the curtains and with her were two waiters, each with a loaded tray.

'Good morning, how is our hero this morning?' The waiters put down their trays and went out as she came across to Sean's bed.

Sean blinked the sleep out of his eyes. 'My throat feels as though I've just finished a meal of broken glass.'

'That's the dust,' Candy told him and laid her hands on his forehead. Sean's hand sneaked round behind her and she squeaked as he pinched her. Standing well away from the bed she rubbed her bottom and made a face at him.

'There's nothing wrong with you!'

'Good, then I'll get up.' Sean started to pull back the bedclothes.

'Not until the doctor's had a look at you, you won't.'

'Candy, if that bastard puts one foot in this room I'll punch him so hard in the mouth his teeth will march out of his backside like soldiers.'

Candy turned to the breakfast trays to cover her smile. 'That's no way to talk in front of a lady. But don't worry, it isn't Symmonds.'

'Where's Duff?' Sean asked.

'He's having a bath, then he's coming to eat breakfast with you.'

'I'll wait for him, but give me a cup of coffee in the meantime, there's a sweetheart.'

She brought the coffee to him. 'Your savage has been camping on my trail all morning, he wants to see you. I've just about had to put an armed guard on this room to keep him out.'

Sean laughed. 'Will you send him in, Candy?'

She went to the door and stopped with a hand on the latch.

'It's nice to have you back, Sean, don't do anything silly like that again, will you?'

'That's a promise,' Sean assured her.

Mbejane came quickly and stood in the doorway. 'Nkosi, is it well with you?'

Sean looked at the iodine-stained bandages on his hands and the maroon and gold livery without answering. Then he rolled on his back and stared at the ceiling. 'I sent for my servant and instead there comes a monkey on a chain.'

Mbejane stood still, his face expressionless but for the hurt in his eyes.

'Go – find my servant. You will know him by his dress which is that of a warrior of Zululand.'

It took a few seconds for the laughter to start rolling around in Mbejane's belly; it shook his shoulders and creased the corners of his mouth. He closed the door very softly behind him and when he came back in his loin cloth Sean grinned at him.

'Ah! I see you, Mbejane.'

'And I see you also.'

He stood by the bed and they talked. They spoke little of the cave-in and not at all of Mbejane's part in the rescue. Between them it was understood, words could only damage it. Perhaps they would talk of it later, but not now.

'Tomorrow, will you need the carriage?' Mbejane asked at last.

'Yes – go now. Eat and sleep.' Sean reached out and touched Mbejane's arm. Just that small physical contact – that almost guilty touching – and Mbejane left him.

Then Duff came in in a silk dressing-gown and they ate eggs and steak from the trays and Duff sent down for a bottle of wine just to rinse the dust out of their throats once more.

'They tell me Francois is still down at the Bright Angels – he's been on the drink ever since he got out of that shaft. When he sobers up he can come to the office and collect his pay packet.'

Sean sat up. 'You're going to fire him?'

'I'm going to fire him so high he'll only touch ground when he reaches Capetown.'

'What the hell for?' demanded Sean.

'What for?' Duff echoed. 'What for? For running – that's what for.'

'Duff, he was in a cave-in at Kimberley, wasn't he?'

'Yes.'

'Broke his legs, didn't you say?'

'Yes.'

'Shall I tell you something? If it were to happen to me a second time I'd run as well.'

Duff filled his wine glass without answering.

'Send down to the Bright Angels, tell him alcohol is bad for the liver – that should sober him – tell him unless he's back at work by tomorrow morning we'll dock it off his pay,' Sean said. Duff looked at him with a puzzled expression. 'What is this?'

'I had some time to think while I was down in that hole. I decided that to get to the top you don't have to stamp on everyone you meet.'

'Ah, I understand.' Duff gave his lopsided grin. 'A good resolution – New Year in August. Well, that's all right, you had me worried there, I thought a rock had fallen on your head. I also make good resolutions.'

'Duff, I don't want Francois fired.'

'All right, all right – he stays on. If you like we can open a soup kitchen at the office and turn Xanadu into a home for the aged.'

'Oh, go and burst. I just don't think it's necessary to fire Francois, that's all.'

'Who's arguing? I agreed with you, didn't I? I have deep respect for good resolutions. I make them all the time.'

Duff pulled his chair up to the bed. 'Quite by chance I happen to have a pack of cards with me.' He took them out of his dressing-gown pocket. 'Would you care for a game of Klabejas?'

Sean lost fifty pounds before he was saved by the arrival of the new doctor. The doctor tapped his chest and tut-tutted, looked down his throat and tut-tutted, wrote out a prescription and confined him to bed for the rest of the day.

He was just leaving when Jock and Trevor Heyns arrived. Jock had a bunch of flowers which he presented to Sean in an embarrassed fashion.

Then the room began to fill in earnest: the rest of the crowd from the Exchange arrived, someone had brought a case of champagne, a poker game started in one corner and a political meeting in another.

'Who does this Kruger think he is, anyway – God or something? You know what he said last time we went to see him about getting the vote, he said "Protest, protest – I have the guns and you have not!"'

'Three Kings wins – you *are* holding cards!'

' – you wait and see. Consolidated Wits. will hit thirty shillings by the end of the month.'

' – and the taxes – they're putting another twenty per cent on dynamite.'

' – a new piece at the Opera, Jock's got a season ticket on her – no one else has had a look in yet.'

'All right, you two – stop that. If you want to fight go outside – this is a sick room.'

'This bottle's empty – break open a new one, Duff.'

Sean lost another hundred to Duff and then a little after five Candy came in. She was horrified. 'Out, all of you, out!'

The room emptied as quickly as it had filled and Candy wandered around picking up cigar butts and empty glasses.

'The vandals! Someone's burnt a hole in the carpet and look at this – champagne spilt all over the table.'

Duff coughed and started pouring himself another drink.

'Don't you think you've had enough of that, Dufford?'

Duff put down his glass. 'And it's time you went and changed for dinner.' Duff winked sheepishly at Sean, but he went.

Duff and Candy came back to his room after supper and had a liqueur with him.

'Now to sleep,' Candy commanded and went across to draw the curtains.

'It's still early,' protested Duff with no effect. Candy blew the lamp out.

Sean was not tired, he had lain in bed all day and now his brain was overactive. He lit a cigar and smoked, listening to the street noises below his window and it was past midnight before he finally drifted off. When he woke, he woke screaming, for the darkness was on him again and the blankets pressed down on him suffocating him. He fought them off and stumbled blindly across the room. He had to have air and light. He ran into the thick velvet curtains and they closed around his face; he tore himself free and hit the french windows with his shoulder; they burst open and he was out on the balcony, out in the cold air with the moon fat and yellow in the sky above him. His gasping slowed until he was breathing normally again. He went back inside and lit the lamp, then he went through to Duff's empty bedroom. There was a copy of *Twelfth Night* on the bedside table and he took it back to his own room. He sat with the lamp at his elbow and forced his eyes to follow the printed words even though they made no sense. He read until the dawn showed grey through the open windows, then he put down the book. He shaved, dressed and went down the back stairs into the hotel yard. He found Mbejane in the stables.

'Put a saddle on the grey.'

'Where are you going, Nkosi?'

'To kill a devil.'

'Then I will come with you.'

'No, I will be back before midday.'

He rode up to the Candy Deep and tied his horse outside the administration buildings. There was a sleepy clerk in the front offices.

'Good morning, Mr Courtney. Can I help you?'

'Yes. Get me overalls and a helmet.'

Sean went to the Number Three shaft. There was a frost on the ground that crunched as he walked on it and the sun had just cleared the eastern ridge of the Witwatersrand. Sean stopped at the hoist shed and spoke to the driver.

'Has the new shift gone on yet?'

'Half an hour ago, sir.' The man was obviously surprised to see him. 'The night shift finished blasting at five o'clock.'

'Good – drop me down to the fourteenth level.'

'The fourteenth is abandoned now, Mr Courtney, there's no one working there.'

'Yes, I know.'

Sean walked across to the head of the shaft. He lit his carbide lamp and while he waited for the skip he looked out across the valley. The air was clear and the sun threw long shadows. Everything stood out in sharp relief. He had not been up this early in the morning for many months and he had almost forgotten how fresh and delicately coloured a new day was. The skip stopped in front of him. He took a deep breath and stepped into it. When he reached the fourteenth level he got out and pushed the recall signal for the skip and he was alone in the earth again. He walked up the tunnel and the echo of his footsteps went with him. He was sweating and a muscle in his cheek started to jerk; he reached the face and set the carbide lamp down on a ledge of rock. He checked to make sure his matches were in his pocket, then he blew out the lamp. The darkness came squeezing down on him. The first half hour was the worst. Twice he had the matches in his hand ready to strike but he stopped himself. The sweat formed cold wet patches under his arms and the darkness filled his open mouth and choked him. He had to fight for each lungful of air, suck in, hold it, breathe out. First he regulated his breathing and then slowly, slowly his mind came under control and he knew he had won. He waited another ten minutes breathing easily and sitting relaxed with his back against the side of the tunnel, then he lit the lamp. He was smiling as he went back to the lift station and signalled for the skip. When he reached the surface he stepped out and lit a cigar; he flicked the match into the square black opening of the shaft.

'So much for you, little hole.'

He walked back towards the administration building. What he could not know was that the Number Three shaft of the Candy Deep was to take something from him just as valuable as his courage and that, next time, what it took it would not give back. But that was many years ahead.

– 22 –

By October Xanadu was nearly finished. The three of them drove out to it as usual one Saturday afternoon.

'The builder is only six months behind schedule – now he says he'll be finished by Christmas and I haven't found the courage yet to ask him which Christmas,' Sean remarked.

'It's all the alterations Candy has thought up,' Duff said. 'She's got the poor man so confused he doesn't know whether he's a boy or a girl.'

'Well, if you'd consulted me in the first place it would have saved a lot of trouble,' Candy told them.

The carriage turned in through the marble gates and they looked around them. Already the lawns were smooth and green and the jacaranda trees lining the drive were shoulder high.

'I think it's going to live up to its name – that gardener's doing a good job,' Sean spoke with satisfaction.

'Don't you call him a gardener to his face or we'll have a strike on our hands. He's a horticulturist,' Duff smiled across at him.

'Talking about names,' Candy interrupted, 'don't you think Xanadu is – well, a bit outlandish?'

'No, I do not,' Sean said. 'I picked it myself. I think it's a damn good name.'

'It's not dignified – why don't we call it Fair Oaks?'

'Firstly, because there isn't an oak tree within fifty miles and secondly because it's already called Xanadu.'

'Don't get cross, it was just a suggestion.'

The builder met them at the top of the drive and they began the tour of the house. That took an hour, then they left the builder and went out into the garden. They found the gardener with a gang of natives near the north boundary.

'How's it going, Joubert?' Duff greeted him.

'Not bad, Mr Charleywood, but it takes time you know.'

'You've done a damn fine job so far.'

'It's kind of you to say so, sir.'

'When are you going to start laying out my maze?'

The gardener looked surprised; he glanced at Candy, opened his mouth, closed it again and looked once more at Candy.

'Oh, I told Joubert not to worry about the maze.'

'Why did you do that? I wanted a maze – ever since I visited Hampton Court as a child I've wanted my own maze.'

'They're silly things,' Candy told him. 'They just take up a lot of space and they're not even nice to look at.'

Sean thought Duff was going to argue, but he didn't. They talked to the gardener a little longer, then they walked back across the lawns in front of the house towards the chapel.

'Dufford, I've left my parasol in the carriage, would you mind getting it for me?' Candy asked.

When Duff was gone Candy took Sean's arm.

'It's going to be a lovely home. We're going to be very happy here.'

'Have you two decided on a date yet?' Sean asked.

'We want the house finished first so we can move straight in. I think we'll make it some time in February next year.'

They reached the chapel and stopped in front of it.

'It's a sweet little church.' Candy spoke dreamily. 'And such a nice idea of Dufford's – a special church of our own.'

Sean shuffled uncomfortably. 'Yes,' he agreed, 'it's a very romantic idea.' He glanced over his shoulder and saw Duff coming back with the parasol.

'Candy – it's none of my business. I don't know anything about marriage, but I know about training horses – you break them to the halter before you put the saddle on their backs.'

'I don't follow you.' Candy looked puzzled. 'What are you trying to say?'

'Nothing – just forget it. Here comes Duff.'

When they got back to the hotel there was a note at the reception desk for Sean. They went through into the main lounge and Candy went off to check the menu for dinner. Sean opened the envelope and read the note:

> 'I should like to meet you and Mr Charleywood to discuss a matter of some importance. I will be at my hotel after dinner this evening and hope that it will be convenient for you to call on me then. N. Hradsky.'

Sean passed the note across to Duff.

'What do you suppose he wants?'

'He has heard of your deadly skill as a Klabejas player. He wants to take lessons,' Duff answered.

'Shall we go?'

'Of course. You know I can't resist Norman's exhilarating company.'

It was a superb dinner. The crayfish, packed in ice, had come up from Capetown by express coach.

'Candy – Sean and I are going across to see Hradsky. We might be back a little late,' Duff told her when they were finished.

'As long as it's Hradsky,' Candy smiled at him. 'Don't get lost – I have my spies at the Opera House you know.'

'Shall we take the carriage?' Duff asked Sean, and Sean noticed that he hadn't laughed at Candy's joke.

'It's only two blocks, we might as well walk.'

They walked in silence. Sean felt his dinner settling down comfortably inside him, he belched softly and took another puff from his cigar. When they had almost reached the Grand National Hotel Duff spoke.

'Sean . . .' He stopped.

'Yes?' Sean prompted him.

'About Candy . . .' He stopped again.

'She's a fine girl,' Sean prompted again.

'Yes, she's a fine girl.'

'Is that all you wanted to say?'

'Well – oh! never mind. Let's go and see what Saul and David want.'

Max met them at the door of Hradsky's suite.

'Good evening, gentlemen, I am so pleased you could come.'

'Hello, Max.' Duff went past him to where Hradsky was standing in front of the fireplace.

'Norman, my dear fellow, how are you?'

Hradsky nodded an acknowledgement and Duff took hold of the lapels of Hradsky's coat and adjusted them carefully; then he picked an imaginary piece of fluff off his shoulder.

'You have a way with clothes, Norman. Don't you agree that Norman has a way with clothes, Sean? I know of no one else who can put on a twenty-guinea suit and make it look like a half-filled bag of oranges.' He patted Hradsky's arm affectionately. 'Yes, thank you – I will have a drink.' He went across to the liquor cabinet and poured one for himself. 'Now, what can you gentlemen do for me?'

Max glanced at Hradsky and Hradsky nodded.

'I will come to the point immediately,' said Max. 'Our two groups of companies are the largest on the Witwatersrand.'

Duff put his glass back on top of the cabinet and dropped his grin. Sean sat down in one of the armchairs, his expression also serious; both of them could guess what was coming.

'In the past,' continued Max, 'we have worked together on numerous occasions and we have both benefited from it. The next logical step, of course, is to combine our strength, pool our resources and go on together to new greatness.'

'I take it that you are proposing a merger?'

'Precisely, Mr Courtney, a merger of these two vast financial ventures.'

Sean leaned back in his chair and started to whistle softly. Duff picked up his glass again and took a sip.

'Well, gentlemen, what are your feelings on the subject?' asked Max.

'Have you got a proposal worked out, Max, something definite for us to think about?'

'Yes, Mr Courtney, I have.' Max went to the stinkwood desk which filled one corner of the room and picked up a sheaf of papers. He carried it across to Sean. Sean scanned through it.

'You've done quite a bit of work here, Max. It's going to take us a day or two to work out exactly what you are offering.'

'I appreciate that, Mr Courtney. Take as long as you

wish. We have worked for a month to draw up that scheme and I hope our labours have not been in vain. I think you will find our offer very generous.'

Sean stood up.

'We'll contact you again in the next few days, Max. Shall we go, Duff?'

Duff finished his drink.

'Goodnight, Max, look after Norman. He's very precious to us, you know.'

They went to their building on Eloff Street. Sean let them in through one of the side doors, lit the lamps in his office and Duff pulled up an extra chair to the desk. By two o'clock the following morning they understood the essentials of Hradsky's offer. Sean stood up and went to open one of the windows, for the room was thick with cigar smoke. He came back and flopped onto the couch, arranged a cushion behind his head and looked at Duff.

'Let's hear what you've got to say.'

Duff tapped his teeth with a pencil while he arranged his words.

'Let's decide first if we want to join with him.'

'If he makes it worth our while, we do,' Sean answered.

'I agree with you – but only if he makes it worth our while.' Duff laid back in his chair. 'Now the next point. Tell me, laddie, what is the first thing that strikes you about this scheme of Norman's?'

'We get nice-sounding titles and fat cash payments and Hradsky gets control,' Sean answered.

'You have laid your finger on the heart of it – Norman wants control. More than money, Norman wants control, so that he can sit at the top of the pile, look down on everyone else and say, "All right, you bastards, what if I do stutter?"'

Duff stood up, he walked round the desk and stopped in front of Sean's couch.

'Now for my next question. Do we give him control?'

'If he pays our price, then we give him control,' Sean answered. Duff turned away and went across to the open window.

'You know I rather like the feeling of being top man myself,' he said thoughtfully.

'Listen, Duff, we came here to make money. If we go in with Hradsky we'll make more,' Sean said.

'Laddie, we've got so much now that we could fill this room waist deep in sovereigns. We've got more than we'll ever be able to spend and I like being top man.'

'Hradsky's more powerful than we are – let's face up to that. He's got his diamond interests as well, so you're not top man even now. If we join him you still won't be top man but you'll be a damn sight richer.'

'Unassailable logic,' Duff nodded. 'I agree with you then. Hradsky gets control but he pays for it; we'll put him through the wringer until he's dry.'

Sean swung his legs off the couch. 'Agreed – now let's take this scheme of his by the throat, tear it to pieces and build it up again to suit ourselves.'

Duff looked at his watch. 'It's after two o'clock. We'll leave it now and start on it when we're fresh in the morning.'

They had their lunch brought down to the office the next day, and ate it at the desk. Johnson, who had been sent up to the Stock Exchange with instructions to keep an eye on prices and call them immediately if anything out of the ordinary happened, reported back after high change.

'It's been as quiet as a graveyard all day, sir, there's all sorts of rumours flying about. Seems someone saw the lights burning in this office at two o'clock this morning. Then when you didn't come to the Exchange but sent me instead – well, I can tell you, sir, there were a lot of questions asked.' Johnson hesitated, then his curiosity got the better of him.

'Can I help you at all, sir?' He started sidling across towards the desk.

'I think we can manage on our own, Johnson. Shut the door as you go out, please.'

At half-past seven they decided it was enough for one day and they went back to the hotel. As they walked into the lobby Sean saw Trevor Heyns disappear into the lounge and heard his voice.

'Here they are!'

Almost immediately Trevor appeared again with his brother.

'Hello, boys.' Jock appeared surprised to see them. 'What are you doing here?'

'We live here,' said Duff.

'Oh, yes, of course. Well, come and have a drink with us.' Jock smiled expansively.

'And then you can pump us and find out what we've been doing all day,' Duff suggested.

Jock looked embarrassed. 'I don't know what you mean, I just thought we'd have a drink together, that's all.'

'Thanks all the same, Jock, we've had a hard day. I think we'll just go on up to bed,' Duff said. They were halfway across the lobby before Duff turned back to where the two brothers were standing.

'I'll tell you boys something,' he said in a stage whisper. 'This is really big – it's so big it takes a while for the mind to grasp it. When you two realize that it's been right there under your noses all the time, you're going to kick yourselves.'

They left the Heyns brothers in the lobby staring after them and went up the stairs.

'That wasn't very kind,' Sean laughed. 'They won't sleep for a week.'

– 23 –

When neither Sean nor Duff put in an appearance at the Exchange the next morning, the rumours surged round the members' lounge and the prices started running amok. Reliable information that Sean and Duff had struck a rich new goldfield across the vaal sent the prices up like rocketing snipe; then twenty minutes later the denial came in and clipped fifteen shillings a share off the Courtney-Charleywood stock. Johnson ran backwards and forwards between the office and the Exchange all morning. By eleven he was so tired he could hardly talk.

'Don't worry any more, Johnson,' Sean told him. 'Here's a sovereign – go down to the Grand National and buy yourself a drink, you've had a hard morning.'

One of Jock Heyns's men, who had been detailed off to watch the Courtney-Charleywood offices, followed Johnson down to the Grand National and heard him place his order with the barman. He raced back to the Exchange and reported to Jock.

'Their head clerk has just gone and ordered himself a bottle of French champagne,' he panted.

'Good God!' Jock nearly jumped out of his chair and beside him Trevor signalled frantically for his clerk.

'Buy,' he whispered in the man's ear. 'Buy every scrap of their script you can lay your hands on.'

Across the lounge Hradsky settled down a little further in his chair; he clasped his hands contentedly over the front of his stomach and he very nearly smiled.

By midnight Sean and Duff had completed their counterproposal to Hradsky's offer.

'How do you think Norman will react to it?' asked Sean.

'I hope his heart is strong enough to stand the shock,'

Duff grinned. 'The only reason that his jaw won't hit the floor is that his great gut will be in the way.'

'Shall we go down to his hotel now and show him?' suggested Sean.

'Laddie, laddie.' Duff shook his head sorrowfully. 'After all the time I've spent on your education, and you still haven't learned.'

'What do we do then?'

'We send for him, laddie, we make him come to us. We play him on the home ground.'

'How does that help?' Sean asked.

'It gives us an advantage immediately – it makes him remember that he's the one doing the asking.'

Hradsky came down to their office at ten o'clock the next morning; he came in state driven behind a four-in-hand and attended by Max and two secretaries. Johnson met them at the front door and ushered them into Sean's office.

'Norman, dear old Norman, I'm delighted to see you,' Duff greeted him and, fully aware of the fact that Hradsky never smoked, Duff thrust a cheroot between his lips. When everyone was seated Sean opened the meeting.

'Gentlemen, we have spent some time examining your proposition and in the main we find it just, fair and equitable.'

'Hear, hear,' Duff agreed politely.

'At the outset I want to make it quite clear,' Sean went on, 'that Mr Charleywood and myself feel strongly that the union of our two ventures is desirable – nay! essential. If you will forgive the quotation, "*ex unitate vires*".'

'Hear, hear – hear, hear.' Duff lit his cigar.

'As I was saying, we have examined your proposition and we accept it readily and happily, with the exception of a few minor details which we have listed.' Sean picked up the thick pile of paper. 'Perhaps you would care to glance through it and then we can proceed to the drawing-up of a formal agreement.'

Max accepted the sheaf gingerly. 'If you want privacy, Mr Charleywood's office which adjoins this room is at your disposal.'

Hradsky took his band next door and an hour later when he led them back again they looked like a party of pallbearers. Max was on the verge of tears, he cleared the lump from his throat.

'I think we should examine each item separately,' he said sadly, and three days later they shook hands on the deal.

Duff poured the drinks and gave each man a glass. 'To the new company, Central Rand Consolidated. It has been a long confinement, gentlemen, but I think we have given birth to a child of which we can be proud.'

Hradsky had control, but it had cost him dearly.

Central Rand Consolidated had its christening party on the main floor of the Johannesburg Stock Exchange; ten per cent of the shares were put out for sale to the public. Before the day's dealings began the crowd had overflowed the Stock Exchange building and jammed in the street for a block in each direction. The President of the Exchange read the prospectus of Central Rand Consolidated; in the cathedral hush his every word carried clearly to the members' lounge. The bell rang and still the hush persisted. Hradsky's authorized clerk broke the silence timidly. 'I sell C.R.C.'s.'

It was nearly a massacre; two hundred men were trying to buy shares from him simultaneously. First his jacket and then his shirt disintegrated beneath the clutching hands; he lost his spectacles, crushed to powdered glass beneath the trampling feet. Ten minutes later he managed to fight his way out of the crowd and report to his masters, 'I was able to sell them, gentlemen.'

Sean and Duff laughed. They had reason to laugh, for in

those ten minutes their thirty per cent holding in C.R.C. had appreciated in value by half a million pounds.

– 24 –

That year Christmas dinner at Candy's Hotel was considerably better than it had been five years previously. Seventy-five people sat down to it at one table and by three o'clock, when it ended, only half of them were able to stand up. Sean used the banisters to get up the stairs and at the top he told Candy and Duff solemnly, 'I love you – I love you both desperately – but now I must sleep.' He left them and set off down the corridor bouncing against the walls like a trick billiard shot until he ricocheted through the door into his suite.

'You'd better make sure he's all right, Dufford.'

'A case of the blind drunk leading the blind drunk,' said Duff indistinctly, and also employing the wall to wall route followed Sean down the corridor. Sean was sitting on the edge of his bed wrestling with one of his boots.

'What you trying to do, laddie, break your ankle?'

Sean looked up and smiled beatifically. 'Come in, come in – all four of you. Have a drink.'

'Thanks, I brought my own.'

Duff closed the door behind him like a conspirator and produced a bottle from under his coat. 'She didn't see me – she didn't know her little Dufford had a big beautiful bottle in his inside pocket.'

'Would you mind helping me with this damn boot?' Sean asked.

'That's a very good question,' said Duff seriously as he set a course across the room for one of the armchairs. 'I'm glad you asked it.' He reached the chair and dropped into it. 'The answer, of course, is, Yes! I would mind.'

Sean let his foot drop and lay back on the bed.

'Laddie, I want to talk to you,' Duff said.

'Talk's free – help yourself.'

'Sean, what do you think of Candy?'

'Lovely pair of titties,' Sean opined.

'Sure, but a man cannot live by titties alone.'

'No, but I suppose she's also got the other basic equipment,' Sean said drowsily.

'Laddie, I'm being serious now – I want your help. Do you think I am doing the right thing – this marriage business, I mean.'

'Don't know much about marriage.' Sean rolled over on his face.

'She's calling me Dufford already – did you notice that, laddie? That's an omen, that's an omen of the most frightful portent. Did you notice, hey?' Duff waited a second for an answer which he didn't receive. 'That's what the other one used to call me. "Dufford," she'd say – I can hear it now – "Dufford, you're a pig".'

Duff looked hard at the bed. 'Are you still with me?'

No answer.

'Sean, laddie, I need your help.'

Sean snored softly.

'Oh, you drunken oaf,' said Duff miserably.

– 25 –

Xanadu was finished by the end of January and the wedding was set for the twentieth of February. Duff sent the Commandant and the entire police force of Johannesburg an invitation: in return they put a twenty-four hour a day guard on the ballroom of Xanadu where the wedding gifts were laid out on long trestle tables. Sean drove up with Duff and Candy on the afternoon of the tenth, as Duff put it, to make the latest count of the booty. Sean gave the constable on duty a cigar and then they went through into the ballroom.

'Look, oh look,' squealed Candy. 'There's a whole lot of new presents!'

'This one's from Jock and Trevor.' Sean read the card.

'Open quickly, please, Dufford, let's see what they've given us.'

Duff prised the lid off the case and Sean whistled softly.

'A solid gold dinner service,' gasped Candy. She picked up one of the plates and hugged it to her chest. 'Oh, I just don't know what to say.'

Sean examined the other boxes. 'Hey, Duff, this one will make you specially happy – "Best wishes, N. Hradsky".'

'This I must see,' said Duff with the first enthusiasm he had shown in a month. He unwrapped the parcel.

'A dozen of them!' Duff hooted gleefully. 'Norman, you priceless little Israelite, a whole dozen dish towels.'

'It's the thought that counts,' laughed Sean.

'Dear old Norman, how it must have hurt him to shell out for them! I'll have him autograph them and I'll frame them and hang them in the front hall.'

They left Candy to arrange the presents and they went out into the garden.

'Have you got this mock priest organized?' asked Duff.

'Yes, he's at a hotel in Pretoria. He's in training now – he'll be able to rattle through the service like an old hand when the time comes.'

'You don't think that faking it is just as bad as doing it properly?' asked Duff dubiously.

'It's a hell of a time to think of that now,' said Sean.

'Yes, I suppose it is.'

'Where are you going for the honeymoon?' Sean asked.

'We'll coach down to Capetown and take the mail boat

to London, then a month or so on the Continent. Be back here about June.'

'You should have a good time.'

'Why don't you get married as well?'

'What for?' Sean looked surprised.

'Well, don't you feel as though you're letting the old firm down a bit – me going into this alone?'

'No,' said Sean. 'Anyway, who is there to marry?'

'What about that lass you brought to the races last Saturday; she's a lovely piece of work.'

Sean raised an eyebrow. 'Did you hear her giggle?'

'Yes, I did,' admitted Duff. 'You couldn't very well miss it.'

'Can you imagine that giggle coming at you across the breakfast table?' Sean asked.

Duff shuddered. 'Yes, I see your point. But as soon as we get back I'll have Candy start picking you out a suitable female.'

'I've got a better idea, you let Candy run your life and I'll run my own.'

'That, laddie, is what I'm very much afraid is going to happen.'

Hradsky reluctantly agreed that the activities of the group – the mines, the workshops, the transport companies, all of them – should be suspended on the twentieth to allow their employees to attend Duff's nuptials. This meant that half the businesses on the Witwatersrand would shut down for the day. Consequently, most of the independent companies decided to close as well. On the eighteenth the wagons carrying the food and liquor started caravanning up the hill to Xanadu. Sean, in a burst of benevolence, that night invited the entire company from the Opera House to the wedding. He remembered it vaguely the next morning and went down to cancel the invitation but Blue Bessie told him that most of the girls had already gone into town to buy new dresses.

'The hell with it then – let them come. I just hope Candy doesn't guess who they are, that's all.'

On the night of the nineteenth Candy gave them the use of the dining-room and all the downstairs lounges of the Hotel for Duff's bachelor party. Francois arrived with a masterpiece made up in the mine workshops – an enormous ball and chain. This was formally locked onto Duff's leg and the party began.

Afterwards there was a school of thought that maintained that the building contractor commissioned to repair the damage to the Hotel was a bandit and that the bill for just under a thousand pounds that he presented was nothing short of robbery. However, none of them could deny that the Bok-Bok game in the dining-room, played by a hundred men, had done a certain amount of damage to the furniture and fittings; nor that the chandelier had not been able to support Mr Courtney's weight and on the third swing had come adrift from the ceiling and knocked a moderately large hole through the floor. Neither did anyone dispute the fact that after Jock Heyns had tried unsuccessfully for half an hour to shoot a glass off the top of his brother's head with champagne corks, the resulting ankle-deep lake of wine in the one lounge made it necessary for the floor to be relaid. Nevertheless they felt that a thousand was a little bit steep. On one point, however, everyone agreed – it was a memorable party.

At the beginning Sean was worried that Duff's heart wasn't in it for Duff stood by the bar with the metal ball under one arm listening to the lewd comments with a lopsided grin fixed on his face. After seven or eight drinks Sean stopped worrying about him and went off to have his way with the chandelier. At midnight Duff talked Francois into releasing him from his chains and he slipped out of the room. No one – least of all Sean – noticed him go.

Sean could never remember how he got up to bed that night but next morning he was tactfully awakened by a waiter with a coffee tray and a note.

'What time is it?' asked Sean as he unfolded the note.

'Eight o'clock, baas.'

'No need to shout,' muttered Sean. His eyes focused with difficulty for the pain in his head was pushing them out of their sockets.

> 'Dear Best Man,
>
> This serves as a reminder that you and Duff have an appointment at eleven o'clock. I am relying on you to get him there, whole or in pieces. Love Candy.'

The brandy fumes in the back of his throat tasted like chloroform, he washed them out with coffee and lit a cigar which started him coughing, and every cough nearly took the top off his head. He stubbed out the cigar and went to the bathroom. Half an hour later he felt strong enough to wake Duff. He went across the sitting-room and pushed open Duff's door; the curtains in the room were still drawn. He pulled them open and was nearly blinded by the sunlight that poured in through them. He turned to the bed and frowned with surprise. He walked slowly across and sat on the edge of it.

'He must have slept in Candy's room,' Sean muttered as he looked at the unused pillows and neatly tucked blankets. It took a few seconds for him to find the fault in his reasoning.

'Then why did she write that note?' He stood up, feeling the first twinge of alarm. A picture of Duff, drunk and helpless lying out in the yard or knocked over the head by one of the busy Johannesburg footpads came very clearly to mind. He ran across the bedroom and into the sitting-room. Halfway to the door he saw the envelope propped up on the mantelpiece and he took it down.

'What is this, a meeting of the authors' guild?' he muttered. 'The place is thick with letters.'

The paper crackled as he opened it and he recognized Duff's back sloping hand.

> 'The first the worst, the second the same. I'm not going through with it. You're the best man so make my excuses to all the nice people. I'll be back when the dust has settled a little. D.'

Sean sat down in one of the armchairs, he read through it twice more. Then he exploded.

'Damn you, Charleywood – "make my excuses". You craven bastard. Walk out and leave me to sweep up the mess.'

He rushed across the room with his dressing-gown flapping furiously round his legs. 'You'll make your own damned excuses – even if I have to drag you back on the end of a rope.'

Sean ran down the back stairs. Mbejane was in the stable yard talking to three of the grooms.

'Where is Nkosi Duff?' Sean roared.

They stared at him blankly.

'Where is he?' Sean's beard bristled.

'The baas took a horse and went for a ride,' answered one of the grooms nervously.

'When?' bellowed Sean.

'In the night – perhaps seven, eight hours ago. He should be back soon.'

Sean stared at the groom, breathing heavily. 'Which way did he go?'

'Baas, he did not say.'

Eight hours ago – he could be fifty miles away by now. Sean turned and went back to his room. He threw himself on the bed and poured another cup of coffee.

'This is going to break her up badly—' He imagined the tears and the chaos of undisciplined grief.

'Oh, hell – damn you to hell, Charleywood.' He sipped the coffee and thought about going as well – taking a horse and getting as far away as possible. 'It's no mess of my making – I want no part of it.' He finished the coffee and started dressing. He looked in the mirror to comb his hair and saw Candy standing alone in the chapel, waiting while the silence turned to murmuring and then to laughter.

'Charleywood, you pig,' Sean scowled. 'I can't let her go up there – it'll be bad enough without that. I'll have to tell her.'

He picked up his watch from the dressing-table, it was past nine.

'Damn you, Charleywood.'

He went down the passage and stopped outside Candy's door. He could hear women's voices inside and he knocked before he went in. There were two of Candy's friends and the coloured girl Martha. They stared at him.

'Where's Candy?'

'In the bedroom – but you mustn't go in. It's bad luck.'

'It's the worst bloody luck in the world,' agreed Sean. He knocked on the bedroom door.

'Who is it?'

'Sean.'

'You can't come in – what do you want?'

'Are you decent?'

'Yes, but you mustn't come in.'

He opened the door and looked in on a confusion of squealing females.

'Get out of here' – he said harshly – 'I have to speak to Candy alone.'

They fled and Sean closed the door behind them. Candy was in a dressing-gown. Her face was quick with anticipation; her hair was pulled back and hung shiny and soft. She was beautiful, Sean realized. He looked at the frothy pile of her wedding-dress on the bed.

'Candy, bad news – I'm afraid. Can you take it?' He spoke almost roughly – hating it, hating every second of it.

He saw the bloom on her face wither until her expression was dead – blank and dead as a statue.

'He's gone,' said Sean. 'He's run out on you.'

Candy picked up a brush from her dressing-table and started stroking it listlessly through her hair. It was very quiet in the room.

'I'm sorry, Candy.'

She nodded without looking at him; instead she was looking down the lonely corridor of the future. It was worse than tears would have been, that silent acceptance. Sean scratched the side of his nose – hating it.

'I'm sorry – I wish I could do something about it.' He turned to the door.

'Sean, thank you for coming and telling me.' There was no emotion in her voice; like her face it was dead.

'That's all right,' Sean said gruffly.

He rode up to Xanadu. There were people clustered about the marquees on the lawn; by the quality of their laughter he could tell they were drinking already. The sun was bright and as yet not too hot, the band was playing from the wide veranda of the mansion, the women's dresses were gay against the green of the lawns. 'Gala day' fluttered the flags above the tents. 'Gala day' shouted the laughter.

Sean rode up the drive, lifting his hand in brief acknowledgement of the greetings that were shouted to him. From the vantage point of his horse's back he spotted Francois and Martin Curtis, glasses in hand, standing near the house talking to two of the Opera girls. He gave his horse to one of the native grooms and strode across towards them.

'Hello, boss,' called Curtis. 'Why so glum – you're not the one getting married.' They all laughed.

'Francois, Martin, come with me please.'

'What's the trouble, Mr Courtney?' Francois asked as he led them aside.

'The party's over,' Sean said grimly. 'There'll be no wedding.'

They gaped at him.

'Go around and tell everybody. Tell them they'll get their presents back.'

He turned to leave them.

'What's happened, boss?' Curtis asked.

'Just tell them that Candy and Duff changed their minds.'

'Do you want us to send them home?'

Sean hesitated. 'Oh, the hell with it – let them stay – let them all get sick drunk. Just tell them there'll be no wedding.'

He went up to the house. He found the pseudo-priest waiting nervously in the downstairs study. The man's Adam's apple had been rubbed raw by the starch-stiff dog collar.

'We won't need you,' Sean told him.

He took out his cheque book, sat down at the desk and filled in a cheque form.

'That's for your trouble. Now get out of town.'

'Thank you, Mr Courtney, thank you very much.' The man looked mightily relieved; he started for the door.

'My friend,' Sean stopped him. 'If you ever breathe a word about what we planned to do today, I'll kill you. Do I make myself clear?'

Sean went through to the ballroom, he slipped a small stack of sovereigns into the constable's hand.

'Get all these people out of here.' He gestured with his head at the crowds that were wandering among the tables looking at the gifts. 'Then lock the doors.'

He found the chef in the kitchen. 'Take all this food outside – give it to them now. Then lock up the kitchens.'

He went round the house closing the doors and drawing the curtains. When he walked into the study there was a couple on the big leather couch and the man's hand was under the girl's skirts; she was giggling.

'This isn't a whore house,' Sean shouted at them and they left hurriedly. He sank into one of the chairs. He could hear the voices and the laughter from outside on the lawn, the band was playing a Strauss waltz. It irritated him and he scowled at the marble fireplace. His head was aching again and the skin of his face felt dry and tight from the night's debauch.

'What a mess – what a bloody mess,' he said aloud. After an hour he went out and found his horse. He rode out along the Pretoria Road until he had passed the last houses, then he turned off into the veld. He cantered into the sea of grass with his hat pushed back on his head so the sun and the wind could find his face. He sat relaxed and loose in the saddle and let his horse pick its own way. In the late afternoon he came back to Johannesburg and left his horse with Mbejane in the stableyard. He felt better; the exercise and the fresh air had cleared his head and helped him to see things in truer perspective. He ran himself a deep hot bath, climbed into it and while he soaked the last of his anger at Duff smoothed out. He had control of himself again. He got out of the bath and towelled, then he slipped on his gown and went through to the bedroom. Candy was sitting on his bed.

'Hello, Sean.' She smiled at him, a brittle smile. Her hair was a little tangled now, her face was pale and unrouged. She had not changed from the dressing-gown he had seen her in that morning.

'Hello, Candy.' He picked up the cut-glass bottle of bay rum and rubbed some into his hair and beard.

'You don't mind me coming to see you, do you?'

'No, of course not.' He started combing his hair. 'I was about to come and see you myself.'

She drew her legs up under her in the double-jointed manner of women that is impossible for a man to copy.

'Can I have a drink, please?'

'I'm sorry – I thought you never touched the stuff.'

'Oh, today is special.' She laughed too gaily. 'It's my wedding day, you know.'

He poured the brandy without looking at her. He hated this suffering and he felt his anger at Duff coming back strongly. Candy took the drink and sipped it. She pulled a face. 'It tastes awful.'

'It'll do you good.'

'To the bride,' she said and drank it down quickly.

'Another one?' asked Sean.

'No thanks.' She stood up and went across to the window. 'It's getting dark now – I hate the darkness. Darkness distorts things so; what is bad in the daylight is unbearable at night.'

'I'm sorry, Candy, I wish I could help you.'

She whirled and came to him, her arms circled tight round his neck and her face pale and frightened pressed to his chest.

'Oh, Sean, please hold me – I'm so afraid.'

He held her awkwardly.

'I don't want to think about it. Not now, not now in the darkness,' she whispered. 'Please help me. Please help me not to think about it.'

'I'll stay with you. Don't get yourself upset. Come and sit down. I'll get you another drink.'

'No, no,' she clung to him desperately. 'I don't want to be alone. I don't want to think. Please help me.'

'I can't help you – I'll stay with you but that's all I can do.' Anger and pity mixed together in Sean like charcoal and saltpetre; his fingers tightened hard on her shoulders, digging into the flesh until they met bone.

'Yes, hurt me. That way I'll forget for a while. Take me to the bed and hurt me, Sean, hurt me deep.'

Sean caught his breath. 'You don't know what you're saying, that's crazy talk.'

'It's what I want – to forget for a little. Please, Sean, please.'

'I can't do that, Candy, Duff's my friend.'

'He's finished with me and I with him. I'm your friend too. Oh, God, I'm so alone. Don't you leave me too. Help me, Sean, please help me.'

Sean felt his anger slide down from his chest and flare up, cobra-headed, from his thighs. She felt it also.

'Yes, oh please, yes.'

He picked her up and carried her to the bed. He stood over her while he tore off his gown. She moved on the bed, shedding her clothing and spreading herself to meet him, to take him in and let him fill the emptiness. He covered her quickly bayoneting through the soft veil and into the warmth of her body. There was no desire in it, it was cruel and hard drawn out to the frontiers of endurance. For him an expression of anger and pity; for her an act of renunciation. Once was not enough. Again and yet again he took her, until there were brown smudges on the bedclothes from his bleeding back, until her body ached and they lay entwined, wet and tired from the fury of it. In the quiescence of after-passion Sean spoke softly. 'It didn't help, did it?'

'Yes, it did.' Physical exhaustion had weakened the barriers that held back her grief. Still holding onto him, she started to cry.

A street lamp outside the room threw a silver square of light on the ceiling. Sean laid on his back and watched it, listening to Candy's sobs. He recognized the moment they reached their climax and followed their decline into silence. They slept then and later before the day woke together as if by arrangement.

'You are the only one who can help him now,' Candy said.

'Help him do what?' asked Sean.

'Find what he is looking for. Peace, himself – whatever you want to call it. He's lost, you know, Sean. He's lost and lonely, almost as lonely as I am. I could have helped him, I'm sure I could.'

'Duff lost?' Sean asked cynically. 'You must be mad!'

'Don't be so blind, Sean, don't be misled by the big talk and the grand manner. Look at the other things.'

'Like what?' asked Sean.

She didn't answer for a while. 'He hated his father, you know.'

'I guessed as much from the little he told me.'

'The way he revolts at any discipline. His attitude to Hradsky, to women, to life. Think about it, Sean, and then tell me if he acts like a happy man.'

'Hradsky did him a disservice once – he just doesn't like him,' Sean defended Duff.

'Oh, no – it's much deeper than that. In a way Hradsky is an image of his father. He's so broken up inside, Sean, that's why he clings to you. You can help him.'

Sean laughed outright. 'Candy, my dear, we like each other that's all, there are no deep and dark motives in our friendship. Don't you start getting jealous of me now.'

Candy sat up and the blankets slipped down to her waist.

She leaned towards Sean and her breasts swung forward, heavy, round and silver-white in the half light.

'There's a strength in you, Sean, a kind of solid sureness in you that you haven't discovered yet. Duff has recognized it and so will other unhappy people. He needs you, he needs you very badly. Look after him for me, help him to find what he seeks.'

'Nonsense, Candy,' Sean muttered with embarrassment.

'Promise me you'll help him.'

'It's time you went back to your room,' Sean told her. 'People will start talking.'

'Promise me, Sean.'

'All right, I promise.'

Candy slipped out of the bed. She dressed quickly. 'Thank you, Sean, goodnight.'

– 26 –

For Sean, Johannesburg was poorer without Duff: the streets were not so busy, the Rand Club was drearier and the thrills at the Stock Exchange not so intense. However, there was work to do; his share and Duff's as well.

It was late every evening when the conferences with Hradsky and Max ended and he went back to the Hotel. In the reaction from the day's tension, when his brain was numb and his eyes burned, there was little energy to spare for regret. Yet he was lonely. He went to the Opera House and drank champagne with the crowd there. One of the girls did the Can-Can on the big table in the centre of the room and when she stopped in front of Sean and Trevor Heyns, with her forehead touching her knees and her petticoats hanging forward over her shoulders, Sean let Trevor whip her pants down – a week before he would have punched Trevor in the nose rather than concede the honour. It wasn't so much fun any more. He went home early.

The following Saturday noon Curtis and Francois came into the office for the weekly progress meeting. When they had finished and Hradsky had left, Sean suggested, 'Come along with me, we'll go and have a pot or twelve at the Grand National Bar, baptize the weekend so to speak.'

Curtis and Francois fidgeted in their chairs.

'We had arranged to meet some of the other boys down at the Bright Angels, boss.'

'That's fine, I'll come along with you,' said Sean eagerly, the prospect of being with ordinary men again was suddenly very attractive to him. He felt sickened of the company of those who shook his hand and smiled at him while they waited for a chance to wipe him off the board. It would be good to go along with these two and talk mining and not stocks and shares, to laugh with men who didn't give a damn if C.R.C.'s hit sixty shillings on Monday. He'd get a little drunk with Francois and Curtis; later on perhaps he'd have a fight – an honest, snorting, stand-up fight. God, yes, it would be good to be with men who were clean inside – even if there was dirt under their nails and the armpits of their shirts were stained with sweat.

Curtis glanced quickly at Francois. 'There'll be just a crowd of roughnecks down there, boss, all the diggers come in on a Saturday.'

'That's fine,' said Sean. 'Let's go.'

He stood up and buttoned his dove-grey coat; the lapels were edged in black watered silk and matched the black pearl pin in his tie. He picked up his cane from the desk.

'Come on – let's get moving.'

They ran into the noise from the Bright Angels a block before they reached the building. Sean grinned and quickened his step like an old gun dog with the scent of the bird in its nostrils again. Francois and Curtis hurried along on either side of him. There was a big digger standing on the bar counter. Sean recognized him as one of his men from the Little Sister Mine; the man's body was tilted back to balance the weight of the demijohn he held to his lips and his throat jerked regularly as he swallowed. The crowd around his feet were chanting:

'Drink it, down, down, down, down.'

The digger finished, he threw the bottle against the far wall and belched like an air-locked geyser. He bowed to acknowledge the applause and then he caught sight of Sean standing in the doorway. He wiped his mouth guiltily with the back of his hand and jumped down off the counter. The other men in the crowd turned and saw Sean and the noise tapered off. They spread out along the bar in silence. Sean led Francois and Curtis into the room. He placed a pile of sovereigns on the counter.

'Set them up, barman, take the orders. Today is Saturday and it's time to tie the dog loose.'

'Cheers, Mr Courtney.'

'Good luck, sir.'

'*Gezondheid*, Mr Courtney.'

Their voices were subdued with respect.

'Drink up, men, there's plenty more where that came from.' Sean stood with Francois and Curtis at the bar. They laughed at his jokes. His voice was loud with good fellowship and his face flushed with happiness. He bought more drinks. After a while his bladder started making its presence felt and he went through the back door into the washrooms. There were men talking in there; he stopped before he rounded the edge of the screen into the room. '. . . what's he want to come here for, hey? This isn't the mucking Rand Club.'

'Shh! He'll hear you, man, do you want to lose your job?'

'I don't give a damn. Who does he think he is – "Drink up, boys, there's plenty more where that came from – I'm the boss, boys, do as you're told, boys, kiss my arse, boys."' Sean stood paralysed.

'Pipe down, Frank, he'll go just now.'

'The sooner the better, say I, the big dandy bastard with his ten-guinea boots and gold cane. Let him go back where he belongs.'

'You're drunk, man, don't talk so loud.'

'Sure I'm drunk, drunk enough to go in there and tell him to his face . . .'

Sean backed out through the door and walked slowly across the bar to Francois and Curtis.

'I hope you'll excuse me; I've just remembered there's something I've got to do this afternoon.'

'That's too bad, boss.' Curtis looked relieved. 'Perhaps some other time, hey?'

'Yes, perhaps some other time.'

They were pleased to see him when he went up to the Rand Club. Three men nearly fought one another to buy him a drink.

– 27 –

He had dinner with Candy that night and over the liqueurs he told her about it. She listened without interruption until he finished.

'They didn't want me there, I don't see what I've done to them that they should dislike me that way.'

'And it worries you?' she asked.

'Yes, it worries me. I've never had people feel like that towards me before.'

'I'm glad it worries you.' She smiled gently at him. 'One day you're going to grow into quite a nice person.'

'But why do they hate me?' Sean followed his original line of thought.

'They're jealous of you – you say this man said, "ten-guinea boots and gold cane" – that is what's behind it. You're different from them now, you're rich. You can't expect them to accept that.'

'But I've never done anything to them,' he protested.

'You don't have to. One thing I've found in this life – for everything you get you have to pay a price. This is part of the payment you have to make for success.'

'Hell, I wish Duff was here,' said Sean.

'Then Duff would explain to you that it doesn't matter, wouldn't he?' said Candy. '"Who gives a damn for them, laddie, the unwashed herd? We can do without them,"' she mimicked. Sean scratched the side of his nose and looked down at the table.

'Please, Sean, don't ever let Duff teach you that people don't matter. He doesn't believe it himself – but he's so convincing. People are important. They are more important than gold or places or – or anything.'

Sean looked up at her. 'I realized that once; when I was trapped in the Candy Deep. I saw it very clearly then in the darkness and the mud. I made a resolution.' He grinned sheepishly. 'I told myself I'd never hurt anyone again if I could help it. I really meant it, Candy. I felt it so strongly at the time – but, but . . .'

'Yes, I think I understand. That's a big resolution to make and a much bigger one to keep. I don't think any single experience is enough to change a person's way of thinking. It's like building a wall brick by brick. You add to it a little at a time until at last it's finished. I've told you before, Sean, that you have a strength in you. I think one day you'll finish building your wall – and when you do, it will have no weak spots.'

– 28 –

The next Tuesday Sean rode up to Xanadu for the first time since Duff had left. Johnson and four of the clerks from the office were at work in the ballroom, packing and labelling the presents.

'Nearly finished, Johnson?'

'Just about, Mr Courtney, I'll send a couple of wagons up tomorrow morning to fetch this lot.'

'Yes, do that. I don't want them lying around here any longer.'

He went up the marble staircase and stood on the top landing. The house had a dead feeling to it: new and sterile, it was waiting for people to come into it and bring it to life. He went down the corridor, stopping to look at the paintings that Candy had chosen. They were oils in soft pastels, woman's colours.

'We can do without these – I'll get some with fire in them, scarlets and blacks and bright blues.'

He pushed open the door to his own bedroom. This was better: vivid Persian rugs on the floor, walls panelled in dark satiny wood and a bed like a polo field. He lay on the bed and looked up at the scrolled ornate plaster ceiling.

'I wish Duff were back – we can do some real living in this house.' He went downstairs again.

Johnson was waiting at the foot of the stairs. 'All finished, sir.'

'Good man! Off you go, then.'

He went through into the study and walked across to the gun rack. He took down a Purdey shotgun, carried it to the french windows and looked at it in the light. His nostrils flared a little at the nostalgic smell of gun oil. He brought the gun up to his shoulder, felt the true exciting balance of it and enjoyed it. He swung the barrels in an arc across the room, following the flight of an imaginary bird, and suddenly Duff's face was in his sights. Sean was taken so by surprise that he stood with the gun trained at Duff's head.

'Don't shoot, I'll come quietly,' said Duff solemnly.

Sean lowered the shotgun and carried it back to the rack.

'Hello.'

'Hello,' Duff answered, still standing in the doorway. Sean made a pretence of fitting the gun into the rack with his back to Duff.

'How are you, laddie?'

'Fine! Fine!'

'How's everybody else?'

'To whom do you refer, in particular?' Sean asked.

'Candy, for one.'

Sean considered the question. 'Well, you could have damaged her more by feeding her into a stamp mill.'

'Bad, hey?'

'Bad,' agreed Sean.

They stood in silence for a while.

'I take it that you are not very well disposed towards me either,' Duff said at last.

Sean shrugged his shoulders and moved across to the fireplace.

'Dufford, you're a pig,' he said conversationally.

Duff winced. 'Well, it was nice knowing you, laddie. I suppose from here on our paths diverge?'

'Don't drivel, Duff, you're wasting time. Pour the drinks and then you can tell me what it feels like being a pig. Also I want to discuss with you those paintings Candy has plastered along the upstairs corridor. I don't know whether to give them away or burn them.'

Duff straightened up from leaning against the door jamb; he tried to stop the relief showing on his face but Sean went on quickly, 'Before we close the lid on the subject and bury it, I want to tell you this. I don't like what you did. I can see why you did it, but I don't like it. That's my piece said. Have you got anything to add to it?'

'No,' said Duff.

'All right then. I think you'll find a bottle of Courvoisier right at the back of the cabinet behind the whisky decanter.'

Sean went down to Candy's Hotel that evening and found Candy in her office.

'He's back, Candy.'

'Oh!' Candy caught her breath. 'How is he, Sean?'

'A little chastened, but not much.'

'I didn't mean that – I meant is he well?'

'The same as ever. He had the grace to ask how you were,' said Sean.

'What did you tell him?' asked Candy.

Sean shrugged and sat down in the chair next to her desk. He looked at the tall stacks of sovereigns that Candy was counting.

'Is that last night's bar takings?' he asked, avoiding her question.

'Yes,' she answered absently.

'You're rich – will you marry me?' he smiled.

Candy stood up and walked across to the window.

'I suppose you two will be moving up to Xanadu now,' she said. Sean grunted and she went on quickly. 'The Heyns brothers will take over the Victoria rooms – they've spoken to me about it already, so don't worry about that. You'll have fun up there, it will be marvellous for you. I bet you'll have parties every night and crowds of people. I don't mind, I've gotten used to the idea now.'

Sean stood up and went to her, he took her gently by the elbow and turned her to face him. He gave her the silk handkerchief out of his top pocket to blow her nose.

'Do you want to see him again, Candy?'

She shook her head, not trusting her voice.

'I'll look after him like I promised.' He gave her a hug and turned to go.

'Sean,' she called after him. He looked back. 'You'll come to see me sometimes. We could have dinner and talk a little. You'll still be my friend, won't you?'

'Of course, Candy, of course, my dear.'

She smiled damply. 'If you pack your things and Duff's I'll have them sent up to Xanadu for you.'

– 29 –

Sean looked across the boardroom table at Duff, seeking his support. Duff blew a thick ring of cigar smoke. It spun and expanded like a ripple in a pond before it hit the table top and disintegrated. Duff wasn't going to back him up, Sean realized bitterly. They had argued half the previous night. He had hoped that Duff might still change his mind. Now he knew he wouldn't. He made one last appeal.

'They have asked for a ten per cent wage increase. I believe they need it – prices have soared in this town, but wages have remained the same. These men have wives and children, gentlemen, can't we take that into account?'

Duff blew another smoke ring and Hradsky pulled his watch from his pocket and looked at it pointedly. Max coughed and interrupted. 'I think we've been over that before, Mr Courtney. Could we put it to the vote now?'

Sean watched Hradsky's hand go up against him. He

didn't want to look at Duff. He didn't want to see him vote with Hradsky, but he forced himself to turn his head. Duff's hands were on the table in front of him. He blew another smoke ring and watched it hit the table top.

'Those in favour of the motion?' asked Max, and Duff and Sean raised their right hands together. Sean realized then how much it would have meant if Duff had voted against him. Duff winked at him and he couldn't help grinning.

'That is thirty votes for, and sixty against,' declared Max. 'Therefore Mr Courtney's motion falls to the ground. I will inform the Mineworkers' Union of the decision. Now is there any other business before we close the meeting?'

Sean walked with Duff back to his own office.

'The only reason I supported you was because I knew Hradsky would win anyway,' said Duff pleasantly. Sean snorted.

'He's right, of course,' Duff went on unperturbed as he held open the door to Sean's office. 'A ten per cent wage increase would jump the group working costs up ten thousand a month.'

Sean kicked the door closed behind them and didn't answer.

'For God's sake, Sean, don't carry this goodwill-towards-men attitude to absurdity. Hradsky's right – Kruger is likely to slap another one of his taxes on us at any moment and we've got to finance all that new development on the East Rand. We can't let production costs creep up now.'

'All right,' gruffed Sean. 'It's all settled. I just hope we don't have a strike on our hands.'

'There are ways of dealing with strikes. Hradsky has got the police on our side and we can have a couple of hundred men up from Kimberley in no time at all,' Duff told him.

'Damn it, Duff, it's wrong. You know it's wrong. That

grotesque Buddha with the little eyes knows it's wrong. But what can I do? Damn it, what can I do?' Sean exploded. 'I feel so bloody helpless.'

'Well, you're the one who wanted to give him control.' Duff laughed at him. 'Stop trying to change the world and let's go home.'

Max was waiting for them in the outer office. He looked nervous. 'Excuse me, gentlemen, could I have a word with you?'

'Who's talking,' Sean asked abruptly, 'you or Hradsky?'

'It's a private matter, Mr Courtney.' Max dropped his voice.

'Can't it wait until tomorrow?' Sean pushed past him and kept going for the door.

'Please, Mr Courtney, it's of the utmost importance.'

Max plucked desperately at Sean's arm.

'What is it, Max?' Duff asked.

'I have to speak to you alone,' Max dropped his voice again and glanced unhappily at the street door.

'Well, speak then,' Duff encouraged him. 'We're alone now.'

'Not here. Can you meet me later?'

Duff raised an eyebrow. 'What is this, Maximilian, don't tell me you are selling dirty pictures.'

'Mr Hradsky is waiting for me at the hotel. I told him I was coming to find some papers, he'll get suspicious if I don't go back immediately.' Max was nearly in tears; his Adam's apple played hide-and-seek behind his high collar, bobbing out and disappearing again. Duff was suddenly very interested in what Max had to say.

'You don't want Norman to know about this?' he asked.

'My goodness, no.' Max came closer to tears.

'When do you want to meet us?'

'Tonight, after ten o'clock when Mr Hradsky has retired.'

'Where?' asked Duff.

'There's a side road round the east end of the Little Sister Mine dump. It's not used any more.'

'I know it,' said Duff. 'We'll ride along there about half past ten.'

'Thank you, Mr Charleywood, you won't regret it.' Max scampered for the door and disappeared.

Duff adjusted his beaver at the correct angle, then he prodded Sean in the belly with the point of his cane.

'Smell it – suck it in.' Duff sniffed appreciatively and Sean did the same.

'I don't smell a thing,' Sean declared.

'The air is thick with it,' Duff told him. 'The sweet smell of treachery.'

They left Xanadu just after half past nine. Duff insisted on wearing a black opera cloak.

'Atmosphere is vital, laddie, you can't go to a rendezvous like this dressed in dirty khaki pants and *veldschoen*. It would ruin the whole thing.'

'Well, I'm damned if I'm going to get into fancy dress. This is a very good suit. It will have to do.'

'Can't I persuade you to wear a pistol in your belt?' asked Duff wistfully.

'No,' laughed Sean.

'No?' Duff shook his head. 'You're a barbarian, laddie. No taste, that's your trouble.'

They avoided the main streets on their way through Johannesburg and met the Cape road half a mile beyond the town. There was only a minute slice of moon left in the dark bowl of the sky. The stars, however, were big and by their light the white mine dumps, each the size of a large hill, stood out like pustules on the earth's face.

Despite himself, Sean felt a little breathless with excitement – Duff's zest was always infectious. They cantered with their stirrups almost touching, Duff's cloak billowing out behind him and the breeze of their passage fanning the tip of Sean's cigar to a fierce red spark.

'Slow down, Duff, the turning's just about here somewhere. It's overgrown, we'll miss it.'

They reined to a walk.

'What's the time?' asked Duff.

Sean drew on his cigar and held his watch close to the glow. 'A quarter after ten. We're early.'

'My bet is Maximilian will be there before us – here's the road.' Duff turned his horse onto it and Sean followed him. The Little Sister Mine dump rose up next to them, steep and white in the starlight. They skirted it but its bulk threw a shadow over them. Duff's horse snorted and shied and Sean gripped with his knees as his own horse danced sideways. Max had stepped out from a scraggy cluster of bushes next to the road.

'Well met by moonlight, Maximilian,' Duff greeted him.

'Please bring your horses off the road, gentlemen.' Max was still showing signs of the afternoon's agitation. They tied their horses next to Max's among the bushes and walked across to join him.

'Well, Max, what's new? How are the folks?' Duff asked.

'Before we go any further in this matter, I want you gentlemen to give me your word of honour that, whether anything comes of it or not, you will never say a word to anybody of what I tell you tonight.' Max was very pale, Sean thought, or perhaps it was just the starlight.

'I agree to that,' said Sean.

'Cross my heart,' said Duff.

Max opened the front of his coat and brought out a long envelope. 'I think if I show you these first it will make it easier to explain my proposition.'

Sean took the envelope from him. 'What are they, Max?'

'The latest statements from all four banks at which Mr Hradsky deals.'

'Matches, Sean, give us a light, laddie,' said Duff eagerly.

'I have a lantern with me,' Max said and he squatted down to light it. Sean and Duff squatted with him and spread the bank statements in the circle of yellow light. They examined them in silence until at last Sean rocked back on his heels and lit another cigar.

'Well, I am glad I don't owe that much money,' Sean announced. Sean folded up the sheets and put them back in the envelope. He slapped the envelope into the palm of his free hand and started chuckling. Max reached across, took it from him and placed it carefully back inside his coat.

'All right, Max, spell it out for us,' said Sean. Max leaned forward and blew out the lantern. What he had to say was easier said in darkness.

'The large cash payment that Mr Hradsky had to make to you gentlemen and the limitation of output from his diamond mines in terms of the new cartel agreements in the diamond industry have forced him to borrow heavily on all his banks.' Max stopped and cleared his throat. 'The extent of this borrowing you have seen. Of course, the banks demanded security for the loans and Mr Hradsky has given them his entire holding of C.R.C. shares. The banks have set a limit on the shares of thirty-five shillings each. As you know C.R.C.'s are currently quoted at ninety shillings, which leaves a wide margin of safety. However, if the shares were to suffer a setback and fall in price to thirty-five shillings the banks would sell. They would dump every single share that Mr Hradsky owns in C.R.C.'s onto the market.'

'Go on, Max,' said Duff. 'I'm beginning to like the sound of your voice.'

'It occurred to me that if Mr Hradsky were temporarily absent from Johannesburg – say if he went on a trip to England to buy new machinery or something of that nature – it would be possible for you gentlemen to force the price of C.R.C.'s down to thirty-five shillings. Done correctly it would only take three or four days to accomplish. You could sell short and start rumours that the Leader Reef had pinched out at depth. Mr Hradsky would not be here to defend his interests and as soon as C.R.C.'s hit thirty-five shillings the banks would off-load his shares. The price would crash and you, with ready cash available, would be in a position to buy up C.R.C. shares at a fraction of their actual value. There is no reason why you shouldn't gain control of the group and make a couple of million to boot.'

There was another silence. It lasted a long time before Sean asked, 'What do you get out of it, Max?'

'Your cheque for one hundred thousand pounds, Mr Courtney.'

'Wages are going up,' remarked Sean. 'I thought the standard pay for this type of work was thirty pieces of silver. The rate, I believe, was set by a countryman of yours.'

'Shut up,' snapped Duff, then more pleasantly to Max, 'Mr Courtney likes his little jokes. Tell me, Max, is that all you want – just the money? I'll be frank with you – it doesn't ring true. You must be a moderately rich man as it is.'

Max stood up quickly and started towards the horses. He hadn't reached them before he swung around. His face was in darkness but his voice was naked as he screamed at them.

'Do you think I don't know what they call me – "The Court Jester", "Hradsky's tongue", "Lick-arse". Do you think I like it? Do you think I enjoy crawling to him every minute of every day? I want to be free again. I want to be a man again.' His voice choked off and his hands came up and covered his face. He was sobbing. Sean couldn't watch him and even Duff looked down at the ground in embarrassment. When Max spoke again it was in his usual soft and sad voice.

'Mr Courtney, if you wear your yellow waistcoat to the office tomorrow, I will take it as a sign that you intend to follow my suggestion and that my terms are acceptable to you. I will then make the necessary arrangements to ensure Mr Hradsky's absence from the country.' He untied his horse, mounted and rode away down the track towards the Cape Road. Neither Sean nor Duff moved to stand up. They listened to the hoof-beats of Max's horse fade into the darkness, before Duff spoke. 'Those bank statements were genuine – I had a good look at the seals.'

'And even more genuine was Max's emotion.' Sean flicked his cigar away into the bushes. 'No one could act that well. It made me feel quite sick listening to him. Hell, how can a man so cold-bloodedly betray his trust?'

'Laddie, let's not turn this into a discussion of Max's morals. Let's concern ourselves with the facts. Norman has been delivered into our hands, neatly trussed, spiced with garlic and with a sprig of parsley behind each ear. I say let's cook him and eat him.'

Sean smiled at him. 'Give me a few good reasons. I want you to convince me. The way I feel towards him after that meeting this afternoon, I shouldn't be surprised if I convince easily.'

'One.' Duff held up a finger. 'Norman deserves it.'

Sean nodded.

'Two.' Another of Duff's fingers came up. 'If we gain control we can run things the way we want. You can indulge your good resolution and give everybody a pay rise and I'll be top man again.'

'Yes!' Sean tugged at his moustache thoughtfully.

'Three. We came here to make money, we'll never get another opportunity like this. And my last reason, but the most potent – you look so beautiful in that yellow waistcoat, laddie, I wouldn't miss seeing you in it tomorrow morning, not for a thousand C.R.C. shares.'

'It is rather natty,' admitted Sean. 'But listen, Duff, I don't want another Lochtkamper business. Messy, you know.'

Duff stood up.

'Norman's a big boy, he wouldn't do that. Anyway, he'll still be rich – he's got his diamond mines. We'll only be relieving him of his responsibilities on the Witwatersrand.'

They walked across to the horses. Sean had his foot in the stirrup when he stiffened and exclaimed, 'My God, I can't do it. It's all off.'

'Why?' Duff was alarmed.

'I spilt gravy on that waistcoat – I can't possibly wear it tomorrow. My tailor would murder me.'

– 30 –

There was no problem in arranging for Hradsky's absence – someone had to go to London. There was machinery to buy for the new areas on the East Rand and they had to select two engineers from the hundred or so applicants waiting in England. Not ungraciously, Hradsky allowed himself to be elected for the job.

'We'll give him a farewell party,' Duff suggested to Sean during dinner that night. 'Well, not really a farewell party – but a wake.'

Sean started whistling the 'Dead March' and Duff tapped it out on the table with the handle of his knife.

'We'll have it at Candy's Hot—' Duff cut himself short. 'We'll have it here. We'll really lay it on for poor old Norman so afterwards he'll be able to say, "The bastards may have cleaned me out, but they certainly gave me a grand party".'

'He doesn't like parties,' said Sean.

'That's an excellent reason why we should give him one,' agreed Duff.

A week later when Hradsky and Max left on the morning coach for Port Natal there were fifty members of the Johannesburg Stock Exchange still in full evening dress from the night's party to wave him goodbye. Duff made a touching, if somewhat slurred, little speech and presented Hradsky with a bouquet of roses. Nervous of the crowd that milled about them, the horses bolted when the driver cracked his whip and Max and Hradsky were thrown together in an undignified heap on the rear seat of the coach. The crowd cheered them out of sight. With an arm around his shoulder Sean led Duff across the street to the office and deposited him in one of the deep leather armchairs.

'Are you sober enough to talk sense?' Sean asked dubiously.

'Sure. Always at your service as the lady said to the customer.'

'I managed to have a word with Max last night,' Sean told him. 'He will send us a telegram from Port Natal when he and Hradsky are safely on the mailboat. We won't start anything until we receive it.'

'Very wise – you're the wisest chap I know,' Duff grinned happily.

'You'd better go to bed,' Sean told him.

'Too far,' said Duff. 'I'll sleep here.'

It was another ten days before Max's telegram arrived. Sean and Duff were eating lunch in the Rand Club when it was delivered to their table. Sean slit open the envelope and read the message to Duff.

'Sailing four o'clock this afternoon. Good luck. Max.'

'I'll drink to that.' Duff lifted his wine glass.

'Tomorrow,' said Sean, 'I'll go up to the Candy Deep and tell Francois to pull all the men out of the bottom levels of the mine. No one's to be allowed in.'

'Put a guard at the fourteenth level,' suggested Duff. 'That'll make it more impressive.'

'Good idea,' agreed Sean. He looked up as someone passed their table and suddenly he started to smile. 'Duff, do you know who that is?'

'Who are you talking about?' Duff looked bewildered.

'That chap who's just gone out into the lounge – there he is, going into the lavatories.'

'Isn't that Elliott, the newspaper fellow?'

'Editor of the *Rand Mail*,' nodded Sean. 'Come with me, Duff.'

'Where are we going?'

'To get a bit of cheap publicity.'

Duff followed Sean out of the dining-room, across the lounge and into the men's lavatories. The door of one of the closets was closed and as they walked in someone farted softly behind it. Sean winked at Duff and went across to the urinal. As he addressed himself to it he said, 'Well, all we can hope for now, Duff, is that Norman will be able to work a miracle in England. Otherwise—' He shrugged his shoulder. Duff picked up his cue.

'We're taking a hell of a chance relying on that. I still say we should sell out now. C.R.C.'s were at ninety-one shillings this morning so it's obvious that the story hasn't leaked out yet. But when it does you won't be able to give the bloody shares away. I say we should get out while the going's good.'

'No,' Sean disagreed. 'Let's wait until we hear from Norman. It's taking a bit of a chance, I know, but we have a responsibility to the men working for us.' Sean took Duff's arm and led him out of the lavatory again; at the door he added the cherry to the top of the pie. 'If and when C.R.C. collapses there are going to be thousands of men out of work – do you realize that?'

Sean closed the door behind them and they grinned delightedly at each other.

'You're a genius, laddie,' whispered Duff.

'I'm happy to say I agree with you,' Sean whispered back.

The next morning Sean woke with the knowledge that something exciting was going to happen that day. He lay and savoured the feeling before he sent his mind out to hunt for the reason. Then he sat up suddenly and reached for the newspaper that lay folded on the coffee tray beside his bed. He shook it open and found what he was looking for on the front page, big headlines: *Is all well with the Central Rand Consolidated? Norman Hradsky's mystery journey*. The story itself was a masterpiece of journalistic evasion. Seldom had Sean seen anyone write so fluently or convincingly on a subject about which he knew nothing. 'It is suggested', 'Usually reliable sources report' and 'There is reason to believe' – all the old phrases of no significance. Sean groped for his slippers and padded down the corridor to Duff's room.

Duff had all the blankets and most of the bed; the girl was curled up like a pink anchovy on the outskirts. Duff was snoring and the girl whimpered a little in her sleep. Sean tickled Duff's lips with the tassel of his dressing-gown cord, Duff's nose twitched and his snores gurgled into silence. The girl sat up and looked at Sean with eyes wide but vacant from sleep.

'Quickly, run,' Sean shouted at her, 'the rebels are coming.'

She leapt straight into the air and landed three feet from the bed quivering with panic. Sean ran a critical eye over her. A pretty filly, he decided, and made a mental note to take her for a trot just as soon as Duff put her out to grass.

'All right,' he reassured her, 'they've gone away now.'

She became aware of her nakedness and Sean's frank appraisal of it. She tried to cover it with hands too small for the task. Sean picked up Duff's gown from the foot of the bed and handed it to her.

'Go and have a bath or something, sweetheart, I want to talk to Mr Charleywood.'

With the gown on she recovered her composure and told him severely, 'I didn't have any clothes on, Mr Courtney.'

'I would never have guessed,' said Sean politely.

'It's not nice.'

'You are too modest – I thought it was better than average. Off you go now, there's a good girl.' With a saucy flick of her head she disappeared into the bathroom and Sean transferred his attention to Duff. Duff had held grimly onto the threads of sleep throughout the exchange but he let go when Sean whacked him across the backside with the folded newspaper. Like a tortoise coming out of its shell his head emerged from the blankets. Sean handed him the paper and sat down on the edge of the bed. He watched Duff's face crease into laughter lines before he spoke.

'You better get down to the Editor's office and shout at him a little – just to confirm his suspicions. I'll go up to the Candy Deep and close all the bottom levels. I'll meet you back at the Exchange at opening time and don't forget to clean that grin off your face before you show it round town. Try and look haggard, it shouldn't be difficult for you.'

When Sean arrived at the Stock Exchange building the crowd had filled the street outside. Mbejane eased the landau into it and it opened to give them a passage. Sean scowled straight ahead and ignored the questions which were shouted at him from all around. Mbejane stopped the carriage outside the main entrance and four police constables held back the mob while Sean hurried across the pavement and through the double doors. Duff was there ahead of him, the centre of a turbulent circle of members and brokers. He saw Sean and waved frantically over the heads of his inquisitors. That was sufficient to switch their attention from Duff to Sean and they flocked to him, ringing him in with anxious angry faces. Sean's hat was knocked forward over his eyes and a button popped off his coat as one of them caught hold of his lapels.

'Is it true?' the man shouted, spittle flying from his lips into Sean's face. 'We've got a right to know if it's true.'

Sean swung his cane in a full overarm stroke onto the man's head and sent him tottering backwards into the arms of those behind him.

'Back, you bastards,' he roared at them using both the point and the edge of his cane to beat them away, scattering them across the floor until he stood alone, glowering at them with the cane still twitching restlessly in his hand.

'I'll make a statement later on. Until then, behave yourselves.' He adjusted his hat, picked the loose thread where the button had been from his coat and stalked across to join Duff. He could see Duff's grin starting to lift the corner of his mouth and he cautioned him silently with his eyes. Grim-faced they walked through into the members' lounge.

'How's it going your end?' Duff kept his voice low.

'Couldn't be better.' Sean contrived a worried expression. 'I've got an armed guard on the fourteenth level. When this bunch hear about that, they'll really start frothing at the mouth.'

'When you make your statement, let it ring with obvious false confidence,' Duff instructed. 'If it goes on like this we'll have the shares down to thirty-five shillings within an hour of opening.'

Five minutes before opening time Sean stood in the President's box and made his address to his fellow members, Duff listened to him with mounting admiration. Sean's hearty reassurances and verbal side-stepping were enough to strike despair into the souls of the most hardened optimists. Sean finished his speech and climbed down from the box amid a gloomy lack of applause. The bell rang and the brokers stood singly or in small disconsolate groups about the floor. The first tentative offer was made. 'I sell C.R.C.'

But there was no rush to buy. Ten minutes later there was a sale recorded at eighty-five shillings, six shillings lower than the previous day's closing price. Duff leaned across to Sean. 'We'll have to start selling some of our own shares to get things moving, otherwise everybody's going to keep sitting on the fence.'

'That's all right,' Sean nodded, 'we'll buy them back later at a quarter of the price. But wait until the news about the Candy Deep gets out.'

It was just before ten o'clock when that happened. The reaction was sharp. In one quick burst of selling C.R.C.'s dropped to sixty shillings. But there they hung, fluctuating nervously in the chaos of hope and doubt.

'We'll have to sell now,' whispered Duff, 'they are short of script. We'll have to give it to them otherwise the price will stick here.'

Sean felt his hands trembling and he clenched them in his pockets. Duff was showing signs of the strain as well, there was a nerve jumping in his cheek and his eyes had receded into their sockets a little. This was a game with high stakes.

'Don't overdo it – sell thirty thousand.'

The price of C.R.C.'s sagged under the weight but levelled out at forty-five shillings. There was still another hour until high change and Sean's whole body was screwed up tight with tension. He felt the cold patches of sweat under his arms.

'Sell another thirty thousand,' he ordered his clerk and

even to himself his voice sounded wheezy. He stubbed out his cigar in the copper ashtray next to his chair; it was already half full of butts. It was no longer necessary for either of them to act worried. This time the price stuck at forty shillings and the sale of sixty thousand more of their shares failed to move it down more than a few shillings.

'Someone's buying up,' muttered Sean uneasily.

'It looks like it,' agreed Duff. 'I'll lay odds it's that bloody Greek Efthyvoulos. It looks as if we'll have to sell enough to glut him before they'll drop any further.'

By high change Duff and Sean had sold three-quarters of their holdings in C.R.C.'s and the price still stood stubbornly at thirty-seven and sixpence. So tantalizingly close to the magic figure that would release a flood of Hradsky's shares onto the unprepared market, but now they were nearing the stage when they would no longer have any shares with which to force the price down that last two and sixpence.

The market closed and left Duff and Sean sitting limply in their armchairs, shaken and tired as prizefighters at the end of the fifteenth round. Slowly the lounge emptied but still they sat on. Sean leaned across and put his hand on Duff's shoulder. 'It's going to be all right,' he said. 'Tomorrow it will be all right.'

They looked at each other and they exchanged strength, each of them drawing it from the other until they were both smiling. Sean stood up. 'Come on, let's go home.'

Sean went to bed early and alone. Although he felt drained of energy, sleep was a long time coming to him and when it did it was full of confused dreams and punctuated with sharp jerks back into wakefulness. It was almost a relief to see the dawn define the windows as grey squares and to be released from his unrewarding rest. At breakfast he drank a cup of coffee and found that his stomach was unable to accept the plateful of steak and eggs that was offered it for it was already screwing up tight in anticipation of the day ahead. Duff was edgy and tired-looking as well; they spoke only a little during the meal and not at all in the carriage when Mbejane drove them down to the Exchange.

The crowd was outside the Stock Exchange again. They forced their way through it and into the building; they took their seats in the lounge and Sean looked round at the faces of his fellow members. In each of them were the marks of worry, the same darkness round the eyes and the jerkiness in movement. He watched Jock Heyns yawn extravagantly and had to do the same; he lifted his hand to cover his mouth and found it was trembling again. He laid the hand on the arm of his chair and kept it still. Across the lounge Bonzo Barnes caught Sean's eye and looked away quickly, then he also gaped into a cavernous yawn. It was the tension. In the years ahead Sean would see men yawn like that while they waited for the dawn to send them against the Boer guns. Duff leaned across to him and broke his line of thought.

'As soon as the trading starts, we'll sell. Try and panic them. Do you agree?'

'Sudden death,' Sean nodded. He couldn't face another morning of that mental agony. 'Couldn't we offer shares at thirty-two shillings and sixpence and get it over with?' he asked.

Duff grinned at him. 'We can't do that, it's too obvious – we'll just have to go on offering to sell at best and let the price fall on its own.'

'I suppose you're right – but we'll play our high cards now and dump the rest of our shares as soon as the market opens. I don't see how the price can possibly hold after that.'

Duff nodded. He beckoned to their authorized clerk who was waiting patiently at the door of the lounge and when the man came up to them he told him, 'Sell one hundred thousand C.R.C.'s at best.'

The clerk blinked but he jotted the order down on his pad and went out onto the main floor where the other brokers were gathering. It was a few minutes from the bell.

'What if it doesn't work?' Sean asked. The tightness in his belly was nauseating him.

'It must work – it's got to work,' Duff whispered as much to himself as to Sean. He was twisting his fingers round the head of his cane and chewing against clenched teeth. They sat and waited for the bell and when it rang Sean jumped then reached sheepishly for his cigar case. He heard their clerk's voice, raised sharply, 'I sell C.R.C.'s,' and then the confused mumble of voices as the trading started. Through the lounge door he saw the recorder chalk up the first sale. 'Thirty-seven shillings.'

He drew hard on his cigar and lay back in his chair forcing himself to relax, ignoring the restless tapping of Duff's fingers on the arm of the chair next to him. The recorder wiped out the figures and wrote again. 'Thirty-six shillings.'

Sean blew out cigar smoke in a long jet. 'It's moving,' he whispered and Duff's hand clenched on the arm of the chair, his knuckles paling from the pressure of his grip.

'Thirty-five.' The elusive number at last. Sean heard Duff sigh next to him and his voice, 'Now! watch it go, laddie, now the banks will come on. Get ready, laddie, get ready now.'

'Thirty-four and six,' wrote the recorder.

'They must come in now,' said Duff again. 'Get ready to get rich, laddie.'

Their clerk was coming back across the floor and into the lounge. He stopped in front of their chairs. 'I managed to sell them, sir.'

Sean straightened up quickly. 'So soon?' he asked.

'Yes, sir, three big sales and I got rid of them all. I'm afraid the last was only at thirty-four and sixpence.'

Sean stared back at the board. The figure was still at thirty-four and sixpence.

'Duff, something's going on here. Why haven't the banks come in yet?'

'We'll force them to off-load.' Duff's voice was unnaturally hoarse. 'We'll force the bastards.' He pulled himself half out of his chair and snarled at the clerk.

'Sell another one hundred thousand at thirty shillings.' The man's face went slack with surprise. 'Hurry, man, do you hear me? What are you waiting for?' The clerk backed away from Duff, then he turned and scurried out of the lounge.

'Duff, for God's sake.' Sean grabbed his arm. 'Have you gone mad?'

'We'll force them,' muttered Duff. 'They'll have to sell.'

'We haven't got another hundred thousand shares.' Sean jumped up. 'I'm going to stop him.' He ran across the lounge but before he reached the door he saw the sale being chalked up on the board at thirty shillings. He pushed his way across the crowded floor until he reached his clerk. 'Don't sell any more,' he whispered.

The man looked surprised. 'I've sold them already, sir.'

'The whole hundred thousand?' There was horrified disbelief in Sean's voice.

'Yes, sir, someone took the lot in one batch.'

Sean walked back across the floor in a daze. He sank into the chair beside Duff.

'They're sold already.' He spoke as though he didn't believe himself.

'We'll force them, we'll force them to sell,' muttered Duff again and Sean turned to him with alarm. Duff was sweating in little dewdrops across his forehead and his eyes were very bright.

'Duff, for God's sake,' Sean whispered to him, 'steady, man.' Sean knew that they were watched by everybody in the lounge. The watching faces seemed as large as those seen through a telescope and the buzz of their voices echoed strangely in his ears. Sean felt confused: everything seemed to be in slow motion like a bad dream. He looked through into the trading floor and saw the crude number thirty still chalked accusingly against C.R.C. Where were the banks? Why weren't they selling?

'We'll force them, we'll force the bastards,' Duff said again. Sean tried to answer him but the words wouldn't come. He looked back across the trading floor and now he knew it was a bad dream for Hradsky and Max were there, walking across the floor towards the members' lounge. Men were crowding around them and Hradsky was smiling and holding up his hands as if to fend off their questions. They came through into the lounge and Hradsky went to his chair by the fireplace. He lowered himself into it with his shoulders sagging forward and his waistcoat wrinkled tightly around the full bag of his belly. He was still smiling and Sean thought that his smile was one of the most unnerving things he had ever seen. He watched it with flesh-crawling fascination and beside him Duff was just as still and stricken. Max spoke quickly to Hradsky and then he stood up and walked across to Sean and Duff. He stopped in front of them.

'The clerk informs us that you have contracted to sell to Mr Hradsky five hundred thousand shares in C.R.C.'s at an average price of thirty-six shillings.' Max's lashes drooped sadly onto his cheeks. 'The total issue of C.R.C.'s, as you know, is one million shares. During the last two days Mr Hradsky was able to purchase another seventy-five thousand shares apart from the ones you sold to him. This makes his total holdings of C.R.C.'s almost six hundred thousand shares. It seems therefore that you have sold shares that don't exist. Mr Hradsky foresees that you will have some difficulty in fulfilling your contract.'

Sean and Duff went on staring at him. He turned to leave them and Duff blurted out. 'But the banks – why didn't the banks sell?'

Max smiled a mournful little smile. 'The day he reached Port Natal Mr Hradsky transferred sufficient funds from his accounts there to liquidate his overdrafts in Johannesburg. He sent you that telegram and returned here immediately. We only arrived an hour ago.'

'But – but, you lied to us. You tricked us!'

Max inclined his head. 'Mr Charleywood, I will not discuss honesty with a man who does not understand the meaning of the word.' He went back to Hradsky's side. Everyone in the lounge had heard him and while Duff and Sean went on sitting amongst the ruins of their fortune the struggle to buy C.R.C. shares started on the main floor. In five minutes the price was over ninety shillings and still climbing. When it reached one hundred shillings, Sean touched Duff's arm.

'Let's go.' They stood up together and started for the door of the members' lounge. As they passed Hradsky's chair he spoke.

'Yes, Mr Charleywood, you can't win all the time.' It came out quite clearly with only a slight catch on the 'c's' – they were always difficult letters for Norman Hradsky.

Duff stopped, he turned to face Hradsky, his mouth open as he struggled to find a reply. His lips moved, groping, groping for words – but there were none. His shoulders drooped, he shook his head and turned away. He stumbled once at the edge of the floor. Sean held his arm and guided him through the excited jabber of brokers. No one took any notice of the two of them. They were bumped and jostled before they were through the crush and out onto the pavement. Sean signalled Mbejane to bring the carriage.

They climbed into it and Mbejane drove them up to Xanadu.

They went through into the drawing-room.

'Get me a drink, please, Sean.' Duff's face was grey and crumpled-looking. Sean poured two tumblers half full of brandy and carried one across to Duff. Duff drank and then sat staring into the empty glass.

'I'm sorry – I lost my head. I thought we'd be able to buy those shares for dirt, when the banks started selling.'

'It doesn't matter,' Sean's voice was tired. 'We were smashed before that happened. Christ! What a well-laid trap it was!'

'We couldn't have known. It was so damn cunning, we couldn't have guessed, could we, Sean?' Duff was trying to excuse himself.

Sean kicked off his boots and loosened his collar. 'That night up at the mine dump – I would have staked my life Max wasn't lying.' He lay back in the chair and stirred his brandy with a circular movement of his hand. 'Christ, how they must have laughed to see us stampede into the pitfall!'

'But we aren't finished, Sean, we aren't completely finished, are we?' Duff was pleading with him, begging for a peg to hang his hope on. 'We'll come out of this all right, you know we will, don't you? We'll save enough out of the wreckage to start again. We'll build it all up again, won't we, Sean?'

'Sure,' Sean laughed brutally. 'You can get a job down at the Bright Angels cleaning out the spittoons and I'll get one at the Opera House playing the piano.'

'But – but – there'll be something left. A couple of thousand even. We could sell this house.'

'Don't dream, Duff, this house belongs to Hradsky. Everything belongs to him.' Sean flicked the brandy that was left in his glass into his mouth and swallowed it. He stood up quickly and went across to the liquor cabinet. 'I'll explain it to you. We owe Hradsky a hundred thousand shares that don't exist. The only way we can deliver them is to buy them from him first and he can set his own price on them. We're finished, Duff, do you know what that means? Smashed! Broken!' Sean poured brandy into his glass, slopping a little on the sideboard. 'Have another drink on Hradsky, it's his brandy now.' Sean swept his arm round the room, pointing at the rich furniture and heavy curtains. 'Take a last look at this lot. Tomorrow the Sheriff will be here to attach it; then through the due processes of the law it will be handed to its rightful owner – Mr Norman Hradsky.' Sean started back towards his chair and then he stopped.

'The due processes of the law,' he repeated softly. 'I wonder – it might just work.'

Duff sat up eagerly in his chair. 'You've got an idea?'

Sean nodded. 'Well, half an idea anyway. Listen, Duff, if I can save a couple of thousand out of this do you agree that we get out of here?'

'Where to – where will we go?'

'We were facing north when we started. It's as good a direction as any. They say there's gold and ivory beyond the Limpopo for those who want it.'

'But, why can't we stay here? We could play the stock market.' Duff looked uncertain, almost afraid.

'Damn it, Duff, we're finished here. It's a different story playing the market when you are paying the fiddler and calling the tune, but with a mere thousand or so we'd be among the dogs fighting for the scraps under Hradsky's table. Let's get out and start again. We'll go north, hunt ivory and prospect for a new reef. We'll take a couple of wagons and find another fortune. I bet you've forgotten how it feels to sit on a horse and handle a rifle, to have the wind in your face and not a whore or a stockbroker within five hundred miles.'

'But it means leaving everything we've worked for,' Duff groaned.

'Sweet merciful heavens, man, are you blind or just plain stupid?' Sean stormed at him. 'You don't own anything, so how the hell can you leave something you haven't got? I'm going down to see Hradsky and try to make a deal with him. Are you coming?'

Duff looked at him without seeing him, his lips were trembling and he was shaking his head. At last he was realizing the position they were in and the impact of it had dazed him. The higher you ride the further there is to fall.

'All right,' said Sean. 'Wait for me here.'

Hradsky's suite was full of talking, laughing men. Sean recognized most of them as the courtiers who used to cluster round the throne on which he and Duff had sat. The King is dead, long live the King! They saw him standing in the doorway and the laughter and loud voices fizzled out. He saw Max take two quick steps to the stinkwood desk in the corner, pull open the top drawer and drop his hand into it. He stood like that watching Sean. One by one the courtiers picked up their hats and canes and hurried out of the room. Some of them mumbled embarrassed greetings as they brushed passed Sean. Then there were only the three of them left: Sean standing quietly in the doorway, Max behind the desk with his hand on the pistol and Hradsky in the chair by the fireplace watching through yellow, half-hooded eyes.

'Aren't you going to invite me in, Max?' Sean asked and Max glanced quickly at Hradsky, saw his barely perceptible nod and looked back at Sean. 'Come in, please, Mr Courtney.'

Sean pushed the door shut behind him. 'You won't need the gun, Max, the game is over.'

'And the score is in our favour, is it not, Mr Courtney?'

Sean nodded. 'Yes, you've won. We are prepared to make over to you all the C.R.C. shares we hold.'

Max shook his head unhappily. 'I'm afraid it's not quite as easy as that. You have undertaken to sell us a certain number of shares and we must insist upon delivery in full.'

'Just where do you suggest we get them?' Sean asked.

'You could buy them on the Stock Exchange.'

'From you?'

Max shrugged but made no reply.

'So you are going to twist the knife, are you?'

'You put it very poetically, Mr Courtney,' agreed Max.

'Have you considered the consequences of forcing us into bankruptcy?'

'I will admit freely that the consequences to you do not concern us.'

Sean smiled. 'That was not very nice, Max, but I was talking about it from your point of view. Sequestration orders, creditors' meetings – you can rest assured that the liquidator appointed will be a member of the *Volksraad* or a relative of one. There will be court actions and counter actions, enforced sale of the shares in the estate and costs to pay. A liquidator with any sense at all could string it out for three or four years, all the time drawing a handsome commission. Have you thought about that, Max?'

The narrowing of Max's eyes showed that he hadn't. He looked at Hradsky with a trace of helplessness in his face, and Sean took a little comfort from that look.

'Now what I suggest is this – you let us draw ten thousand, take our horses and personal belongings. We in exchange will give you the rest. Shares, bank accounts, property, everything. You cannot possibly get more out of it if you force us into bankruptcy.'

Hradsky gave Max a message in their private facial code and Max interpreted it to Sean.

'Would you mind waiting outside, please, while we discuss this offer of yours.'

'I'll go down and have a drink in the bar,' said Sean. He pulled his watch from his waistcoat pocket and checked the time. 'Will twenty minutes be enough?'

'Ample, thank you, Mr Courtney.'

Sean had his drink by himself although the bar was nowhere near empty. This was not an arrangement of his own choosing, but he was flying the fever flag of failure and so he had to take an isolation berth at one end of the bar while all the other ships steered wide of him. No one looked in his direction and the conversation that went on round him was carefully arranged so as to exclude him. While he waited out the twenty minutes he amused himself by imagining the reactions of these his friends if he were to ask them for a loan. This helped to take the sting out of their snubs but still he felt it rankling. He looked at his watch again. The twenty minutes were up. Sean walked back along the counter towards the door. Jock and Trevor Heyns saw him coming, they turned away abruptly and immediately became absorbed in staring at the bottle-lined shelves behind the bar counter. Sean stopped level with Jock and cleared his throat deferentially. 'Jock, could you spare a minute?'

Jock turned slowly. 'Ah, Sean. Yes, what is it?'

'Duff and I are leaving the Rand. I have something for you, just something to remember us by. I know Duff would want you to have it too.'

Jock reddened with embarrassment. 'That's not necessary,' he said and started to turn back to his drink.

'Please, Jock.'

'Oh, all right,' Jock's voice was irritable. 'What is it?'

'This,' Sean said and stepped forward, moving his weight behind the fist. Jock's large and whisky-flushed nose was a target to dream about. It was not one of Sean's best punches, he was out of training, but it was good enough to send Jock in a spectacular back-somersault over the counter. Dreamily Sean picked up Jock's glass and emptied it over Trevor's head.

'Next time you meet me smile and say "Hello",' he told Trevor. 'Until then – stay out of mischief.'

He went up the stairs to Hradsky's suite in much better spirits. They were waiting for him.

'Give me the word, Max,' Sean could even grin at him.

'Mr Hradsky has very generously—'

'How much?' Sean cut him short.

'Mr Hradsky will allow you to take fifteen hundred and your personal effects. As part of the agreement you will give an undertaking not to embark on any business venture on the Witwatersrand for a period of three years.'

'That will be too soon,' said Sean. 'Make it two thousand and you've got a deal.'

'The offer is not open to discussion.'

Sean could see they meant it. They didn't have to bargain; it was a statement.

'All right, I accept.'

'Mr Hradsky has sent for his lawyer to draw up the agreement. Would you mind waiting, Mr Courtney?'

'Not at all, Max, you forget I am a gentleman of leisure now.'

– 31 –

Sean found Duff still sitting in the chair where he had left him in the drawing-room of Xanadu. The bottle clutched in his hand was empty and he was unconscious. He had spilt brandy down the front of his waistcoat and three of the buttons were undone. Huddled in the big chair, his body seemed to have shrunk and the curly hair hanging onto his forehead softened the gaunt lines of his face. Sean loosened his fingers from the neck of the bottle and Duff moved restlessly, muttering and twisting his head.

'Bedtime for small boys,' said Sean. He lifted him out of the chair and hung him over one shoulder.

Duff sicked up copiously.

'That's the way, show Hradsky what you think of his bloody carpet,' Sean encouraged him. 'Give him another one for luck, but not on my boots.'

Duff did as he was bid and, chuckling, Sean carried him up the stairs. At the top he stopped and with Duff still bundled over one shoulder tried to analyse his own feelings. Damn it, he felt happy. It was ridiculous to feel so happy in the midst of disaster. He went on down the passage still wondering at himself and into Duff's room. He dropped Duff on the bed and stripped his clothes off, then he rolled him under the blankets. He brought the enamel wash basin from the bathroom and placed it next to the bed.

'You may need this – sleep well. There's a long ride ahead of us tomorrow.'

He stopped again at the top of the stairs and looked down their marble slope into the splendour of the lobby. He was leaving all of it and that was nothing to feel happy about. He laughed aloud. Perhaps it was because he had faced complete annihilation and at the last instant had changed it into something less; by avoiding the worst he had made defeat into a victory. A pathetic little victory to be sure, but at least they were no worse off now than they had been when they had arrived on the Rand. Was that the reason? Sean thought about it and found that it wasn't the whole truth. There was also a feeling of release. That was another part of it. To go on his way: north to a new land. He felt the tingle of anticipation.

'Not a whore or a stockbroker within five hundred miles,' he said aloud and grinned. He gave up trying to find words for his feeling. Emotion was so damned elusive: as soon as you cornered it, it changed its shape and the net of words which you had ready to throw over it was no longer suitable. He let it go free to range through his body, accepting and enjoying it. He ran down the stairs, out through the kitchens and into the stableyard.

'Mbejane!' he shouted, 'where the hell are you?'

The clatter of a stool overturning in the servants' quarters and the door of one of the rooms burst open.

'Nkosi – what is it?' The urgency of Sean's voice had alarmed Mbejane.

'Which are the six best horses we have?'

Mbejane named them, making no attempt to hide his curiosity.

'Are they all salted against the Nagana?'*

'All of them, Nkosi.'

'Good – have them ready before tomorrow's light. Two with saddles, the others to carry the packs.'

Mbejane turned on his smile. 'Could it be we are going hunting, Nkosi?'

'It could easily be,' Sean agreed.

'How long will we be gone, Nkosi?'

'How long is for ever? Take leave of all your women,

* Sleeping sickness. Salting involved deliberate exposure to the sting of the tsetse fly. Animals that recovered were then immune.

bring your kaross and your spears and we will see where the road leads.'

Sean went back to his bedroom. It took him half an hour to pack. The pile of discarded clothing in the centre of the room grew steadily and what he kept made only half a horseload. He crammed it into two leather valises. He found his sheepskin coat in the back of one of the closets and threw it over a chair with his leather breeches and slouch hat, ready to wear in the morning. He went down to the study and made his selection from the gun rack, ignoring the fancy doubles and obscure calibres. He took down a pair of shotguns and four Mannlichers.

Then he went to tell Candy goodbye. She was in her suite but she opened quickly to his knock.

'Have you heard?' he asked her.

'Yes, the whole town knows. Oh! Sean, I'm so sorry – please come in.' She held the door open for him. 'How is Duff?'

'He'll be all right – right now he's both drunk and asleep.'

'I'll go to him,' she said quickly. 'He'll need me now.'

For answer Sean raised an eyebrow and looked at her until she dropped her eyes.

'No, you're right, I suppose. Perhaps later, when he's got over the first shock.' She looked up at Sean and smiled. 'I suppose you need a drink. It must have been hell for you as well.' She went across to the cabinet. She had on a blue gown and it clung to the womanish thrust of her hips and did not go high enough to cover the cleft of her breasts. Sean watched her pour his drink and bring it to him. She was lovely, he thought.

'Till we meet again, Candy.' Sean lifted his glass.

Her eyes went wide and very blue. 'I don't understand. Why do you say that?'

'We're going, Candy, first thing tomorrow.'

'No, Sean – you're joking.' But she knew he wasn't. There wasn't much to say after that. He finished his drink and they talked for a while, then he kissed her.

'Be happy, please,' he ordered her.

'I'll try. Come back one day soon.'

'Only if you promise to marry me.' He smiled at her and she caught hold of his beard and tugged his head from side to side.

'Get away with you – before I hold you to that.' He left her then because he knew she was going to weep and he didn't want to watch it.

The next morning Duff packed his gear under Sean's direction. He followed each instruction with a dazed obedience, answering when Sean spoke but otherwise withdrawn in a protective shell of silence. When he had finished Sean made him pick up his bags and marched him down to where the horses waited in the chill gloom of not-yet day. With the horses were men, four shapes in the darkness. Sean hesitated before going out into the yard.

'Mbejane,' he called. 'Who are these with you?'

They came forward into the light that poured through the doorway and Sean chuckled.

'Hlubi, of the noble belly! Nonga! And is it you, Kandhla?' Men who had worked beside him in the trenches of the Candy Deep, had plied the spades that had uncovered his fortune, had plied the spears that protected it from the first predators. Happy at his recognition of them, for it had been many years, they crowded forward smiling as widely and whitely as only a Zulu can.

'What brings you three rogues together so early in the day?' Sean asked, and Hlubi answered for them.

'Nkosi, we heard talk of a trek and our feet burned, we heard talk of hunting and we could not sleep.'

'There is no money for wages,' Sean spoke gruffly to cover the sudden rush of affection he felt for them.

'We made no talk of wages,' Hlubi answered with dignity. Sean nodded, it was the reply he had expected. He cleared his throat and went on.

'You would come with me when you know that I have the Tagathi on me?' He used the Zulu word for witchcraft. 'You would follow me knowing that behind me I leave a spoor of dead men and sorrow?'

'Nkosi,' Hlubi was grave as he answered. 'Something always dies when the lion feeds – and yet there is meat for those that follow him.'

'I hear the chatter of old women at a beer drink,' Mbejane observed drily. 'There is no more to say and the horses grow restless.'

They rode down the driveway of Xanadu between the jacaranda trees and the smooth wide lawns. Behind them the mansion was grey and unlighted in the half darkness. They took the Pretoria road, climbed to the ridge and checked their horses at the crest. Sean and Duff looked back across the valley. The valley was filled with early morning mist, and the mine headgears probed up out of it. They watched the mists turn to gold as the low sun touched them and a mine hooter howled dismally.

'Couldn't we stay for just a week longer – perhaps we could work something out?' Duff asked softly.

Sean sat silently staring at the golden mist. It was beautiful. It hid the scarred earth and it hid the mills – it was a most appropriate cloak for that evil, greedy city. Sean turned his horse away towards Pretoria and slapped the loose end of his reins across its neck.

– III –

The Wilderness

– 1 –

They stayed five days in Pretoria, just long enough to buy the wagons and commission them, and when they left on the morning of the sixth day they went north on the Hunters Road. The wagons moved in column urged on by the Zulus and a dozen new servants that Sean had hired. They were followed by a mixed bag of black and white urchins and stray dogs; men called good luck after them and women waved from the verandas of the houses which lined the road. Then the town was behind them and they were out into the veld with only a dozen of the more adventurous mongrels still following them.

They made fifteen miles the first day and when they camped that night beside the ford of a small stream, Sean's back and legs ached from his first full day in the saddle in over five years. They drank a little brandy and ate steaks grilled over wood embers, then they let the fire die and sat and looked at the night. The sky was a curtain at which a barrel of grape-shot had been fired, riddling it with the holes through which the stars shone. The voices of the servants made a hive murmur as a background to the wailing of a jackal in the darkness beyond the firelight. They went to their living wagon early and for Sean the feel of rough blankets instead of silk sheets and the hardness of a straw mattress were not sufficient to keep him long from sleep.

From an early start the following morning they put another twenty miles behind them before outspan that night and twenty more the next day. The push and urgent drive were habits Sean had acquired on the Rand when every minute was vital and the loss of a day was a disaster. They were habits that stuck, and he pushed the caravan northward as impatiently as he would have chivvied the men on the Candy Deep who were cutting a drive to intersect the Reef. Then one morning, when they were inspanning the oxen at the usual hour of dawn, Mbejane asked him, 'Do we go to meet someone, Nkosi?'

'No. Why do you ask?'

'When a man moves fast there is usually a reason. I was seeking the reason for our haste.'

'The reason is—' Sean stopped. He looked around him quickly as if to find it, then he cleared his throat and scratched the side of his nose, ' – outspan an hour before high sun,' he finished abruptly and went to his horse. He and Duff rode out a mile or two ahead of the wagons that day, then instead of keeping to the track or hurrying back to chase up the caravan Sean suggested, 'Let's ride across to that kopje over there. We'll leave the horses at the bottom and climb up to the top.'

'What for?' asked Duff.

'For the hell of it – come on.'

They hobbled the horses and set off up the steep side of the kopje, picking their way over the tumbled boulders and through the tangle of tree trunks. They were sweating and blowing hard when they came out on the summit and found a place with shade and a flat rock ledge on which to sit. Sean gave Duff a cheroot and they smoked and looked out across the land that was spread like a map below them.

Here the grasslands of the high veld were starting to blend into the forests and hilly country of the bushveld. There were vleis open as wheatfields, ending suddenly against a hill or bounded by haphazard plantations of tall trees. From the height at which they sat they could trace the courses of underground rivers by the dark green and superior height of the trees that grew above them. Everything else was the colour of Africa – brown, a thousand different shades of brown. Pale brown grass on red brown soil, with twisted, chocolate-brown tree trunks reaching up to the moving masses of brown leaves at their tips. Flickering indefinite brown were the herds of springbok that fed amongst the trees and on the slopes of the bare bulging brown hills, and the brown land reached away vast and unhurried into immeasurable distance, unmarred by the scratchings of man: tranquil and dignified in its immensity.

'It makes me feel small, but sort of safe – as though no one will notice me here,' said Duff, then laughed self-consciously.

'I know what you mean,' Sean answered him. He saw that for the first time since they had left the Rand the strain was gone from Duff's face. They smiled at each other and leaned back against the rock face behind them. They watched their wagons, far below them, coil into the tight circle of the laager and the cattle turned free move out to graze. The sun sank and the shadows stretched out longer and longer across the land. At last they went down the hill and found their horses. That night they stayed later than usual next to the fire and though they talked little there was the old feeling between them again. They had discovered a new reef that was rich with the precious elements of space and time. Out here there was more of those two treasures than a man could use in a dozen lifetimes. Space to move, to ride or to fire a rifle; space spread with sunlight and wind, grass and trees, but not filled with them. There was also time. This was where time began: it was a quiet river, moving but not changed by movement; draw on it as much as you would and still it was always full. It was measured by the seasons but not restricted by them, for the summer that was now standing back to let autumn pass was the same summer that had flamed a thousand years before and would flame again a thousand years hence. In the presence of so much space and time all striving was futile.

From then on their lives took their tempo from the leisurely turning of wagon-wheels. Sean's eyes which had been pointing straight ahead along the line of travel now turned aside to look about him. Each morning he and Duff would leave the wagons and wander out into the bush. Sometimes they would spend the day panning for gold in the sands of a stream, another day they would search for the first signs of elephant, but mostly they just rode and talked or lay hidden and watched the herds of game that daily became more numerous. They killed just enough to feed themselves, their servants and the pack of dogs that had followed them when they left Pretoria. They passed the little Boer settlement at Pietersburg and then the Zoutpansberg climbed up over the horizon, its sheer sides dark with rain forest and high rock cliffs. Here under the mountains they spent a week at Louis Trichardt, the most northerly permanent habitation of white men.

In the town they spoke with men who had hunted to the north of the mountains, across the Limpopo. These were taciturn brown-faced Boers with tobacco-stained beards – big men with the peace of the bush in their eyes. In their courteous, unhurried speech Sean sensed a fierce possessive love of the animals that they hunted and the land through which they moved so freely. They were a different breed from the Natal Afrikanders and those he had met on the Witwatersrand, and he conceived the respect for them that would grow stronger in the years ahead when he would have to fight them.

There was no way through the mountains, they told him, but wagons could pass around them. The western passage skirted the edge of the Kalahari desert and this was bad country where the wagon wheels sank into the sandy soil and the marches between water became successively longer. To the east there was good rich forest land, well watered and stocked with game: low country, hotter the nearer one went to the coast, but the true bushveld where a man could find elephant.

So Sean and Duff turned east and, holding the mountains always in sight at their left hand, they went down into the wilderness.

– 2 –

Within a week's trek they saw elephant sign: trees broken and stripped of their bark. Although it was months old – the trees already dried out – nevertheless Sean felt the thrill of it and that night spent an hour cleaning and oiling his rifles. The forest thickened until the wagons had to weave continually between the trunks of the trees. But there were clearings in the forest – open vleis filled with grass where buffalo grazed like herds of domestic cattle and white tick birds squawked about them. This country was well watered with streams as clear and merry as a Scottish trout stream, but the water was blood-warm and the banks thick with bush. Along the rivers, in the forest and in the open were the herds of game: impala twisting and leaping away at the first approach with their crumpled horns laid back, kudu with big ears and soft eyes, black sable antelope with white bellies and horns curved like a naval cutlass, zebra trotting with the dignity of fat ponies, while about them frolicked their companions, the gnu, waterbuck, nyala, roan antelope and – at last – elephant.

Sean and Mbejane were ranging a mile ahead of the wagons when they found the spoor. It was fresh, so fresh that sap still oozed from the mahoba-hoba tree where the bark had been prised loose with the tip of a tusk and then stripped off. The wood beneath was naked and white.

'Three bulls,' said Mbejane. 'One very big.'

'Wait here.' Sean spun his horse and galloped back to the column. Duff lay on the driver's seat of the first wagon rocking gently to its motion, his hat covering his face and his hands behind his head.

'Elephant! Duff,' Sean yelled. 'Not an hour ahead of us. Get saddled up, man!'

Duff was ready in five minutes. Mbejane was waiting for them; he had already worked the spoor a short distance and picked up the run of it and now he went away on it. They followed him, riding slowly side by side.

'You've hunted elephant before, laddie?' asked Duff.

'Never,' said Sean.

'Good grief!' Duff looked alarmed. 'I thought you were an expert. I think I'll go back and finish my sleep, you can call me when you've had a little more experience.'

'Don't worry,' Sean laughed with excitement. 'I know all about it; I was raised on elephant stories.'

'That sets my heart at ease,' Duff murmured sarcastically and Mbejane glanced over his shoulder at them, not trying to conceal his irritation.

'Nkosi, it is not wise to talk now for we will soon come up with them.'

So they went on in silence: passing a knee-high pile of yellow dung that looked like the contents of a coir mattress, following the oval pad marks in the dust and the trail of torn branches.

It was a good hunt, this first one. The small breeze held steadily into their faces and the spoor ran straight and hot. They closed in, each minute strengthening the certainty of the kill. Sean sat stiff and eager in the saddle with his rifle across his lap, his eyes restlessly moving over the frieze of bush ahead of him. Mbejane stopped suddenly and came back to Sean's stirrup.

'Here they halted for the first time. The sun is hot and they will rest but this place was not to their liking and they have moved on. We will find them soon now.'

'The bush becomes too thick,' Sean grunted; he eyed the untidy tangle of catbush into which the spoor had led them. 'We will leave the horses here with Hlubi and go in on foot.'

'Laddie,' Duff demurred. 'I can run much faster on horseback.'

'Off!' said Sean and nodded to Mbejane to lead. They moved forward again. Sean was sweating and the drops clung heavily to his eyebrows and trickled down his cheeks; he brushed them away. The excitement was an indigestible ball in his stomach and a dryness in his throat.

Duff sauntered casually next to Sean with that small half smile on his face, but there was a quickness in his breathing. Mbejane cautioned them with a gesture of his hand and they stopped. Minutes passed slowly and then Mbejane's hand moved again, pink-palmed eloquence.

'It was nothing,' said the hand. 'Follow me.'

They went on again. There were Mopani flies swarming at the corners of Sean's eyes, drinking the moisture, and he blinked them away. Their buzzing was so loud in his ears that he thought it must carry to their quarry. His every sense was tuned to its limit: hearing magnified, vision sharp and even his sense of smell so clear that he could pick up the taint of dust, the scent of a wild flower and Mbejane's faintly musky body-smell.

Suddenly in front of him Mbejane was still; his hand moved again gently, unmistakably.

'They are here,' said the hand.

Sean and Duff crouched behind him, searching with eyes

that could see only brown bush and grey shadows. The tension coarsened their breathing and Duff was no longer smiling. Mbejane's hand came up slowly and pointed at the wall of vegetation in front of them. The seconds strung together like beads on the string of time and still they searched.

An ear flapped lazily and instantly the picture jumped into focus. Bull elephant, big and very close, grey among grey shadow. Sean touched Mbejane's arm. 'I had seen it,' said that touch.

Slowly Mbejane's hand swivelled and pointed again. Another wait, another searching and then a belly rumbled, a great grey belly filled with half-digested leaves. It was a sound so ridiculous in the silence that Sean wanted to laugh – a gurgling sloshy sound – and Sean saw the other bull. It was standing in shadow also, with long yellow ivory and small eyes tight-closed. Sean put his lips to Duff's ear.

'This one is yours,' he whispered. 'Wait until I get into position for the other,' and he began moving out to the side, each step exposing a little more of the second bull's flank until the shoulder was open to him and he could see the point of the elbow beneath the baggy, wrinkled skin. The angle was right; from here he could reach the heart. He nodded at Duff, brought his rifle up – leaning forward against the recoil, aiming close behind the massive shoulder – and he fired.

The gunfire was shockingly loud in the confined thorn bush; dust flew in a spurt from the bull's shoulder and it staggered from the strike of the bullet. Beyond it the third elephant burst from sleep into flight and Sean's hands moved neatly on his weapon, ejecting and reloading, swinging up and firing again. He saw the bullet hit and he knew it was a mortal wound. The two bulls ran together and the bush opened to them and swallowed them: they were gone, crashing away wounded, trumpeting in pain.

Sean ran after them, dodging through the catbush, oblivious to the sting of the thorns that snatched at him as he passed.

'This way, Nkosi,' Mbejane shouted beside him. 'Quickly or we will lose them.' They sprinted after the sounds of flight – a hundred yards, two hundred, panting now and sweating in the heat. Suddenly the catbush ended and in front of them was a wide riverbed with steep banks. The river sand was blindingly white and in the middle was a sluggish trickle of water. One of the bulls was dead, lying in the stream with the blood washing off him in a pale brown stain. The other bull was trying to climb the far bank; it was too steep for him and he slid back wearily. The blood dripped from the tip of his trunk, and he swung his head to look at Sean and Mbejane. His ears cocked back defiantly and he began his charge, blundering towards them through the soft river sand.

Sean watched him come and there was sadness in him as he brought up his rifle, but it was the proud regret that a man feels when he watches hopeless courage. Sean killed with a brain shot, quickly.

They climbed down the bank into the riverbed and went to the elephant; it knelt with its legs folded under it and its tusks driven deep into the sand with the force of its fall. The flies were already clustering at the little red mouths of the bullet wounds. Mbejane touched one of the tusks and then he looked up at Sean.

'It is a good elephant.' He said no more, for this was not the time to talk. Sean leaned his rifle against the bull's shoulder; he felt in his top pocket for a cheroot and stood with it unlit between his teeth. He would kill more elephant, he knew, but always this would be the one he would remember. He stroked his hand over the rough skin and the bristles were stiff and sharp.

'Where is Nkosi Duff?' Sean remembered him suddenly. 'Did he also kill?'

'He did not shoot,' answered Mbejane.

'What!' Sean turned quickly to Mbejane. 'Why not?'

Mbejane sniffed a pinch of snuff and sneezed, then he shrugged his shoulders.

'It is a good elephant,' he said again, looking down at it.

'We must go back and find him.' Sean snatched up his rifle and Mbejane followed him. They found Duff sitting alone in the catbush with his rifle propped beside him and a water-bottle to his lips. He lowered the bottle as Sean came up and saluted him with it.

'Hail! the conquering hero comes.' There was something in his eyes that Sean could not read.

'Did you miss yours?' Sean asked.

'Yes,' said Duff, 'I missed mine.' He lifted the bottle and drank again. Suddenly and sickeningly Sean was ashamed for him. He dropped his eyes, not wanting to acknowledge Duff's cowardice.

'Let's get back to the wagons,' he said. 'Mbejane can come with packhorses for the tusks.'

They did not ride together on the way home.

– 3 –

It was almost dark when they arrived back at the laager. They gave their horses to one of the servants and washed in the basin that Kandhla had ready for them, then they went to sit by the fire. Sean poured the drinks, fussing over the glasses to avoid looking at Duff. He felt awkward. They'd have to talk about it and he searched his brain for a way to bring it into the open. Duff had shown craven and Sean started to find excuses for him – he may have had a misfire or he may have been unsighted by Sean's shot. At all events Sean determined not to let it stay like this, sour and brooding between them. They'd talk it out then forget it. He carried Duff's glass to him and smiled at him.

'That's right, try and cover it with a grin,' Duff lifted his glass. 'To our big brave hunter. Dammit, laddie, how could you do it?'

Sean stared at Duff. 'What do you mean?'

'You know what I mean, you're so damned guilty you can't even look me in the face. How could you kill those bloody great animals – but even worse how could you *enjoy* doing it?'

Sean subsided weakly into his chair. He couldn't tell which of his emotions was uppermost – relief or surprise. Duff went on quickly.

'I know what you're going to say, I've heard the arguments before – from my dear father. He explained it to me one evening after we'd ridden down a fox. When I say "we", I mean twenty horsemen and forty hounds.'

Sean had not yet rallied from the shock of finding himself in the dock after preparing himself to play the role of prosecutor.

'Don't you like hunting?' he asked incredulously. The way he might have asked, 'don't you like eating?'

'I'd forgotten what it was like. I was carried away by your excitement, but when you started to kill them it all came back to me.' Duff sipped his brandy and stared into the fire. 'They never had a chance. One minute they were sleeping and the next you were ripping them with bullets the way the hounds ripped that fox. They didn't have a chance.'

'But, Duff, it wasn't meant to be a contest.'

'Yes, I know, my father explained that to me. It's a ritual – a sacred rite to Diana. He should have explained it to the fox as well.'

Sean was getting angry now. 'We came out here to hunt ivory – and that's what I'm doing.'

'Tell me that you killed those elephant only for their

teeth, laddie, and I'll call you a liar. You loved it. Christ! You should have seen your face and the face of your damned heathen.'

'All right! I like hunting and the only other man I ever met who didn't was a coward,' Sean shouted at him.

Duff's face paled and he looked up at Sean. 'What are you trying to say?' he whispered. They stared at each other and in the silence Sean had to choose between letting his temper run or keeping Duff's friendship, for the words that would spoil it for ever were crowding into his mouth. He made his hands relax their grip on the arms of his chair.

'I didn't mean that,' he said.

'I hope you didn't.' Duff's grin came precariously back onto his face. 'Tell me why you like hunting, laddie. I'll try and understand but don't expect me to hunt with you again.'

It was like explaining colour to a blind man, describing the lust of the hunter to someone who was born without it. Duff listened in agonized silence as Sean tried to find the words for the excitement that makes a man's blood sing through his body, that heightens his senses and allows him to lose himself in an emotion as old as the urge to mate. Sean tried to show him how the nobler and more beautiful was the quarry, the stronger was the compulsion to hunt and kill it, that it had no conscious cruelty in it but was rather an expression of love: a fierce possessive love. A devouring love that needed the complete and irrevocable act of death for its consummation. By destroying something, a man could have it always as his own: selfish perhaps, but then instinct knows no ethics. It was all very clear to Sean, so much a part of him that he had never tried to voice it before and now he stumbled over the words, gesticulating in helpless inarticulateness, repeating himself, coming at last to the end and knowing by the look on Duff's face that he had failed to show it to him.

'And you were the gentleman who fought Hradsky for the rights of man,' Duff said softly, 'the one who always talked about not hurting people.'

Sean opened his mouth to protest but Duff went on. 'You get ivory for us and I'll look for gold – each of us to what he is best suited. I'll forgive you your elephants as you forgave me my Candy – still equal partners. Agreed?'

Sean nodded and Duff held up his glass.

'It's empty,' he said. 'Do me a favour, laddie.'

– 4 –

There was never any after-taste to their disputes, no rankling of unspoken words or lingering of doubt. What they had in common they enjoyed, where there were differences they accepted them. So when after each hunt the packhorses brought the tusks into the camp there was no trace of censure in Duff's face or voice; there was only the genuine pleasure of having Sean back from the bush. Sometimes it was a good day and Sean would cut the spoor, follow, kill and be back in the laager the same night. But more often, when the herd was moving fast or the ground was hard or he could not kill at the first approach, he would be gone for a week or more. Each time he returned they celebrated, drinking and laughing far into the night, lying late in bed the next morning, playing Klabejas on the floor of the wagon between their cots or reading aloud out of the books that Duff had brought with him from Pretoria. Then a day or two later Sean would be gone again, with his dogs and his gunboys trotting behind him.

This was a different Sean from the one who had whored it up at the Opera House and presided over the panelled offices in Eloff Street. His beard, no longer groomed and shaped by a barber, curled onto his chest. The doughy colour of his face and arms had been turned by the sun to the rich brown of a newly-baked loaf. The seat of his pants that had been stretched to danger point across his rump now hung loosely; his arms were thicker and the soft swell of fat had given way to the flatness and bulge of hard muscle. He walked straighter, moved quicker and laughed more easily.

In Duff the change was less noticeable. He was lean and gaunt-faced as ever, but now there was less of the restlessness in his eyes. His speech and movements were slower and the golden beard he was growing had the strange effect of making him appear younger. Each morning he left the wagons, taking one of the servants with him, and spent the days wandering in the bush, tapping with his prospecting hammer at the occasional outcrops of rock or squatting beside a stream and spinning the gravel in his pan. Every evening he came back to camp and analysed the bag of rock samples he had collected during the day; then he threw them away, bathed and set out a bottle and two glasses on the table beside the fire. While he ate his supper he listened and waited for the dogs to bark, for the sound of horses in the darkness and Sean's voice. If the night remained silent he put the bottle away and climbed up into his wagon. He was lonely then, not with a deep loneliness but just enough to add relish to Sean's return.

Always they moved east, until gradually the silhouette of the Zoutpansberg softened as the mountains became less steep and began to fade into the tail of the range. Scouting along their edge Sean found a pass and they took the wagons up and over and down into the Limpopo valley beyond. Here the country changed character again; it became flat, the monotony of thorn scrub relieved only by the baobab trees with their great, swollen trunks crowned in a little halo of branches. Water was scarce and Sean rode ahead from each camp to find the next waterhole before they moved. However, the hunting was good for the game was concentrated on the isolated drinking places, and before they were halfway from the mountains to the Limpopo Sean had filled another wagon with ivory.

'We'll be coming back this way, I suppose?' Duff asked.

'I suppose so,' agreed Sean.

'Well then, I don't see any point in carrying a ton of ivory with us. Let's bury it and we can pick it up on our way back.'

Sean looked at him thoughtfully. 'About once in every year you come up with a good idea – we'll do exactly that.'

The next camp was a good one. There was water – an acre of muddy liquid not as heavily salted with elephant urine as some of the previous ones had been; there was shade provided by a grove of wild fig trees and the grazing was of a quality that promised to restore the condition that the oxen had lost since crossing the mountains. They decided to make it a rest camp: bury the ivory, do some repairs and maintenance on the wagons and let the servants and animals fatten up a little. The first task was to dig a hole large enough to contain all the hundred-odd tusks they had accumulated and it was evening on the third day before they finished.

– 5 –

Sean and Duff sat together inside the laager and watched the sun go down, bleeding below the land, and after it had gone the clouds were oyster and lilac-coloured in the brief twilight. Kandhla threw wood on the fire and it burnt up fiercely. They ate grilled kudu liver, and thick steaks with a rind of yellow fat on them, and they drank brandy with their coffee. The conversation lagged into contented silence for they were both tired. They sat staring into the fire, too lazy to make the effort required for bed. Sean watched the fire pictures form in the coals, the faces and the phantoms flickering and fading. He saw a tiny temple have its columns pulled out from under it by a fiery Samson and collapse in a shower of sparks – a burning horse changed magically into a dragon of blue flame. He looked away to rest his eyes and when he turned back there was a small black scorpion scuttling out from under the loose bark on one of the logs. It lifted its tail like the arm of a flamenco dancer and the flames that ringed it shone on its glossy body armour. Duff was also watching it, leaning forward with his elbows on his knees.

'Will he sting himself to death before the flames reach him?' he asked softly. 'I have heard that they do.'

'No,' said Sean.

'Why not?'

'Only man has the intelligence to end the inevitable; in all other creatures the instinct of survival is too strong,' Sean answered him, and the scorpion crabbed sideways from the nearest flames and stopped again with its raised sting jerking slightly. 'Besides he's immune to his own poison so he has no choice.'

'He could jump down into the fire and get it over with,' murmured Duff, subdued by the little tragedy.

The scorpion started its last desperate circuit of the closing ring. Its tail drooped and the grip of its claws was unsteady on the rough bark; it was shrivelling with the heat, its legs curling up and its tail subsiding. The flames caressed it with swift yellow hands and smeared its shiny body with the dullness of death. The log tipped sideways and the speck was gone.

'Would you?' asked Sean. 'Would you have jumped?'

Duff sighed softly. 'I don't know,' he said and stood up. 'I'm going to pump out my bilges and crawl into bed.' He walked away and went to stand at the edge of the circle of firelight.

Since they had left Pretoria the small voices of the jackals had yapped discreetly around each outspan – they were so much a part of the African night that they went unnoticed – but now suddenly there was a difference. Only one jackal spoke, and with a voice that stammered shrilly – a sound of pain, a crazy hysterical shrieking that made Sean's skin prickle. He scrambled to his feet and stood staring undecided into the darkness. The jackal was coming towards the camp, coming fast – and suddenly Sean knew what was happening.

'Duff!' he called. 'Come back here! Run, man, run!'

Duff looked back at Sean helplessly, his hands held low in front of him and his water arcing down, curving silver in the firelight from his body to the ground.

'Duff!' Sean's voice was a shout. 'It's a rabid jackal. Run, damn you, run!' The jackal was close now, very close, but at last Duff started to move. He was halfway back to the fire before he tripped. He fell and rolled over and brought his feet up under his body to rise. His head turned to face the darkness from which it would come. Then Sean saw it. It flitted out of the shadows like a grey moth in the bad light and went straight for where Duff knelt. Sean saw him try to cover his face with his hands as the jackal sprang at him. One of the dogs twisted out of Mbejane's hand and brushed past Sean's legs. Sean snatched up a piece of firewood and sprinted after it, but already Duff was on his back, his arms flailing frantically as he tried to push away the terrier-sized animal that was slashing at his face and hands. The dog caught it and dragged it off, worrying it, growling through locked jaws. Sean hit the jackal with the club – breaking its back. He swung again and again, beating its body into shapelessness before he turned to Duff. Duff was on his feet now. He had unwound the scarf from his neck and was mopping with it at his face but the blood dribbled down his chin and blotched the front of his shirt. His hands were trembling. Sean led him close to the fire, pulled Duff's hands down and examined the bites. His nose was torn and the flesh of one cheek hung open in a flap.

'Sit down!'

Duff obeyed, holding the scarf to his face again. Sean went quickly to the fire: with a stick he raked embers into a pile, then he drew his hunting-knife and thrust the blade into the coals.

'Mbejane,' he called, without taking his eyes off the knife. 'Throw that jackal onto the fire. Put on plenty of wood. Do not touch its body with your hands. When you have done that tie up that dog and keep the others away from it.' Sean turned the knife in the fire. 'Duff, drink as much of that brandy as you can.'

'What are you going to do?'

'You know what I've got to do.'

'He bit my wrist as well.' Duff held up his hand for Sean to see the punctures, black holes from which the blood oozed watery and slow.

'Drink.' Sean pointed at the brandy bottle. For a second they looked at each other and Sean saw the horror moving in Duff's eyes: horror of the hot knife and horror of the germs which had been injected into him. The germs that must be burnt out before they escaped into his blood, to breed and ferment there until they ate into his brain and rode him to a screaming, gibbering death.

'Drink,' said Sean again. Duff took up the bottle and lifted it to his mouth. Sean stooped and pulled the knife out of the fire. He held the blade an inch from the back of his hand. It was not hot enough. He thrust it back into the coals.

'Mbejane, Hlubi, stand on each side of the Nkosi's chair.

Be ready to hold him.' Sean loosened his belt, doubled the thick leather and handed it to Duff. 'Bite on this.'

He turned back to the fire and this time when he drew the knife its blade was pale pink. 'Are you ready?'

'The work you are about to do will break the hearts of a million maids.' A last hoarse attempt at humour from Duff.

'Hold him,' said Sean.

Duff gasped at the touch of the knife – a great shuddering gasp – and his back arched, but the two Zulus held him down remorselessly. The edges of the wound blackened and hissed as Sean ran the blade in deeper. The stink of burning brought the vomit into his throat. He clenched his teeth. When he stepped back Duff hung slackly in the Zulus' hands, sweat had soaked his shirt and wet his hair. Sean heated the knife again and cleaned the bites in Duff's wrist while Duff moaned and writhed weakly in the chair. He smeared axle grease over the burns and bandaged the wrist loosely with strips torn from a clean shirt. They lifted Duff into the wagon and laid him on his cot. Sean went out to where Mbejane had tied the dog. He found scratches beneath the hair on its shoulder. They put a sack over its head to stop it biting and Sean cauterized its wounds also.

'Tie it to the far wagon, do not let the other dogs near it, see it has food and water,' he told Mbejane.

Then he went back to Duff. Delirious with pain and brandy Duff did not sleep at all that night and Sean stayed by his cot until the morning.

– 6 –

About fifty yards from the laager under one of the wild fig trees the servants built Duff a hut. The framework was of poles and over it they stretched a tarpaulin. They made a bed for him and brought his mattress and blankets from the wagon. Sean joined four trekchains together, forging new links and hammering them closed. He passed one end of the chain round the base of the fig tree and riveted it back up on itself. Duff sat in the shade of a wagon and watched them work. His hurt hand was in a sling and his face was swollen, the wound crusty-looking and edged in angry red. When he was finished with the chain, Sean walked across to him.

'I'm sorry, Duff, we have to do it.'

'They abolished the slave trade some time ago – just in case you didn't know.' Duff tried to grin with his distorted face. He stood up and followed Sean to the hut. Sean looped the loose end of the chain round Duff's waist. He locked it with a bolt through two of the links then flattened the end of the bolt with a dozen strokes of the hammer.

'That should hold you.'

'An excellent fit,' Duff commended him. 'Now let us inspect my new quarters.'

Sean followed him into the hut. Duff lay down on the bed. He looked very tired and sick.

'How long will it take before we know?' he asked quietly.

Sean shook his head. 'I'm not sure. I think you should stay here at least a month – after that we'll allow you back into society.'

'A month – it's going to be fun. Lying here expecting any minute to start barking like a dog and lifting my leg against the nearest tree.'

Sean didn't laugh. 'I did a thorough job with the knife.

It's a thousand to one you'll be all right. This is just a precaution.'

'The odds are attractive – I'll put a fiver on it.' Duff crossed his ankles and stared up at the roof. Sean sat down on the edge of the bed. It was a long time before Duff ended the silence.

'What will it be like, Sean? Have you ever seen someone with rabies?'

'No.'

'But you've heard about it, haven't you? Tell me what you've heard about it,' Duff persisted.

'For Chrissake, Duff, you're not going to get it.'

'Tell me, Sean, tell me what you know about it.' Duff sat up and caught hold of Sean's arm.

Sean looked steadily at him for a moment before he answered. 'You saw that jackal, didn't you?'

Duff sank back onto his pillows. 'Oh, my God!' he whispered.

Together they started the long wait. They used another tarpaulin to make an open shelter next to the hut and under it they spent the days that followed.

In the beginning it was very bad. Sean tried to pull Duff out of the black despair into which he had slumped, but Duff sat for hours at a time gazing out into the bush, fingering the scabs on his face and only occasionally smiling at the banquet of choice stories that Sean spread for him. But at last Sean's efforts were rewarded – Duff began to talk. He spoke of things he had never mentioned before and listening to him Sean learned more about him than he had in the previous five years. Sometimes Duff paced up and down in front of Sean's chair with the chain hanging down behind him like a tail; at other times he sat quietly, his voice filled with longing for the mother he had never known.

' – there was a portrait of her in the upper gallery, I used to spend whole afternoons in front of it. It was the kindest face I had ever seen—'

Then it hardened again as he remembered his father, 'that old bastard'.

He talked of his daughter. ' – she had a fat chuckle that would break your heart. The snow on her grave made it look like a big sugar-iced cake, she would have liked that—'

At other times his voice was puzzled as he examined some past action of his, angry as he remembered a mistake or a missed opportunity. Then he would break off and grin self-consciously. 'I say, I am talking a lot of drivel.'

The scabs on his face began to dry up and come away, and more often now his old gaiety bubbled to the surface.

On one of the poles that supported the tarpaulin roof he started a calendar, cutting a notch for each day. It became a daily ceremony. He cut each notch with the concentration of a sculptor carving marble and when he had finished he would stand back and count them aloud as if by doing so he could force them to add up to thirty, the number that would allow him to shed his chain.

There were eighteen notches on the pole when the dog went mad. It was in the afternoon. They were playing Klabejas. Sean had just dealt the cards when the dog started screaming from among the wagons. Sean knocked over his chair as he jumped up. He snatched his rifle from where it leant against the wall and ran down to the laager. He disappeared behind the wagon to which the dog was tied and almost immediately Duff heard the shot. In the abrupt and complete stillness that followed, Duff slowly lowered his face into his hands.

It was nearly an hour before Sean came back. He picked up his chair, set it to the table and sat down.

'It's you to call – are you going to take on?' he asked as he picked up his cards. They played with grim intensity, fixing their attention on the cards, but both of them knew that there was a third person at the table now.

'Promise you'll never do that to me,' Duff blurted out at last.

Sean looked up at him. 'That I'll never do what to you?'

'What you did to that dog.'

The dog! The bloody dog. He should never have taken a chance with it, he should have destroyed it that first night.

'Just because the dog got it doesn't mean that you—'

'Swear to me,' Duff interrupted fiercely, 'swear you won't bring the rifle to me.'

'Duff, you don't know what you're asking. Once you've got it—' Sean stopped; anything he said would make it worse.

'Promise me,' Duff repeated.

'All right, I swear it then.'

– 7 –

It was worse now than it had been in the beginning. Duff abandoned his calendar and with it the hope that had been slowly growing stronger. If the days were bad then the nights were hell, for Duff had a dream. It came to him every night – sometimes two or three times. He tried to keep awake after Sean had left, reading by the light of a lantern; or he lay and listened to the night noises, the splash and snort of buffalo drinking down at the waterhole, the liquid half-warble of night birds or the deep drumming of a lion. But in the end he would have to sleep and then he dreamed.

He was on horseback riding across a flat brown plain: no hills, no trees, nothing but lawnlike grass stretching away on all sides to the horizon. His horse threw no shadow – he always looked for a shadow and it worried him that there never was one. Then he would find the pool – clear water, blue and strangely shiny. The pool frightened him but he could not stop himself going to it. He would kneel beside it and look into the water; the reflection of his own face looked up at him – animal-snouted, shaggy-brown with wolf teeth, white and long. He would wake then and the horror of that face would last until morning.

Nearly desperate with his own utter helplessness, Sean tried to help him. Because of the accord they had established over the years and because they were so close to each other, Sean had to suffer with him. He tried to shut himself off from it; sometimes he succeeded for an hour or even half a morning, but then it came back with a stomach-swooping shock. Duff was going to die – Duff was going to die an unspeakable death. Was it a mistake to let someone get too deep inside you, so that you must share his agony in every excruciating detail? Didn't a man have enough of his own that he must share the full measure of another's suffering?

By then the October winds had started, the heralds of the rain: hot winds full of dust, winds that dried the sweat on a man's body before it had time to cool him, thirsty winds that during daylight brought the game to the water-hole in full view of the camp.

Sean had half a case of wine hoarded under his cot. That last evening he cooled four bottles, wrapping them in wet sacking. He took them up to Duff's shelter just before supper and set them on the table. Duff watched him. The scars on his face were almost completely healed now, glassy red marks on his pale skin.

'Chateau Olivier,' said Sean and Duff nodded.

'It's a good wine – most probably travel-sick.'

'Well, if you don't want it, I'll take it away again,' said Sean.

'I'm sorry, laddie,' Duff spoke quickly. 'I didn't mean to be ungrateful. This wine suits my mood tonight. Did you know that wine is a sad drink?'

'Nonsense!' Sean disagreed as he twisted the corkscrew into the first cork. 'Wine is gay.' He poured a little into Duff's glass and Duff picked it up and held it towards the fire so the light shone through it.

'You see only the surface, Sean. A good wine has the elements of tragedy within it. The better the wine the more sad it is.'

Sean snorted. 'Explain yourself,' he invited.

Duff put his glass down on the table again and stared at it. 'How long do you suppose this wine has taken to reach its present perfection?'

'Ten or fifteen years, I suppose,' Sean answered.

Duff nodded. 'And now all that remains is to drink it – the work of years destroyed in an instant. Don't you think that is sad?' Duff asked softly.

'My God, Duff, don't be so damned morbid.'

But Duff wasn't listening to him. 'Wine and mankind have this in common. They can find perfection only in age, in a lifetime of seeking. Yet in the finding they find also their own destruction.'

'So you think that if a man lives long enough he will reach perfection?' Sean challenged him, and Duff answered him still staring at the glass.

'Some grapes grew in the wrong soil, some were diseased before they went to the press and some were spoiled by a careless vintner – not all grapes make good wine.' Duff picked up his glass and tasted from it, then he went on. 'A man takes longer and he must find it not within the quiet confines of the cask but in the cauldron of life; therefore his is the greater tragedy.'

'Yes, but no one can live for ever,' Sean protested.

'So you think that makes it less sad?' Duff shook his

head. 'You're wrong, of course. It does not detract from it, it enhances it. If only there were some escape, some way of ensuring that what is good could endure instead of this complete hopelessness.'

Duff lay back in his chair, his face pale and gaunt-looking. 'Even that I could accept, if only they had given me more time.'

'I've had enough of this talk. Let's discuss something else. I don't know what you're worrying about. You're not fit to drink yet, you've got another twenty or thirty years to go,' Sean said gruffly and Duff looked up at him for the first time.

'Have I, Sean?'

Sean couldn't meet his eyes. He knew Duff was going to die. Duff grinned his lopsided grin and looked down again at his glass. Slowly the grin disappeared and he spoke again.

'If only I had more time, I could have done it. I could have found the weak places and fortified them. I could have seen the answers.' His voice rose higher. 'I could have! I know I could have! Oh God, I'm not ready yet. I need more time.' His voice was shrill and his eyes wild and haunted. 'It's too soon – it's too soon!'

Sean couldn't stand it, he jumped up and caught Duff's shoulders and shook him.

'Shut up, God damn you, shut up,' he shouted at him. Duff was panting, his lips were parted and quivering. He touched them with the tips of his fingers as though to stop them.

'I'm sorry, laddie, I didn't mean to let go like that.' Sean dropped his hands from Duff's shoulders.

'Both of us are too damned edgy,' he said. 'It's going to be all right, you wait and see.'

'Yes – it will be all right.' Duff ran his fingers through his hair, combing it back from his eyes. 'Open another bottle, laddie.'

– 8 –

That night after Sean had gone to bed, Duff had his dream again. The wine he had drunk slowed him down and prevented him from waking. He was trapped in his fancy, struggling to escape into wakefulness but only reaching the surface before he sank back to dream that dream again.

Sean went up to Duff's shelter the next morning early. Although the night's coolness still lingered under the spreading branches of the wild figs the rising day promised to blow dry and burn hot. The animals could sense it. The trek oxen were clustered among the trees and a small herd of eland was moving from the waterhole. The bull, with his short thick horns and the dark tuft on his forehead, was leading his cows away to find shade. Sean stood in the doorway of the hut and waited while his eyes adjusted themselves to its gloom. Duff was awake.

'Get out of bed or you'll have bed sores to add to your happiness.'

Duff swung his feet off the litter and groaned.

'What did you put in that wine last night?' He massaged his temples gently. 'I've got a hundred hobgoblins doing a Cossack dance around the roof of my skull.'

Sean felt the first twinge of alarm. He put his hand on Duff's shoulder feeling for the heat of fever, but Duff was quite cool. He relaxed.

'Breakfast's ready,' said Sean. Duff played with his porridge and barely tasted the grilled eland liver. He kept screwing his eyes up against the glare of the sun and when they had finished their coffee he pushed back his chair.

'I'm going to take my tender head to bed.'

'All right.' Sean stood up as well. 'We're a bit short of meat. I'll go and see if I can get a buck.'

'No, stay and talk to me,' Duff said quickly. 'We can have a few hands of cards.'

They hadn't played in days and Sean agreed readily. He sat on the end of Duff's bed and within half an hour he had won thirty-two pounds from him.

'You must let me teach you this game sometime,' he gloated.

Petulantly, Duff threw his hand in. 'I don't feel like playing any more.' He pressed his fingers to his closed eyelids. 'I can't concentrate with this headache.'

'Do you want to sleep?' Sean gathered up the cards and put them in their box.

'No. Why don't you read to me?'

Duff picked up a leather-bound copy of *Bleak House* from the table beside the bed and tossed it into Sean's lap.

'Where shall I start?' Sean asked.

'It doesn't matter, I know it almost by heart.' Duff lay back and closed his eyes. 'Start anywhere.'

Sean read aloud. He stumbled on for half an hour with his tongue never quite catching the rhythm of the words. Once or twice he glanced up at Duff, but Duff lay still with a faint sheen of sweat on his face and the scars very noticeable. He was breathing easily. Dickens is a powerful sleeping-draught for a hot morning and Sean's eyelids sagged down and his voice slowed and finally stopped. The book slid off his lap.

The small tinkle of Duff's chain disturbed him; he awoke and looked at the bed. Duff crouched apelike. The madness was a fire in his eyes and his cheeks twitched. A yellowish froth coated his teeth and formed a thin line of scum along his lips.

'Duff—' Sean said, and Duff lunged at him with fingers hooked and a noise in his throat that was not human nor yet animal. It was a sound that jellied Sean's stomach and took the strength from his legs.

'Don't!' screamed Sean, and the chain caught on one of the posts of the bed, jerking Duff back sprawling onto the bed before he could sink his teeth into Sean's paralysed body.

Sean ran. He ran out of the hut and into the bush. He ran with terror trembling in his legs and choking his breath. He ran with his heart taking its beat from his racing feet and his lungs pumping in disordered panic. A branch ripped across his cheek and the sting of it served to steady him. His feet slowed – he stopped and stood gasping, staring back towards the camp. He waited while his body settled and he forced his terror down until it was only a sickening sensation in his stomach. Then he circled through the thorn bush and approached the laager from the side farthest away from Duff's shelter. The camp was empty, the servants had fled in the same terror that had driven Sean. He remembered that his rifle was still in the hut beside Duff's bed. He slipped into his wagon and quickly opened the case of unused rifles. His hands were unsteady again as he fumbled with the locks, for the chain might have parted and at every second he expected to hear that inhuman sound behind him. He found his bandolier hanging on the end of his cot and he took cartridges from it. He loaded the rifle and cocked it. The weight of steel and wood in his hands gave him comfort. It made him a man again.

He jumped down out of the wagon and with the rifle held ready he went cautiously out of the circle of wagons. The chain had held. Duff stood in the shade of the wild fig plucking at it. He was making a sound like a new-born puppy. His back was turned to Sean and he was naked, his torn clothing scattered about him. Sean walked slowly towards him. He stopped outside the reach of the chain.

'Duff!' Sean called uncertainly. Duff spun and crouched, the froth was thick in his golden beard; he looked at Sean and his teeth bared. Then he charged screaming until the chain caught him and threw him onto his back once more. He scrambled to his feet and fought the chain, his eyes fastened hungrily on Sean. Sean backed away. He brought up the rifle and aimed between Duff's eyes.

Swear to me. Swear to me you won't bring the rifle to me.

Sean's aim wavered. He kept moving backwards. Duff was bleeding now. The steel links had smeared the skin off his hips, but still he pulled against them fighting to get at Sean – and Sean was shackled just as effectively by his promise. He could not end it. He lowered the rifle and watched in impotent pity.

Mbejane came to him at last.

'Come away, Nkosi. If you will not end it, come away. He no longer has need of you. The sight of you inflames him.'

Duff still struggled and screamed against his chain. From his torn waist the blood trickled down and clung in the hair of his legs with the stickiness of molten chocolate. With each jerk of his head the froth sprayed from his mouth and splattered his chest and arms.

Mbejane led Sean back into the laager. The other servants were there and Sean roused himself to give orders.

'I want everyone away from here. Take blankets and food – go camp on the far side of the water. I will send for you when it is over.' He waited until they had gathered their belongings and as they were leaving he called Mbejane back. 'What must I do?' he asked.

'If a horse breaks a leg?' Mbejane answered him with a question.

'I gave him my word,' Sean shook his head desperately, still facing towards the sound of Duff's raving.

'Only a rogue and a brave man can break an oath,' Mbejane answered simply. 'We will wait for you.' He turned and followed the others. When they were gone Sean hid in one of the wagons and through a tear in the canvas he watched Duff. He saw the idiotic shaking of his head, the curious shambling gait as he moved around the circle of the chain. He watched when the pain made him roll on the ground and claw at his head, tearing out tufts of hair and leaving long scratches down his face. He listened to the sounds of insanity: the bewildered bellows of pain, the senseless giggling and that growl, that terrible growl.

A dozen times he sighted along the rifle barrel, holding his aim until the sweat ran into his eyes and blurred them and he had to take the butt from his shoulder and turn away.

Out there on the end of the chain, its exposed flesh reddening in the sun a piece of Sean was dying. Some of his youth, some of his laughter, some of his carefree love of life – so he had to creep back to the hole in the canvas and watch.

The sun reached its peak and started down again and the thing on the chain grew weaker. It fell and was a long time crawling on its hands and knees before it regained its feet again.

An hour before sunset Duff had his first convulsion. He was standing facing Sean's wagon, swinging his head from side to side, his mouth working silently. The convulsion took him and he stiffened; his lips pulled up grinning, showing his teeth, his eyes rolled back and disappeared leaving only the whites, and his body started to bend backwards. That beautiful body, still slim as a boy's with the long moulded legs, bending tighter and tighter until with a brittle crack the spine snapped and he fell. He lay wriggling, moaning softly and his trunk was twisted at an impossible angle from the broken spine.

Sean jumped from the wagon and ran to him: standing over him he shot Duff in the head and turned away. He flung his rifle from him and heard it clatter on the hard earth. He walked back to his wagon and took a blanket off

Duff's cot. He came back and wrapped Duff in it, averting his eyes from the mutilated head. He carried him to the shelter and laid him on the bed. The blood soaked through the blanket, spreading on the cloth, like ink spilled on blotting-paper. Sean sank down on the chair beside the bed.

Outside the darkness gathered and became complete. Once in the night a hyena came and snuffled at the blood outside on the earth, then it moved away. There was a pride of lions hunting in the bush beyond the waterhole; they killed two hours before dawn and Sean sat in the darkness and listened to their jubilant roaring.

In the morning, Sean stood up stiffly from his chair and went down to the wagons. Mbejane was waiting beside the fire in the laager.

'Where are the others?' Sean asked.

Mbejane stood up. 'They wait where you sent them. I came alone – knowing you would need me.'

'Yes,' said Sean. 'Get two axes from the wagon.'

They gathered wood, a mountain of dry wood, and packed it around Duff's bed – then Sean put fire to it. Mbejane saddled a horse for Sean and he mounted up and looked down at the Zulu.

'Bring the wagons on to the next waterhole. I will meet you there.'

Sean rode out of the laager. He looked back only once and saw that the breeze had spread the smoke from the pyre in a mile long smudge across the tops of the thorn trees.

– 9 –

Like a bag of pus at the root of an infected tooth the guilt and grief rotted in Sean's mind. His guilt was double-edged. He had betrayed Duff's trust, and he had lacked the courage to make the betrayal worthwhile. He had waited too long. He should have done it at the beginning, cleanly and quickly, or he should not have done it at all. He longed with every fibre of his body to be given the chance to do it again, but this time the right way. He would gladly have lived once more through all that horror to clear his conscience and clean the stain from the memory of their friendship.

His grief was a thing of emptiness, an aching void – so immense that he was lost in it. Where before there had been Duff's laughter, his twisted grin and his infectious zest there was now only a grey nothingness. No glimmer of sun penetrated it and there were no solid shapes in it.

The next waterhole was shallow soup in the centre of a flat expanse of dry mud the size of a polo field. The mud was cracked in an irregular chequered pattern forming small brickettes, each the size of a hand. A man could have jumped across the water without wetting his feet. Scattered thickly round its circumference were the droppings of the animals that had drunk there. Back and forth across its surface, changing direction as the wind veered, a few loose feathers sailed. The water was brackish and dirty. It was a bad camp. On the third day Mbejane went to Sean's wagon. Sean lay in his cot. He had not changed his clothes since leaving Duff. His beard was beginning to mat, sticky with sweat for it was hot as an oven under the wagon canvas.

'Nkosi, will you come and look at the water. I do not think we should stay here.'

'What is wrong with it?' Sean asked without interest.

'It is dirty, I think we should go on towards the big river.'

'Do whatever you think is right.' Sean rolled away from him, his face towards the side of the wagon.

So Mbejane took the wagon-train down towards the Limpopo. It was two days later that they found the ribbon of dark green trees that lined the banks. Sean stayed in his cot throughout the trek, jolting over the rough ground, sweating in the heat but oblivious to all discomfort. Mbejane put the wagons into laager on the bank above the riverbed, then he and all the other servants waited for Sean to come to life again. Their talk round the fire at nights was baited with worry and they looked often towards Sean's living wagon, where it stood unlit by lantern, dark as the mood of the man that lay within.

Like a bear coming out of its cave at the end of winter, Sean came out of the wagon at last. His clothes were filthy. The dogs hurried to meet him, crowding round his knees, begging for attention and he did not notice them. Vaguely he answered the greetings of his servants. He wandered down the bank into the riverbed.

The summer had shrunk the Limpopo into a sparse line of pools strung out down the centre of the watercourse. The pools were dark olive green. The sand around them was white, glaring snowfield white, and the boulders that choked the barely moving river were black and polished smooth. The banks were steep, half a mile apart and walled in with trees. Sean walked through the sand, sinking to his ankles with each step. He reached the water and sat down at the edge, he dabbled his hand in it and found it warm as blood. In the sand next to him was the long slither mark of a crocodile, and a troop of monkeys were shaking the branches of a tree on the far bank and chattering at him. A pair of Sean's dogs splashed across the narrow neck between two pools and went off to chase the monkeys. They went half-heartedly with their tongues flapping at the corners of their mouths for it was very hot in the whiteness of the riverbed. Sean stared into the green water. It was lonely without Duff; he had only his guilt and his sorrow for company. One of the dogs that had stayed with him touched his cheek with its cold nose. Sean put his arm round its neck and the dog leaned against him. He heard footsteps in the sand behind him, he turned and looked up. It was Mbejane.

'Nkosi, Hlubi has found elephant not an hour's march up stream. He has counted twenty who show good ivory.'

Sean looked back at the water. 'Go away,' he said.

Mbejane squatted down beside him with his elbows on his knees. 'For whom do you mourn?' he asked.

'Go away, Mbejane, leave me alone.'

'Nkosi Duff does not need your sorrow – therefore I think that you mourn for yourself.' Mbejane picked up a pebble and tossed it into the pool.

'When a traveller gets a thorn in his foot,' Mbejane went on softly, 'and he is wise he plucks it out – and he is a fool who leaves it and says "I will keep this thorn to prick me so that I will always remember the road upon which I have travelled." Nkosi, it is better to remember with pleasure than with pain.' Mbejane lobbed another pebble into the pool, then he stood up and walked back to the camp. When Sean followed him ten minutes later he found a saddle on his horse, his rifle in the scabbard and Mbejane and Hlubi waiting with their spears. Kandhla handed him his hat, he held it by the brim, turning it in his hands. Then he clapped it onto his head and swung up onto the horse.

'Lead,' he ordered.

During the next weeks Sean hunted with a single-mindedness that left no time for brooding. His returns to the wagons were short and intermittent; his only reasons for returning at all were to bring in the ivory and change his horse. At the end of one of these brief visits to camp and as Sean was about to mount up for another hunt, even Mbejane complained. 'Nkosi, there are better ways to die than working too hard.'

'You look well enough,' Sean assured him, although Mbejane was now as lean as a greyhound and his skin shone like washed anthracite.

'Perhaps all men look healthy to a man on horseback,' Mbejane suggested and Sean stopped with one foot in the stirrup. He looked at Mbejane thoughtfully, then he lowered his leg again. 'We hunt on foot now, Mbejane, and the first to ask for mercy earns the right to be called "woman" by the other.'

Mbejane grinned; the challenge was to his liking. They crossed the river and found spoor before midday – a small herd of young bulls. They followed it until nightfall and slept huddled together under one blanket, then they went on again next morning. On the third day they lost the spoor in rocky ground and they cast back towards the river. They picked up another herd within ten miles of the wagons, went after them and killed that evening – three fine bulls, not a tusk between them under fifty pounds weight. A night march back to the wagons, four hours' sleep and they were away again. Sean was limping a little now and on the second day out, during one of their infrequent halts, he pulled off his boot. The blister on his heel had burst and his sock was stiff with dried blood. Mbejane looked at him expressionlessly. 'How far are we from the wagons?' asked Sean.

'We can be back before dark, Nkosi.' Mbejane carried Sean's rifle for him on the return. Not once did his mask of solemnity slip. Back in camp Kandhla brought a basin of hot water and set it in front of Sean's chair. While Sean soaked his feet in it his entire following squatted in a circle about him. Every face wore an expression of studied concern and the silence was broken only by the clucking sounds of

Bantu sympathy. They were loving every minute of it and Mbejane, with the timing of a natural actor, was building up the effect, playing to his audience. Sean puffed at a cheroot, scowling to stop himself laughing. Mbejane cleared his throat and spat into the fire. Every eye was on him; they waited breathlessly.

'Nkosi,' said Mbejane, 'I would set fifty head of oxen as your marriage price – if you were my daughter.'

One instant more of silence, then a shout of laughter. Sean laughed with them at first, but after a while when Hlubi had nearly staggered into the fire and Nonga was sobbing loudly on Mbejane's shoulder with tears of mirth streaming down his cheeks, Sean's own laughter stopped. It wasn't *that* funny.

He looked at them sourly – at their wide open pink mouths and their white teeth, at their shaking shoulders and heaving chests and suddenly it came to him very clearly that they were no longer laughing at him. They were laughing for the joy of it. They were laughing because they were alive. A chuckle rattled up Sean's throat and escaped before he could stop it, another one bounced around inside his chest and he lay back in his chair, opened his mouth and let it come. The hell with it, he was alive, too.

In the morning when he climbed out of his wagon and limped across to see what Kandhla was cooking for breakfast, there was a faint excitement in him again, the excitement of a new day. He felt good. Duff's memory was still with him, it always would be, but now it was not a sickening ache. He had plucked out the thorn.

– 10 –

They moved camp three times in November, keeping to the south bank of the river, following it back towards the west. Slowly the wagons which they had emptied of ivory beside the waterhole began to fill again, for the game was concentrated along the river. The rest of the land was dry but now each day there was promise of relief.

The clouds that had been scattered across the sky began to crowd together, gathering into rounded dark-edged masses or rearing proudly into thunderheads. All of nature seemed impressed by their growing importance. In the evenings the sun dressed them in royal purple and during the day the whirlwinds did dervish dances for their entertainment. The rains were coming. Sean had to make a decision, cross the Limpopo and cut himself off from the south when the river flooded, or stay where he was and leave the land beyond undisturbed. It wasn't a difficult decision. They found a place where the banks flattened out a little on both sides of the river. They unloaded the first wagon and double-teamed it; then with everybody shouting encouragement the oxen galloped down the steep slope into the riverbed. The wagon bounced behind them until it hit the sand where it came to a halt, tilted at an abandoned angle, with its wheels sunk axle-deep into the sand.

'Onto the spokes,' shouted Sean. 'They flung themselves on the wheels and strained to keep them turning, but half the oxen were down on their knees, powerless in the loose footing.

'Damn it to hell.' Sean glared at the wagon. 'Outspan the oxen and take them back. Get out the axes.'

It took them three days to lay a bridge of corduroyed branches across the river and another two to get all the wagons and ivory to the far bank. Sean declared a holiday when the last wagon was manhandled into the laager and the whole camp slept late the next morning. The sun was high by the time Sean descended from his wagon. He was still muzzy and a little liverish from lying abed. He yawned wide and stretched like a crucifix. He ran his tongue round his mouth and grimaced at the taste, then he scratched his chest and the hair rasped under his fingers.

'Kandhla, where's the coffee? Don't you care that I am near dead from thirst?'

'Nkosi, the water will boil very soon.'

Sean grunted and walked across to where Mbejane squatted with the other servants by the fire watching Kandhla.

'This is a good camp, Mbejane.' Sean looked up at the roof of leaves above them. It was a place of green shade, cool in the late morning heat. Christmas beetles were squealing in the wide stretched branches.

'There is good grazing for the cattle,' Mbejane agreed; he stretched out his hand towards Sean.

'I found this in the grass – someone else has camped here.' Sean took it from him and examined it, a piece of broken china with a blue fig-leaf pattern. It was a shock to Sean, that little fragment of civilization in the wilderness; he turned it in his fingers and Mbejane went on. 'There are the ashes of an old fire there against the shuma tree and I found the ruts where wagons climbed the bank at the same place as ours.'

'How long ago?'

Mbejane shrugged. 'A year perhaps. Grass has grown in the wagon tracks.'

Sean sat down in his chair, he felt disturbed. He thought about it and grinned as he realized he was jealous; there were strangers here in the land he was coming to regard as his own, those year-old tracks gave him a feeling of being in a crowd. Also there was the opposite feeling, that of longing for the company of his own kind. The sneaking desire to see a white face again. It was strange that he could resent something and yet wish for it simultaneously.

'Kandhla, am I to have coffee now or at supper tonight?'

'Nkosi, it is done.' Kandhla poured a little brown sugar into the mug, stirred it with a stick and handed it to him. Sean held the mug in both hands, blowing to cool it, then sipping and sighing with each mouthful. The talk of his Zulus passed back and forth about the circle and the snuff-boxes followed it, each remark of worth being greeted with a solemn chorus of 'It is true, it is true,' and the taking of snuff. Small arguments jumped up and fell back again into the leisurely stream of conversation. Sean listened to them, occasionally joining in or contributing a story until his stomach told him it was time to eat. Kandhla started to cook, under the critical supervision and with the helpful suggestions of those whom idleness had made garrulous. He had almost succeeded in grilling the carcass of a guinea-fowl to the satisfaction of the entire company, although Mbejane felt that he should have added a pinch more salt, when Nonga, sitting across the fire from him, jumped to his feet and pointed out towards the north. Sean shaded his eyes and looked.

'For Chrissake,' said Sean.

'Ah! ah! ah!' said his servants.

A white man rode towards them through the trees; he cantered with long stirrups, slouched comfortably, close enough already for Sean to make out the great ginger beard that masked the bottom half of his face. He was a big man; the sleeves of his shirt rolled high around thick arms.

'Hello,' shouted Sean and went eagerly to meet him. The rider reined in at the edge of the laager. He climbed stiffly out of the saddle and grabbed Sean's outstretched hand. Sean felt his finger-bones creak in the grip.

'Hello, man! How goes it?' He spoke in Afrikaans. His voice matched the size of his body and his eyes were on a level with Sean's. They pumped each other's arms mercilessly, laughing, putting sincerity into the usual inanities of greeting.

'Kandhla – get out the brandy bottle,' Sean called over his shoulder, then to the Boer, 'Come in, you're just in time for lunch. We'll have a dram to celebrate. Hell, it's good to see a white man again!'

'You're on your own, then?'

'Yes – come in, man, sit down.'

Sean poured drinks and the Boer took one up.

'What's your name?' he asked.

'Courtney – Sean Courtney.'

'I'm Jan Paulus Leroux – glad to meet you, meneer.'

'Good health, meneer,' Sean answered him and they drank. Jan Paulus wiped his whiskers on the palm of his hand and breathed out heavily, blowing the taste of the brandy back into his mouth.

'That was good,' he said and held out his mug. They talked excitedly, tongues loose from loneliness, trying to say everything and ask all the questions at once – meetings in the bush are always like this. Meanwhile the tide was going out in the bottle and the level dropped quickly.

'Tell me, where are your wagons?' Sean asked.

'An hour or two behind. I came ahead to find the river.'

'How many in your party?' Sean watched his face, talking just for the sound of it.

'Ma and Pa, my little sister and my wife – which reminds me – you had better move your wagons.'

'What?' Sean looked puzzled.

'This is my outspan place,' the Boer explained to him. 'See, there are the marks of my fire – this is my camp.'

The smile went out of Sean's voice. 'Look around you,

Boer, there is the whole of Africa. Take your pick – anywhere except where I am sitting.'

'But this is my place.' Jan Paulus flushed a little. 'I always camp at the same place when I return along a spoor.'

The whole temper of their meeting had changed in a few seconds. Jan Paulus stood abruptly and went to his horse. He stooped and tightened the girth, hauling so savagely on the strap that the animal staggered off balance. He flung himself onto its back and looked down at Sean.

'Move your wagons,' he said. 'I camp here tonight.'

'Would you like to bet on that?' Sean asked grimly.

'We'll see!' Jan Paulus flashed back.

'We certainly shall,' agreed Sean.

The Boer wheeled his horse and rode away. Sean watched his back disappear among the trees and only then did he let his anger slip. He rampaged through the laager working himself into a fury, pacing out frustrated circles, stopping now and then to glare out in the direction from which the Boer's wagons would come – but under all the external signs of indignation was his unholy anticipation of a fight. Kandhla brought him food, hurrying along behind him with the plate. Sean waved him away impatiently and continued his pugnacious patrol. At last a trek whip popped in the distance and an ox lowed faintly, to be answered immediately by Sean's cattle. The dogs started barking and Sean crossed to one of the wagons on the north side of the laager and leaned against it with assumed nonchalance. The long line of wagons wound out of the trees towards him. There were bright blobs of colour on the high box seat of the lead wagon. Women's dresses! Ordinarily they would have made Sean's nostrils flare like those of a stud stallion, but now his whole attention was concentrated on the larger of the two outriders. Jan Paulus cantered ahead of his father, and Sean, with his fists clenched into bony hammers at his sides, watched him come. Jan Paulus sat straight in the saddle; he stopped his horse a dozen paces from Sean and shoved his hat onto the back of his head with a thumb as thick and as brown as a fried sausage; he tickled his horse a little with his spurs to make it dance and he asked with mock surprise, 'What, *Rooi Nek*, still here?'

Sean's dogs had rushed forward to meet the other pack and now they milled about in a restrained frenzy of mutual bottom-smelling, stiff-limbed with tension, backs abristle and legs cocking in the formal act of urination.

'Why don't you go and climb a tree? You'll feel more at home there,' Sean suggested mildly.

'Ah! so?' Jan Paulus reared in his stirrups. He kicked loose his right foot, swung it back over his horse's rump to dismount and Sean jumped at him. The horse skittered nervously, throwing the Boer off balance and he clutched at the saddle. Sean reached up, took a double handful of his ginger beard and leaned back on it with all his weight. Jan Paulus came over backwards with his arms windmilling, his foot caught in the stirrup and he hung suspended like a hammock, held at one end to the plunging horse and at the other by his chin to Sean's hands. Sean dug his heels in, revelling in the Boer's bellows.

Galvanized into action by Sean's example, the dogs cut short the ceremony and went at each other in a snarling, snapping shambles; the fur flew like sand in a Kalahari dust-storm.

The stirrup-leather snapped; Sean fell backwards and rolled to his feet just in time to meet Jan Paulus's charge. He smothered the punch that the Boer bowled overarm at him, but the power behind it shocked him; then they were chest to chest and Sean felt his own strength matched. They strained silently with their beards touching and their eyes inches apart. Sean shifted his weight quickly and tried for a fall, but smoothly as a dancer Jan Paulus met and held him. Then it was his turn; he twisted in Sean's arms and

Sean sobbed with the effort required to stop him. Oupa Leroux joined in by driving his horse at them, scattering the dogs, his hippo-hide sjambok hissing as he swung it.

'Let it stand! you thunders, give over – hey! Enough, let it stand!'

Sean shouted with pain as the lash cut across his back and at the next stroke Jan Paulus howled as loudly. They let go of each other and massaging their whip-weals retreated before the skinny old white-beard on the horse.

The first of the wagons had come up now and two hundred pounds of woman, all in one package, called out from the box seat, 'Why did you stop them, Oupa?'

'No sense in letting them kill each other.'

'Shame on you – so you must spoil the boys' fun. Don't you remember how you loved to fight? Or are you now so old you forget the pleasures of your youth? Leave them alone!'

Oupa hesitated, swinging the sjambok and looking from Sean to Jan Paulus.

'Come away from there, you old busybody,' his wife ordered him. She was solid as a granite kopje, her blouse packed full of bosom and her bare arms brown and thick as a man's. The wide brim of her bonnet shaded her face but Sean could see it was pink and pudding-shaped, the kind of face that smiles more easily than it frowns. There were two girls on the seat beside her but there was no time to look at them. Oupa had pulled his horse out of the way and Jan Paulus was moving down on him. Sean went up on his toes, crouching a little, preoccupied with the taste he had just had of the other's strength, watching Jan Paulus close in for the main course and not too certain he was going to be able to chew this mouthful.

Jan Paulus tested Sean with a long right-hander but Sean rolled his head with it and the thick pad of his beard cushioned the blow; he hooked Jan Paulus in the ribs under his raised arm and Jan Paulus grunted and circled away.

Forgetting his scruples, Oupa Leroux watched them with rising delight. It was going to be a good fight. They were well matched – both big men, under thirty, quick and smooth on their feet. Both had fought before and that often; you could tell it by the way they felt each other out, turning just out of reach, moving in to offer an opening that a less experienced man might have attempted and regretted, then dropping back.

The fluid, almost leisurely pattern of movement exploded. Jan Paulus jumped in, moving left, changed direction like the recoil of a whip lash and used his right hand again; Sean ducked under it and laid himself open to Jan Paulus's left. He staggered back from its kick, bleeding where it had split the flesh across his cheek-bone, and Jan Paulus followed him eagerly, his hands held ready, searching for the opening. Sean kept clear, instinct moving his feet until the blackness faded inside his head and he felt the strength in his arms again. He saw Jan Paulus following him and he let his legs stay rubbery; he dropped his hands and waited for Jan Paulus to commit himself. Too late Jan Paulus caught the cunning in Sean's eyes and tried to break from the trap, but clenched bone raked his face. He staggered away and now he was bleeding also.

They fought through the wagons with the advantage changing hands a dozen times. They came together and used their heads and their knees, they broke and used their fists again. Then locked chest to chest once more they rolled down the steep bank into the riverbed of the Limpopo. They fought in the soft sand and it held their legs, it filled their mouths when they fell and clung like white icing-sugar to their hair and beards. They splashed into one of the pools and they fought in the water, coughing with the agony of it in their lungs, floundering like a pair of bull hippos, their movements slowing down until they knelt facing each other, no longer able to rise, the water running from them and the only sound their gasping for air.

Not sure whether the darkness was actuality or a fantasy of fatigue, for the sun had set by the time they were finished, Sean watched Jan Paulus starting to puke, retching with a tearing noise to bring up a small splash of yellow bile. Sean crawled to the edge of the pool and lay with his face in the sand. There were voices echoing in his ears and the light of a lantern – the light was red – filtered through the blood that had trickled into his eyes. His servants lifted him and he hardly felt them. The light and the voices faded into blackness as he slipped over the edge of consciousness.

The sting of iodine woke him and he struggled to sit up but hands pushed him down.

'Gently, gently, the fight is over.' Sean focused his one eye to find the voice. The pinkness of Ouma Leroux hung over him. Her hands touched his face and the antiseptic stung him again. He exclaimed through puffed lips.

'So! Just like a man,' Ouma chuckled. 'Your head nearly knocked off without a murmur but one touch of medicine and you cry like a baby.'

Sean ran his tongue round inside his mouth; one tooth loose but all the others miraculously present. He started to lift his hand to touch his closed eye but Ouma slapped it down impatiently and went on working over him.

'Glory, what a fight!' She shook her head happily. 'You were good, *kerel*, you were very good.'

Sean looked beyond her and saw the girl. She was standing in shadow, a silhouette against the pale canvas. She was holding a basin. Ouma turned and dipped the cloth in it, washing out the blood before she came back to his face. The wagon rocked under her weight and the lantern that hung from the roof swung, lighting the girl's face from the side. Sean's legs straightened on his cot and he moved his head slightly to see her better.

'Be still, *jong*,' Ouma commanded. Sean looked past her at the girl at the full serene line of her lips and the curve of her cheek. He saw the pile of her hair fluff up in happy disarray and then, suddenly – penitent – slide down behind her neck, curl over her shoulder and hang to her waist in a plait as thick as his wrist.

'Katrina, do you expect me to reach right across to the basin each time? Stand closer, girl.'

She stepped into the light and looked at Sean. Green, laughing, almost bubbling green was the colour of her eyes. Then she dropped them to the basin. Sean stared at her, not wanting to miss the moment when she would look up again.

'My big bear,' Ouma spoke with grudging approval. 'Steal our camp site, fight my son and ogle my daughter. If you go on like this I might have to knock the thunder out of you myself. Glory, but you are a dangerous one! Katrina, you had better go back to our wagons and help Henrietta see to your brother. Leave the basin on the chest there.'

She looked at Sean once more before she left. There were secret shadows in the green – she didn't have to smile with her mouth.

– 11 –

Sean woke to the realization that something was wrong. He started to sit up but the pain checked him: the stiffness of bruised muscle and the catch of half-dried scab. He groaned and the movement hurt his lips. Slowly he swung his legs off the cot and roused himself to take stock of the damage. Dark through the hair of his chest showed a heel imprint of Jan Paulus's boot. Sean prodded round it gently, feeling for the give of a broken rib; then, satisfied with that area, he went on to inspect the raw graze that wrapped round onto his back, holding his left arm high and peering closely at the broken skin. He picked a bit of blanket fluff from the scab. He stood up, only to freeze as a torn muscle in his shoulder knifed him. He started to swear then softly, monotonously, and he kept it up all through the painful business of climbing down out of the wagon.

His entire following watched his descent – even the dogs looked worried. Sean reached the ground and started to shout.

'What the hell—' He stopped hurriedly as he felt his lip crack open again and start to bleed.

'What the hell' – he said again, keeping his lips still – 'are you doing standing round like a bunch of women at a beer drink – is there no work here? Hlubi, I thought I sent you out to look for elephant.' Hlubi went. 'Kandhla, where's breakfast? Mbejane, get me a basin of water and my shaving-mirror.' Sean sat in his chair and morosely inspected his face in the mirror.

'If a herd of buffalo had stampeded across it they would have done less damage.'

'Nkosi, it is nothing compared to his face,' Mbejane assured him.

'Is he bad?' Sean looked up.

'I have spoken to one of his servants. He has not left his bed yet and he lies there, growling like a wounded lion in a thicket; but his eyes are as tightly closed as those of a new cub.'

'Tell me more, Mbejane. Say truly, was it a good fight?'

Mbejane squatted down next to Sean's chair. He was silent a moment as he gathered his words.

'When the sky sends its cloud impis against the peaks of the Drakensberg, with thunder and the spears of lightning, it is a thing to thrill a man. When two bull elephants fight unto death there is no braver show in all the veld. Is this not so?'

Sean nodded, his eyes twinkling.

'Nkosi, hear me when I tell you these things were as the play of little children beside this fight.'

Sean listened to the praises. Mbejane was well versed in the oldest art of Zululand and when he had finished he looked at Sean's face. It was happy. Mbejane smiled and took a fold of paper out of his loin cloth. 'A servant from the other camp brought this while you slept.'

Sean read the note. It was written in a big round schoolgirl hand and worded in High Dutch. He liked that writing. It was an invitation to dinner.

'Kandhla, get out my suit and my number one boots.' He picked up the mirror again. There wasn't very much he could do about his face – trim the beard, perhaps, but that was all. He laid the mirror down and looked up stream to where the Leroux wagons were half hidden among the trees.

Mbejane carried a lantern in front of Sean. They walked slowly to enable Sean to limp with dignity. When they reached the other laager, Jan Paulus climbed stiffly out of his chair and nodded an equally stiff greeting. Mbejane had lied – except for a missing tooth there was little to choose between their faces. Oupa slapped Sean's back and pressed a tumbler of brandy into his hand. He was a tall man, but twenty thousand suns had burnt away his flesh and left only stringy muscle, had faded his eyes to a pale green and toughened his skin to the texture of a turkey's neck. His beard was yellowish-white with still a touch of ginger round the mouth. He asked Sean three questions without giving him time to answer the first, then he led him to a chair.

Oupa talked, Sean listened and Jan Paulus sulked. Oupa talked of cattle and hunting and the land to the north. After a few minutes Sean realized that he was not expected to take part in the conversation: his few tentative efforts were crushed under Oupa's verbal avalanche. So Sean listened half to him and half to the whisper of women's voices from the cooking fires behind the laager. Once he heard her laugh. He knew it was her for it was the rich sound of the thing that he had seen in her eyes. At last the women's business with food and pots was finished and Ouma led the girls to where the men sat. Sean stood up and saw that Katrina was tall, with shoulders like a boy. As she walked towards him the movement pressed her skirt against her legs – they were long but her feet were small. Her hair was red-black and tied behind her head in an enormous bun.

'Ah, my battling bear,' Ouma took Sean's arm, 'let me present my daughter-in-law, Henrietta – here is the man that nearly killed your husband.' Jan Paulus snorted from his chair and Ouma laughed, her bosom wobbling merrily. Henrietta was a small dark-eyed girl. *She doesn't like me*, Sean guessed instantly. He bowed slightly and took her hand. She pulled it away.

'This is my youngest daughter, Katrina. You met her last night.'

She does like me. Her fingers were long and square-tipped in his. Sean risked his lips with a smile.

'Without her ministrations I might have bled to death,' he said. She smiled straight back at him but not with her mouth.

'You wear your wounds well, maneer, the blue eye has an air of distinction.'

'That will be enough from you, girl,' Oupa spoke sharply. 'Go and sit by your mother.' He turned to Sean. 'I was telling you about this horse – I said to the fellow, "He's not worth five pounds let alone fifteen, look at those hocks, thin as sticks." So he says to me, trying to get me away, you follow, he says, "Come and look at the saddle." But I can see he's worried—'

The thin cotton of the girl's blouse could hardly contain the impatient push of her breasts. Sean thought that he had never seen anything so wonderful.

There was a trestle-table next to the cooking fire; they went to it at last. Oupa said grace. Sean watched him through his lashes. Oupa's beard waggled as he spoke and at one point he thumped the table to emphasize the point he was making to the Almighty. His 'amen' had such an impressive resonance that Sean had to make an effort to stop himself applauding and Oupa fell back spent.

'Amen,' said Ouma and ladled stew from a pot the size of a bucket. Henrietta added pumpkin fritters and Katrina stacked slices of fresh mealie bread on each plate. A silence fell on the table, spoiled only by the clank of metal on china and the sound of Oupa breathing through his nose.

'Mevrouw Leroux, I have waited a long time to taste food like this again.' Sean mopped up the last bit of gravy with a piece of mealie bread. Ouma beamed.

'There's plenty more, meneer. I love to see a man eat. Oupa used to be a great trencherman. My father made him take me away for he could not afford to feed him every time he came courting.' She took Sean's plate and filled it. 'You look to me like a man who can eat.'

'I think I'll hold my own in most company,' Sean agreed.

'So?' Jan Paulus spoke for the first time. He passed his plate to Ouma. 'Fill it up, please, Mother, tonight I am hungry.'

Sean's eyes narrowed, he waited until Jan Paulus had his plate back in front of him, then he took up his fork deliberately. Jan Paulus did the same.

'Glory,' said Ouma happily. 'Here we go again. Oupa, you may have to go out and shoot a couple of buffalo before dinner is finished tonight.'

'I will bet one sovereign on Jan Paulus,' Oupa challenged

his wife. 'He is like an army of termites. I swear that if there was nothing else he'd eat the canvas off the wagons.'

'All right,' agreed Ouma. 'I've never seen the Bear eat before, but it seems to me he has plenty of room to put it.'

'Your woollen shawl against my green bonnet that Jan Paulus gives up first,' Katrina whispered to her sister-in-law.

'When Jannie has finished the stew he'll eat the English man,' Henrietta giggled. 'But it's a pretty bonnet – I'll take the wager.'

Plateful for plateful, Ouma measuring out each ladle with scrupulous fairness, they ate against each other. The talk round the table dwindled and halted.

'More?' asked Ouma each time the plates were clean, and each time they looked at each other and nodded. At last the ladle scraped the bottom of the pot.

'That's the end of it, my children, we will have to call it another draw.'

The silence went on after she had spoken. Sean and Jan Paulus sat very still looking at their respective plates. Jan Paulus hiccupped, his expression changed. He stood up and went into the darkness.

'Ah! listen! listen!' crowed Ouma. They waited and then she exploded into laughter. 'The ungrateful wretch, is that what he thinks of my food? Where's your sovereign, Oupa?'

'Wait, you greedy old woman, the game's not finished yet.' He turned and stared at Sean. 'To me it looks as though your horse is nearly blown.'

Sean closed his eyes. The sounds of Jan Paulus's distress came to him very clearly.

'Thank you for a—' He didn't have time to finish. He wanted to get far away so the girl couldn't hear him.

– 12 –

The following morning during breakfast Sean thought about his next move. He would write an invitation to dinner and then he would deliver it himself. They would have to ask him to stay for coffee and then, if he waited, there would be a chance. Even Oupa would have to stop talking sometime and Ouma might relax her vigilance. He was sure there'd be a chance to talk to the girl. He didn't know what he would say to her but he'd worry about that when the time came. He climbed into the wagon and found pencil and paper in his chest. He went back to the table and spread the paper in front of him. He chewed the end of the pencil and stared out into the bush. Something moved against the trees. Sena put the pencil down and stood up. The dogs barked then stopped as they recognized Hlubi. He was coming at a trot – he was coming with news. Sean waited for him.

'A big herd, Nkosi, with many showing ivory. I saw them drink at the river and then go back into the bush, feeding quietly.'

'When?' asked Sean to gain time. He was searching for a plausible excuse to stay in camp – it would have to be good to satisfy Mbejane who was already saddling one of the horses.

'Before the sun this morning,' answered Hlubi and Sean was trying to remember which was his sore shoulder – he couldn't hunt with a sore shoulder. Mbejane led the horse into the laager. Sean scratched the side of his nose and coughed.

'The tracker from the other camp follows close behind me, Nkosi, he too has seen the herd and brings the news to his master. But I, being as swift as a springbok when I run, have outdistanced him,' Hlubi ended modestly.

‘Is that so?’ For Sean it changed the whole problem, he couldn’t leave the herd to that red-headed Dutchman. He ran across to the wagon and snatched his bandolier from the foot of the cot. His rifle was already in the scabbard.

‘Are you tired, Hlubi?’ Sean buckled the heavy ammunition belt across his chest. The sweat had run in oily streaks down the Zulu’s body; his breathing was deep and quick.

‘No, Nkosi.’

‘Well, then, lead us to these elephant of yours, my fleet-footed springbok.’ Sean swung up onto his horse. He looked over his shoulder at the other camp. She would still be there when he came back.

Sean was limited to the speed of Hlubi’s feet while the two Leroux had only to gallop along the easy spoor left by Sean’s party and they caught up with him before he had gone two miles.

‘Good morning to you,’ Oupa greeted him as he drew level and pulled his horse in to a trot. ‘Out for a morning’s ride, I see.’

Sean made the best of it with a grin. ‘If we are all to hunt then we must hunt together. Do you agree?’

‘Of course, meneer.’

‘And we must share the bag equally, one third to each man.’

‘That is always the way.’ Oupa nodded.

‘Do you agree?’ Sean turned in his saddle towards Jan Paulus. Jan Paulus grunted. He showed little inclination to open his mouth since he had lost his tooth.

They found the spoor within an hour. The herd had wrecked a road through the thick bush along the river. They had stripped the bark from the saplings and left them naked and bleeding. They had knocked down bigger trees to reach the tender top leaves and they had dropped their great piles of dung in the grass.

'We need no trackers to follow this.' Jan Paulus had the first excitement on him. Sean looked at him and wondered how many elephant had died in front of his rifle. A thousand perhaps, and yet the excitement was on him again now.

'Tell your servants to follow us. We'll go ahead. We'll catch them within an hour.' He smiled at Sean, gap-toothed, and Sean felt the excitement lift the hair on his own forearms. He smiled back.

They cantered in a rough line abreast, slack-reined to let the horses pick their own way among the fallen trees. The river bush thinned out as they moved north and soon they were into parkland. The grass brushed their stirrups and the ground beneath it was firm and smooth.

They rode without talking, leaning forward in their saddles, looking ahead. The rhythmic beat of hooves was a war drum. Sean ran his fingers along the row of bullets strapped across his chest, then he drew his rifle, checked the load and thrust it back into its scabbard.

'There!' said Oupa and Sean saw the herd. It was massed among a grove of fever trees a quarter of a mile ahead.

'Name of a name,' Paulus whistled. 'There must be two hundred at least.'

Sean heard the first pig-squeal of alarm, saw ears fan out and trunks lift. Then the herd bunched together and ran with their backs humped, a thin screen of dust trailing behind them.

'Paulus take the right flank. You, meneer, in the middle and I'll ride left,' shouted Oupa.

Sean jammed his hat down over his ears and his horse jumped under him as he hit it with his heels. Like a thrown trident the three horsemen hurled themselves at the herd. Sean rode into the dust. He picked an old cow elephant from the moving mountain range in front of him and pressed his horse so close upon her that he could see the bristles in her tail tuft and the erosion of her skin, wrinkled as an old man's scrotum. He touched his hand to his horse's neck and it plunged – from full gallop to standstill in half a dozen strides. Sean threw his feet free of the stirrups and hit the ground, loose-kneed to ride the shock. The cow's spine was a line of lumps beneath the grey skin – Sean broke it with his first bullet and she dropped, sliding on her hindquarters like a dog with worms. His horse started to run again before he was properly in the saddle and everything became movement and noise, dust and the smell of burnt powder. Chase them, coughing in the dust. Close with them. Off the horse and shoot. Wet blood on grey skin. Slam, slam of the rifle – its barrel hot, recoiling savagely. Sweat in the eyes, stinging. Ride. Shoot again. Two more down, screaming, anchored by paralysed legs. Blood-red as a flag. Load, cramming cartridges into the rifle. Ride. Chase them, shoot again and again. The bullets striking on flesh with a hollow sound, then up and ride again. Ride – until the horse could no longer keep up with them and he had to let them go. He stood holding his horse's head, the dust and the thirst closed his throat. He could not swallow. His hands trembled in reaction. His shoulder was aching again. He untied his silk scarf, wiped his face with it and blew the mud out of his nose, then he drank from his water-bottle. The water tasted sweet.

The hunt had led from parkland into mopani bush. It was very thick, shiny green leaves hanging to the ground and pressing close around him. The air was still and warm to breathe. He turned back along the line of the chase. He found them by their squealing. When they saw him they tried to charge, dragging themselves towards him – using the front legs only and groping with their trunks. They sagged into stillness after the head shot. This was the bad part. Sean worked quickly. He could hear the other rifles in the mopani forest around him and when he came to one of the long clearings among the trees he saw Jan Paulus walking towards him, leading his horse.

'How many?' called Sean.

'*Gott*, man, I didn't count. What a killing, hey? Have you got a drink for me? I dropped my water-bottle somewhere.'

Jan Paulus's rifle was in its saddle scabbard. The reins were slung over his shoulder and his horse followed him with its head drooping from exhaustion. The clearing was walled in with the dense mopani trees and a wounded elephant broke into the open. It was lung shot – the side of its chest painted with froth – and when it squealed the blood sprayed in a pink spout from the end of its trunk. It went for Jan Paulus, streaming the black battle ensigns of its ears. His horse reared, the reins snapped, it turned free and galloped away, leaving him full in the path of the charge. Sean went up onto his horse's back without touching stirrups. His horse threw its head, dancing in a tight circle, but he dragged it around and drove it to intercept the charge.

'Don't run, for God's sake, don't run!' he shouted as he cleared his rifle from the scabbard. Jan Paulus heard him. He stood with his hands at his sides, his feet apart and his body braced. The elephant heard Sean shout also and it swung its head and Sean saw the first hesitation in its run. He fired, not trying to pick his shot, hoping only to hurt it, to bring it away from Jan Paulus. The bullet slapped into it with the sound of a wet towel flicked against a wall. The elephant turned, clumsy with the weakness of its shattered lungs. Sean gathered his horse beneath him and wheeled it away and the elephant followed him.

Sean fumbled as he reloaded, his hands were slippery with sweat. One of the brass shells slipped through his fingers, tapped against his knee and dropped into the grass under his horse's hooves. The elephant gained on him. He loosened his bed-roll from the saddle and let it fall – they would sometimes stop to savage even a fallen hat, but not this one. He turned in the saddle and fired into it. It squealed again so close upon him that the blown blood splattered into his face. His horse was almost finished; he could feel its legs flopping with every stride and they were nearly at the end of the clearing racing towards the solid wall of green mopani. He pushed another round into the breech of his rifle and swung his body across the saddle. He slid down until his feet touched the ground and he was running next to his horse. He let go and was flung forward, but he fought to keep his balance, his body jarring with the force of his run. Then, still on his feet, he turned for his first steady shot. The elephant was coming in fast, almost on top of him, hanging over him like a cliff. Its trunk coiled on its chest and the curves of its ivory were lifted high.

It's too close, much too close, I can't hit the brain from here.

He aimed at the hollow in its forehead just above the level of its eyes. He fired and the elephant's legs folded up; its brain burst like an overripe tomato within the bone castle of its skull.

Sean tried to jump aside as the massive body came skidding down upon him, but one of its legs hit him and threw him face down into the grass. He lay there. He felt sick, for his stomach was still full of warm oily fear.

After a while he sat up and looked at the elephant. One of its tusks had snapped off flush with the lip. Jan Paulus came, panting from his run. He stopped next to the elephant and touched the wound in its forehead, then he wiped his fingers on his shirt.

'Are you all right, man?'

He took Sean's arm and helped him to his feet; then he picked up Sean's hat and dusted it carefully before handing it to him.

– 13 –

In the three-sided shelter formed by the belly and out-thrust legs of one of the dead elephants they made their camp that night. They drank coffee together and Sean sat between the two Leroux with his back against the rough skin of the elephant's belly. The silhouettes of the tree against the night sky were deformed by the shapes of the vultures that clustered in them and the darkness was ugly with the giggling of hyena. They had set a feast for the scavengers. They spoke little for they were tired, but Sean could feel the gratitude of the men who sat beside him and before they rolled into their blankets Jan Paulus said gruffly, 'Thank you, *kerel*.'

'You might be able to do the same for me one day.'

'I hope so, *ja*! I hope so.'

In the morning Oupa said, 'It's going to take us three or four days to cut out all this ivory.' He looked up at the sky. 'I don't like these clouds. One of us had better ride back to camp to fetch more men and wagons to carry the ivory.'

'I'll go.' Sean stood up quickly.

'I was thinking of going myself.' But Sean was already calling to Mbejane to saddle his horse and Oupa couldn't really argue with him, not after yesterday.

'Tell Ouma to take the wagons across the river,' he acquiesced. 'We don't want to be caught on this side when the river floods. Perhaps you wouldn't mind helping her.'

'No,' Sean assured him. 'I don't mind at all.'

His horse was still tired from the previous day's hunt and it was three hours before he reached the river.

He tied his horse on the bank and went down to one of the pools. He stripped off his clothes and lowered himself into the water. He scrubbed himself with handfuls of the coarse sand and when he waded out of the pool and dried on his shirt his skin was tingling. He rode along the bank and the temptation to gallop his horse was almost unbearable. He laughed to himself a little.

'The field's almost clear, though I wouldn't put it past that suspicious old Dutchman to follow me.'

He laughed again and thought about the colour of her eyes, green as *crème-de-menthe* in a crystal glass, and the shape of her bosom. The muscles in his legs tightened and the horse lengthened its stride in response to the pressure of his knees. 'All right, run then,' Sean encouraged it, 'I don't insist on it, but I would be grateful.'

He went to his own wagons first and changed his sweaty shirt for a fresh one, his leather breeches for clean calico and his scuffed boots for soft polished leather. He scrubbed his teeth with salt and dragged a comb through his hair and beard. He saw in the mirror that the battle damage to his face was fading and he winked at his image. 'How can she resist you?' He gave his moustache one more twirl, climbed out of the wagon and was immediately aware of a most uncomfortable feeling in his stomach. He walked towards the Leroux laager thinking about it, and he recognized it as the same feeling he used to have when Waite Courtney called him to the study to do penance for his boyhood sins.

'That's odd,' he muttered. 'Why should I feel like that?' His confidence faded and he stopped. 'I wonder if my breath smells – I think I'd better go back and get some cloves.' He turned with relief, knew it as cowardice and stopped again. 'Get a grip on yourself. She's only a girl, an uneducated little Dutch girl. You've had fifty finer women.'

'Name me two,' he shot back at himself.

'Well, there was – Oh! for Chrissake, come on.' Resolutely he set off for the Leroux's laager again.

She was sitting in the sun within the circle of wagons. She was leaning forward on the stool and her newly-washed hair fell thickly over her face almost to the ground. With each stroke of the brush it leapt like a live thing and the sun sparkled the red lights in it. Sean wanted to touch it – he wanted to twist fistfuls of it round his hands and he wanted to smell it, it would smell warm and slightly milky like a puppy's fur. He stepped softly towards her but before he reached her she took the shiny mass with both hands and threw it back over her shoulders – a startled flash of green eyes, one despairing wail, 'Oh, no! not with my hair like this.' A swirl of skirts that sent the stool flying and she was gone into her wagon. Sean scratched the side of his nose and stood awkwardly.

'Why are you back so soon, meneer?' she called through the canvas. 'Where are the others? Is everything all right?'

'Yes, they're both fine. I left them and came to fetch wagons to carry the ivory.'

'Oh, that's good.' Sean tried to interpret the inflection of her voice: was it good that they were fine, or good that he had left them? So far the indications were favourable; her confusion at seeing him boded well.

'What's wrong?' Ouma bellowed from one of the other wagons. 'It's not Oupa, don't tell me something has happened to him?' The wagon rocked wildly and her pink face, puckered with sleep, popped out of the opening. Sean's reassurances were smothered by her voice.

'Oh, I knew this would happen. I had a feeling. I shouldn't have let him go.'

'Paulus, oh, Jan Paulus – I must go to him. Where is he?'

Henrietta came running from the cooking fire behind the wagons and then the dogs started barking and the servants added their chatter to the confusion. Sean tried to shout them all down and watch Katrina emerging from her wagon at the same time. She had disciplined her hair now – it had a green ribbon in it and hung down her back. She was laughing and she helped him to quieten Ouma and Henrietta.

They brought him coffee, then they sat round him and listened to the story of the hunt. Sean went into detail on the rescue of Jan Paulus and was rewarded by a softening of the dislike in Henrietta's eyes. By the time Sean had finished talking it was too late to start moving the wagons across the river. So he talked some more, it was most agreeable to have three women as an attentive audience, and then they ate supper.

With ostentatious tact Ouma and Henrietta retired early to their respective living wagons and left Sean and Katrina sitting by the fire. At carefully-spaced intervals there was a stage cough from Ouma's wagon, a reminder that they were not entirely alone. Sean lit a cheroot and frowned into the fire searching desperately for something intelligent to say, but all his brain could dredge up was, 'Thank God, Oupa isn't here.' He sneaked a glance at Katrina: she was staring into the fire as well and she was blushing. Instantly Sean felt his own cheeks starting to heat up. He opened his mouth to talk and made a squawking noise. He shut it again.

'We can speak in English if you like, meneer.'

'You speak English?' Sean's surprise brought his voice back.

'I practise every night – I read aloud out of my books.'

Sean grinned at her delightedly – it was suddenly very important that she could speak his language. The dam, holding back all the questions that there were to ask and all the things there were to say, burst and the words came pouring out over each other. Katrina fluttered her hands when she couldn't find the word she wanted and then lapsed back into Afrikaans. They killed the short taut silences with a simultaneous rush of words, then laughed together in confusion. They sat on the edges of their chairs and watched each other's faces as they talked. The moon came up, a red rain moon, and the fire faded into a puddle of ashes.

'Katrina, it's long past the time decent people were asleep. I'm sure Meneer Courtney is tired.'

They dropped their voices to a whisper, drawing out the last minutes.

'In just one minute, girl, I'm coming out to fetch you to bed.'

They walked to her wagon and with each step her skirts brushed against his leg. She stopped with one hand on the wagon step. She wasn't as tall as he'd imagined, the top of her head came to his chin. The seconds slid by as he hesitated, reluctant to touch, strangely frightened to test the delicate thread they had spun together lest he destroy it before it became strong. Slowly he swayed towards her and something surged up inside him as he saw her chin lift slightly and the lashes fall over her eyes.

'Goodnight, Meneer Courtney.' Ouma's voice again, loud and with an edge to it. Sean started guiltily.

'Goodnight, mevrouw.'

Katrina touched his arm just above the elbow, her fingers were warm.

'Goodnight, meneer, I shall see you in the morning.'

She rustled up the steps and slipped through the opening of the canvas. Sean scowled at Ouma's wagon.

'Thanks very much – and if there is ever anything I can do for you, please don't hesitate to ask.'

– 14 –

They started moving the wagons early next morning. There was no time to talk to Katrina in the bustle of inspanning and working the wagons across the corduroy bridge. Sean spent most of the morning in the riverbed and the white sand bounced the heat up at him. He threw off his shirt and sweated like a wrestler. He trotted beside Katrina's wagon when they ran it through the riverbed. She looked once at his naked chest and arms; her cheeks darkened in the shadow of her bonnet and she dropped her eyes and didn't look at him again. With only the two wagons that were going back to fetch the ivory still on the north bank and the rest safely across, Sean could relax. He washed in one of the pools, put on his shirt and went across to the south bank looking forward to a long afternoon of Katrina's company.

Ouma met him. 'Thank you, my dear, the girls have made you a parcel of cold meat and a bottle of coffee to eat on your way.' Sean's face went slack. He had forgotten all about that stinking ivory; as far as he was concerned Oupa and Paulus could keep the lot of it.

'Don't worry about us any more now, maneer. I know how it is with a man who is a man. When there's work to do everything else comes after.'

Katrina put the food in his hands. Sean looked for a sign from her. One sign and he'd defy even Ouma.

'Don't be too long,' she whispered. The thought that he might shirk work had obviously not even occurred to her. Sean was glad he hadn't suggested it.

It was a long ride back to the elephant.

'You've taken your time, haven't you?' Oupa greeted him with sour suspicion. 'You'd better get to work if you don't want to lose some of your share.'

Taking out the tusks was a delicate task: a slip of the axe would scar the ivory and halve its value. They worked in the heat with a blue haze of flies around their faces, settling on their lips and crawling into their nostrils and eyes. The carcasses had started to rot and the gases ballooned their bellies and escaped in posthumous belches. They sweated as they worked and the blood caked their arms to the elbows, but each hour the wagons filled higher until on the third day they loaded the last tusk. Sean reckoned his share at twelve hundred pounds, the equivalent of a satisfactory day on the Stock Exchange.

He was in a good mood on the morning that they started back to the camp, but it deteriorated as the day wore on and they struggled with the heavily-loaded wagons. The rain seemed to have made up its mind at last and now the sky's belly hung down as heavily as that of a pregnant sow. The clouds trapped the heat beneath them and the men panted and the oxen complained mournfully. At mid-afternoon they heard the first far thunder.

'It will be on us before we pass the river,' fretted Oupa. 'See if you can't get some pace out of those oxen.'

They reached Sean's camp an hour after dark and threw his share of the ivory out of the wagons almost without stopping; then they went down to the river and across the bridge to the south bank.

'My mother will have food ready,' Jan Paulus called back to Sean. 'When you have washed come across and eat with us.'

Sean had supper with the Leroux, but his attempts to get Katrina by herself were neatly countered by Oupa whose suspicions were now confirmed. The old man played his trump card immediately after supper and ordered Katrina to bed. Sean could only shrug helplessly in reply to Katrina's appealing little glance. When she had gone Sean went back to his own camp. He was dizzy with fatigue and he fell onto his cot without bothering to undress.

The rains opened their annual offensive with a midnight broadside of thunder. It startled Sean to his feet before he was awake. He pulled open the front of the wagon and heard the wind coming.

'Mbejane, get the cattle into the laager. Make sure all the canvas is secure.'

'It is done already, Nkosi. I have lashed the wagons together so the oxen cannot stampede and I have—' Then the wind whipped his voice away.

It came out of the east and it frightened the trees so they thrashed their branches in panic; it drummed on the wagon canvas and filled the air with dust and dry leaves. The oxen turned restlessly within the laager. Then came the rain: stinging like hail, drowning the wind and turning the air to water. It swamped the sloping ground that could not drain it fast enough, it blinded and it deafened. Sean went back to his cot and listened to its fury. It made him feel drowsy. He pulled the blankets up to his chin and slept.

In the morning he found his oilskins in the chest at the foot of his cot. They crackled as he pulled them on. He climbed out of the wagon. The cattle had churned the inside of the laager to calf-deep mud and there was no chance of a fire for breakfast. Although the rain was still falling the noise was out of proportion to its strength. Sean paused in his inspection of the camp; he thought about it and suddenly he knew that it was the flood voice of the Limpopo that he heard. Sliding in the mud, he ran out of the laager and stood on the bank of the river. He stared at the mad water. It was so thick with mud it looked solid and it raced so fast it appeared to be standing still. It humped up over piles of submerged rock, gullied through the deeps and hissed in static waves through the shallows. The branches and tree trunks in it whisked past so swiftly that they did little to dispel the illusion that the river was frozen in this brown convulsion.

Reluctantly Sean lifted his eyes to the far bank. The Leroux's wagons were gone.

'Katrina,' he said with the sadness of the might-have-been, then again, 'Katrina,' with the sense of his loss melting in the flame of his anger; and he knew that his wanting was not just the itch that is easily scratched and forgotten, but that it was the true ache, the one that gets into your hands and your head and your heart as well as your loins. He couldn't let her go. He ran back to his wagon and threw his clothes onto the cot.

'I'll marry her,' he said and the words startled him. He stood naked, with an awed expression on his face.

'I'll marry her,' he said again; it was an original thought and it frightened him a little. He took a pair of shorts out of his chest and put his legs into them; he pulled them up and buttoned the fly.

'I'll marry her!' He grinned at his own daring. 'I'm damned if I won't!' He buckled his belt on and tied a pair of *veldschoen* to it by their laces. He jumped down into the mud. The rain was cold on his bare back and he shivered briefly. Then he saw Mbejane coming out of one of the other wagons and he ran.

'Nkosi, Nkosi, what are you doing?' Sean put his head down and ran faster with Mbejane chasing him out onto the bank of the river.

'It's madness . . . let us talk about it first,' Mbejane shouted. 'Please, Nkosi, please.' Sean slipped in the mud and slithered down the bank. Mbejane jumped down after and caught him at the edge of the water, but the mud had coated Sean's body like grease and Mbejane couldn't hold him. Sean twisted out of his hands and sprang far out. He hit the water flat and swam on his back trying to avoid the undertow. The river swept him away. A wave slapped into his mouth and he doubled up to cough; immediately the river caught him by the heels and pulled him under the surface. It let him go again, just long enough to snatch air then it stirred him in a whirlpool and sucked him under once more. He came up beating at the water with his arms, then it tumbled him over a cascade and he knew by the pain in his chest that he was drowning. He swooped down a chute of swift water between rocks and it didn't matter anymore. He was too tired. Something scraped against his chest and he put out his hand to protect himself; his fingers closed round a branch and his head lifted out of the water. He drank air and then he was clinging to the branch, still alive and wanting to live. He started kicking, edging across the current, riding the river with his arms around the log.

One of the eddies beneath the south bank swung the log in, under the branches of a tree. He reached up, caught them and dragged himself out. He knelt in the mud and water came gushing up out of him, half through his mouth and half through his nose. He had lost his *veldschoen*. He belched painfully and looked at the river. How fast was it moving, how long had he been in the water? He must be fifteen miles below the wagons. He wiped his face with his hand. It was still raining. He stood shakily and faced upstream.

It took him three hours to reach the spot opposite his wagons. Mbejane and the others waved in wild relief when they saw him, but their shouts could not carry across the river. Sean was cold now and his feet were sore. The tracks of the Leroux wagons were dissolving in the rain. He followed them and at last the pain in his feet healed as he saw the flash of canvas in the rain mist ahead of him.

'Name of a name,' shouted Jan Paulus. 'How did you cross the river?'

'I flew, how else?' said Sean. 'Where's Katrina?'

Paulus started to laugh, leaning back in the saddle. 'So that's it then, you haven't come all this way to say goodbye to me.'

Sean flushed. 'All right, laughing boy. That's enough merriment for today . . . Where is she?'

Oupa came galloping back towards them. He asked his first question when he was fifty yards away and his fifth as he arrived. From experience Sean knew there was no point in trying to answer them. He looked beyond the two Leroux and saw her coming. She was running back from the lead wagon, her bonnet hanging from its ribbon around her throat and her hair bouncing loosely with each step. She held her skirts out of the mud, her cheeks flushed darker than the brown of her face and her eyes were very green. Sean ducked under the neck of Oupa's horse and went wet, muddy and eager to meet her.

Then the shyness stopped them and they stood paces apart. 'Katrina, will you marry me?'

She went pale. She stared at him then turned away, she was crying and Sean felt the bottom drop out of his stomach.

'No,' shouted Oupa furiously. 'She won't marry you. Leave her alone, you big baboon. You've made her cry. Get out of here. She's only a baby. Get out of here.' He forced his horse between them.

'You hold your mouth, you old busybody.' Ouma came panting back to join the discussion. 'What do you know about it anyway? Just because she's crying doesn't mean she doesn't want him.'

'I thought he was going to let me go,' sobbed Katrina. 'I thought he didn't care.'

Sean whooped and tried to dodge around Oupa's horse.

'You leave her alone,' shouted Oupa desperately, manoeuvring his horse to cut Sean off. 'You made her cry. I tell you she's crying.'

Katrina was undoubtedly crying. She was also trying to get around Oupa's horse.

'*Vat haar*,' shouted Jan Paulus. 'Get her, man, go and get her!'

Ouma caught the horse by the reins and dragged it away: she was a powerful woman. Sean and Katrina collided and held tight.

'Hey, that's it, man.' Jan Paulus jumped off his horse and pounded Sean's back from behind. Unable to protect himself Sean was driven forward a pace with each blow.

Much later Oupa muttered sulkily, 'She can have two wagons for her dowry.'

'Three!' said Katrina.

'Four!' said Ouma.

'Very well, four. Take your hands off him, girl. Haven't you any shame?' Hastily Katrina dropped her arm from Sean's waist. Sean had borrowed a suit of clothing from Paulus and they were all standing round the fire. It had stopped raining but the low clouds were prematurely bringing on the night.

'And four of the horses,' Ouma prompted her husband.

'Do you want to beggar me, woman?'

'Four horses,' repeated Ouma.

'All right, all right . . . four horses.' Oupa looked at Katrina, his eyes were stricken. 'She's only a baby, man, she's only fifteen years.'

'Sixteen,' said Ouma.

'Nearly seventeen,' said Katrina, 'and anyway you've promised, Pa, you can't go back on your word now.'

Oupa sighed; then he looked at Sean and his face hardened.

'Paulus, get the Bible out of my wagon. This big baboon is going to swear an oath.'

Jan Paulus put the Bible on the tailboard of the wagon. It was thick and the cover was of black leather, dull with use.

'Come here,' Oupa said to Sean. 'Put your hand on the book . . . don't look at me. Look up, man, look up. Now say after me, "I do most solemnly swear to look after this woman" – don't gobble, speak slower – "until I can find a priest to say the proper words. Should I fail in this then I ask you, God, to blast me with lightning, sting me with serpents, burn me in eternal fire – "' Oupa completed the list of atrocities, then he grunted with satisfaction and tucked the Bible under his arm. 'He won't have a chance to do all that to you . . . I'll get you first.'

Sean shared Jan Paulus's wagon that night; he wasn't in a mood for sleep and anyway Jan Paulus snored. It was raining again in the morning, depressing weather for farewells. Jan Paulus laughed, Henrietta cried and Ouma did both. Oupa kissed his daughter.

'Be a woman like your mother,' he said, then he scowled at Sean.

'Remember, just you remember!'

Sean and Katrina stood together and watched the trees and the curtain of rain hide the wagon train. Sean held Katrina's hand. He could feel the sadness on her; he put his arm round her and her dress was damp and cold. The last wagon disappeared and they were alone in a land as vast as solitude. Katrina shivered and looked up at the man beside her. He was so big and overpoweringly male; he was a stranger. Suddenly she was frightened. She wanted to hear her mother's laugh and see her brother and father riding ahead of her wagon, the way it had always been.

'Oh, please, I want . . .' She pulled out from his arm. She never finished that sentence, for she looked at his mouth and his lips were full and burnt dark by the sun – they were smiling. Then she looked at his eyes and her panic smoothed away. With those eyes watching over her she was never to feel frightened again, not until the very end and that was a long time away. Going into his love was like going into a castle, a thick-walled place. A safe place where no one else could enter. The first feeling of it was so strong that she could only stand quietly and let the warmth wrap her.

– 15 –

That evening they outspanned Katrina's wagons back at the south bank of the river. It was still raining. Sean's servants waved and signalled to them, but the brown water bellowed down between them cutting off all sound and hope of passage. Katrina looked at the water. 'Did you really swim that, meneer?'

'So fast that I hardly got wet.'

'Thank you,' she said.

Despite the rain and smoky fire Katrina served up a meal as good as one of Ouma's. They ate it in the shelter of the tarpaulin beside her wagon. The wind guttered the hurricane lamp, flogged the canvas and blew a fine haze of rain in on them. It was so uncomfortable that when Sean suggested that they go into the wagon Katrina barely hesitated before agreeing. She sat on the edge of her cot and Sean sat on the chest opposite her. From an awkward start their conversation was soon running as fast as the river outside the wagon.

'My hair is still wet,' Katrina exclaimed at last. 'Do you mind if I dry it while we talk?'

'Of course not.'

'Then let me get my towel out of the chest.'

They stood up at the same time. There was very little space in the wagon. They touched. They were on the cot. The movement of his mouth on hers, the warm taste of it, the strong pleading of his fingers at the nape of her neck and along her spine – all these things were strangely confusing. She responded slowly at first, then faster with bewildered movements of her own body and little graspings at his arms and shoulders. She did not understand and she did not care. The confusion spread through her whole body and she could not stop it, she did not want to. She reached up and her fingers went into his hair. She pulled his face down on hers. His teeth crushed her lips – sweet, exciting pain. His hand came round from her back and enclosed a fat round breast. Through the thin cotton he found the erectness of her nipple and rolled it gently between his fingers. She reacted like a filly feeling the whip for the first time. One instant she lay under the shock of his touch and then her convulsive heave caught him by surprise. He went backwards off the cot and his head cracked against the wooden chest. He sat on the floor and stared up at her, too surprised even to rub the lump on his head. Her face was flushed and she pushed the hair back from her forehead with both hands. She was shaking her head wildly in her effort to speak through her gasping. 'You must go now, meneer – the servants have made a bed for you in one of the other wagons.'

Sean scrambled to his feet. 'But, I thought . . . surely we are . . . well, I mean.'

'Keep away from me,' she warned anxiously. 'If you touch me again tonight, I'll . . . I'll bite you.'

'But, Katrina, please, I can't sleep in the other wagon.' The thought appalled him.

'I'll cook your food, mend your clothes . . . everything! But until you find a priest . . .' She didn't go on, but Sean got the idea. He started to argue. It was his introduction to Boer immovability and at last he went to find his own bed. One of Katrina's dogs was there before him – a three-quarters-grown brindle hound. Sean's attempts to persuade it to leave were as ill-fated as had been his previous arguments with its mistress. They shared the bed. During the night a difference of opinion arose between them as to what constituted a half-share of the blankets. From it the dog earned its name – Thief.

– 16 –

Sean determined to show Katrina just how strongly he resented her attitude. He would be polite but distant. Five minutes after they had sat down to breakfast the next morning this demonstration of disapproval had deteriorated to the stage where he was unable to take his eyes off her face and he was talking so much that breakfast lasted an hour.

The rain held steady for three more days and then it stopped. The sun came back, as welcome as an old friend, but it was another ten days before the river regained its sanity. Time, rain or river meant very little to the two of them. They wandered out into the bush together to pick mushrooms; they sat in camp and when Katrina was working Sean followed her around. Then, of course, they talked. She listened to him. She laughed at the right places and gasped with wonder when she was meant to. She was a good listener. As for Sean, if she had repeated the same word over and over the sound of her voice alone would have held him entranced. The evenings were difficult. Sean would start getting restless and make excuses to touch her. She wanted him to, but she was frightened of the confusion that had so nearly trapped her the first night. So she drew up a set of rules and put them to him. 'Do you promise not to do anything more than kiss me?'

'Not unless you say I can,' Sean agreed readily.

'No.' She saw the catch in that.

'You mean, I must never do anything but kiss you even if you say I can?'

She started to blush. 'If I say so in the daytime, that's different . . . but anything I say at night doesn't count, and if you break your promise I'll never let you touch me again.'

Katrina's rules stood unchanged by the time the river

had dropped enough for the wagons to be taken across to the north bank. The rains were resting, gathering their strength, but soon they would set in once more. The river was full but no longer murderous. Now was the time to cross. Sean took the oxen across first, swimming them in a herd. Holding on to one of their tails he had a Nantucket sleigh-ride across the river and when he reached the north bank there was a joyous welcome awaiting him.

They took six thick coils of unused rope from the stores wagon and joined them together. With the end of the rope round his waist Sean made one of his horses tow him back across the river, Mbejane paying out the line to him as he went. Then Sean supervised Katrina's servants as they emptied all the water barrels and lashed them to the sides of the first wagon to serve as floats. They ran the wagon into the water, tied on the rope and adjusted the barrels so that the wagon floated level. Sean signalled to Mbejane and waited until he had made the other end of the rope fast to a tree on the north bank. Then they pushed the wagon into the current and watched anxiously as it swung across the river like a pendulum, the current driving it but the tree anchoring it. It hit the north bank a distance the exact width of the river downstream of the tree, and Sean's party cheered as Mbejane and the other servants ran down the bank to retrieve it. Mbejane had a team of oxen standing ready and they dragged it out. Sean's horse towed him across the river again to fetch the rope.

Sean, Katrina and all her servants rode across on the last wagon. Sean stood behind Katrina with his arms round her waist, ostensibly to steady her, and the servants shouted and chattered like children on a picnic.

The water piled up brown against the side of the wagon, tilting it and making it roll, and with an exhilarating swoop they shot across the river and crashed into the far bank. The impact tumbled them overboard, throwing them into the knee-deep water beside the bank. They scrambled ashore. The water streamed out of Katrina's dress, her hair melted wetly over her face; she had mud on one cheek and she was gasping with laughter. Her sodden petticoats clung to her legs, tripping her, and Sean picked her up and carried her to his own laager. His servants shouted loud encouragement after him and Katrina shrieked genteelly to be put down, but held tight round his neck with both arms.

– 17 –

Now that the rains had changed every irregularity in the land into a waterhole and sowed new green grass where before had been dust and dry earth, the game scattered away from the river. Every few days Sean's trackers came into camp to report that there were no elephant. Sean condoled with them and sent them out again. He was well satisfied; there was a new quarry now, more elusive and therefore more satisfying than an old bull elephant with a hundred and fifty pounds of ivory on each side of his face. Yet to call Katrina his quarry was a lie. She was much more than that.

She was a new world – a place of endless mysteries and unexpected delights, an enchanting mixture of woman and child. She supervised the domestic routine with deceptive lack of fuss. With her there, suddenly his clothes were clean and had their full complement of buttons; the stew of boots and books and unwashed socks in his wagon vanished. There were fresh bread and fruit preserves on the table; Kandhla's eternal grilled steaks gave way to a variety of dishes. Each day she showed a new accomplishment. She could ride astride, though Sean had to turn his back when she mounted and dismounted. She cut Sean's hair and made as good a job of it as his barber in Johannesburg. She had a medicine chest in her wagon from which she produced remedies for every ailing man or beast in the company. She handled a rifle like a man and could strip and clean Sean's Mannlicher. She helped him load cartridges, measuring the charges with a practised eye. She could discuss birth and procreation with a clinical objectivity and a minute later blush all over when he looked at her that way. She was as stubborn as a mule, haughty when it suited her, serene and inscrutable at times and at others a little girl. She would push a handful of grass down the back of his shirt and run for him to chase her, giggle for minutes at a secret thought, play long imaginative games in which the dogs were her children and she talked to them and answered for them. Sometimes she was so naive that Sean thought she was joking until he remembered how young she was. She could drive him from happiness to spitting anger and back again within the space of an hour. But, once he had won her confidence and she knew that he would play to the rules, she responded to his caresses with a violence that startled them both. Sean was completely absorbed in her. She was the most wonderful thing he had ever found and, best of all, he could talk to her. He told her about Duff. She saw the extra cot in his wagon and found clothing that was obviously too small for him. She asked about it and he told her all of it and she understood.

The days became weeks. The cattle grew fat, their skins sleek and tight. Katrina planted a small vegetable garden and reaped a crop from it. Christmas came and Katrina baked a cake. Sean gave her a kaross of monkey skins that Mbejane had worked on in secret. Katrina gave Sean handsewn shirts, each with his initials embroidered on the top pocket, and she relaxed the rules a fraction.

Then when the new year had begun and Sean hadn't killed an elephant in six weeks, Mbejane headed a deputation from the gunboys. The question he had to ask, though tactfully disguised, was simply, 'Did we come here to hunt, or what?'

They broke camp and moved north again and the strain was showing on Sean at last. He tried to sweat it out by long days of hunting but this didn't help for conditions were so bad that they added to his irritability. The grass in most places was higher than a mounted man's head, its sharp edges cut as he passed through it. But the grass seeds were the worst: half an inch long and barbed like an arrow they worked their way quickly through clothing and into the skin. In the humid heat the small wounds they made festered within hours. Then there were the flies. Hippo-flies, greenheaded flies, sand-flies all with one thing in common – they stung. The soft skin behind the ears was their favourite place. They'd creep upon him, settle so lightly he wouldn't feel it – then, ping with the red-hot needle. Always wet, sometimes with sweat, other times with rain, Sean would close with a herd of elephant. He would hear them moving in the long grass around him and see the white canopy of egrets fluttering over them, but it was seldom he could get a shot at them. If he did he had to stand in the centre of a storm of blundering bodies. Often they would be following a herd, almost upon them, when Sean would lose interest and they'd all go back to camp. He couldn't keep away.

He was miserable, his servants were miserable, and Katrina was happy as a bird at daybreak. She had a man, she was mistress of a household which she ran with confidence and, because her senses were not yet as seasoned as Sean's, she was physically content. Even with Sean's strict adherence to the rules, their evenings in her wagon would end for her with a sigh and a shudder and she would go dreamy-eyed to bed and leave Sean with a burning devil inside of him. The only person Sean could complain to was Thief. He would lie with his snout buried in Sean's armpit, with at least his share of the blankets over him, and listen quietly.

The Zulus could see what the trouble was but they didn't understand it. They didn't discuss it, of course, but if one of them spread his hands expressively or coughed in a certain way the others knew what he meant. Mbejane came closest to actually putting it into words. Sean had just thrown a tantrum. It was a matter of a lost axe and who was responsible. Sean lined them up and expressed doubts as to their ancestry, present worth and future prospects, then he stormed off to his wagon. There was a long silence and Hlubi offered his snuff-box to Mbejane.

Mbejane took a pinch and said, 'It's a stupid stallion that doesn't know how to kick down a fence.'

'It is true, it is true,' they agreed, and there the matter rested.

– 18 –

A week later they reached the Sabi river. The mountains on the far side were blue-grey with distance and the river was full – brown and full.

The next morning was fresh and cool from the night's rain. The camp smelt of wood-smoke, cattle and wild mimosa. From one of the ostrich eggs that Mbejane had found the day before, Katrina made an omelette the size of a soup-plate. It was flavoured with nutmeg and chunks of mushroom, yellow and rich. Afterwards there were scones and wild honey, coffee and a cheroot for Sean.

'Are you going out today?' Katrina asked.

'Uh huh.'

'Oh!'

'Don't you want me to?'

'You haven't stayed in camp for a week.'

'Don't you want me to go?'

She stood up quickly and started clearing the table. 'Anyway you won't find any elephant . . . you haven't found anything for ages.'

'Do you want me to stay?'

'It's such a lovely day.' She signed to Kandhla to take the plates away.

'If you want me to stay, ask me properly.'

'We could look for mushrooms.'

'Say it,' said Sean.

'All right then, please!'

'Mbejane! Take the saddle off that horse, I won't be using him.'

Katrina laughed. She ran to her wagon, skirts swirling around her legs, calling to the dogs. She came back with her bonnet on and a basket in her hand. The dogs crowded round them, jumping up and barking.

'Go on . . . seek up then,' Sean told them and they raced ahead, circling back barking, chasing one another. Sean and Katrina walked holding hands. The brim of Katrina's bonnet kept her face in shadow, but even then her eyes when she looked at him were bright green. They picked the new mushrooms, round and hard, brown and slightly sticky on top, fluted underneath delicately as a lady's fan. In an hour they had filled the basket and they stopped under a marula tree. Sean lay on his back. Katrina broke off a blade of grass and tickled his face with it until he caught her wrist and pulled her down onto his chest. The dogs watched them, sitting around them in a circle, their tongues hanging out pink and wet.

'There's a place in the Cape, just outside Paarl. The mountains stand over it and there's a river . . . the water's very clear, you can see the fish lying on the bottom,' said Katrina. Her ear was against his chest and she was listening to his heart. 'Will you buy me a farm there one day?'

'Yes,' said Sean.

'We'll build a house with a wide veranda and on Sundays we'll drive to church with the girls and the little ones in the back and the bigger boys riding next to the buggy.'

'How many will there be?' asked Sean. He lifted the side of her bonnet and looked at her ear. It was a very pretty ear, in the sunlight he could see the fine fur on the lobe.

'Oh lots . . . boys mostly, but a few girls.'

'Ten?' suggested Sean.

'More than that.'

'Fifteen?'

'Yes, fifteen.'

They lay and thought about it. To Sean it seemed a fairly well-rounded number.

'And I'll keep chickens, I want lots of chickens.'

'All right,' said Sean.

'You don't mind?'

'Should I?'

'Some people mind chickens, some people don't like them at all,' said Katrina. 'I'm glad you don't mind them. I've always wanted them.'

Stealthily Sean advanced his mouth towards her ear but she felt him move and sat up.

'What are you doing?'

'This,' said Sean and his arm shot out.

'No, Sean, they're watching us.' She waved her hand at the dogs.

'They'll understand,' said Sean and then they were both quiet for a long time.

The dogs burst out together in full hunting chorus. Katrina sat up and Sean turned his head and saw the leopard. It stood fifty yards away on the edge of the thick bush along the river bank watching them, poised elegantly in tights of black and gold, long and small-bellied. It moved then, blurring with speed, touching the ground as lightly as a swallow touches the water when it drinks in flight. The dogs went after it in a pack, Thief leading them, his voice cracking with excitement.

'Back, come back,' shouted Sean. 'Leave it, damn you, come back.'

'Stop them, Sean, go after them. We'll lose them all.'

'Wait here,' Sean told her.

He ran after the sound of the pack. Not shouting, saving his wind. He knew what would happen and he listened for it. He heard the tone of the hunt change – sharper now. Sean stopped and stood panting, peering ahead. The dogs were not moving. The sound of their barking was steady in volume.

'The swine has stopped; he's going to take them.'

He started running again and almost immediately heard the first dog scream. He kept running. He found the dog lying where the leopard had flung it – the old bitch with white ears, her stomach was stripped out. Sean went on. The tan ridgeback next, disembowelled, still alive and crawling to meet him. He ran on; always the hunt was out of sight ahead of him but he kept after it. He no longer stopped to help the dogs that had been mauled. Most of them were dead before he reached them. The saliva thickened in his mouth, his heart jumped against his ribs and he reeled as he ran.

Suddenly he was in the open and the hunt was spread out before him. There were three dogs left. One of them was Thief. They were circling the leopard, belling him, darting in at his back legs, snapping, then jumping back as the leopard spun snarling. The grass was short and green in the clearing. The sun was directly overhead: it threw no shadow, it lit everything with a flat, even light. Sean tried to shout but his throat wouldn't let the sound out. The leopard dropped onto its back and lay with the sprawled grace of a sleeping cat, its legs open and its belly exposed.

The dogs hung back, hesitating. Sean shouted again but his voice still would not carry. That creamy yellow belly, soft and fluffy, was too much temptation. One of the dogs went for it, dipping its head, its mouth open. The leopard closed on it like a spring trap. It caught and held the dog with its front paws and its back legs worked quickly. The dog yammered at the swift surgeon strokes and then it was thrown aside, its bowels hanging out. The leopard relaxed again to show the yellow bait of its belly. Sean was close now and this time the two dogs heard his shout. The leopard heard it also. It flashed to its feet and tried to break, but the instant it turned Thief was at it, slashing at its back legs forcing it to swing and crouch.

'Here, boy, leave him! Here, Thief, come here!'

Thief took Sean's shout as encouragement. He danced just out of reach of the flicking paws, shrilly taunting the leopard. The hunt was finely balanced now. Sean knew if he could get the dogs to slacken their attack the leopard would run. He went forward a pace, stooped to pick up a stone to throw at Thief and his movement tipped the balance. When he straightened up the leopard was watching him and he felt the eel of fear move in his stomach. It was going to come for him. He knew it by the way its ears flattened against its head and its shoulders bunched like loaded springs. Sean dropped the stone and reached for the knife on his belt.

The leopard's lips peeled back. Its teeth were yellow, its head with the ears flattened was like a snake's. It came fast and low against the ground, brushing the dogs aside. Its run was long-reaching, smoothly beautiful. It snaked towards him, fast over the short grass. It came into the air, lifting high, very fast and very smoothly. Sean felt the shock and the pain together. The shock threw him backwards and the pain sucked the breath from his lungs. Its claws hooked into his chest, he felt them scrape his ribs. He held its mouth from his face, his forearm against its throat and he smelt the overripe grave smell of its breath. They rolled together in the grass, its front claws still holding in the flesh of his chest, and he felt its back legs coming up to rake his stomach. He twisted desperately to keep clear of them, using his knife at the same time, slipping the blade into its back. The leopard screamed, its back legs came up again; he felt the claws go into his hip and tear down his thigh. The pain was deep and strong and he knew he was badly hurt. The legs came up again. This time they would kill him.

Thief locked his teeth in the leopard's leg before the claws could catch in Sean's flesh, he dragged back, digging in with his front feet, holding the leopard stretched out across Sean's body. Sean's vision was dissolving into blackness and bright lights. He pushed the knife into the leopard's back, close to the spine and pulled it down between the ribs the way a butcher cuts a chop. The leopard screamed again with its body shuddering and its claws curling in Sean's flesh. Sean cut again, deep and long – and again, then again. Tearing at it, mad with the pain, its blood gushed out and mixed with his and he rolled away from it. The dogs were worrying it, growling. It was dead. Sean let the knife slip out of his hand and touched the tears in his leg. The blood was dark red, pouring with the thickness of treacle, much blood. He was looking down a funnel of darkness. The leg was far away, not his – not his leg.

'Garry,' he whispered. 'Garry, oh God! I'm sorry. I slipped, I didn't mean it, I slipped.' The funnel closed and there was no leg – only darkness. Time was a liquid thing, all the world was liquid, moving in darkness. The sun was dark and only the pain was steady, steady as a rock in the dark moving sea. He saw Katrina's face indistinct in the darkness. He tried to tell her how sorry he was. He tried to tell her it was an accident, but the pain stopped him. She was crying. He knew she would understand so he went back into the dark sea. Then the surface of the sea boiled and he choked in the heat, but always the pain was there like a rock to hold onto. The steam from the sea coiled up around him and it hardened into the shape of a woman and he thought it was Katrina, then he saw its head was a leopard's head and its breath stank like the rotting of a gangrenous leg.

'I don't want you – I know who you are,' he shouted at it. 'I don't want you. It's not my child,' and the thing broke into steam, twisting grey steam, and came back gibbering at him on a chain that tinkled, frothing yellow from the grey misty mouth, and terror came with it. He twisted and covered his face, holding onto the pain for the pain was real and steady.

Then after a thousand years the sea froze and he walked on it and the white ice stretched away wherever he looked. It was cold and lonely on the ice. There was a small wind, a cold small wind, the wind whispered across the ice and its whispering was a sad sound, and Sean held his pain, hugging it close to him for he was lonely and only the pain was real. Then there were other figures moving around him on the ice, dark figures all hurrying one way, crowding him, pushing him along with them and he lost his pain, lost it in the desperate hurrying press. And though they had no faces, some of the figures wept and others laughed and they hurried forward until they came to the place where the crevasse split across the ice in front of them. The crevasse was wide and deep and its sides were white, then pale-green shading to blue and at last to infinite blackness, and some of the figures threw themselves joyfully into it singing as they fell. Others clung to edges, their formless faces full of fear, and still others stepped off into the void, tiredly, like travellers at the end of a long journey. When Sean saw the crevasse he began to fight, throwing himself back against the crowd that bore him forward, carrying him to the edge of the pit, and his feet slid over the edge. He clawed with his fingers at the slippery edge of the ice. He fought and he shouted as he fought for the dark drop sucked at his legs. Then he lay quietly and the crevasse had closed and he was alone. He was tired – wasted and terribly tired. He closed his eyes and the pain came back to him, throbbing softly in his leg.

He opened his eyes and he saw Katrina's face. She was pale and her eyes were big and heavily underscored in blue. He tried to lift his hand to touch her face but he couldn't move.

'Katrina,' he said. He saw her eyes go green with surprise and happiness.

'You've come back. Oh, thank God. You've come back.'

Sean rolled his head and looked at the canvas of the wagon tent.

'How long?' he asked. His voice was a whisper.

'Five days . . . Don't talk – please, don't talk.'

Sean closed his eyes. He was very tired so he slept.

– 19 –

Katrina washed him when he woke. Mbejane helped her lift and turn him, his big pink-palmed hands very gentle as he handled the leg. They washed the smell of fever off him and changed the dressings. Sean watched Katrina as she worked and every time she looked up they smiled at each other. Once he used a little of his strength to ask Mbejane, 'Where were you when I needed you?'

'I slept in the sun, Nkosi, like an old woman,' Mbejane half-laughed, half-apologized. Katrina brought him food and when he smelt it he was hungry. He ate it all and then he slept again.

Mbejane built a shelter with open sides and a roof of thatch. He sited it in the shade on the bank of the Sabi. Then he made a bed of poles and laced leather thongs. They carried Sean from the wagon, Katrina fussing around them until they had laid him in the shelter. Katrina went back to the wagon for pillows and when she returned she found Thief and Sean settling down comfortably.

'Sean, get that monster out of there – those blankets have just been washed.'

Thief flattened his body and hid his head in Sean's armpit.

'It's all right, he's quite clean,' Sean protected him.

'He smells.'

'He does not.' Sean sniffed at Thief. 'Well, not much anyway.'

'You two!' She put the pillows under Sean's head and went round to his leg. 'How does it feel?'

'It's fine,' said Sean. Thief inched himself up the bed until he reached the pillows.

In the slow slide of days Sean's body healed and the well of his strength filled. The moving air under the shelter dried the scabs off his chest and leg, but there would be scars. In the mornings, after breakfast, Sean held court from his couch. Katrina sat on the end of the bed and his servants squatted around him. First they talked over domestic matters – the health of the oxen, mentioning them by name, discussing their eyes, hooves and stomachs. There was a tear in the canvas of one wagon. The single remaining bitch was in season – was Thief man enough for the job yet? There was meat to kill – perhaps the Nkosikaze would take the rifle later today. Hlubi had caught four barbel of medium size in his fish trap, and here the talk turned to the bush around them. A lion had killed a buffalo below the first bend in the river – there you could see the vultures. During the night a herd of cow elephant had drunk a mile upstream. Each item was considered by the meeting. Everyone felt free to comment or argue against any view which conflicted with his own. When everything had been said Sean gave them their tasks for the day and sent them away. Then he and Katrina could be alone.

From the shelter they could see the full sweep of the river, with the crocodiles lying on the white sandbars and the kingfishers plopping into the shallows. They sat close to each other and they talked of the farm they would have. Sean would grow grapes and breed horses and Katrina would keep chickens. By the next rainy season they would have filled all the wagons; one more trip after that and they would have enough to buy the farm.

Katrina kept him in bed long after he was strong enough to leave it. She mothered him and he loved it. Shamelessly, in the fashion of the male, he accepted her attentions and even exaggerated his injuries a little. Finally but reluctantly Katrina let him up. He stayed in camp a week more, until his legs stopped wobbling, then one evening he took his rifle and went with Mbejane to shoot fresh meat. They went slowly, Sean favouring his leg, and he shot a young eland not far from the laager. Sean sat against a msasa tree and smoked a cheroot while Mbejane went back to fetch servants to carry the meat. Sean watched them butcher the carcass; there were slabs of white fat on the meat. They slung it on poles and carried it between them, two men to a pole, and when they got back to camp Sean found Katrina in one of her inscrutable moods. When he talked to her at supper she answered him from far away and afterwards by the fire she sat detached from him. She was very lovely and Sean was puzzled and a little resentful. At last he stood up.

'It's time for bed – I'll see you to your wagon.'

'You go. I'll sit a little longer.'

Sean hesitated. 'Is there something wrong? Have I done something wrong?'

'No,' she said quickly. 'No. I'm all right. You go to bed.'

He kissed her cheek. 'If you need me I'll be close. Goodnight, sleep sweet.'

He straightened up. 'Come on, Thief,' he said. 'Time for bed.'

'Leave Thief with me, please.' Katrina caught the skin at the back of the dog's neck and restrained him.

'Why?'

'I just feel like company.'

'Then I'll stay as well.' Sean moved to sit down again.

'No, you go to bed.' She sounded desperate and Sean looked hard at her.

'Are you sure you're all right?'

'Yes, please go.'

He went to his wagon and looked back at her. She was sitting very straight, holding the dog. He climbed into the wagon. The lamp was lit and he stopped in surprise when he saw his cot. There were sheets on it, not just the rough blankets. He ran his hand over the smooth fabric; it was crisp from new ironing. He sat on the cot and pulled off his boots. He undid his shirt and threw it onto the chest, then he lay back and looked up at the lamp.

'There's something bloody funny going on here,' he said.

'Sean' – her voice just outside the wagon. Sean jumped up and opened the flap. 'Can I come in?'

'Yes, of course.' He gave her his hand and lifted her into the wagon. He looked at her face. She was frightened.

'There *is* something wrong,' he said.

'No, don't touch me. There's something I've got to tell you. Sit down on the cot.'

Sean watched her face. He was worried.

'I thought I loved you when I came away with you. I thought we had for ever to be together.' She swallowed painfully. 'Then I found you there in the grass – torn and dead. Before our life together had begun you were dead.'

Sean saw the pain come back into her eyes; she was living it again. He put out his hand to her but she held his wrist.

'No, wait . . . please let me finish. I have to explain to you. It's very important.'

Sean dropped his hand and she went on speaking quickly.

'You were dead and I, too, was dying inside. I felt empty. There was nothing left. Nothing . . . just the hollowness inside and the dry dead feeling on the outside. I touched your face and you looked at me. I prayed then, Sean, and I prayed through the days when you fought the rotting of your body.'

She knelt in front of him and held him around the waist.

'Now we are alive and together again, but I know that it cannot be for ever. A day more, a year, if we are lucky, twenty. But not for ever. I see how small I have been to us. I want to be your wife.'

He bent to her quickly but she pulled away and stood up. She slipped the buttons and her clothing fell away. She loosed her hair and let it drop shiny bright down the whiteness of her body.

'Look at me, Sean, I want you to look at me. This and my love I can give you . . . is it enough?'

There was smoothness, hollow and swell, hair like black fire and soft light on soft skin. He saw the flush from her cheeks spread onto her breasts until they glowed, pink and shy but proud in their perfection. He looked no further. He took her to him and covered her nakedness with his big body. She was trembling and he put her between the sheets and gentled her with his voice until the trembling stopped and she lay with her face pressed up under his beard into his neck.

'Show me how . . . I want to give everything to you. Please show me how,' she whispered.

So they married each other and their marriage was a comingling of many things. There was the softness of the wind in it and wanting, the way the baked earth wants the rain. There was pain sharp and swift, movement like running horses, sound low as voices in the night but glad as a greeting, joy climbing on eagles' wings, the triumphant surge and burst of wild water on a rock shore and then there was stillness and warmth within and the snuggling of drowsy puppies, and sleep. Yet it did not end in the sleep, it went on to another seeking and finding, another union and a stranger mystery in the secret depths of her body.

– 20 –

In the morning she brought her Bible to him.

'Hey, hey,' protested Sean, 'I've already sworn one oath.' Katrina laughed at him, the memory of the night still warm and happy inside her. She opened the book at its fly leaf.

'You've got to write your name in it . . . here, next to mine.'

She watched him, standing next to his chair with her hip touching his shoulder.

'And your date of birth,' she said.

Sean wrote: 'Ninth Jan. 1862.' Then he said: 'What's this "date of death" . . . do you want me to fill that in as well?'

'Don't talk like that,' she said quickly and touched the wooden table.

Sean was sorry he'd said it. He tried to cover up. 'There's only space for six children.'

'We can write the others in the margin. That's what Ma

did . . . hers even go over onto the first page of Genesis. Do you think we'll get that far, Sean?'

Sean smiled at her. 'The way I feel now we should reach the New Testament without much trouble.'

They had made a good start. By June the rains were over and Katrina walked with her shoulders back to balance her load. There was a good feeling in the camp. Katrina was more woman than child now. She was big and radiant, pleased with the awe her condition inspired in Sean. She sang to herself often and sometimes in the night she would let him share in it. She would let him pull the nightdress back from the mound of her stomach and lay his ear against the tight-stretched, blue-veined skin. He listened to the suck and gurgle and felt the movement against his cheek. When he sat up his eyes would be full of the wonder of it and she would smile proudly at him and take his head on her shoulder and they would lie together quietly. In the daytime things were right as well. Sean laughed with the servants and hunted without the intensity of before.

They moved north along the Sabi river. Sometimes they camped for a month at one place. The game came back to the rivers as the veld dried out and once more the ivory started piling up in the wagons.

One afternoon in September Sean and Katrina left the camp and walked along the bank. The land was brown again and smelt of dry grass. The river was pools and white sand.

'Hell, it's hot.' Sean took off his hat and wiped the sweat off his forehead. 'You must be cooking under all those clothes.'

'No, I'm all right.' Katrina was holding his arm.

'Let's have a swim.'

'You mean with no clothes on?' Katrina looked shocked.

'Yes, why not?'

'It's rude.'

'Come on.' He took her down the bank protesting every step and at a place where boulders screened the water he prised her out of her dress. She was laughing and gasping and blushing all at the same time. He carried her into the pool and she sat down thankfully with the water up to her chin.

'How's that feel?' Sean asked.

She let her hair down and it floated out round her, she wriggled her toes in the sand and her stomach showed through the water like the back of a white whale.

'It's nice,' she admitted. 'It feels like silk underwear against my skin.'

Sean stood over her with only his hat on. She looked at him.

'Sit down,' she said uncomfortably and looked away from him.

'Why?' he asked.

'You know why . . . you're rude, that's why.'

Sean sat down beside her.

'You should be used to me by now.'

'Well, I'm not.'

Sean put his arm round her under the water.

'You're lovely,' he said. 'You're my fancy.'

She let him kiss her ear.

'What's it going to be?' He touched the ripe swelling. 'Boy or girl?' This was currently the favourite topic of conversation.

'Boy.' She was very definite.

'What shall we call him?'

'Well, if you don't find a *predikant* soon we'll have to call him the name you're always giving to the servants.'

Sean stared at her. 'What do you mean?'

'You know what you call them when you're cross.'

'Bastard,' said Sean, then really concerned, 'Hell, I hadn't thought of that! We'll have to find a priest. No child of mine will be a bastard. We'll have to go back to Louis Trichardt.'

'You've got about a month,' Katrina warned him.

'My God, we'll never make it. We've left it too late.' Sean's face was ghastly. 'Wait, I've got it. There are Portuguese settlements across the mountains on the coast.'

'Oh, Sean, but they're Roman Catholics.'

'They all work for the same boss.'

'How long will it take to cross the mountains?' Katrina asked doubtfully.

'I don't know. Perhaps two weeks to reach the coast on horseback.'

'On horseback?' Katrina looked still more doubtfully.

'Oh hell . . . you can't ride!' Sean scratched the side of his nose. 'I'll have to go and fetch one. Will you stay on your own? I'll leave Mbejane to look after you.'

'Yes, I'll be all right.'

'I won't go if you don't want me to. It's not that important.'

'It is important, you know it is. I'll be all right, truly I will.'

Before he left the next morning Sean took Mbejane aside. 'You know why you're not coming with me, don't you?'

Mbejane nodded, but Sean answered his own question. 'Because there is more important work for you to do here.'

'At night,' said Mbejane, 'I will sleep beneath the Nkosikazi's wagon.'

'You'll sleep?' asked Sean threateningly.

'Only once in a while and then very lightly,' Mbejane grinned.

'That's better,' said Sean.

– 21 –

Sean said goodbye to Katrina. There were no tears, she understood necessity and helped him to a quiet acceptance of it. They stood a long while beside their wagon, holding each other, their lips almost touching as they whispered together and then Sean called for his horse. Hlubi followed him leading the packhorse when he crossed the Sabi and when Sean reached the far bank he turned and looked back. Katrina was still standing by their wagon and behind her hovered Mbejane. In her bonnet and green dress she looked very young. Sean waved his hat over his head and then set off towards the mountains.

The forests dwindled into grassland as they climbed and each night was colder than the last. Then, in its turn the grassland conceded to the sheer bluffs and misty gorges of the mountain back. Sean and Hlubi struggled upwards, following the game trails, losing them, turning back from impassable cliffs, scouting for a pass, leading the horses over the steep pitches and at night sitting close to the fire and listening to the baboons barking in the kranses around them. Then suddenly, in the middle of a morning that was bright as a cut diamond, they were at the top. To the west the land lay spread out like a map and the distance they had travelled in a week was pathetically small. By straining his eyes and his imagination Sean could make out the dark-green belt of the Sabi watercourse. To the east the land merged with a blueness that was not the sky and for a while he failed to recognize it. Then – 'The sea,' he shouted and Hlubi laughed with him for it was a godlike feeling to stand above the world. They found an easier route down the eastern slopes and followed it onto the coastal plain. At the bottom of the mountains they came to a native village. To see cultivated lands and human dwellings again was a small shock to Sean. He had come to accept the fact that he and his retinue were the only people left on earth.

The entire population of the village fled when they saw him. Mothers snatched up a child in each hand and ran as fast as their menfolk – memories of the slave-traders still persisted in this part of Africa. Within two minutes of his arrival Sean again had the feeling that he was the only person left on earth. With the contempt of the Zulu for every other tribe in Africa, Hlubi shook his head sadly.

'Monkeys,' he said.

They dismounted and tied their horses under the big tree that was the centre of the village. They sat in the shade and waited. The huts were grass beehives, their roofs blackened with smoke, and a few chickens picked and scratched at the bare earth between them. Half an hour later Sean saw a black face watching him from the edge of the bush and he ignored it. Slowly the face emerged, followed closely by a reluctant body. With a twig, Sean went on drawing patterns in the dust between his feet. Out of the corner of his eye he watched the hesitant approach. It was an old man with stork thin legs and one eye glazed into a white jelly by tropical ophthalmia. Sean concluded that his fellows had picked him to act as ambassador on the grounds that of all their number he would be the least loss.

Sean looked up and gave him a radiant smile. The old man froze and then his lips twitched into a sickly grin of relief. Sean stood up, dusted his hands on the sides of his breeches and went to shake the old man's hand. Immediately the bush around them swarmed with people, they poured back into the village jabbering and laughing: they crowded round Sean and felt his clothing, peered into his face and exclaimed delightedly. It was obvious that most of them had never seen a white man before. Sean was trying to shake off One-Eye, who still had a possessive hold on Sean's right hand, and Hlubi leaned disdainfully against the tree, taking no part in the welcome. One-Eye ended the confusion by screeching at them in a voice rusty with age. The courage he had displayed earlier now earned its reward. At his command a dozen of the younger women scampered off and came back with a carved wooden stool and six earthenware pots of native beer. By the hand, on which he had not for an instant relaxed his grip, One-Eye led Sean to the stool and made him sit; the rest of the villagers squatted in a circle round him and one of the girls brought the biggest beer-pot to Sean. The beer was yellow and it bubbled sullenly. Sean's stomach shied at the sight of it. He glanced at One-Eye who was watching him anxiously, he lifted the pot and sipped. Then he smiled with surprise; it was creamy and pleasantly tart.

'Good,' he said.

'Goot,' chorused the villagers.

'Your health,' said Sean.

''ealt,' said the village as one man, and Sean drank deep. One of the girls took another beer-pot to Hlubi. She knelt in front of him and shyly offered it. She had a plaited-grass string around her waist from which a small kilt hung down in front, but her stern was completely exposed and her bosoms were the size and shape of ripe melons. Hlubi looked at them until the girl hung her head, then he lifted the beer-pot.

Sean wanted a guide to the nearest Portuguese settlement. He looked at One-Eye and said, 'Town? Portagee?'

One-Eye was almost overcome by Sean's attention. He grabbed Sean's hand again before he could pull it away and shook it vigorously.

'Stop that, you bloody fool,' said Sean irritably and One-Eye grinned and nodded, then without releasing Sean's hand he began an impassioned speech to the other villagers. Sean meanwhile was searching his memory for the name of one of the Portuguese ports on this coast.

'Nova Sofala,' he shouted as he got it.

One-Eye broke off his speech abruptly and stared at Sean.

'Nova Sofala,' said Sean again pointing vaguely towards the east and One-Eye showed his gums in his biggest grin yet.

'Nova Sofala,' he agreed pointing with authority and then it was only a matter of minutes before it was understood between them that he would act as guide. Hlubi saddled the horses, One-Eye fetched a grass sleeping mat and a battle-axe from one of the huts. Sean mounted and looked at Hlubi to do the same but Hlubi was acting strangely.

'Yes?' Sean asked with resignation. 'What is it?'

'Nkosi.' Hlubi was looking at the branches of the tree above them. 'The Old One could lead the packhorse.'

'You can take it in turns,' said Sean.

Hlubi coughed and transferred his eyes to the fingernails of his left hand.

'Nkosi, is it possible that you will return to this village on the way back from the sea?'

'Yes, of course,' said Sean, 'we'll have to leave the Old One here. Why do you ask?'

'I have a thorn in my foot, Nkosi, it gives me pain. If you do not require me I will wait here for you. Perhaps the thorn wound will have healed by then.' Hlubi looked up at the tree again and shuffled his feet with embarrassment. Sean had not noticed him limping and he was puzzled as to why Hlubi should start malingering now. Then Hlubi could not stop himself from glancing at where the girl stood in the circle of villagers. Her kilt was very small and from the sides gave her no cover at all. Understanding came to Sean and he chuckled.

'The thorn you have is painful, but it's not in your foot.'

Hlubi shuffled his feet again. 'You said they were monkeys . . . have you changed your mind?' Sean asked.

'Nkosi, they are indeed monkeys,' Hlubi sighed. 'But very friendly monkeys.'

'Stay then . . . but do not weaken yourself too much. We have mountains to cross on the way home.'

– 22 –

One-Eye led the packhorse – this made him very proud. Through tall grass, mangrove swamp and thick hot jungle, then through white coral sand and the curving stems of palm trees, they came at last to the sea. Nova Sofala was a fort with brass cannon and thick walls. The sea beyond it was muddy brown from the estuary that flowed into it.

The sentry at the gates said, '*Madre de Dio*' when he saw Sean, and took him to the Commandant. The Commandant was a small man with fever-yellowed face and a tired, sweat-darkened tunic. The Commandant said, '*Madre de Dio*,' and shot his chair back from his desk. It took some time for him to realize that contrary to appearance this dirty, bearded giant was not dangerous. The Commandant could speak English and Sean laid his problem before him.

For a certainty he could be of assistance. There were three Jesuit missionaries in the fort, freshly arrived from Portugal and eager for employment. Sean could take his pick but first he must bath, eat dinner with the Commandant and help him sample the wines that had arrived on the same boat as the missionaries. Sean thought that was a good idea.

At dinner he met the missionaries. They were young men, pink-faced still, for Africa had not yet had a chance to mark them. All three of them were willing to go with him and Sean selected the youngest – not for his appearance but rather for his name. 'Father Alphonso' had a heroic ring to it. The Jesuits went early to bed and left the Commandant, the four junior officers and Sean to the port. They drank toasts to Queen Victoria and her family and to the King of Portugal and his family. This made them thirsty so they drank to absent friends, then to each other. The Commandant and Sean swore a mutual oath of friendship and loyalty and this made the Commandant very sad. He cried and Sean patted his shoulder and offered to dance the Dashing White Sergeant for him. The Commandant said that he would esteem it as a very great honour and furthermore he would be delighted. He himself did not know this dance but perhaps Sean would instruct him. They danced on the table. The Commandant was doing very well until in his enthusiasm he misjudged the size of the table. Sean helped the junior officers put him to bed and in the morning Sean, Father Alphonso and One-Eye started back towards the mountains.

Sean was impatient of any delay now; he wanted to get back to Katrina. Father Alphonso's English was on a par with Sean's Portuguese. This made conversation difficult, so Alphonso solved the problem by doing all the talking. At first Sean listened but when he decided that the good father was trying to convert him he no longer bothered. Alphonso did not seem put out – he just went on talking and clinging to the horse with both hands while his cassock flapped about his legs and his face sweated in the shade of his wide-brimmed hat. One-Eye followed them like an ancient stork.

It took them two days back to One-Eye's village and their entry was a triumphal procession. Father Alphonso's face lit up when he saw so many prospective converts. Sean could see him mentally rubbing his hands together, and he decided to keep going before Alphonso forgot the main object of the expedition. He gave One-Eye a hunting-knife in payment for his services. One-Eye sat down under the big tree in the centre of the village, his own thin legs no longer able to support his weight and the knife clutched to his chest.

'Hlubi, you've had enough of that . . . come on now!' Sean had not dismounted and was restlessly waiting for Hlubi to say his farewells to three of the village girls. Hlubi had displayed traditional Zulu taste – all three of them were big-breasted, big-bottomed and young. They were also crying.

'Come on, Hlubi . . . what's the trouble?'

'Nkosi, they believe that I have taken them for my wives.'

'What made them think that?'

'Nkosi, I do not know.' Hlubi broke the armhold that the plumpest and youngest had around his neck, he snatched up his spears and fled. Sean and Alphonso galloped after him. The villagers shouted farewells and Sean looked back and saw One-Eye still sitting at the base of the big tree.

The pace which Sean set was at last telling on Alphonso. His verbal spring-tides slackened and he showed a measure of reluctance to let his backside touch the saddle; he rode crouched forward on his horse's neck with his buttocks in the air. They crossed the mountains and went down the other side; the ground levelled out into the Sabi Valley and they rode into the forest. On the ninth day out from Nova Sofala they reached the Sabi river. It was late afternoon. Flocks of guinea-fowl were drinking in the riverbed. They went up in a blue haze of whirling wings as Sean led his party down the bank. While the horses watered Sean spoke with Hlubi.

'Do you recognize this part of the river?'

'Yes, Nkosi, we are two hours' march upstream from the wagons . . . we held too far to the north coming through the forest.'

Sean looked at the sun, it was on the tree-tops.

'Half an hour's light left . . . and there's no moon tonight.'

'We could wait until morning,' Hlubi suggested hopefully. Sean ignored him and motioned to Alphonso to mount up. Alphonso was prepared to debate the advisability of moving on. Sean took a handful of his cassock and helped him into the saddle.

– 23 –

In the darkness the lantern burning in Katrina's wagon glowed through the canvas and guided them the last half mile into camp. Thief bayed them welcome and Mbejane ran out at the head of the other servants to take Sean's horse. His voice was loud with worry and relief.

'Nkosi, there is little time . . . it has begun.'

Sean jumped off his horse and ran to the wagon. He tore open the canvas flap.

'Sean.' She sat up. Her eyes were very green in the lantern light, but they were dark-ringed. 'Thank God, you've come.'

Sean knelt beside her cot and held her. He said certain things to her and she clung to him and moved her lips across his face. The world receded and left one wagon standing in darkness, lit by a single lamp and the love of two people.

Suddenly she stiffened in his arms and gasped. Sean held her, his face suddenly helpless and his big hands timid and uncertain on her shoulders.

'What can I do, my fancy? How can I help you?'

Her body relaxed slowly and she whispered, 'Did you find a priest?'

'The priest!' Sean had forgotten about him. Still holding onto her he turned his head and bellowed, 'Alphonso . . . Alphonso. Hurry, man.'

Father Alphonso's face in the opening of the wagon was pale with fatigue and grimy with dust.

'Marry us,' said Sean. 'Quickly, man, che-cha, chop-chop . . . you savvy?'

Alphonso climbed into the wagon. The skirts of his cassock were torn and his knees were white and bony through the holes. He stood over them and opened his book. 'Ring?' he asked in Portuguese.

'I do,' said Sean.

'No! No! Ring?' Alphonso held up a finger and made an encircling gesture. 'Ring?'

'I think he wants a wedding ring,' whispered Katrina.

'Oh, my God,' said Sean. 'I'd forgotten about that.' He looked round desperately. 'What can we use? Haven't you got one in your chest or something?'

Katrina shook her head, opened her lips to answer but closed them again as another pain took her. Sean held her while it lasted and when she relaxed he looked up angrily at Alphonso.

'Marry us . . . damn you. Don't you see there's no time for all the trimmings?'

'Ring?' said Alphonso again. He looked very unhappy.

'All right, I'll get you a ring.' Sean leapt out of the wagon and shouted at Mbejane.

'Bring my rifle, quickly.'

If Sean wanted to shoot the Portuguese that was his business and Mbejane's duty was to help him. He brought Sean the rifle. Sean found a gold sovereign in the pouch on his belt, he threw it on the ground and held the muzzle of the rifle on it. The bullet punched a ragged hole through it.

He tossed the rifle back to Mbejane, picked up the small gold circle and scrambled back into the wagon.

Three times during the service the pains made Katrina gasp and each time Sean held her tight and Alphonso increased the speed of his delivery. Sean put the punctured sovereign on Katrina's finger and kissed her. Alphonso gabbled out the last line of Latin and Katrina said, 'Oh, Sean, it's coming.'

'Get out,' Sean told Alphonso and made an expressive gesture towards the door – thankfully Alphonso went.

It did not take long then, but to Sean it was an eternity – like that time when they had taken Garrick's leg. Then in a slippery rush it was finished. Katrina lay very quiet and pale, while on the cot below her, still linked to her, purple-blotched and bloody lay the child that they had made.

'It's dead,' croaked Sean. He was sweating and he had backed away against the far wall of the wagon.

'No.' Katrina struggled up fiercely. 'No, it's not . . . Sean, you must help me.'

She told him what to do and at last the child cried.

'It's a boy,' said Katrina softly. 'Oh, Sean . . . it's a boy.' She was more beautiful than he had ever seen her before; pale and tired and beautiful.

– 24 –

Sean's protests were in vain – Katrina left her bed the next morning and squeezed into one of her old dresses. Sean hovered between her and the child on the cot.

'I'm still so *fat*,' she lamented.

'Fancy, please stay in bed another day or two.'

She pulled a face at him and went on struggling with the lacing of her bodice.

'Who's going to look after the baby?'

'I will!' said Sean earnestly. 'You can tell me what to do.'

Arguing with Katrina was like trying to pick up quicksilver with your fingers, not worth the effort. She finished dressing and took up the child.

'You can help me down the steps.' She smiled at him. Sean and Alphonso set a chair for her in the shade of one of the big shuma trees and the servants came to see the child. Katrina held him in her lap and Sean stood over them in uncertain possession. For Sean it seemed unreal yet . . . too much for his mind to digest in so short a time. He grinned dazedly at the steady stream of comment from his servants and his arm was limp when Alphonso shook his hand for the twentieth time that morning.

'Hold your child . . . Nkosi. Let us see you with him on your arm,' called Mbejane and the other Zulus took up the cry. Sean's expression changed slowly to one of apprehension.

'Pick him up, Nkosi.'

Katrina proffered the bundle and a hunted look came into Sean's eyes.

'Have no fear, Nkosi, he has no teeth, he cannot harm you,' Hlubi encouraged him. Sean held his first-born awkwardly and assumed the hunchbacked posture of the new father. The Zulus cheered him and slowly Sean's face relaxed and his smile was a glow of pride.

'Mbejane, is he not beautiful?'

'As beautiful as his father,' Mbejane agreed.

'Your words are a blade with two edges,' laughed Sean. He looked at the child closely. It wore a cap of dark hair, its nose was flat as a bulldog's, its eyes were milky-grey and its legs were long, skinny and red.

'How will you name him?' asked Hlubi. Sean looked at Katrina.

'Tell them,' he said.

'He shall be called Dirk,' she said in Zulu.

'What is the meaning?' asked Hlubi, and Sean answered him.

'It means a dagger . . . a sharp knife.'

There was immediate nodded approval from all the servants. Hlubi produced his snuff-box and passed it among them and Mbejane took a pinch.

'That,' he said, 'is a good name.'

– 25 –

Paternity, the subtle alchemist, transformed Sean's attitude to life within twelve hours. Never before had anything been so utterly dependent upon him, so completely vulnerable. That first evening in their wagon he watched Katrina sitting cross-legged on her cot, stooping forward over the child to give it her breast. Her hair hung in a soft wing across one cheek, her face was fuller, more matronly and the child in her lap fed with a red face and small wheezings. She looked up at him and smiled and the child tugged her breast with its tiny fists and hunting mouth.

Sean crossed to the cot, sat beside them and put his arm around them. Katrina rubbed her cheek against his chest and her hair smelt warm and clean. The boy went on feeding noisily. Sean felt vaguely excited as though he were on the threshold of a new adventure.

A week later, when the first rain clouds built up in the sky, Sean took the wagons across the Sabi and onto the slopes of the mountains to escape the heat of the plains. There was a valley he had noticed when he and Hlubi had made their journey to the coast. The valley bottom was covered with short sweet grass and cedar trees grew along a stream of clean water. Sean took them to this place.

Here they would wait out the rainy season and when it was finished and the baby was strong enough to travel they could take the ivory south and sell it in Pretoria. It was a happy camp. The oxen spread out along the valley, filling it with movement and the contented sound of their lowing; there was laughter among the wagons and at night when the mist slumped down off the mountains the camp fire was bright and friendly. Father Alphonso stayed with them for nearly two weeks. He was a pleasant young man and although he and Sean never understood what the other was saying yet they managed well enough with sign language. He left at last with Hlubi and one of the other servants to escort him back over the mountains, but before he did he managed to embarrass Sean by kissing him goodbye. Sean and Katrina were sorry to see him go. They had grown to like him and Katrina had almost forgiven him his religion.

The rains came with the usual flourish and fury. Weeks drifted into months. Happy months, with life centring around Dirk's cot. Mbejane had made the cot for him out of cedarwood and one of Katrina's chests produced the sheets and blankets for it. The child grew quickly: each day he seemed to occupy more of his cot, his legs filled out, his skin lost its blotchy-purple look and his eyes were no longer a vague milky-blue. There was green in them now – they would be the same colour as his mother's.

To fill the long lazy days Sean started to build a cabin beside the stream. The servants joined in and from a modest first plan it grew into a thing of sturdy plastered walls and neatly thatched roof with a stone fireplace at one end. When it was finished Sean and Katrina moved into it. After their wagon with its thin canvas walls, the cabin gave a feeling of permanence to their love. One night, when the rain hissed down in darkness outside and the wind whined at the door like a dog wanting to be let in, they spread a mattress in front of the fireplace and there in the moving firelight they started another baby.

Christmas came, and after it the New Year. The rains stuttered and stopped and still they stayed on in their valley. Then at last they had to go, for their supplies of basic stores – powder, salt, medicines, cloth – were nearly finished. They loaded the wagons, inspanned and left in the early morning. As the line of wagons wound down the valley towards the plains Katrina sat on the box-seat of the lead wagon holding Dirk on her lap and Sean rode beside her. She looked back – the roof of their cabin showed brown through the branches of the cedar trees. It seemed forlorn and lonely.

'We must come back one day, we've been so happy here,' she said softly. Sean leaned out of the saddle towards her and touched her arm.

'Happiness isn't a place, my fancy, we aren't leaving it here, we're taking it with us.'

She smiled at him. The second baby was starting to show already.

– 26 –

They reached the Limpopo river at the end of July and found a place to cross. It took three days to unload the wagons, work them through the soft sand and then carry the ivory and stores across. They finished in the late afternoon of the third day and by then everyone was exhausted. They ate an early supper and an hour after sunset the Zulus were rolled in their blankets, and Sean and Katrina were sleeping arms-around and head-on-chest in the wagon. In the morning Katrina was quiet and a little pale. Sean didn't notice it until she told him that she felt tired and was going to lie down – immediately he was all attentive. He helped her into the wagon and settled the pillows under her head.

'Are you sure you're all right?' he kept asking.

'Yes . . . it's nothing, I'm just a bit tired. I'll be all right,' she assured him. She appreciated his concern but was relieved when finally he went to see to the business of reloading the wagons for Sean's ministrations were always a little clumsy. She wanted to be left alone, she felt tired and cold.

By midday the wagons were loaded to Sean's satisfaction. He went to Katrina's wagon, lifted the canvas and peeped in. He expected her to be asleep. She was lying on the cot with her eyes open and two of the thick grey blankets wrapped around her. Her face was as pale as a two-day corpse. Sean felt the first leap of alarm. He scrambled into the wagon.

'My dear, you look ghastly. Are you sick?' He put his hand on her shoulder and she was shivering. She didn't answer him, instead her eyes moved from his face to the floor near the foot of the bed and Sean's eyes followed hers. Katrina's luxury was her chamberpot; it was a massive china thing with red roses hand-painted on it. She loved it dearly and Sean used to tease her when she was perched on top of it. Now the pot stood near the foot of the bed and when Sean saw what was in it his breathing stopped. It was half full of a liquid the colour of milk stout. 'Oh, my God,' he whispered. He went on staring at it, standing very still while a gruesome snatch of doggerel he remembered hearing sung in the canteens of the Witwatersrand began trotting through his brain like an undertaker's hack.

Black as the Angel,
Black as disgrace
When the fever waters flow
They're as black as the ace.

Roll him in a blanket
Feed him on quinine
But all of us we know
It's the end of the line.

Black as the Angel
Black as disgrace
Soon we'll lay him down below
And chuck dirt in his face.

He raised his head and looked steadily at her, searching for the signs of fear. But just as steadily she looked back at him.

'Sean, it's blackwater.'

'Yes . . . I know,' Sean said, for there was nothing to be gained by denial, no room for extravagant hope. It was blackwater fever: malaria in its most malignant form, attacking the kidneys and turning them to fragile sacks of black blood that the slightest movement could rupture. Sean knelt by her cot. 'You must lie very still.' He touched her forehead lightly with the tips of his fingers and felt the heat of her skin.

'Yes,' she answered him, but already the expression in her eyes was blurring and she made the first restless movement of delirium. Sean put his arm across her chest to hold her from struggling.

By nightfall Katrina was deep in the nightmare of malaria. She laughed, she screamed in senseless terror, she shook her head and fought him when he tried to make her drink. But she had to drink, it was her one chance, to flush out her kidneys that she might live. Sean held her head and forced her.

Dirk started crying, hungry and frightened by the sight of his mother.

'Mbejane!' shouted Sean, his voice pitched high with

desperation. Mbejane had waited all afternoon at the entrance of the wagon.

'Nkosi, what can I do?'

'The child . . . can you care for him?'

Mbejane picked up the cot with Dirk still in it. 'Do not worry about him again. I will take him to the other wagon.'

Sean turned his whole attention back to Katrina. The fever built up steadily within her. Her body was a furnace, her skin was dry and with every hour she was wilder and her movements more difficult to control.

An hour after dark Kandhla came to the wagon with a pot of steaming liquid and a cup. Sean's nose wrinkled as he caught the smell of it.

'What the hell is that?'

'I have stewed the bark from a maiden's breast tree . . . the Nkosikazi must drink it.'

It had the same musty smell as boiling hops and Sean hesitated. He knew the tree. It grew on high ground, it had a diseased-looking lumpy bark and each lump was the size and shape of a breast surmounted by a thorn.

'Where did you get it? I have seen none of these trees near the river.' Sean was marking time while he decided whether to make Katrina drink the brew. He knew these Zulu remedies, what they didn't kill they sometimes cured.

'Hlubi went back to the hills where we camped four days ago . . . he brought the bark into the camp an hour ago.'

A thirty-mile round journey in something under six hours – even in his distress Sean could smile.

'Tell Hlubi the Nkosikazi will drink his medicine.'

Kandhla held her head and Sean forced the evil-smelling liquid between her lips – he made her finish the whole potful. The juice of the bark seemed to relieve the congestion of her kidneys; four times before morning she passed frothy black water. Each time Sean held her gently, cushioning her body from any movement that might have killed her. Gradually her delirium became coma; she lay huddled and still in the cot, shaken only by the brief fits of shivering. When the morning sun hit the wagon canvas and lit the interior, Sean saw her face, and he knew that she was dying. Her skin was an opaque yellowish white, her hair had lost its glow and was lifeless as dry grass. Kandhla brought another pot of the medicine and they fed it to her. When the pot was empty Kandhla said, 'Nkosi, let me lay a mattress on the floor beside the Nkosikazi's bed. You must sleep and I will stay here with you and wake you if the Nkosikazi stirs.'

Sean looked at him with haunted eyes. 'There will be time to sleep later, my friend.' He looked down at Katrina and went on softly. 'Perhaps, very soon there will be time.'

Suddenly Katrina's body stiffened and Sean dropped on his knees beside her cot. Kandhla hovered anxiously behind him. It took Sean a while to understand what was happening and then he looked up at Kandhla.

'Go! Go quickly!' he said and the suffering in his voice sent Kandhla stumbling blindly from the wagon. Sean's second son was born that morning and while Kandhla watched over Katrina Sean wrapped the child in a blanket, took him into the veld and buried him. Then he went back to Katrina and stayed with her while days and nights blended together into a hopeless muddle of grief. As near as Katrina was to death, that near was Sean to insanity. He never moved out of the wagon, he squatted on the mattress next to her cot, wiping the perspiration from her face, holding a cup to her lips or just sitting and watching her. He had lost his child and before his eyes Katrina was turning into a wasted yellow skeleton. Dirk saved him. Mbejane brought the boy to him and he romped on the mattress, crawling into Sean's lap and pulling his beard. It was the one small glimmer of light in the darkness.

– 27 –

Katrina survived. She came back slowly from the motionless coma that precedes death and with her hesitant return Sean's despair changed to hope and then to a wonderful relief. Her water was no longer black but dark pink and thick with sediment. She was aware of him now and, although she was so weak that she could not lift her head off the pillow, her eyes followed him as he moved about the wagon. It was another week before she learned about the baby. She asked him, her voice a tired whisper, and Sean told her with all the gentleness of which he was capable. She did not have the strength for any great show of emotion; she laid quietly staring up at the canvas above her head and her tears slid down across her yellow cheeks.

The damage that the fever had done to her body was hardly credible. Her limbs were so thin that Sean could completely encircle her thigh with one hand. Her skin hung in loose yellow folds from her face and body and pink blood still stained her water. This was not all: the fever had sucked all the strength from her mind. She had nothing left to resist the sorrow of her baby's death, and the sorrow encased her in a shell through which neither Sean nor Dirk could reach her. Sean struggled to bring her back to life, to repair the terrible damage to her mind and body. Every minute of his time he employed in her service.

He and the servants scoured the veld for thirty miles around the laager to find delicacies to tempt her appetite, wild fruits, honey, giraffe marrows, the flesh of a dozen animals: kabobs of elephant heart and duiker liver, roasted iguana lizard as white and tender as a plump pullet, golden fillets of the yellow-mouthed bream from the river. Katrina picked at them listlessly then turned away and lay staring at the canvas wall of the cot.

Sean sat beside her and talked about the farm they would buy, trying vainly to draw her into a discussion of the house they would build. He read to her from Duff's books and the only reaction he received was a small quivering of her lips when he read the words 'death' or 'child'. He talked about the days on the Witwatersrand, searching his mind for stories that might amuse her. He brought Dirk to her and let him play about the wagon. Dirk was walking now, his dark hair had started to curl and his eyes were green. Dirk, however, could not be too long confined in the wagon. There was too much to do, too much to explore. Before long he would stagger to the entrance and issue the imperial summons: 'Bejaan! Bejaan!'

Almost immediately Mbejane's head would appear in the opening and he would glance at Sean for permission.

'All right, take him out then . . . but tell Kandhla not to stuff him full of food.'

Quickly, before Sean changed his mind, Mbejane would lift Dirk down and lead him away. Dirk had nearly two dozen Zulus to spoil him. They competed hotly for his affections, no effort was too much – dignified Mbejane down on his hands and knees being ridden mercilessly in and out among the wagons, Hlubi scratching himself under the arms and gibbering insanely in his celebrated imitation of a baboon while Dirk squealed with delight, fat Kandhla raiding Katrina's store of fruit preserves to make sure Dirk was properly fed and the others keeping in the background, anxious to join the worship but fearful of incurring the jealousy of Mbejane and Hlubi. Sean knew what was happening but he was powerless to prevent it. His time was completely devoted to Katrina.

For the first time in his life Sean was giving more than just a superficial part of himself to another human being. It was not an isolated sacrifice: it went on throughout the months it took for Katrina to regain sufficient of her strength to enable her to sit up in bed without assistance; it continued through the months that she needed before Sean judged it safe to resume the trek towards the south. They built a litter for her – Sean would not risk the jarring of the wagon – and the first day's trek lasted two hours. Four of the servants carried the litter and Katrina lay in it, protected from the sun by a strip of canvas spread above her head. Despite the gentleness with which the Zulus handled her, at the end of the two hours Katrina was exhausted. Her back ached and she was sweating in small beads from her yellow skin. The next week they travelled two hours daily and then gradually increased the time until they were making a full day's journey.

They were halfway to the Magaliesberg, camped at a muddy waterhole in the thorn flats, when Mbejane came to Sean.

'There is still one wagon empty of ivory, Nkosi.'

'The others are full,' Sean pointed out.

'Four hours' march from this place there is enough ivory buried to fill those wagons.'

Sean's mouth twisted with pain. He looked away towards the south-east and he spoke softly. 'Mbejane, I am still a young man and yet already I have stored up enough ugly memories to make my old age sad. Would you have me steal from a friend not only his life but his share of ivory also?'

Mbejane shook his head. 'I asked, that is all.'

'And I have answered, Mbejane. It is his . . . let it lie.'

– 28 –

They crossed the Magaliesberg and turned west along the mountain range. Then, two months after they had left the Limpopo river, they reached the Boer settlement at Louis Trichardt. Sean left Mbejane to outspan the wagons on the open square in front of the church and he went to search for a doctor. There was only one in the district. Sean found him in his surgery above the general dealer's store and took him to the wagons. Sean carried his bag for him and the doctor, a greybeard and unused to such hardships, trotted to keep up with Sean. He was panting and pouring sweat by the time they arrived. Sean waited outside while the doctor completed his examination and when he finally made his descent from the wagon Sean fell on him impatiently. 'What do you think, man?'

'I think, meneer, that you should give hourly thanks to your Maker.' The doctor shook his head in amazement. 'It seems hardly possible that your wife could have survived both the fever and the loss of the child.'

'She is safe then, there's no chance of a relapse?' Sean asked.

'She is safe now . . . but she is still a very sick woman. It may take a year before her body is fully mended. There is no medicine I can give you. She must be kept quiet, feed her well and wait for time to cure her.' The doctor hesitated. 'There is other damage—' He tapped his forehead with his forefinger. 'Grief is a terrible destroyer. She will need love and gentleness and after another six months she will need a baby to fill the emptiness left by the one she lost. Give her those three things, meneer, but most of all give her love.' The doctor hauled his watch from his waistcoat and looked at it. 'Time! There is so little time. I must go, there are others who need me.' He held out his hand to Sean. 'Go with God, meneer.'

Sean shook his hand. 'How much do I owe you?'

The doctor smiled, he had a brown face and his eyes were pale blue; when he smiled he looked like a boy. 'I make no charge for words. I wish I could have done more.' He hurried away across the square and when he walked you could see that his smile lied, he was an old man.

'Mbejane,' said Sean. 'Get a big tusk out of the wagon and take it to the doctor's room above the store.'

Katrina and Sean went to the morning service in the church next day. Katrina could not stand through the hymns. She sat quietly in her pew, watching the altar, her lips forming the words of the hymn and her eyes full of her sorrow.

They stayed on for three more days in Louis Trichardt and they were made welcome. Men came to drink coffee with them and see the ivory and the women brought them eggs and fresh vegetables, but Sean was anxious to move south. So on the third day they started the last stage of their trek.

Katrina regained her strength rapidly now. She took over the management of Dirk from the servants, to their ill-concealed disappointment, and soon she left her litter and rode on the box seat of the lead wagon again. Her body filled out and there was colour showing once more through the yellow skin of her cheeks. Despite the improvement to her body the depression of her mind still persisted and there was nothing that Sean could do to lift it.

A month before the Christmas of 1895 Sean's wagon train climbed the low range of hills above the city and they looked down into Pretoria. The jacaranda trees that filled every garden were in bloom – masses of purple – and the busy streets spoke well of the prosperity of the Transvaal

Republic. Sean outspanned on the outskirts of the city, simply pulling the wagons off the road and camping beside it, and once the camp was established and Sean had made certain that Katrina no longer needed his help he put on his one good suit and called for his horse. His suit had been cut to the fashion of four years previously and had been made to encompass the belly he had acquired on the Witwatersrand. Now it hung loosely down his body but bunched tightly around his thickened arms. His face was burnt black by the sun and his beard bushed down onto his chest and concealed the fact that the stiff collar of his shirt could no longer close around his neck. His boots were scuffed almost through the uppers, there was not a suspicion of polish on them and they had completely lost their shape. Sweat had soaked through his hat around the level of the band and left dark greasy marks; the brim drooped down over his eyes so he had to wear it pushed onto the back of his head. There was, therefore, some excuse for the curious glances that followed him that afternoon as he rode down Church Street with a great muscular savage trotting at his one stirrup and an overgrown brindle hound at the other. They pushed their way between the wagons that cluttered the wide street; they passed the Raadsaal of the Republican Parliament, passed the houses standing back from the road in their spacious purple and green gardens and came at last to the business area of the city that crowded round the railway station. Sean and Duff had bought their supplies at a certain general dealer's stores and now Sean went back to it. It was hardly changed – the signboard in front had faded a little but still declared that I. Goldberg, Importer & Exporter, Dealer in Mining Machinery, Merchant & Wholesaler, was prepared to consider the purchase of gold, precious stone, hides and skins, ivory and other natural produce. Sean swung down from the saddle and tossed his reins to Mbejane. 'Unsaddle, Mbejane. This may take time.'

Sean stepped up onto the sidewalk, lifted his hat to two passing ladies and went through into the building where Mr Goldberg conducted his diverse activities. One of the assistants hurried to meet him, but Sean shook his head and the man went back behind the counter. He had seen Mr Goldberg with two customers at the far end of the store. He was content to wait. He browsed around among the loaded shelves of merchandise, feeling the quality of a shirt, sniffing at a box of cigars, examining an axe, lifting a rifle down off the rack and sighting at a spot on the wall, until Mr Goldberg bowed his customers through the door and turned to Sean. Mr Goldberg was short and fat. His hair was cropped short and his neck bulged over the top of his collar. He looked at Sean and his eyes were expressionless while he rifled through the index cards of his memory for the name. Then he beamed like a brilliant burst of sunlight. 'Mr Courtney, isn't it?'

Sean grinned. 'That's right. How are you, Izzy?' They shook hands. 'How's business?'

Mr Goldberg's face fell. 'Terrible, terrible, Mr Courtney. I'm a worried man.'

'You look well enough on it.' Sean prodded his stomach. 'You've put on weight.'

'You can joke, Mr Courtney, but I'm telling you it's terrible. Taxes and worry, taxes and worry.' Mr Goldberg sighed, 'And now there's talk of war.'

'What's this?' Sean frowned.

'War, Mr Courtney, war between Britain and the Republic.'

Sean's frown dissolved and he laughed. 'Nonsense, man, not even Kruger could be such a bloody fool! Get me a cup of coffee and a cigar and we'll go through to your office and talk business.'

Mr Goldberg's face went blank and his eyelids drooped almost sleepily.

'Business, Mr Courtney?'

'That's right, Izzy, this time I'm selling and you're buying.'

'What are you selling, Mr Courtney?'

'Ivory!'

'Ivory?'

'Twelve wagon loads of it.'

Mr Goldberg sighed sadly. 'Ivory's no good now, the bottom's fallen out of it. You can hardly give it away.' It was very well done; if Sean had not been told the ruling prices two days before he might have been convinced.

'I'm sorry to hear that,' he said. 'If you're not interested, I'll see if I can find someone else.'

'Come along to my office anyway,' said Mr Goldberg. 'We can talk about it. Talk costs nothing.'

Two days later they were still talking about it. Sean had fetched his wagons and had off-loaded the ivory in the back yard of the store. Mr Goldberg had personally weighed each tusk and written the weights down on a sheet of paper. He and Sean had added the columns of figures and agreed on the total. Now they were in the last stages of agreeing the price.

'Come on, Izzy, we've wasted two days already. That's a fair price and you know it . . . let's get it over with,' Sean growled.

'I'll lose money on this,' protested Mr Goldberg. 'I've got to make a living, every man's got to live.'

'Come on.' Sean held out his right hand. 'Let's call it a deal.'

Mr Goldberg hesitated a second longer, then he put his pudgy hand in Sean's fist and they grinned at each other, both well satisfied. One of Mr Goldberg's assistants counted out the sovereigns, stacking them in piles of fifty along the counter, then Sean and Mr Goldberg checked them and agreed once more. Sean filled two canvas bags with the gold, slapped Mr Goldberg's back, helped himself to another cigar and headed heavily laden for the bank.

'When are you going into the veld again?' Mr Goldberg called after him.

'Soon!' said Sean.

'Don't forget to get your supplies here.'

'I'll be back,' Sean assured him.

Mbejane carried one of the bags and Sean the other. Sean was smiling and streamers of cigar smoke swirled back from his head as he strode along the sidewalk. There's something in the weight of a sack of gold that makes the man who holds it stand eight feet tall.

That night as they lay together in the darkness of the wagon Katrina asked him.

'Have we enough money to buy the farm yet, Sean?'

'Yes,' said Sean. 'We've got enough for the finest farm in the whole Cape peninsular . . . and, after one more trip, we'll have enough to build the house and the barns, buy the cattle, lay out the vineyard and still have some left over.'

Katrina was silent for a moment then, 'So we are going back into the bushveld again?'

'One more trip,' said Sean. 'Another two years and then we'll go down to the Cape.' He gave her a hug. 'You don't mind, do you?'

'No,' she said. 'I think I'd like that. When will we leave?'

'Not just yet awhile,' Sean laughed. 'First we're going to have some fun.' He hugged her again, her body was still painfully thin; he could feel the bones of her hips pressed against him.

'Some pretty clothes for you, my fancy, and a suit for me that doesn't look like a fancy dress. Then we'll go out and see what this burg has to offer in the way of entertainment—' He stopped as the idea swelled up in his mind. 'Damn it! I know what we'll do. We'll hire a carriage and go across to Jo'burg. We'll take a suite at the Grand National Hotel and do some living. Bath in a china bath, sleep in a real bed; you can have your hair prettied-up and I'll have my beard trimmed by a barber. We'll eat crayfish and penguin eggs . . . I can't remember when I last tasted pork or mutton . . . we'll wash it down with the old bubbling wine and waltz to a good band—' Sean raced on and when he stopped for breath Katrina asked softly, 'Isn't the waltz a very sinful dance, Sean?'

Sean smiled in the darkness. 'It certainly is!'

'I'd like to be sinful just once . . . not too much; just a little with you to see what it's like.'

'We will be,' said Sean, 'as wicked as hell.'

– 29 –

The next day Sean took Katrina to the most exclusive ladies' shop in Pretoria. He chose the material of half a dozen dresses. One of them was to be a ball gown in canary-yellow silk. It was extravagance and he knew it, but he didn't care once he saw the flash of guilty delight in Katrina's cheeks and the old green sparkle in her eyes. For the first time since the fever she was living again. He spilled out his sovereigns with thankful abandon. The sales girls were delighted with him, they crowded round him with trays of feminine accessories.

'A dozen of those,' said Sean and, 'yes, those will do.' Then a flash of green on the racks across the room caught his eye – it was Katrina's green.

'What's that?' He pointed and two sales girls nearly knocked each other down in the rush to get it for him. The winner carried the shawl back to him and Sean took it and placed it around Katrina's shoulders. It was a beautiful thing.

'We'll take it,' said Sean and Katrina's lips quivered – then suddenly she was crying, sobbing brokenly. The excitement had been too much. There was immediate consternation among the shop assistants, they flapped around Sean like hens at feeding time while he picked Katrina up and carried her out to the hired carriage. At the door he paused and spoke over his shoulder.

'I want those dresses finished by tomorrow evening. Can you do it?'

'They'll be ready, Mr Courtney, even if my girls have to work all night on them.'

He took Katrina back to the wagons and laid her on her cot.

'Please forgive me, Sean, I've never done that in my life before.'

'It's all right, my fancy, I understand. Now you just go to sleep.'

The following day Katrina stayed at the camp resting, while Sean went to see Mr Goldberg again and buy from him the stores they would need for the next expedition. It took another day to load the wagons and by then Katrina seemed well enough to make the trip to Johannesburg.

They left in the early afternoon. Mbejane driving, Sean and Katrina sitting close together on the back seat holding hands under the travelling rug and Dirk bouncing round the interior of the carriage, pausing now and then to flatten his face against a window and keeping up a flow of comment in the peculiar mixture of English, Dutch and Zulu that Sean called Dirkese. They reached Johannesburg long before Sean expected to. In four years the town had doubled its size and had spread out into the veld to meet them. They followed the main road through the new areas and came to the centre. There were changes here as well but it was, in the main, the way he remembered it. They threaded their way through the babble of Eloff Street, and around them, mingling with the crowds on the sidewalks, were the ghosts of the past. He heard Duff laugh and twisted quickly in his seat to place the sound; a dandy in a boater hat with gold fillings in his teeth laughed again from a passing carriage and Sean heard that it was not Duff's laugh. Very close, but not the same. All of it was like that – similar but subtly changed, nostalgic but sad with the knowledge of loss. The past was lost – and he knew then that you can never go back. Nothing is the same, for reality can exist at one time only and in one place only. Then it dies and you have lost it and you must go on to find it at another time and in another place.

They took a suite at the Grand National, with a sitting-room and two bedrooms, a private bathroom and a balcony that looked out over the street – over the rooftops to where the headgears and white dumps stood along the ridge. Katrina was exhausted. They had supper sent up to the room early and when they had eaten Katrina went to bed and Sean went down alone to drink a nightcap at the bar. The bar-room was crowded. Sean found a seat in the corner and sat silently in the jabber of conversation. In it, but no longer a part of it.

They had changed the picture above the bar – it used to be a hunting print; but now it was a red-coated general, impressively splattered with blood, taking leave of his staff in the middle of a battlefield. The staff looked bored. Sean let his eyes wander on along the dark panelled walls. He remembered – there was so much to remember! Suddenly he blinked. Near the side door was a star-shaped crack in the wooden panelling. Sean started to grin and put down his glass and massaged the knuckles of his right hand. If Oakie Henderson hadn't ducked under that punch it would have taken his head off.

Sean signalled to the barman. 'Another brandy, please.'

While the man was pouring, Sean asked, 'What happened to that panel near the door?'

The man glanced up and then back at the bottle. 'Some fellow put his fist through it in the old days. Boss left it like that, sort of souvenir, you know.'

'He must have been quite a fellow . . . that wood's an inch thick. Who was he?' Sean asked expectantly.

The man shrugged. 'One of the drifters. They come and they go. Make a few pounds, piss it against the wall and then go back where they came from.' He looked at Sean with bored eyes. 'That'll be half a dollar, mate.' Sean drank the brandy slowly, turning the glass in his hands between sips and watching the liquor cling to its sides like thin oil. By a cracked panel in a bar-room they shall remember you.

And now I shall go to bed, he decided, this is no longer my world. My world is upstairs sleeping – I hope! He smiled a little to himself and finished the brandy in his glass.

'Sean' – a voice at his ear and a hand on his shoulder as he turned to leave. 'My God, Sean, is it really you?'

Sean stared at the man beside him. He did not recognize the neatly clipped beard and the big sun-burned nose with the skin peeling off the tip, but suddenly he knew the eyes.

'Dennis, you old rogue. Dennis Petersen from Ladyburg. That's right isn't it?'

'You didn't recognize me!' laughed Dennis. 'So much for our friendship – you disappear without a word and ten years later you don't even know me!'

Now they were both laughing.

'I thought they would have hanged you long ago—' Sean defended himself. 'What on earth are you doing in Johannesburg?'

'Selling beef – I'm on the committee of the Beef Growers' Association.' There was pride in Dennis's voice. 'I have been up here negotiating the renewal of our contracts.'

'When are you going back?'

'My train leaves in an hour.'

'Well, there's time for a drink before you go – what will it be?'

'I'll have a small brandy, thanks.'

Sean ordered the drinks and they took them up and stood, suddenly awkward in the awareness that ten years were between their once complete accord.

'So, what have you been doing with yourself?' Dennis ended the pause.

'This and that, you know – a bit of mining, just come back from the bushveld. Nothing very exciting.'

'Well, it's good to see you again anyway. Your health.'

'And yours,' said Sean, and then suddenly he realized that here was news of his family – news he had been without for many years.

'How's everyone at Ladyburg – your sisters?'

'Both married – so am I, with four sons,' and the pride was in Dennis's voice again.

'Anyone I know?' asked Sean.

'Audrey – you know old Pye's daughter.'

'No!' Sean ripped out the word, and then quickly, 'That's wonderful, Dennis. I'm pleased for you – she was a lovely girl.'

'The best,' agreed Dennis complacently. He had the sleek well-fed, well-cared for look of a married man, fatter in the face and his stomach starting to show. I wonder if I have it yet, Sean thought. 'Of course, old man Pye's dead now – that's one creditor he couldn't buy off. Ronnie's taken over the bank and the store.'

'The bat-eared bush rat,' said Sean and knew immediately that he had said the wrong thing. Dennis frowned slightly. 'He's family now, Sean. A very decent chap really – and a clever business man.'

'I'm sorry, I was joking. How's my mother?' Sean changed

the subject by asking the question that had been in the forefront of his mind and he had picked the right topic. Dennis's expression softened immediately – you could see the warmth in his eyes.

'The same as ever. She's got a dress shop now, next door to Ronnie's store. It's a gold mine – no one would think of buying anywhere else but at Aunt Ada's. She's godmother to my two eldest, I guess she's godmother to half the kids in the district,' and then his expression hardened again. 'The least you could have done was write to her sometime, Sean. You can't imagine the pain you have caused her.'

'There were circumstances.' Sean dropped his eyes to his glass.

'That's no excuse – you have a duty which you neglected. There is no excuse for it.'

You little man. Sean lifted his head and looked at him without trying to disguise his annoyance. You pompous, preaching little man peering out at the world one-eyed through the keyhole of your own self-importance. Dennis had not noticed Sean's reaction and he continued. 'That's a lesson a man must learn before he grows up – we all have our responsibilities and our duties. A man grows up when he faces those duties, when he accepts the burdens that society places on him. Take my own case: despite the vast amount of work I have on the farms – I now own Mahoba's Kloof as well – and despite the demands made on me by my family, yet I have time to represent the district on the committee of the Beef Growers' Association, I am a member of the Church Council and the village management board, and I have every reason to believe that next month I will be asked to accept the office of mayor.' Then he looked steadily at Sean. 'What have *you* done with your life so far?'

'I've lived it,' Sean answered, and Dennis looked a little perplexed – then he gathered himself.

'Are you married yet?'

'I was – but I sold her to the Arab slavers up north.'

'You did what?'

'Well,' grinned Sean, 'she was an old wife and the price was good.'

'That's a joke, hey? Ha, ha!' You couldn't fool good old Dennis – Sean laughed out loud. This unbelievable little man!

'Have a drink, Dennis,' he suggested.

'Two is my limit, thanks, Sean.' Dennis pulled the gold hunter from his waistcoat pocket and inspected it. 'Time to go – I'm afraid. Nice seeing you again.'

'Wait,' Sean stopped him. 'My brother – how's Garry?'

'Poor old Garry.' Dennis shook his head solemnly.

'What's wrong with him?' Sean's voice was sharp with his sense of dread.

'Nothing – ' Dennis reassured him quickly. 'Well, I mean nothing more than ever was.'

'Why did you say "poor old Garry" then?'

'I don't really know – except that everybody says it. It's habit, I suppose – he's just one of those people you say *poor old* in front of.'

Sean suppressed his irritation, he wanted to know. He had to know.

'You haven't answered me – how is he?'

Dennis made a significant gesture with his right hand. 'Looking into the bottle quite a bit these days – not that I blame him with that woman he married. You were well out of it there if I may say so, Sean.'

'You may,' Sean acquiesced, 'but is he well? How are things at Theunis Kraal?'

'We all took a bit of a beating with the rindepest* but Garry – well, he lost over half of his herds. Poor old Garry, everything happens to him.'

* An epidemic cattle disease.

'My God – fifty per cent!'

'Yes – but, of course, Ronnie helped him out. Gave him a mortgage on the farm to tide him over.'

'Theunis Kraal bonded again,' groaned Sean. 'Oh Garry, Garry.'

'Yes – well.' Dennis coughed uneasily. 'Well, I think I'd better be going. *Totsiens*, Sean.' He held out his hand. 'Shall I tell them I saw you?'

'No,' said Sean quickly. 'Just leave it stand.'

'Very well then.' Dennis hesitated. 'Are you all right, Sean? I mean' – he coughed again – 'are you all right for money?'

Sean felt his unhappiness dissolve a little; this pompous little man was going to offer him a loan. 'That's very good of you, Dennis. But I've got a couple of pounds saved up – enough to eat on for a few days,' he spoke seriously.

'All right then.' Dennis looked mightily relieved. 'All right then – *totsiens*, Sean,' and he turned and walked quickly out of the bar. As he left the room so he went out of Sean's mind, and Sean was thinking of his brother again.

Then suddenly Sean decided. I will go back to Ladyburg when this next trip is over. The dream farm outside Paarl would not lose anything in being transplanted to Natal – and he suddenly longed to sit in the panelled study at Theunis Kraal again, and to feel the mist come cold down the escarpment in the mornings, and see the spray blowing off the white falls in the wind. He wanted to hear Ada's voice again and to explain to her, knowing she would understand and forgive.

But more, much more it was Garry – poor old Garry. I must go back to him – ten years is a long time and he will have lost the bitterness. I must go back to him – for his sake and for Theunis Kraal. With the decision made, Sean finished his drink and went up the stairs to his suite.

Katrina was breathing softly in her sleep, the dark mass

of her hair spread out on the pillow. While he undressed he watched her and slowly the melancholy dissolved. Gently he pulled back the blankets on his side of the bed and just then Dirk whimpered from the next room. Sean went through to him. 'All right, what's the trouble?'

Dirk blinked owlishly and searched for an excuse, then the relief flooded into his face and he produced the one that creaked with age. 'I want a drink a water.'

The delay while Sean went through to the bathroom gave Dirk an opportunity to rally his forces and when Sean came back he opened the offensive in earnest.

'Tell me a story, Daddy.' He was sitting up now, bright-eyed.

'I'll tell you a story about Jack and a Nory—' said Sean.

'Not that one—' protested Dirk. The saga of Jack and his brother lasted five seconds and Dirk knew it. Sean sat down on the edge of the bed and held the glass for him.

'How about this one? There once was a king who had everything in the world . . . but when he lost it he found out that he had never had anything and that he now had more than he ever had before.'

Dirk looked stunned.

'That's not a very good one,' he gave his opinion at last.

'No,' said Sean. 'It isn't . . . is it? But I think we should be charitable and admit that it's not too bad for this time of night.'

– 30 –

Sean woke feeling happy. Katrina was sitting up in bed filling cups from a pewter coffee pot and Dirk was hammering at the door to be let in. Katrina smiled at him. 'Good morning, meneer.'

Sean sat up and kissed her. 'How did you sleep, fancy?'

'Well, thank you,' but there were dark rings under her eyes. Sean went across to the bedroom door.

'Prepare to receive cavalry,' he said and swung it open. Dirk's charge carried him onto the bed and Sean dived after him. When two men are evenly matched, weight will usually decide and within seconds Dirk had straddled Sean's chest, pinning him helplessly and Sean was pleading for quarter.

After breakfast Mbejane brought the carriage round to the front of the hotel. When the three of them were settled in it, Sean opened the small window behind the driver's seat and told Mbejane, 'To the office first. Then we have to be at the Exchange by ten o'clock.'

Mbejane grinned at him. 'Yes, Nkosi, then lunch at the Big House.' Mbejane had never been able to master the word Xanadu.

They went to all the old places. Sean and Mbejane laughing and reminiscing at each other through the window. There was a panic at the Exchange, crowds on the pavement outside. The offices on Eloff Street had been refaced and a brass plate beside the front door carried the roll of the subsidiaries of Central Rand Consolidated. Mbejane stopped the carriage outside and Sean boasted to Katrina. She sat silently and listened to him, suddenly feeling inadequate for a man who had done so much. She misinterpreted Sean's enthusiasm and thought he regretted the past and wished he were back.

'Mbejane, take us up to the Candy Deep,' Sean called at last. 'Let's see what's happening there.'

The last five hundred yards of the road was overgrown and pitted with disuse. The administration block had been demolished and grass grew thick over the foundations. There were new buildings and headgears half a mile farther along the ridge, but here the reef had been worked out and abandoned. Mbejane pulled up the horses in the circular drive in front of where the offices had stood. He jumped down and held their heads while Sean helped Katrina out of the carriage. Sean lifted Dirk and sat him on his shoulder and they picked their way through the waist-high grass and piles of bricks and rubbish towards the Candy Deep Number Three Shaft.

The bare white concrete blocks that had held the machinery formed a neat geometrical pattern in the grass. Beyond them reared the white mine dump; some mineral in the powdered rock had leaked out in long yellow stains down its sides. Duff had once had the mineral identified. It was of little commercial value, used occasionally in the ceramics industry. Sean had forgotten the name of it; it sounded like the name of a star – Uranus perhaps.

They came to the shaft. The edges of it had crumbled and the grass hung into it, the way an unkempt moustache hangs into an old man's mouth. The headgear was gone and only a rusty barbed-wire fence ringed the shaft. Sean bent his knees: keeping his back straight for Dirk still sat on his shoulder, he picked up a lump of rock the size of a man's fist and tossed it over the fence. They stood quietly and listened to it clatter against the sides as it fell. It fell for a long time and when at last it hit the bottom the echo rang faintly up from a thousand feet below.

'Throw more!' commanded Dirk, but Katrina stopped him.

'No, Sean, let's go. It's an evil place.' She shuddered slightly. 'It looks like a grave.'

'It very nearly was,' said Sean softly, remembering the darkness and the rock pressing down upon him.

'Let's go,' she said again, and they went back to where Mbejane waited with the carriage.

Sean was gay at lunch, he drank a small bottle of wine, but Katrina was tired and more miserable than she had been since they left Louis Trichardt. She had begun to realize the type of life he had led before she met him and she was frightened that now he wanted to return to it. She had only known the bush and the life of the Trek-Boer. She knew she could never learn to live like this. She watched as he laughed and joked during the meal, she watched the easy assurance with which he commanded the white head waiter, the way he picked his way through the maze of cutlery that was spread out on the table before them and at last she could hold it in no longer.

'Let's go away, let's go back into the bush.'

Sean stopped with a loaded fork halfway to his mouth. 'What?'

'Please, Sean, the sooner we go the sooner we'll be able to buy the farm.'

Sean chuckled. 'A day or two more won't make any difference. We're starting to have fun. Tonight I'll take you dancing – we were going to be sinful, remember?'

'Who will look after Dirk?' she asked weakly.

'Mbejane will—' Sean looked at her closely. 'You have a good sleep this afternoon and tonight we'll go out and tie the dog loose.' He grinned at the memories that expression invoked.

When Katrina woke from her rest that evening she found the other part of the reason for her depression. For the first time since the baby her periodic bleeding had started again, the tides of her body and mind were at their lowest ebb. She said nothing to Sean, but bathed and put on the yellow gown. She brushed her hair furiously, dragging the brush through it until her scalp tingled, but still it hung dull and lifeless – as dull as the eyes that looked back at her out of the yellow face in the mirror.

Sean came up behind her and leaned over her to kiss her cheek. 'You look,' said he, 'like a stack of gold bars five-and-a-half feet high.' But he realized that the yellow gown had been a mistake: it matched too closely the fever colour of her skin. Mbejane was waiting in the sitting-room when they went through.

'It may be late before we return,' Sean told him.

'That is of no account, Nkosi.' Mbejane's face was as impassive as ever, but Sean caught a sparkle of anticipation in his eyes and realized that Mbejane could hardly wait to get Dirk to himself.

'You are not to go into his room,' Sean warned.

'What if he cries, Nkosi?'

'He won't . . . but if he does see what he wants, give it to him then leave him to sleep.'

Mbejane's face registered his protest.

'I'm warning you, Mbejane, if I come home at midnight and find him riding you round the room I'll have both your hides for a kaross.'

'His sleep shall be unspoiled, Nkosi,' lied Mbejane.

In the hotel lobby Sean spoke to the receptionist. 'Where can we find the best food in this town?' he asked.

'Two blocks down, sir, the Golden Guinea. You can't miss it.'

'It sounds like a gin palace.' Sean was dubious.

'I assure you, sir, that you'll have no complaint when you get there. Everyone goes there. Mr Rhodes dines there when he's in town, Mr Barnato, Mr Hradsky—'

'Dick Turpin, Cesare Borgia, Benedict Arnold,' Sean

continued for him. 'All right, you have convinced me. I'll take a chance on having my throat cut.'

Sean went out through the front entrance with Katrina on his arm. The splendour of the Golden Guinea subdued even Sean a little. A waiter with a uniform like a major-general's led them down a marble staircase, across the wide meadow of carpet between the group of elegant men and women to a table that even in the soft light dazzled with its bright silver and snowy linen. Chandeliers of crystal hung from the vaulted ceiling, the band was good, and the air was rich with the fragrance of perfume and expensive cigars.

Katrina stared helplessly at the menu until Sean came to her rescue and ordered the meal in a French accent that impressed her but not the waiter. The wine came and with it Sean's high spirits returned. Katrina sat quietly opposite him and listened. She tried to think of something witty to answer him with; in their wagon or alone in the veld they could talk for hours at a time but here she was dumb.

'Shall we dance?' Sean leaned across the table and squeezed her hand. She shook her head.

'Sean, I couldn't. Not with all these people watching. I'd only make a fool of myself.'

'Come on, I'll show you how . . . it's easy.'

'No, I couldn't, truly I couldn't.'

And to himself Sean had to admit that the dance floor of the Golden Guinea on a Saturday night was not the best place for a waltz lesson. The waiter brought the food, great steaming dishes of it. Sean addressed himself to it and the one-sided conversation wilted. Katrina watched him, picking at the too rich food herself, acutely conscious of the laughter and voices around them, feeling out of place and desperately miserable.

'Come on, Katrina,' Sean smiled at her. 'You've hardly touched your glass. Be a devil and get a little of that in you to warm you up.'

Obediently she sipped the champagne. She didn't like the taste. Sean finished the last of his crayfish thermidor and, leaning back in his chair glowing with wine and good food, said, 'Man . . . I only pray the chef can keep the rest of the meal up to that standard.' He belched softly behind his fingers and ran his eyes contentedly round the room. 'Duff used to say that a well-cooked crayfish was proof that—'

Sean stopped abruptly. He was staring at the head of the marble staircase – a party of three had appeared there. Two men in evening dress hovering attentively on each side of a woman. The woman was Candy Rautenbach. Candy with her blonde hair piled on top of her head. Candy with diamonds in her ears and at her throat, her bosom overflowing her gown as white as the frothy head on a beer tankard. Candy with bright blue eyes above a red mouth, Candy poised and lovely. Laughing, she glanced towards him and her eyes met his across the room. She stared in open disbelief, the laughter frozen on her lips, then suddenly her poise was gone and she was running down the stairs towards him, holding her skirts up to her knees, her escorts cantering after her in alarm, waiters scattering out of her path and every head in the room turning to watch her. Sean pushed back his chair, stood up to meet her and Candy reached him and jumped up to throw her arms around his neck. There was a long incoherent exchange of greetings and at last Sean prised her loose from his neck and turned her to face Katrina. Candy was flushed and panting with excitement; with every breath her bosom threatened to spring out of her bodice, and she was still holding on to Sean's arm.

'Candy, I want you to meet my wife, Katrina. My dear, this is Candy Rautenbach.'

'How do you do.' Katrina smiled uncertainly and Candy said the wrong thing.

'Sean, you're joking! You married?'

Katrina's smile faded. Candy noticed the change and went on quickly, 'But I must applaud your choice. I am so pleased to meet you, Katrina. We must get together sometime and I'll tell you all about Sean's terrible past.'

Candy was still holding Sean's arm and Katrina was watching her hand – the long tapered fingers against the dark cloth of Sean's suit. Sean saw the direction of Katrina's eyes and tried tactfully to disengage himself but Candy held on. 'Sean, these are my two current beaux.' They were standing to heel behind her like well-trained gundogs. 'They are both so nice I can't make up my mind about them. Harry Lategaan and Derek Goodman. Boys, this is Sean Courtney. You've heard lots about him.'

They shook hands all round.

'Do you mind if we join you?' asked Derek Goodman.

'I'd be upset if you didn't!' said Sean. The men spread out to find chairs while Candy and Katrina studied each other. 'Is this your first visit to Johannesburg, Mrs Courtney?' Candy smiled sweetly. *I wonder where Sean found her, she's thin as a stick and that complexion! – that accent! He could have done better for himself – he could have had his pick.*

'Yes, we won't be here very long though.' *She's a harlot. She must be – her breasts half-naked and the paint on her face and the way she touches Sean. She must have been his mistress. If she touches him again I'll – I'll kill her.*

Sean came back to the table carrying a chair and set it down for Candy. 'Candy's one of my old friends, my dear, I'm sure you two will like each other.'

'I'm sure we will,' said Candy but Katrina didn't answer and Candy turned back to him. 'Sean, how wonderful it is to see you again. You look so well . . . as sunburnt and handsome as the first time I met you. Do you remember that day you and Duff came to eat at the Hotel?'

A shadow fell across Sean's face at the mention of Duff's name. 'Yes, I remember.' He looked round and snapped his fingers for the waiter. 'Let's have some more champagne.'

'I'll get it,' Candy's escorts cut in simultaneously and then started wrangling good-naturedly as to whose turn it was.

'Is Duff with you tonight, Sean?' Candy asked.

'Candy, didn't Derek get the drinks last time? It's my turn now.' Harry sought her support. Candy ignored them and looked at Sean for a reply but he turned and went round the table to the seat beside Katrina.

'I say, old girl, can I have the first dance?' asked Derek.

'I'll spin you for it, Derek, winner pays but gets first dance,' Harry suggested.

'You're on.'

'Sean, I said is Duff here tonight?' Candy looked at him across the table.

'No, he's not. Listen, you two, how about letting me in on this.' Sean avoided her eyes and joined in the haggle with Harry and Derek. Candy bit her lip – she wanted to press Sean further. She wanted to know about Duff – then suddenly she turned on her smile again. She wasn't going to plead with him.

'What is this?' She tapped Harry's shoulder with her fan. 'Am I going to be the prize in a game of chance? Derek will pay for the wine and Sean gets first dance.'

'I say old girl, that's a bit rough, you know.' But Candy was already standing up.

'Come on, Sean, let's see if you can still tread a stately measure.'

Sean glanced at Katrina. 'You don't mind, do you . . . just one dance?'

Katrina shook her head.

I hate her. She's a harlot. Katrina had never in her life spoken the word out loud, she had seen it only in her Bible, but now it gave her a fierce pleasure to think it. She watched Sean and Candy walk arm-in-arm to the dance floor.

'Would you care to dance, Mrs Courtney?' said Derek. Katrina shook her head again without looking at him. She was staring at Sean and Candy. She saw Sean take her in his arms and a cold lump settled in her stomach. Candy was looking up into Sean's face, laughing at him, her arm on his shoulder, her hand in his.

She's a harlot. Katrina felt her tears very near the surface and thinking that word held them back. Sean swirled Candy into a turn – Katrina stiffened in her chair, her hands clenching in her lap – their legs were touching, she saw Candy arch her back slightly and press her thighs against Sean. Katrina felt as though she were suffocating, jealousy had spread up cold and tight through her chest.

I could go and pull him away, she thought. *I could stop him doing that. He has no right. It's as though the two of them are doing – doing it together. I know they have before, I know it now – Oh God, make them stop it. Please make them stop.*

At last Sean and Candy came back to the table. They were laughing together and when he reached her chair Sean dropped his hand on Katrina's shoulder. She moved away from it but Sean seemed not to notice. Everybody was having a good time. Everybody except Katrina. Harry and Derek were jostling for position. Sean's big laugh kept booming out and Candy was sparkling like the diamonds she wore. Every few minutes Sean turned to Katrina and tried to draw her into the conversation but Katrina stubbornly refused to be drawn. She sat there hating them all. Hating even Sean – for the first time she was unsure of him, jealous and frightened for him. She stared down at her hands on the tablecloth in front of her and saw how bony they were, chapped and reddened by the sun and wind, ugly compared to Candy's. She pulled them quickly into her lap and leaned across towards Sean. 'Please, I want to go back to the hotel. I don't feel well.'

Sean stopped in the middle of a story and looked at her with a mixture of concern and dismay. He didn't want to leave and yet he knew she was still sick. He hesitated one second and then he said, 'Of course, my fancy, I'm sorry. I didn't realize—' He turned to the others. 'We'll have to be going . . . my wife's not too strong . . . she's just had one hell of a go of blackwater.'

'Oh, Sean, must you?' Candy couldn't hide her disappointment. 'There's still so much to talk about.'

'I'm afraid so. We'll get together another night.'

'Yes,' agreed Katrina quickly, 'next time we come to Johannesburg we'll see you.'

'Oh, I don't know . . . perhaps before we go,' Sean demurred. 'Some night next week. How about Monday?'

Before Candy could answer Katrina interrupted. 'Please, Sean, can we go now. I'm very tired.' She started towards the stairs but looked back to see Candy jump up and take Sean's arm, hold her lips close to his ear and whisper a question. Sean answered her tersely and Candy turned back to the table and sat down. When they were out on the street Katrina asked, 'What did she say to you?'

'She just said goodbye,' muttered Sean and Katrina knew he was lying. They didn't talk again on the way back to the hotel. Katrina was preoccupied with her jealousy and Sean was thinking about what Candy had asked and what he had answered.

'Sean, where's Duff? You must tell me.'

'He's dead, Candy.'

The second before she turned back to the table Sean had seen her eyes.

– 31 –

Sean woke with a headache and Dirk's jumping on his chest did not help to ease it at all. Sean had to bribe him off with the promise of sweets. Dirk, sensing his advantage, raised his price to a packet of bull's eyes and two lollipops, the kind with red stripes, before he allowed Katrina to lead him away to the bathroom. Sean sighed and settled back under the blankets. The pain moved up and crouched just behind his eyes. He could taste stale champagne on his own breath and his skin smelt of cigar smoke. He drowsed back in half sleep and the ache faded a little.

'Sean, it's Sunday you know. Are you coming to church with us?' Katrina asked coldly from the bedroom door. Sean squeezed his eyelids tighter closed.

'Sean!' No answer.

'Sean!' He opened one eye.

'Are you going to get up?'

'I don't feel very well,' he croaked. 'I think I have a touch of malaria.'

'Are you coming?' Katrina demanded remorselessly. Her feelings towards him had not softened during the night.

'I don't feel up to it this morning, truly I don't. I'm sure the Good Lord will understand.'

'Thou shalt not take the Lord's name in vain,' Katrina warned him with ice in her voice.

'I'm sorry.' Sean pulled the blankets up to his chin defensively. 'But truly, fancy, I can't get up for another couple of hours. My head would burst.'

Katrina turned back into the sitting-room and Sean heard her speak to Dirk in a voice purposely pitched to reach him.

'Your father's not coming with us. We will have to go

down to breakfast by ourselves. Then we will have to go to church on our own.'

'But,' Dirk pointed out, 'he's going to buy me a packet of bull's eyes and *two* lollipops with red stripes.' In Dirk's opinion that levelled the score. Sean heard the door of the suite close and Dirk's voice receded down the passage. Sean relaxed slowly and waited for the ache behind his eyes to diminish. After a while he became aware of the coffee tray on the table beside the bed and he weighed the additional pain that the effort of sitting up would involve against the beneficial effect of a large cup of coffee. It was a difficult decision but in the end he carefully raised his body to a sitting position and poured a cupful. There was a small jug of fresh cream on the tray. He took it in his right hand and was just about to add a little to the cup when there was a knock on the sitting-room door.

'Come in!' called Sean. He supposed it was the waiter coming to collect the tray. Sean searched his mind for a really scathing remark to send him on his way. He heard the sitting-room door open.

'Who is it?' he asked. There were quick footsteps and then Sean started so violently that the cream slopped out of the jug onto his sheets and his new nightshirt.

'Good God, Candy, you shouldn't have come here.' Sean was in a frenzy of agitation. He put the jug back on the tray with nervous haste and wiped ineffectually at the mess on his nightshirt with his hands. 'If my wife . . . Did anyone see you? You mustn't stay. If Katrina knows you've been here she'll . . . well I mean, she won't understand.'

Candy's eyes were puffy and rimmed with red. She looked as though she hadn't slept. 'It's all right, Sean, I waited across the street until I saw your wife leave. One of my servants followed her, she went to the Dutch church on Commissioner Street and there the service lasts about fifty years.' She came into the room and sat down on the edge of his bed.

'I had to talk to you alone. I couldn't let you go without knowing about Duff. I want you to tell me about it . . . everything about it. I promise not to cry, I know how you hate it.'

'Candy, let's not torture ourselves with it. He's dead. Let's remember him alive.' Sean had forgotten his headache for its place had been taken by pity for her and worry at the position in which she had placed him.

'Tell me, please. I must know. I'd never rest again if I didn't,' she said quietly.

'Candy, don't you see that it doesn't matter? The way in which he went is not important. All that you need to know is he's gone.' Sean's voice faded but went on softly almost to himself, 'He's gone, that is the only thing that matters, he's gone and left us richer for knowing him and a little poorer for having lost him.'

'Tell me,' she said again and they looked at each other, their emotions locked behind expressionless faces. Then Sean told her, his words limping at first, then faster and stronger as the horror of it came back to him. When he had finished she said nothing. She sat on the edge of the bed staring down at the patterned carpet. Sean moved closer to her and put his arm around her.

'There is nothing we can do. That's the thing about death, there is nothing you can do to make it change its mind.'

She leaned against him, against the comfort of his big body and they sat silently until suddenly Candy pulled away from him and smiled her gay brittle smile.

'And now tell me about you. Are you happy? Was that your son with Katrina? He's a lovely child.'

With relief Sean followed her away from the memory of

Duff. They talked about each other, filling in the blanks from the time they had last met until suddenly Sean returned to reality.

'Good God, Candy, we've been talking for ages. Katrina will be back at any moment. You had better run.'

At the door she turned, buried her fingers in his beard and tugged his head from side to side. 'If she ever throws you out, you magnificent brute, here's somebody who'll have a place for you.'

She stood up on her toes and kissed him. 'Be happy,' she commanded and the door closed softly behind her.

Sean rubbed his chin, then he pulled off his nightshirt, screwed it into a ball, tossed it through the open door of the bedroom and went to the bathroom. He was towelling himself and whistling the waltz that the band had played the night before, sweating a little in the steamy warmth of the bathroom when he heard the front door open. 'Is that you, Fancy?'

'Daddy! Daddy! Mummy got sweets for me.' Dirk hammered on the bathroom door, and Sean wrapped the towel round his waist before opening it.

'Look! Look at all my sweets,' gloated Dirk. 'Do you want one, Pa?'

'Thank you, Dirk,' Sean put one of the huge striped humbugs in his mouth, moved it to one side and spoke around it.

'Where's your Mummy?'

'There.' Dirk pointed at the bedroom. He closed the sweet packet carefully. 'I'll keep some for Bejaan,' he announced.

'He'll like that,' Sean said and went across to the bedroom. Katrina lay on the bed; as soon as he saw her he knew something was desperately wrong. She lay staring up at the ceiling, her eyes unseeing, her face as yellow and set as that of a corpse. Two quick strides carried him to her.

He touched her cheek with his fingers and the sense of dread settled on him again, heavily, darkly.

'Katrina?' There was no response. She lay still without a flicker of life in her eyes. Sean swung round and ran out of the suite, down the corridor to the head of the stairs. There were people in the lobby below him and he yelled over their heads to the clerk behind the desk.

'Get a doctor, man, as fast as you can . . . my wife's dying.'

The man stared up at him blankly. He had a neck too thin for his high stiff collar and his black hair was parted down the centre and polished with grease.

'Hurry, you stupid bastard, get moving,' roared Sean. Everybody in the lobby was looking at him. He still wore only a small towel around his waist and, heavy with water, his hair hung down over his forehead.

'Move, man! Move!' Sean was dancing with impatience. There was a heavy stone vase on the banister at Sean's side, he picked it up threateningly and the clerk jerked out of his trance and scuttled for the front door. Sean ran back to the suite.

Dirk was standing by Katrina's bed, his face distorted by the humbug it contained and his eyes large with curiosity. Sean snatched him up, carried him through to the other bedroom and locked the door on his outraged howls. Dirk was unused to being handled in that manner. Sean went back to Katrina and knelt beside her bed. He was still kneeling there when the doctor arrived. Tersely Sean explained about the blackwater, and the doctor listened then sent him to wait in the sitting-room. It was a long wait before the doctor came through to him and Sean sensed that behind his professional poker face the man was puzzled.

'Is it a relapse?' Sean demanded.

'No, I don't think so. I've given her a sedative.'

'What's wrong with her? What is it?' Sean pursued him and the doctor hedged.

'Has your wife had some sort of shock . . . some bad news, something that could have alarmed her? Has she been under nervous strain?'

'No . . . she's just come back from church. Why? What's wrong?' Sean caught the doctor's lapels and shook him in his agitation.

'It appears to be some sort of paralytic hysteria. I've given her laudanum. She'll sleep now and I'll come back to see her this evening.'

The doctor was trying to loosen Sean's hands from his jacket. Sean let him go and pushed past him to the bedroom.

The doctor called again just before dark. Sean had undressed Katrina and put her into the bed, but apart from that she had not moved. Her breathing was shallow and fast despite the drug she had been given. The doctor was baffled.

'I can't understand it, Mr Courtney. There is nothing I can find wrong with her apart from her general run-down condition. I think we'll just have to wait and see. I don't want to give her any more drugs.'

Sean knew the man could be of no more help to him and he hardly noticed when he left with a promise to come again in the morning. Mbejane gave Dirk his bath, fed him and put him to bed and then he slipped quietly out of the suite and left Sean alone with Katrina. The afternoon of worry had tired Sean. He left the gas burning in the sitting-room and stretched out on his own bed. After a while he slept.

When the rhythm of his breathing changed Katrina looked across at him. Sean lay fully clothed on top of his blankets, one thickly-muscled arm thrown above his head and his tension betrayed by the twitching of his lips and the frown that puckered his face. Katrina stood up and moved across to stand over him, lonely as she had never been in the solitude of the bush, hurt beyond the limits of physical pain and with everything that she believed in destroyed in those few minutes that it had taken for her to discover the truth.

She looked down at Sean and with surprise realized that she still loved him, but now the security that she had found with him was gone. The walls of her castle had proved paper. She had felt the first cold draughts blowing in through them as she watched him reliving his past and regretting it. She had felt the walls tremble and the wind howl stronger outside when he danced with that woman – then, they had collapsed into ruin around her. Standing in the half-darkened room, watching the man she trusted so completely and who just as completely had betrayed her, she went carefully over the ground again to make sure there was no mistake.

That morning, she and Dirk had stopped at the sweet shop on the way back from church. It was almost opposite the hotel. It had taken Dirk a long time to select his tuppenny worth. The profusion of wares on display unmanned him and reduced him to a state of dithering indecision. Finally, with the assistance of the proprietor and a little prompting from Katrina, his purchases were made and packed into a brown paper bag. They were just about to go when Katrina looked out through the large front window of the shop and saw Candy Rautenbach leaving the hotel. She came quickly down the front steps, glanced about her, crossed the street to a waiting carriage and her coachman whisked her away. Katrina had stopped the instant she caught sight of her. A pang of last night's jealousy returned, for Candy looked very lovely even in the morning sunlight. It was not until Candy's carriage disappeared that Katrina began to question her presence at their hotel at eleven o'clock on a Sunday morning. Her jealousy was a bayonet thrust up under her ribs: it made her catch her breath. Vividly she remembered Candy's whispered question as they left the Golden Guinea the previous night. She remembered the way Sean had answered and the way he had lied about it afterwards. Sean knew that Katrina would go to church that morning. How simple it all was! Sean had arranged to meet her, he had refused to accompany Katrina and while Katrina was out of the way that harlot had gone to him.

'Mummy, you're hurting me.' Unconsciously she had tightened her grip on Dirk's hand. She hurried out of the shop, dragging Dirk with her. She almost ran across the hotel lobby, up the stairs and along the passage. The door was closed. She opened it and the smell of Candy's perfume met her. Her nostrils flared at it. There was no mistaking it, she remembered it from the previous evening – the smell of fresh violets. She heard Sean call from the bathroom, Dirk ran across the room and hammered on the door.

'Daddy! Daddy! Mummy got sweets for me.'

She put her Bible down on top of the writing desk and moved across the thick carpet with the smell of violets all around her. She stood in the doorway of the bedroom. Sean's nightshirt lay on the floor, there were still damp stains on it. She felt her legs begin to tremble. She looked up and saw the stains on the bed, grey on the white sheets. She felt giddy, her cheeks burned; she only just managed to reach her own bed.

– 32 –

She knew there was no mistake. Sean had taken that woman in such a casually blatant manner – in their own bedroom, almost before her eyes, that his rejection of her could hardly have been more final if he had slapped her face and thrown her into the street. Weakened by fever, depressed by the loss of her child and the phase of her cycle, she had not the resilience to fight against it. She had loved him but she had proved insufficient for him. She could not stay with him: the stubborn pride of her race would not allow it. There was only one alternative.

Timidly she bent over him and as she kissed him she smelt the warm man-smell of his body and felt his beard brush her cheek. Her determination wavered; she wanted to throw herself across his chest, lock her arms around his neck and plead with him. She wanted to ask for another chance. If he could tell her how she had failed him she could try to change, if only he could show her what she had done wrong. Perhaps if they went back into the bush again – She dragged herself away from his bed. She pressed her knuckles hard against her lips. It was no use. He had decided and even if she begged him to take her back there would always be this thing between them. She had lived in a castle and she would not change it now for a mud hut. Driven by the trek whip of her pride she moved quickly across to the wardrobe. She put on a coat and buttoned it – it reached to her ankles and covered her nightdress; she spread the green shawl over her head, winding the loose end around her throat. Once more she looked across at Sean. He slept with his big body sprawled and the frown still on his face.

In the sitting-room she stopped beside the writing desk. Her Bible lay where she had left it. She opened the front cover, dipped the pen and wrote. She closed the book and went to the door. There she hesitated once more and looked back at Dirk's bedroom. She could not trust herself to see him again. She lifted an end of the shawl to cover her mouth, then she went out into the passage and closed the door softly behind her.

– 33 –

Sean was surprised to find himself fully dressed and lying on top of his bed when he woke next morning. It was still half dark outside the hotel windows and the room was cold. He propped himself up on one elbow and rubbed at his eyes with the back of a clenched fist. Then he remembered and he swung his legs off the bed and looked at Katrina's bed. The blankets were thrown back and it was empty. Sean's first feeling was relief, she had recovered enough to get up on her own. He went through to the bathroom, stumbling a little from the stiffness of uneasy sleep. He tapped on the closed door.

'Katrina?' he questioned and then again louder. 'Katrina, are you in there?'

The handle turned when he tried it and the door swung open without resistance. He blinked at the empty room, white tiles reflecting the uncertain light, a towel thrown across a chair where he had left it. He felt the first twinge of alarm. Dirk's room – the door was still locked, the key on the outside. He flung it open. Dirk sat up in bed, his face flushed, his curls standing up like the leaves of a sisal bush. Sean ran out into the passage, along it and looked down into the lobby. There was a light burning behind the reception desk. The clerk slept with his head on his arms, sitting forward on his chair snoring. Sean went down the stairs three at a time. He shook the clerk.

'Has anybody been out through here during the night?' Sean demanded.

'I . . . I don't know.'

'Is that door locked?' Sean pointed at the front door.

'No, sir, there's a night latch on it. You can get out but not in.'

Sean ran out onto the pavement. Which way, which way to search for her? Which way had she gone? Back to Pretoria to the wagons? Sean thought not. She would need transport and she had no money to hire it. Why should she leave without waking him, leave Dirk, leave her clothing and disappear into the night? She must have been unbalanced by the drugs the doctor had given her. Perhaps there was something in his theory that she had suffered a shock, perhaps she was wandering in her nightdress through the streets with no memory, perhaps – Sean stood in the cold grey Transvaal morning, the city starting to murmur into wakefulness around him, the questions crowding into his head and finding there no answers with which to mate.

He turned and ran back through the hotel, out of the rear door into the stable yard.

'Mbejane,' he shouted. 'Mbejane, where the hell are you?'

Mbejane appeared quickly from the stall where he was currying one of the hired horses.

'Nkosi.'

'Have you seen the Nkosikazi?'

Mbejane's face creased into a puzzled frown. 'Yesterday—'

'No, man,' shouted Sean. 'Today, last night . . . have you seen her?'

Mbejane's expression was sufficient reply.

Sean brushed impatiently past him and ran into the stable. He snatched a saddle off the rack and threw it onto the back of the nearest horse. While he clinched the girth and forced a bit between its teeth he spoke to Mbejane.

'The Nkosikazi is sick. She has left during the night. It is possible that she walks as one who still sleeps. Go quickly among your friends and tell them to search for her, tell them that there's ten pounds in gold for the one who finds her. Then come back here and care for Dirk until I return.'

Sean led the horse from the stable and Mbejane hurried off to spread the word. Sean knew that within minutes half the Zulus in Johannesburg would be looking for Katrina – tribal loyalty and ten pounds in gold were strong incentives. He swung up onto the horse and galloped out of the yard. He tried the Pretoria road first. Three miles out of town a native herd boy grazing sheep beside the road convinced him that Katrina had not passed that way. He turned back. He paid a visit to the police station at Marshal Square. The Commandant remembered him from the old days; Sean could rely on his cooperation. Sean left him and rode fast through the streets that were starting to fill with the bustle of a working day. He hitched his horse outside the hotel and took the front steps three at a time. The clerk had no news for him. He ran up the stairs and along the passage to his suite. Mbejane was feeding Dirk his breakfast. Dirk beamed at Sean through a faceful of egg and spread his arms to be picked up but Sean had no time for him.

'Has she come back?'

Mbejane shook his head. 'They will find her, Nkosi. Fifty men are searching for her now.'

'Stay with the child,' said Sean and went down to his horse. He stood beside it ready to mount but not knowing which way to go. 'Where the hell has she got to?' he demanded aloud. In her night clothes with no money, where the hell had she gone?

He mounted and rode with aimless urgency through the streets, searching the faces of the people along the sidewalks, turning down the sanitary lanes and peering into backyards and vacant plots. By midday he had tired his horse and worked himself into a ferment of worry and bad temper. He had searched every street in Johannesburg, made a nuisance of himself at the police station and sworn at the hotel clerk, but there was still no sign of Katrina. He was riding down Jeppe Street for the fifth time when the imposing double-storey of Candy's Hotel registered through his preoccupation.

'Candy,' he whispered. 'She can help.'

He found her in her office among Persian rugs and gilt furniture, walls covered with pink and blue patterned wallpaper, a mirrored ceiling hung with six crystal waterfalls of chandeliers and a desk with an Indian mosaic top. Sean pushed aside the little man in the black alpaca coat who tried to stop him entering and burst into the room. Candy looked up and her small frown of annoyance smoothed as she saw who it was.

'Sean . . . oh, how nice to see you.' She came round from behind the desk, the bell tent of her skirts covering the movement of her legs so she seemed to float. Her skin was smooth white and her eyes were happy blue. She held out her hand to him, but hesitated as she saw his face. 'What is it, Sean?'

He told her in a rush and she listened and when he had finished she rang the bell on her desk.

'There's brandy in the cabinet by the fireplace,' she said, 'I expect you are in need of one.'

The little man in the alpaca coat came quickly to the bell. Sean poured himself a large brandy and listened to Candy giving orders.

'Check the railway station. Telegraph the coach stages on each of the main roads. Send someone up to the hospital. Check the registers of every hotel and boarding-house in town.'

'Very well, madame.' The little man bobbed his head as he acknowledged each instruction and then he was gone.

Candy turned back to Sean.

'You can pour a drink for me also and then sit down and simmer down. You're behaving just the way she wanted you to.'

'What do you mean?' demanded Sean.

'You are being given a little bit of wifely discipline, my dear. Surely you have been married long enough to recognize that?'

Sean carried the glass across to her and Candy patted the sofa next to her.

'Sit down,' she said. 'We'll find your little Cinderella for you.'

'What do you mean . . . wifely discipline?' he demanded again.

'Punishment for bad behaviour. You may have eaten with your mouth open, answered back, taken more than your share of the blankets, not said good morning with the right inflection or committed one of the other mortal sins of matrimony, but—' Candy sipped her drink and gasped slightly, 'I see that time has not given you a lighter hand with the brandy bottle. One Courtney tot always did equal an imperial gallon . . . but, as I was saying, my guess is that little Katy is having an acute attack of jealousy. Probably her first, seeing that the two of you have spent your whole married life out in the deep sticks and she has never had an opportunity of watching the Courtney charm work on any other female before.'

'Nonsense,' said Sean. 'Who's she got to be jealous of?'

'Me,' said Candy. 'Every time she looked at me the other night I felt as though I'd been hit in the chest with an axe.' Candy touched her magnificent bosom with her fingertips, skilfully drawing Sean's attention to it. Sean looked at it. It was deeply cleft and smelt of fresh violets. He shifted restlessly and looked away.

'Nonsense,' he said again. 'We're just old friends, almost like—' he hesitated.

'I hope, my dear, that you weren't going to say "brother and sister" . . . I'll not be party to any incestuous relationship . . . or had you forgotten about that?'

Sean had not forgotten. Every detail of it was still clear. He blushed and stood up.

'I'd better be going,' he said. 'I'm going to keep looking for her. Thanks for your help, Candy, and for the drink.'

'Whatever I have is yours, m'sieur,' she murmured, lifting an eyebrow at him, enjoying the way he blushed. 'I'll let you know as soon as we hear anything.'

The assurance that Candy had given him wore thinner as the afternoon went by with no news of Katrina. By nightfall Sean was again wild with worry, it had completely swamped his bad temper and even anaesthetized his fatigue. One by one Mbejane's tribesmen came in to report a blank score, one by one the avenues Candy's men were exploring proved empty, and long before midnight Sean was the only hunter left. He rode hunched in the saddle, a lantern in his hand, riding the ground that had already been covered a dozen times, visiting the mining camps along the ridge, stopping to question late travellers he met along the network of roads between the mines. But the answer was always the same. Some thought he was joking: they laughed until they saw that his face was haunted and dark-eyed in the lantern light, then they stopped laughing and moved hurriedly on. Others had heard about the missing woman; they started to question him, but as soon as Sean realized they could not help him, he pushed past them and went on searching. At dawn he was back at the hotel. Mbejane was waiting for him.

'Nkosi, I have had food ready for you since last night. Eat now and sleep a little. I will send the men out to search again today, they will find her.'

'Tell them, I will give one hundred pounds to the one who finds her.' Sean passed his hand wearily across his face. 'Tell them to hunt the open veld beyond the ridges, she may not have followed a road.'

'I will tell them . . . but now you must eat.'

Sean blinked his eyes, they were red-veined and each had a little lump of yellow mucus in the corner.

'Dirk?' he asked.

'He is well, Nkosi, I have stayed with him all the while.'

Mbejane took Sean firmly by the arm. 'There is food ready. You must eat.'

'Saddle me another horse,' said Sean. 'I will eat while you do it.'

Without sleep, unsteady in the saddle as the day wore on, Sean widened the circle of his search until he was out into the treeless veld and the mine headgears were small spidery triangles on the horizon.

A dozen times he met Zulus from the city, big black men in loin cloths, moving at their businesslike trot, hunting the ground like hounds. There was a concealed sympathy behind their greetings.

'Mbejane has told us, Nkosi. We will find her.' And Sean left them and rode on alone, more alone than he had ever been in his life before. After dark he rode back into Johannesburg, the faint flutter of hope inside him stilled as he limped stiffly into the gas-lit lobby of the hotel and saw the pity in the reception clerk's face.

'No word, I'm afraid, Mr Courtney.'

Sean nodded. 'Thanks anyway. Is my son all right?'

'Your servant has taken good care of him, sir. I sent dinner up to him an hour ago.'

The stairs seemed endless as he climbed them. By God, he was tired – sick-tired and sick with worry. He pushed open the door of his suite and Candy stood up from a chair across the room. The hope flared up in him again.

'Have you—' he started eagerly.

'No,' she said quickly. 'No, Sean, I'm sorry.' He flopped into one of the chairs and Candy poured a drink for him from a decanter that was waiting on the writing desk. He smiled his thanks and took a big gulp at the glass. Candy lifted his legs one at a time and pulled off his boots, ignoring his faint protest. Then she took up her own glass and went to sit across the room from him.

'I'm sorry I joked yesterday,' she apologized softly. 'I don't think I realized how much you love her.' She lifted her glass to him. 'Here's a speedy end to the search.'

Sean drank again, half a glass at a swallow.

'You do love her, don't you?' Candy asked.

Sean answered her sharply. 'She's my wife.'

'But it's not only that,' Candy went on recklessly, knowing his anger was just below the surface of his fatigue.

'Yes, I love her. I'm just learning how much, I love her as I'll never be able to love again.' He drained his glass and stared at it, his face grey under the brown and his eyes dark with unhappiness. 'Love,' he said. 'Love,' mouthing the word, weighing it. 'They've dirtied that word . . . they sell love at the Opera House . . . they have used that word so much that now when I want to say "I love Katrina" it doesn't sound what I mean.' Sean hurled the glass against the far wall, it shattered with a crack and a tingle and Dirk stirred in the bedroom. Sean dropped his voice to a fierce whisper. 'I love her so it screws my gut, I love her so that to think of losing her now is like thinking of dying.'

He clenched his fists and leaned forward in his chair. 'I'll not lose her now, by Christ, I'll find her and when I do I'll tell her this. I'll tell her just like I'm telling you.' He stopped and frowned. 'I don't think I've ever said to her "I love you." I've never liked using that word. I've said "Marry me" and "You're my fancy," but I've never said it straight before.'

'Perhaps that's part of the reason she ran away, Sean,

perhaps because you never said it she thought you never felt it.' Candy was watching him with a strange expression – pity and understanding and a little yearning.

'I'll find her,' said Sean, 'and this time I'll tell her . . . if it's not too late.'

'You'll find her and it won't be too late. The earth can't have swallowed her, and she'll be glad to hear you say it.' Candy stood up. 'You must rest now, you have a hard day ahead of you.'

Sean slept fully dressed in the chair in the sitting-room. He slept brokenly, his mind struggling and kicking him back to half wakefulness every few minutes. Candy had turned the gas low before she left and its light fell in a soft pool onto the writing desk beneath it. Katrina's Bible lay where she had left it and each time Sean started awake the fat, leather-covered book caught his eye. Some time before dawn he woke for the last time and knew he could not sleep again.

He stood up and his body still ached and his eyes felt gritty. He moved across to the gas lamp and turned it up high, he let his hand drop from the lamp onto the Bible. Its leather was cool and softly polished beneath his fingers. He opened the front cover and caught his breath with a hiss.

Beneath Katrina's name, in her carefully rounded writing, the ink still freshly blue, *she had filled in the date of death.*

The page magnified slowly in front of his eyes until it filled the whole field of his vision. There was a rushing sound in his ears, the sound of a river in flood, but above it he heard voices, different voices.

'Let's go, Sean, it looks like a grave.'

'But more than anything she needs love.'

'The earth can't have swallowed her.'

And his own voice, 'If it's not too late, if it's not too late.'

The morning light was gathering strength as he reached the ruins of the old Candy Deep office block. He left his horse and ran through the grass towards the mine dump. The wind was small and cold; it moved the tops of the grass and went on to where Katrina's green shawl was caught on the barbed wire fence that ringed the shaft. In the wind the shawl flapped its wings like a big green bird of prey.

Sean reached the fence and looked down into the mouth of the shaft. At one place the grass had been torn away from the edge as though someone had snatched at it as they fell.

Sean loosed the shawl from the spikes of the barbed wire, he balled the heavy material in his fists, then he held it out over the shaft and let it drop. It spread out as it floated down into the blackness, and it was the bright green of Katrina's eyes.

'Why?' whispered Sean. 'Why have you done this to us, my fancy?' He turned away and walked back to his horse, stumbling carelessly in the rough footing.

Mbejane was waiting for him in the hotel suite.

'Get the carriage,' Sean told him.

'The Nkosikazi – ?'

'Get the carriage,' Sean repeated.

Sean carried Dirk downstairs. He paid his bill at the reception desk and went out to where Mbejane had the carriage ready. He climbed up into it and held Dirk on his lap.

'Drive back to Pretoria,' Sean said.

'Where's Mummy?' Dirk demanded.

'She's not coming with us.'

'Are we going alone?' Dirk insisted and Sean nodded wearily.

'Yes, Dirk, we are going alone.'

'Is Mummy coming just now?'

'No, Dirk. No, she's not.'

It was finished, Sean thought. It was all over – all the

dreams and the laughter and the love. He was too numbed to feel the pain yet – it would come later.

'Why are you squeezing me so hard, Daddy?'

Sean slackened his grip and looked down at the child on his lap. It was not finished, he realized; it was only a new beginning.

But first I must have time for this to heal: time – and a quiet place to lie up with this wound. The wagons are waiting and I must go back into the wilderness.

Perhaps after another year I will have healed sufficiently to start again, to go back to Ladyburg with my son, back to Ladyburg, and to Ada and to Garry – he thought. Then suddenly and sickeningly he felt the pain again, and the deep raw ache of it frightened him. *Please God*, prayed Sean who had never prayed before, *please God give me the strength to endure it.*

'Are you going to cry, Daddy? You look like you're going to cry.' Dirk was watching Sean's face with solemn curiosity. Sean pulled the child's head gently against his shoulder and held it there.

If tears could pay both our debts, thought Sean, if with my tears I could buy for you an indulgence from all pain, if by weeping now I could do all your weeping for you – then I would cry until my eyes were washed away.

'No, Dirk,' he answered. 'I am not going to cry – crying never helps very much.'

And Mbejane took them to where the wagons waited at Pretoria.